UNREPENTANT

BRIDGET E. BAKER

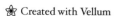

For Whitney
True Soul Mates Aren't Found
They're Made
One Choice at a Time

PROLOGUE

For a jet flying at nearly six hundred miles per hour, a deviation of a few degrees will send the plane to the wrong country during the course of a single flight.

Similarly, a crooked sapling, even if it steadily aims for the sun, will often become a permanently deformed tree.

A single lie can reroute someone's entire life.

It can skew the future of a nation.

It can alter the fate of the world.

But frequently, you don't realize the problem until it's too late. Until the trunk cannot possibly be repaired, and the plane has veered desperately off course.

I told several lies, both small and large, and I told some of them a very long time ago.

"Hello?" Chancery's voice fills the room, and I'm sure it spills into the other rooms of the bunker as well.

Silence.

I press play again on the recording device, the sound quality impressively good for a portable unit. "Is anyone down here? Hello?"

Silence.

I walk closer to the partition that divides the main bunker from the expansion rooms. They're usually completely sealed off, conserving energy in the event that no extra people need to be sheltered in an emergency, but I know that beyond the solid wooden door, the rooms have been opened and the lights are on, two people constrained within their depths. The partition may be locked, but that wouldn't stop Melina and Aline if they wanted through.

Only their vow keeps them on the other side.

I press the button again. "Hello?" Chancery's voice, slightly different each time, querulous, unsure. So perfectly her. "I thought I heard a noise. Is someone here?" I hit pause again.

A grinding sound, and then a sequence of clicks. My heart falls. I don't want to do this—not even a little bit. The thought of the pain on Melina's face when I do it—but I can't avoid it, not now.

When Melina bursts through that door, I sigh.

"Oh." Her eyes widen.

Aline bursts through next to her. "It's not Chancery."

I shake my head. "No, it's definitely not."

Beating Aline is as awful as I expected it would be, especially when Melina tries to stop me. But she's evian, and if I don't beat her badly enough, it won't be a deterrent. Our training prepares us to withstand a lot—and Aline is tough. Given the likelihood that eventually Chancery will check the bunker—since Melina is missing—I have to ensure that Melina and Aline don't give me away.

This is the only way.

I finally stop, Aline groaning piteously in the corner. Melina realized that I don't mean to kill her and stopped fighting me, but she's sobbing on the carpet where I restrained her.

"How?" she chokes out. "How can you defeat us so easily?"

I sit on the edge of the sofa in the main family room of the bunker. "If you had honored your word not to attempt to escape until I had explained myself, we wouldn't be in this situation."

"I didn't try to escape," Melina protests.

My head tilts, my heart sore. "In my opinion, if Chancery does come down, and you make yourself known to her, that's an attempted escape. Do you understand?"

Aline groans and shifts, healing more slowly than I expected from the damage I was forced to inflict. Melina's eyes are drawn to the sound as mine were. She tears her eyes away and looks up at me. "Yes, I do. It won't happen again."

"Then this won't happen again, either." I cross my arms. "Although I can't promise not to test your assurances that it won't happen."

"When are you going to explain?" Melina calms down as her wife's healing progresses, becoming notably less agitated, less upset. Perhaps she has begun to understand that sometimes pawns must be sacrificed in a game, no matter how detestable it is. Can she forgive what I had to do when I captured her? Will my explanation make a difference?

"I have time to begin," I say. "And your question is a good place to start."

She frowns.

"You asked how I'm able to fight you both at once, no weapons drawn, and still defeat you soundly."

Aline drags herself upright and wipes her bloody face with the back of her hand. "I want to know the answer to that, too."

"To understand, I'll have to go back quite a while, to 1830. To the year I discovered who I really am—or perhaps I should say, *what* I really am."

1830

Every time another empress arrives without notice, Mother stomps and scowls and fumes—only in private, of course. It's a good thing it doesn't happen often, or we'd need new rugs double quick.

"I should never have agreed to share the details of my freedom model with any of them." Mother shoves back from her chair and drops her fork on the table. "Leamarta has been the worst. She only started to implement it when Senah made inroads with Spain—and now she's trying to use it to fragment the Spanish control of Mexico, as if I meant for it to be a tool with which to pry away holdings from other families."

"You use it as a tool as well." Dad spears his last bite of sausage and pops it in his mouth. "Productivity and innovation more than tripled under the new models, and you've used the ideas to spread your control in other empresses' lands."

Mother's eyebrow quirks upward. "I didn't *share* the idea so that they could use it against one another, upsetting the balance of power. More pie means all of us have more to eat. That's the point."

Dad has never been one to concede a point. "However she uses it, her people will surely appreciate the shift. They don't care *why* she's giving them more autonomy or freedom—they benefit from the results."

Mother stands up and begins to pace along the wall with the window, but she doesn't even glance at the lavishly maintained gardens outside. "She's not taking my advice. Providing more freedom to your people works to motivate them to produce more, but it's not an effective stopgap when they revolt against you. She's using it all wrong. Is it any wonder she needs me to hold her hand?" She stops and glares at Dad, as if he's the one demanding she save him from himself.

"But you were complaining last week that Senah has been gaining ground," Dad says. "So do Leamarta's job for her a while longer with a fake smile plastered on your face. It's obnoxious, but it benefits us in the long run, and it's a public service for all her humans."

"I have too many other things to do—I don't have time to babysit the other empresses." Mother crosses her arms, her eyes flashing.

"Maintaining the delicate balance between the families has always been a time vortex. If it helps, I'm happy to train Inara for you today. It'll free up a few hours, guilt free."

"Doing favors isn't really my forte." Mom frowns. "But if I don't help Leamarta. . ."

"And Senah succeeds in taking Spain because she stumbles," Dad practically whispers, "Lenora might fall."

Mother laughs. "Balthasar would throw a party."

A smile spreads slowly across Dad's face, and he stands up. "Do you think it's time?"

Mother glances my direction. "For the prophecy?"

He nods slowly, intent on her face.

"With a thirteen-year-old Heir?" She shakes her head. "Soon, perhaps, but not yet. It's too large a gamble."

"Then you need to shore up Leamarta's position." Dad wipes his mouth with his napkin and tosses it on the center of his plate.

Mother sighs. "You've been hounding me about taking over Inara's training for years. Is this all the backdrop of a domestic coup?"

"That's not the reason I think you should help her, but now that you mention it." Dad wraps an arm around Mother's shoulders. "I know you've been putting off the next step in our daughter's training, and I understand why, but it's time to move her to bladed weapons. Past time, really."

Mother's eyes meet Dad's and soften. She melts against him, her head resting against his shoulder. There's no trace of irritation in her voice, not anymore. Somehow, Dad always knows just how to soothe her. "Maybe it's better that I not be there—try blades today, and be prepared to give me a full report on how she does."

My heart soars. I've been ready for bladed combat for two years at least, but Mother has been too nervous, ever since Tanvi died in her first bladed training three years ago. It was a tragedy, sure, but it was Lainina's fault for pushing her too hard, by all counts. Either that, or it's all some kind of cover-up for major weakness in her former Heir.

"It'll probably be better if no one is around to watch," Dad says. "Maybe I should take her on a little trip off the main estate. There are too many guards at Windsor."

"You and Balthasar trained and set each one of those guards." Mother kisses his lips lightly. "Which makes complaining about them. . ."

"Ironic?" Dad asks.

"I was going to say juvenile." Mother smirks. "But it's not a bad idea to start away from the stress of other people's expectations."

Dad points at me. "Grab a bag with flasks and jerky, and

I'll meet you on the steps of the Long Walk in ten minutes."

I race to my room and rummage around for a bag. I fill two water flasks and toss them inside, but I have to stop at the kitchen for the jerky. I don't often go to the kitchen, so when I push through the doorway, the staff freezes. Angel meets my eye and quirks one eyebrow.

"Inara." She walks toward me briskly. "Is anything the matter?"

"Mother is—"

"Dealing with Leamarta," Angel says. "Let me guess. Althuselah's taking you for a jog."

I shrug. "Right—he understands why Mother needs to do it, but he's bored with the tedium of explaining how to implement Mother's idea over and over." I'm proud of how easily I covered what we're really doing, especially to Angel. It's hard to lie to a spymaster about anything, even something as silly as where we're going.

She grabs a loaf of bread and a bag of jerky and extends them to me. "I'm assuming, since I haven't heard from your father, that you need enough for both of you."

I open the bag for her to drop it inside. "I'm not sure."

She hands me a second loaf of bread and a hunk of cheese. "Better too much than too little."

"Thanks," I say.

"Of course," Angel says. "We have to keep the Heir in top condition."

By the time I reach Dad, his foot is already tapping as his eyes scan the trees that line the Long Walk. The guards standing along the Walk are just a little more alert, their shoulders a little more square, knowing Dad's watching. I wonder how long he's been waiting for me.

"I'm two minutes early," I protest.

Dad smiles. "I didn't complain."

I want to argue that we can complain with our body as

well as our words, but I don't. I'm expected to listen and learn all the time, but parents don't abide by the same rules. "Where are we going?"

"Your mother taught you basics—and sladius basics transfer quite simply from practice instruments to true bladed weapons. Even so, she hasn't put you through a rigorous enough training, in my opinion." Dad leans over and pulls a sword from his pack. He extends it toward me, the tooled leather sheath sparkling where rubies, emeralds, and sapphires are mounted.

"What's this?"

Dad yanks it back. "Maybe you aren't ready after all, if you don't know what a *sword* is."

I roll my eyes. "I know it's a sword, but *whose* sword is it?"

He beams at me. "I had it made for you three years ago as a gift for your tenth birthday. Your mother wouldn't allow me to give it to you then, but I kept it and waited."

"Because of Tanvi."

Dad nods.

"But I get it now?"

"You can finally have it, I assume." He extends it slowly.

My hands tremble slightly as my fingers close over the tooled scabbard. *Accept the world as it is* has been embroidered on one side. I flip it over to see the rest of our family motto. *Or do something to change it.*

"You're finally a proper Heir," Dad says.

It's silly, but it almost feels like that's true, as if I've been treading water up until now, not fully prepared for my role as Mother's replacement.

"Well, strap that on your back," Dad says. "We've got quite a jog before you'll get to use it. I'm thinking we circle around and head up the Thames. There's a decent alcove where the Thames hits the Jubilee. If we time this right. . ." He eyes the sun, not yet high in the sky. "We'll jog right past shift change and no obnoxious guards will insist on following to watch us either."

I fumble once, and then again, before I manage to lash the straps in place across my shoulders and settle the sword against my shoulder blades. "Thank you," I whisper.

"Don't thank me yet," Dad says. "Once I've sliced you open and you're screaming in agony, see if you're still grateful then."

I don't mention that I've taken to gouging my arms and legs every night while I study my assigned topics. I'm years behind where Alora was at thirteen, thanks to this Tanvi scare. Pain training while focusing on something else should be second nature to me by now, but instead I'm doing it in secret. Ridiculous. I'll welcome those screams of agony—then who I am won't be so far away from who I should be. Evians aren't weak—we push through the pain. It's who we are. It's who I'll finally become, my birthright.

By the time Dad finally stops running, my thighs burn and sweat beads across my brow, thanks to the humid midsummer air of Southern England. Even so, adrenaline rushes through my entire body, my palms tingling to grip my new sword. I've waited so long that it hardly feels real that the moment is here: I will finally grip a bladed weapon and Dad will treat me like a real opponent, a threat.

Dad drops his pack near a palm tree and reaches over his shoulders to pull both his swords: Uzhastik and the slightly shorter Strakh. Horror and fear in his native Russian. "My father gave me these when I turned ten."

"Why didn't your mother sell you and Balthasar?" I ask, not for the first time.

"Pull your sword," Dad says. "Or you won't be ready for me."

I toss my pack against a tree trunk near Dad's and try to unsheathe my blade in one smooth movement like he just did. I fail miserably. The dumb sword is stuck, and I practically wrench my shoulder pulling it out.

"That's the wrong angle," Dad says softly. "You need to lift it straight out first, and then pull it downward. You'll practice that tonight until it looks easy."

I duck my head, hoping he won't notice how much blood has rushed into my cheeks. "I will."

"Good." He taps the end of my blade with his own and the vibrations travel down into my hand and wrist. "It's heavier than a wooden practice blade, and it won't bruise like even the hardest woods do. That blade is sharp. It'll part skin and bone and sinew. Are you ready?"

I force myself to meet his eyes. "I am Inara Alamecha, daughter of Althuselah and Enora. I am ready now, and I will always be ready. Tomorrow, next week, and for all time."

"Ambitious," Dad says. "I like it."

And then he's swinging, and I'm blocking as quickly as I can. He's going easy on me, and I don't even care. I'm using a real weapon. The sound when I throw my blade up in front of his is a clang, not a whack. The heft of the sword leaves my shoulder screaming in agony.

I love every single painful second.

But I can't block forever. I know what's coming. Before much longer, Dad will begin to slice and dice me, little by little. My leg, my arm, my side. He'll take it slow and easy, watching the level of injury by the widening of my eyes, the heave of my inhalation, the volume of my groan.

I can't have that. His report to Mother cannot be that I healed well and moved relatively well for a brand new fighter. No, if he tells her that, she'll take over again, and we'll be back to square one. I need to show him that I'm something special—I've felt it for years—this is my chance to *prove* it. Mother's only 710 years old. Everyone knows I'll be replaced eventually, which means I need to make my mark. I need to do something impressive, something valuable, something memorable. If I don't, I'll never carve out a place for myself, and when I'm replaced, I'll be relegated to the long list of retired heirs. I'll be nothing, worthless, unimportant. Nothing sounds worse to me.

So I kick dirt into Dad's eyes and swing wide with my very late birthday present.

My ploy doesn't work, not at all. Dad chuckles and blocks my swing with a glint in his eye. His laughing distracts him more than my attempt to take him down. So much for that idea. I can already imagine the sparkle in his eyes, both mischievous and patronizing, when he recounts this to Mother later. I grit my teeth at the image.

But then he freezes.

I have no idea what has worried him now, but I know exactly what to do about it. I thrust toward him, meeting no resistance whatsoever. My blade slides through the gap between his lower right ribs, sliding far deeper than I expected. I choke and yank it back, blood spurting from the puncture.

Oh no. Oh no. Oh no.

Why didn't he stop me? I force myself to swallow, noticing Dad still hasn't made any effort to fight back. My entire world had narrowed to this tiny stretch along the river, closed off on one side by an enormous abandoned windmill, and on the other by an overgrowth of trees. We've entirely isolated ourselves from the invasive eyes of the palace guards. It was Dad's intention from the beginning, so that I'm not under a microscope for my first session with a blade.

But it's bad news if we're surrounded by enemies.

I glance quickly at Dad's side and notice that he has already healed the wound I caused. I swallow and force myself to assess the threat that froze him in place.

A dozen warriors stand in a semicircle around us, their

boat half shoved on the riverbank behind them, all of them armed with bladed weapons. I wrack my brain for anything that will tell me who we're fighting. Who would have forced themselves this far up the Thames, in the center of our control? I can tell from their heart rates that they're all evian. That makes our odds twelve to two, if at thirteen years old I even count as a tally on our side, which I probably shouldn't. Twelve to one is—impossible. Beyond impossible. That means that we're dead.

"You don't want to kill me," Dad says softly.

"We do, actually," a woman says, her eyes flinty. "We'd rather capture you, of course, but the odds of us being caught in the act is too high. Melamecha sent us to kill *you* specifically, so finding you out here alone is a stroke of luck. Enora's still absurdly besotted with you after all these years, which means your loss will cut deeply."

"That's exactly why you should let us go—if you kill Enora's Heir *and* her Consort, she'll be forced to move against my little sister. We may be overextended right now, what with the shifting landscape in the Americas and the expansion into the Indies, but we'd still decimate Shamecha. Surely Melamecha knows that it would be a sanctioned response—no one would come to your aid."

"Ah, that's where you're mistaken. There's nothing to tie us to our queen whether we succeed or fail. She merely wants Enora to be vulnerable and hurting, you see. But if we were to fail, well." The woman spreads her hands wide.

The fact that she's disclosing who she answers to means she's utterly confident in their ability to kill us. One glance at Dad tells me that she's not wrong. No matter what skill he may have, he can't protect me and save himself, not against twelve armed soldiers. Even if a sentry hears us, it would only be two and a half against twelve.

"Keep your blade up, Inara, until the end." Dad leaps forward then, rushing toward the warriors standing ankle

14

deep in the flow of the river. An animalistic shout tears from his throat, and my knees tremble unsteadily.

But I keep my blade up.

Two women and a tall man peel away from Dad and head toward me. My heart thunders in my chest. I knew I'd never rule for Mother, but I didn't think I'd die, not like this, not so young. A woman with long, ebony hair that falls in a braid down her back strikes at me first. I block her and spin to face the other woman, but I can't face three directions at once. No one can.

A knife sinks into my shoulder blade, pain radiating outward in sharp spikes toward my shoulder, my lower back, and my spine. I crouch down involuntarily, the hilt of my gift slipping from my hand.

"We just chop off her head?" The man asks gruffly. "She's still a little girl."

"We have orders. может сделать правильно." Might makes right. The Shamecha motto. The black-haired woman steps toward me, stopping only inches away. My cowardly face is reflected back at me in the shine on the toes of her boots.

Tears well in my eyes and fall with soft splashes on the shiny leather. Mother would be *disgusted*.

I'm ashamed of myself.

My dad's fighting in spite of the odds—he's a true evian. His shouts and grunts are interspersed with swearing from his opponents. He's fighting furiously against nine warriors while I'm huddled and sobbing. But his blood runs in my veins. I might die, but I should do it standing—snarling in the face of my murderers. My fingers shoot forward and tighten on the hilt of my new blade. I leap to my feet, bringing my blade upward with all the force I can muster. It slices into the ebony haired woman's chest, blood pouring downward onto my hand. With the last ounces of strength in my body, as every part of my being rebels against what I'm doing, I wrench my wrist to the left.

I partially behead the woman, her eyes frozen wide in shock and horror.

I'm quite sure my expression matches hers, but I can't stop, not now. I am my father's daughter. A strangled sound behind me tells me that her companions are aware of what I've done. I arc my blade to the right, separating the rest of her neck from her head and eliminating any possibility of her healing what I've done.

A red haze descends over my vision and the world shifts around me, my footing suddenly unsteady. The unease I felt, my fear, my confusion, it all melts away as something else entirely suffuses my entire body. The man behind me growls and leaps toward me, but he does it slowly, as though he's moving at half the speed he should be moving. I pivot and bump his elbow, sending his blade wide, and slide mine underneath, gutting him with his own momentum.

I watch, morbidly fascinated, as his intestines tumble downward, and with a quick shift and plunge, I sever his spine. A grunt from the right alerts me to the movements of the other woman, this one howling in rage. I know just how she feels. I leap above her parry and sever her sword hand at the wrist, watching with idle curiosity as it thumps against the pebbles at the edge of the rushing river water. A pool of blood expands steadily around the large man whose spine I cut.

I spin in it carefully and stab the second woman, whose rage has morphed into horror, through the heart. A quick turn of my wrist slices through her aorta and separates the left and right ventricles. "Heal that," I whisper.

The haze deepens. A heartbeat behind me beats too loudly. The sound grates against my ears, making me twitch. I realize it's coming from the big man whose spine I severed—he's still alive. I remove his head from his body, and with light steps, I shoot toward where the other fighters still struggle. One man is bleeding in dozens of places, but two attackers lie motionless on the sand next to him, and the others all attack him—utterly unfair.

Not enough have died. I analyze the scene impassively, knowing they must all die. I can barely see clearly for the crimson film that obscures my view no matter how many times I blink. The critical details, they're crystal clear. I surrender to the dance then, as I was taught. Except, instead of pirouettes and plies, I slice, I carve, I terminate. People beg and scream and sob, and I smile, mirthlessly. They're pathetic. They deserve to die, all of them. Their beating hearts taunt me, enrage me.

The more I shred, the more I eliminate, the darker the haze around me descends until I almost can't see anything at all. But I can hear them, and it's enough. It's more than enough. My world narrows to the destruction, the satiation of the scarlet fury that consumes me.

"Stop!"

The simple command infuriates me and my lip curls upward from my teeth. Who dares order my actions? I can't stop—I'll never stop. This is my life, my purpose, my calling: death, destruction, the end of everything. And then, finally, the void.

"Inara! You'll kill me! Stop!"

A name. I know the name, somehow. *Inara.* I pause and blink. *Inara Alamecha.* It's someone I know. It's someone I respect.

The blood haze clears, a little.

I stumble backward. I shake my head. But wrath envelops me in a comforting blanket, and I growl.

"Inara Alamecha, daughter of Enora, daughter of Althuselah, you will STOP. Now."

I blink again. I clench my hand, the heft of the hilt

comforting. It's all that keeps me safe. I can't stop. The world must burn, and I hold the key to setting it afire.

"I'm your *father*, and I order you to stand down."

He *orders* me? Fury rises inside of me, exploding outward and my legs shift, my fingers tighten and I coil, ready to terminate this person who thinks to tell me what to do, how to behave. The red haze redoubles, my muscles tightening, my hands trembling, and I strike out again.

"I'm sorry. I didn't mean to command you." The voice trembles, the voice is terrified, the voice pleads.

I know the voice. How do I know the voice?

"I beseech you to spare me. I beg you to stop. Inara, it's Althuselah. It's your father. Don't kill me."

The man in front of me drops to his knees.

I kicked dirt into his face.

Laughing eyes.

A gift, glinting in the sun.

His arms around me, warm and comforting.

The flashes of memory confuse me.

The haze recedes.

I draw in a ragged breath.

"Please, Inara, please forgive me. I love you. I'm your father. You know me. Don't kill me, too." He draws a breath and this time, when he speaks, his voice is ragged, desperate. "Please remember me. I'm your dad."

Dad. More flashes. A spoon being lifted to my mouth. His face looking down on me and singing. Tossing me in the air, a smile splitting his face. Swinging me around. Picking me up and carrying me on his hip.

As if a drain opens up beneath me, the haze recedes in a rush. I can't bring myself to release my sword, but I use my free hand to wipe at my eyes. They burn in their sockets, like banked embers, like they'll never work properly again.

My hands tingle. My shoulders scream with the frustration of overtaxed muscles.

And then, like a wave crashing over a rock, like a bird lighting on a windowsill, like the first of the sun's rays falling on a windowpane, the anger evaporates entirely, and my vision clears.

The world is still soaked in red, but it's not because of whatever ungodly thing just overtook me. No, this is different.

The red all around me is blood spatter.

Oozing body parts.

Heads.

Hands.

Guts.

Scalps.

I drop my sword and stumble toward the river, gripping the side of the boat on the shore with one hand. Once the current reaches my knees, I lean forward, brace my hands against my thighs and vomit until there's nothing left in my stomach. I lift one hand to wipe my mouth and realize that I'm entirely coated in blood and gore. Sobs wrack my body, and I shake uncontrollably. I reach into the Thames and splash water against my arms, my body, my face, my legs. I scrub and scrub, but no matter how much I chafe against myself, blood still condemns me, marks me as guilty.

Murderer.

Destroyer.

I nearly killed my own dad.

Finally, finally, my arms at least are clean. My hands are the simple pinkish color of my skin. I stare at them, transfixed—my hands. They look exactly as they always have, but now I remember them doing *things*. Awful things. Unspeakable things. Gutting and slicing and severing. I shudder violently.

My mind rejects the memories, bucking forcibly against the things that scroll through my head on repeat. I would never—I couldn't even possibly do those things. I was about to die—maybe I did. Maybe I imagined the killing, the gore, and the guilt. Maybe I didn't do what I think I did. Something worse occurs to me. The last memory that makes sense was stabbing my dad. I remember doing that. What if he died and my mind made up the rest?

Did I kill my own father?

My heart stops in my chest. Did I? It's all such a blur. I shoved my sword into his side, the blade sliding smoothly between his ribs. I recall that moment perfectly. I stabbed him and then. . . Did I kill him, and lose touch with reality? Did I invent an attack to excuse my sins? I spin around as quickly as I can, but the riverbank looks the same as it did before. Red. So much red. Blood and gore everywhere—far too much to be explained by the death of only one man.

In the center of it all, my father stands tall—blood-soaked, but hale.

He's alive, but his eyes are sad. Bottomless pools of sorrow and regret.

And fear?

Tears roll freely down my cheeks.

Dad rushes toward me then, his strong arms outstretched. "Oh, Inara, are you there? Is it really you again?"

I stumble backward and throw my hands outward. "Stay away. Don't come closer."

He stops, his eyes wide. "Are you alright Inara, daughter mine?"

"Why do you keep saying my name?"

He smiles then. "You know your name?"

I scowl. "Of course I know my name."

He steps forward again, his arms rising toward me.

I shake my head. I can't seem to stop shaking it. "I'm—" I cover my face with my hands. "I don't know what I am, or what's happening to me. But I know that I'm a monster." I sink to my knees and drop my face in my hands. "This is all my fault. My fault." I rock back and forth, chanting. "My fault, my fault, my fault."

"It is not," Dad says. "None of this is your fault."

I can't stop chanting. "My fault my fault my fault my fault." But the word running through my head is different. *Monster monster monster monster MONSTER.*

"I know what happened, and I know what you are." His voice is calm. Clear. Confident.

I fall back on my butt without thinking, plunging myself up to my armpits in icy water. I wish the current would drag me under. I wouldn't struggle against it. I wanted Dad to have something notable to report to Mother, but not this, nothing like this. Never in my wildest, worst dreams, did I ever imagine anything this awful.

The daughter of Althuselah and Enora Alamecha. The daughter of the two most powerful rulers in the world— and I'm broken beyond repair. I almost killed my own father.

I chopped and sliced and *pureed* ten other people.

"You feel repulsed now, like you've done something you shouldn't have done, but you have to let that go. Because like my father, your grandfather, you're a berserker," Dad says softly. He takes another step toward me, his eyes scanning me carefully, but not fearfully. Watchfully. As if he's worried *for me,* not afraid *of me.*

A what? "I'm an abomination."

He laughs, the familiar sound traveling from his chest and out his throat. "No more than a bear or a wolf is an abomination. You did what your body forced you to do, what you were designed to do." He sits down next to me and takes my hand in his. "You're not the first, darling, and you're unlikely to be the last."

I look up, finally facing his face, his eyes, his feelings about me. "What?"

But he doesn't look disgusted, or scared, or angry. He looks concerned. "It's a closely guarded secret," he says. "And it's certainly not present on your mother's refined side of the family. If you swear never to breathe a word of this to another soul, I'll tell you the identity of the other berserker in our family, even though only your mother and I know it."

"Your dad, you mean?" He already told me about him. He might be in shock.

Dad laughs. "No, the other living berserker."

Oh. "Okay." I gulp. "I swear."

"Balthasar," he says. "My darling little brother is just like you. We discovered it when he was only eight years of age."

"Eight?"

Dad shrugs. "He killed a wild boar on a hunt."

"Huh?"

"That's what does it—killing a mammal. If you're a berserker and you take a life, you completely lose control. You'll kill everything anywhere near you—enemy, friend, the distinction ceases to matter."

My jaw drops.

Dad's face moves closer. His index finger gently pushes my jaw upward until my mouth clicks shut. "It's not all bad, darling. You'll be faster, stronger, and more skilled than any other fighter in the world." His lips purse. "Which makes me wonder." He mouth curls into a beautiful smile. "I would dearly love to see someone destroy my brother in a fight, you know."

"I never want to fight again," I say.

Dad smiles. "Actually."

I want to bawl and never stop. "That's not an option for me now, is it? Uncle Balthasar is Mother's Warlord for a reason." I might be sick again. I never want to go through anything like that again.

"Oh no, you misunderstood me. If your mother found out, she'd use your. . . skill set just as you fear. She wouldn't want to, but when things were hard, she'd use what she had to in order to solve the problem. Just as she has unwillingly used Balthasar for nearly seven centuries, hating herself for it every time."

I dig my fingers into the sand beneath me.

"Which is why you can never tell her, or anyone else." Dad's eyes pin mine. "And I don't say this lightly. I never keep anything from your mother. Not in the entire time I've known her, not a single secret."

"But you won't tell her about me?" I lift both eyebrows in disbelief. "Why not?"

Dad looks down at his hands. "It's for her own good—she really does want what's best for you, but the weight on her is incomprehensible in many ways. Your mother is my whole world, as you well know. She is everything to me, but if she knew, this would eclipse your life. It has been hard enough on me to watch my brother used as a tool. I can't allow that for you. Knowing you're unlikely to ever take over for Mother and rule after her, I think our plans for your future have shifted a little bit."

I've known Mother would likely have another daughter after me for a while—after all, she's only seven hundred years old—but hearing it spoken aloud stings a bit. "What does that mean?"

"You're a smart girl, so this will make sense. Your new job is not to *excel* at anything. You're not to be the smartest, the fastest, or the scariest. You're to be perfectly acceptable at everything, but the best at nothing."

"Why?"

Dad smooths the furrow between my eyebrows. "It rankles, the thought of being acceptable but not extraordinary, especially as you *are*. But dear one, no one sees the threat they don't expect. You'll be right there, the best of them all, but no one will ever suspect you, because people believe what they see, always. The most powerful weapon we have is perception. And you need to control everything about the perception surrounding you to guard this secret, and in so doing, to maintain your own freedom."

Freedom.

Dad wants to keep me free—to allow me to make my own decisions, to choose my own path.

I don't care at all about freedom. I want to follow Mother—to rule in her place once she's gone. I want to make her proud. I want to destroy anyone who stands in our way. I want to decimate the other families and rule the entire earth.

But do I want to be free? Not even a little bit.

The thought of Mother always being a little disappointed in me sinks deep into my soul. She will always wish I could do more, do things faster, be better. "I don't want anyone thinking I'm not quite enough." I purse my lips and look at the ground. "I'd rather just tell Mother—tell everyone—and let them fear me." I think about the gibbering, remorseful mess I was moments before, and I wonder whether I really want that. But I know that I *want* to want it.

"You can," Dad says. "You definitely can. And maybe that's the right call. But when I envision the life I want for you, it's not as your mother's executioner or battle commander. I don't want you to be her blunt instrument, wiping out her enemy armies brutally, relentlessly. I've seen firsthand the toll it takes on my brother. Believe me when I tell you that the glory isn't worth the pain."

I look back at the grotesque landscape behind us and shudder. "You might be right."

"Great." Dad stands up. "Then we have a lot of work to do."

"What?"

"We need to clean up the evidence of your particular skill set."

My eyes widen. "How?"

Dad laughs. "Well, I imagine the proximity to the river will help us, and the way in which you sort of chopped everything into small pieces won't hurt either. Fish will eat most anything that bleeds." He bobs his head at the churning and hungry fish that have gathered not far from us.

I leap to my feet and slosh back toward the riverbank.

"As to the rest, I think we'll keep a few of the carcasses, maybe the ones I killed to show your mother that Melamecha's sore with her again."

I gulp. "Okay. Tell me what to do."

3

1842

Sweat drenches Diablo's neck and shoulders, but he loves racing as much as I do. Instead of pulling back, I lean forward and ask for more. "Push a little harder! I think we can take this."

The cove of trees at the far end of the Queen's Walk barrels into view, barely.

And Nephtali's mare pulls a hair ahead.

I growl.

"H'ya!" The deep bass from behind me sets my teeth on edge. Kohl is always nipping at my heels on his stupid dappled stallion.

"It's close, sweetheart," I whisper to Diablo. "It's time to *go*." I whip him lightly and the powerful muscles in his haunches contract and catapult us ahead. We pull out front just in time, sandy loam flying in chunks around us, cheers and shouts and swearing coming from behind me.

We won!

I pull back gently. "Amazing, boy, just wonderful." I lean forward and pat the side of his neck, but then his front left leg stumbles and twists. He lurches forward, the back of his body tumbling over the front. I shoot over the front of him, landing in a pile of excess vegetation, snapping my collarbone when I hit a pile of cobblestones wrong.

The collarbone has to be the world's most useless bone —it breaks far too easily and far too often. I grit my teeth and shove it back into place so it won't heal wrong and need to be rebroken later. I bite my lip and shove up to standing. In spite of excellent boots, I've managed to break my ankle, too. How embarrassing. I turn around to see how many people are watching and realize that Diablo didn't stumble. His hoof fell into some lazy farmer's pile of rocks from the adjacent field that sank into the ground after years of neglect.

He thrashes and lifts his shattered leg, the bottom a mangled mess above his shining black hoof. The hole into which his hoof sunk snapped his cannon bone and displaced his fetlock joint.

My heart crumples inside my chest.

No. No, no, no. Not Diablo. Not my favorite stallion. I rush to his side, my hands cradling his huge face. He snaps at my hands—which means he's in bad shape. He never bites. Well, he never bites me, anyway.

"Oh, boy, no, not like this."

"You know what has to be done," Mother says quietly behind me. I turn my head slowly. She's still mounted on Napoleon—the Lipizzaner stallion she named just to rub Senah's face in her most recent epic loss.

As if killing my sweetheart wouldn't be hard enough for a normal person—I *can't* do it. Mother sees my reticence as a sign of weakness, but she doesn't know the reality for me. For the millionth time, I wonder whether Dad was right not to tell Mother. I have no idea what he had to do to convince her to surrender my training to him, but I'm sure it was something huge. And we've made no progress whatsoever, not in twelve years.

If Mother knew the truth, she wouldn't be demanding

that I trigger an episode. If she forces me to kill my precious stallion, I'll kill the thirty people present and then keep going. As hard as it was to stop that first day, it has only grown harder since. Not to mention, my skill has grown commensurately as well. I'm not even sure Balthasar would be able to stop me.

"I know what you want me to do, yes," I say.

"The bone is shattered. It can't be repaired. Any other course of action is cruel and beyond that, deluded." She looks away, as if that settles it.

"Surely I don't have to do it in front of all of these people."

Mother quirks an eyebrow. "Death is a part of life, as evians are taught from an early age."

"Technically, it's the opposite of life," I say.

She doesn't smile. "I'll steer everyone back, but if you don't take care of this quickly, we'll have words later."

The further away everyone is when I do this, the better. I wish Dad were here. He always thinks of a reason to get me out of situations like this.

When Mother heads back, almost everyone follows her. Almost.

One of Alora's personal guards lingers. Gideon. Why does it have to be him? His ebony hair and golden eyes draw my eye no matter where he is in the palace.

It would be a real pity if I killed someone so devastatingly beautiful.

He glances over his shoulder at the receding crowd, but instead of turning his deep bay gelding to follow them, he swings his right leg over the saddle, dismounting. Worse and worse. "Need a hand?" His eyes darken a shade, nearing copper. I wish they didn't radiate pity. "I'm not sure I could kill Verian here, no matter how badly he was injured."

A knot forms in my chest. "Mother insists that I do it myself."

28

He glances over his shoulder. "How would she ever know?"

My lip curls. Not many people on the island would risk defying Mother. "Blood spatter."

"Don't worry. I'll sling some blood at you when I'm done." He holds out his hand for my blade.

"And you'll do it with my blade? Attention to detail," I say. "I like it." I unsheathe my blade and hand it to him. When I turn to cradle poor Diablo's head in my arms, tears roll freely down my face. It's a good thing Mother's not here to witness this. She'd be furious with me for everything about how I'm handling this.

"Emotion isn't a weakness, you know." Gideon's standing closer than I expected. When I turn toward him, he's towering over me. Since I stand only a few inches under six feet, not many people tower over me, but he manages.

"You sure about that?"

"Oh, I know it's a liability to let anyone know how you feel when you're negotiating the fate of nations. I get that —I'm not a simpleton. But we should be allowed to *feel*. In fact, if we carved all emotion out of ourselves entirely, I think we'd be a sorry bunch indeed, don't you?"

The rush of emotion that fills my chest when I nod almost overpowers me. Tears flow even more freely, dripping off my chin. "I'm such a mess. I'm sorry."

He wraps his free hand around my shoulders. "You shouldn't have to apologize for being fond of an animal, especially one this fine. Take a minute to grieve. Let me know when you're ready. And I was kidding about the blood spray. Clear out if you'd like. There's no way your mother will ever know, and no reason for you to witness something like this."

I wipe my face against Diablo's jaw. His huge brown eyes watch me trustingly. One more glance at his leg, blood covered and twisted all wrong, and I know Mother's right. Horses have light bones in their legs, and the front legs bear more than half their weight. Unlike a human, Diablo can't recover from this. "I love you, boy. And if there is a heaven somewhere, I hope I'll see you there." I drop to a whisper. "I doubt very much that I'll make it. But I hope you find green pastures and blue skies—and no piles of rocks."

"As hard as it is, this is the right thing to do," Gideon says. "When a creature is suffering like he is, putting it down is hard, but it's the right call."

I know he's right, but it seems so unfair. My body has already healed from more extensive injuries than he suffered, but for him, this one misstep is the end. I wipe my face again, this time with my hand, and press a kiss against his velvety nose.

Then I walk into the trees, leading Gideon's mount behind me as quickly as I can.

Gideon is efficient.

And he waits patiently while I figure out how to recover from the loss of Diablo. Once I realize I'm not in danger of going on a killing spree, the reality of the loss hits me in the gut. Gideon's horse, Verian, lets me hug him and cry into his silvery mane.

But I am Inara Alamecha, daughter of Enora and Althuselah Alamecha. I don't have the luxury of falling apart. So I think about those seconds at the end of the race when we won. I think about the dozens and dozens of times we've won in the past. The wind in my hair, the feel of Diablo's body beneath me, transporting me away from my stress, my fear, my anger, and my misery.

I think about what I loved about him, and I try not to think about how he'll never do that again, for me or anyone else. Because of a pile of rocks.

Why are things in life so senseless?

When I can finally head back without fear of sobbing, I square my shoulders and accept my sword. He even cleaned it for me. "Thank you."

"You're welcome," Gideon says. "I'm sorry it happened at all. I'll let the guards know to take care of the mess—did you want him buried somewhere close, or incinerated?"

"Outside my courtyard," I say. "If they can do it without drawing attention."

He lifts his eyebrows.

I sigh. "Mother wouldn't approve."

"I'm not daughter of the empress, but I think I have enough pull to manage an unobtrusive burial." Gideon's lips don't smile, but his eyes dance a little. It's perfect: self-deprecating and humble, but also confident. Why haven't I ever spoken to him before?

I want to thank him for averting a disaster likely involving his own death, but I don't dare. I can't ever tell anyone, especially not one of my sister's guards whom I don't know at all.

"Well, I appreciate it, but I don't need an escort from here. I'll be fine. Feel free to hop back up on Verian and ride to the stables."

"Where's your guard?" He lifts one unimpressed eyebrow. "Shouldn't they be taking care of this sort of thing for you?"

I snort. "They're all training with Balthasar right now—something about the new protocols for the new Springfield musket technology. Mother told him it was fine—that she'd be happy to make sure her guards kept an eye on me."

"It's a good thing I'm not a villain," Gideon says. "Because your mother's guards didn't really keep her word."

"Not that this area is really dangerous." Not since Dad quadrupled the perimeter guards and put in several outposts at intervals several hundred yards apart all the way down the river, anyway.

"Even so, I think I'll accompany you the rest of the way back."

"Will Alora be annoyed that you stayed to help me?"

"Alora?" Gideon laughs. "I think she blocked my name from her brain years ago. She always looks at me as though she's seeing me for the first time."

"That can't be right," I say without thinking. "You're the best looking guard at the palace." Heat rises in my cheeks in spite of my best efforts to prevent it.

Gideon glances at my face, and his nostrils flare. I find him attractive, and now he knows it. With as long as evians live, many consider relationships with a huge age gap to be perfectly acceptable. Some do not. Based on his reaction, he's one of the latter. And I've just stuck my foot so far into my mouth that I don't even know how to extricate it. I'm twenty-five and he's got to be at least a hundred years older than me, since he was one of Alora's purchased consort options.

"Inara!" Dad sprints toward us.

He must have heard that Mother left me to kill Diablo. I meet his eyes steadily, and he slows to a stop in front of us.

"You're fine," he says.

Gideon straightens his shoulders. "I may not be the most intimidating guard on the island, but I'm competent."

"No disrespect meant," Dad says. "I'm an unabashedly nervous father. Speaking of which, I owe you a huge thank you. Her Majesty forgot to task a few of her guards to look over Inara." Dad always recovers quickly.

"Gideon was just walking me back," I say.

"Of course he was, but now his services are no longer needed." Dad claps him on the shoulder, and Gideon salutes. He swings back up into Verian's saddle and wheels him around toward the stable, kicking right into an easy canter.

At least Dad saved me from dealing with the aftermath of my gaffe.

"He killed your stallion for you."

"He did." My voice is flat. Emotionless.

"We need to get this under control," Dad says.

"Really? I had no idea it was a problem." I start toward Windsor Castle again. "Thanks for reminding me."

"You could have killed dozens of people today, your mother among them."

"You think *I don't know that?* I would have thought of something to put her off." I don't mention that it was his stupid idea not to tell Mother in the first place.

"I know you hate it, but we need to practice pulling you out of the haze more often than we have been, not less. Twice a year isn't working."

I spin on the ball of my foot. "Fourteen people last time, Dad." My fingers curl into fists, and I drop my voice to the barest of whispers. "I killed fourteen people last time, because you couldn't pull me out of it before then."

"My research told me that the town was abandoned." Dad closes his eyes. "None of that was your fault, but until—"

"It *is* my fault." I force my hands to relax at my side. "I recall every single one of them. Every one. But Dad, are you one hundred percent positive that there isn't something else?"

"I've asked Balthasar over and over—enough times that he's becoming suspicious."

"He still maintains it's just a matter of discipline and practice?" Despair threatens to drown me. "It's getting worse, Dad, not better. I thought I killed you last time—that's the only thing that brought me back, recognizing your cry of terror at the end. I can't do that again. I can't. There has to be more to it than he's telling us."

"No."

"I have to tell Balthasar. I need someone who knows what I'm up against to train me. It's been *twelve years* of failure and every single mistake has an unacceptable cost."

Dad's arms envelop me. "I know," he whispers into my hair. "But you can't tell him. I've become more and more convinced that you cannot trust my brother with your secret. As much as Balthasar loves you, he would use it against you—he wouldn't be able to help himself. He's a predator in his heart of hearts."

I sob against his chest. "I hate everything about myself."

"I love you, and God loves you, and what you are is how He made you. You are beautiful and terrible, and this is a horrible burden to bear, but we will figure it out together, I swear it."

"I need help." My voice breaks.

"I'll press him again, but for now, you will be with me all the time, and no matter what, until we learn more, you will not kill so much as a mosquito. Is that clear?"

My laugh sounds forced. "I can kill bugs, Dad."

"I know; it's only those stupid furry mammals that set you off."

"It's not funny," I say, laughing through my tears.

"Sometimes in life, you must laugh and cry in tandem or you won't survive."

Frederick runs toward us, another guard trailing him.

Dad and I spring apart, and I wipe at my eyes.

Frederick pulls up short and brushes his uniform down, his eyes aimed pointedly at the bush next to us. "Your Highness," he says. "I'm very sorry for interrupting. Her Majesty sent me to inform you that Senah's Consort has died."

"Oh," Dad says. "That's terrible. I'm sorry to hear it."

Frederick swallows. "It's my understanding that he died at the hand of Senah's new. . ." Frederick clears his throat.

"I'm twenty-five years old," I say. "You can say it. Senah's new boyfriend killed her Consort."

"From the reports of our agents, that appears to be the case."

"You ran all the way out here to tell us that?" Dad raises one eyebrow.

"Not exactly," Frederick says. "We've received an invite to Senah's wedding. It will take place on Sunday."

"Sunday, as in four days from now?" Dad asks.

Frederick shrugs. "The king is dead."

"Long live the king," I say. "And if we want any hope of making it there in time, we better hurry."

4

1842

Mother doesn't even ask about Diablo when I reach the throne room where she must have met the delegate from Malessa. "I am not going."

Dad meets my pointed sideways glance and shrugs.

"Mother, you have to go," I say. "Senah is your closest ally."

"Her personal life is a mess, and she persists in rubbing our faces in it."

"You've been lucky," I remind her. "Dad is practically perfect, but not everyone finds someone like him."

Mother rolls her eyes. "Practically perfect?"

"Inara gets confused sometimes. She meant to say I'm perfect, no qualifier." He smirks. "But if you won't go, then she will go in your place."

"She's old enough now." Mother steeples her hands and stares at nothing.

"Senah will be offended." I sit on the steps in front of Mother instead of crossing the dais to my throne on her left. She isn't hearing petitions, so the throne room is nearly empty, and if I take my seat we can't all see one another.

Dad takes his place on her right side, always perfect in spite of his self-mocking, always in harmony with his wife without even trying. He takes her hand in his easily, as if he's done it ten million times. Perhaps he has.

Her shoulders relax, but her face collapses into a scowl. "I hope she is offended. She can't crook her finger and expect to set me racing." Mother's eyes roll skyward. "Four days."

"I'm sure it has more to do with who *won't* be able to reach her in that timeframe and less to do with forcing you to hurry," Dad says reasonably. "She knows you aren't in the Americas right now, and that there's no chance Adika could possibly arrive in time, for instance."

Sometimes I hate being evian. Every single action, every single communication is fraught with underlying meanings beneath subtext, piled around hidden messages.

It's unbearably exhausting.

Mother assumes this is some kind of power play, when it might not be. Maybe Senah is mourning and making bad decisions. Maybe she's embarrassing herself, but it's her life to live, and some of her choices might not have anything to do with us. "Could she be hoping no one makes it in time? Maybe she wants a small ceremony, not an affair of state."

Mother makes a sound of disgust low in her throat. "If she wanted privacy, she wouldn't be formally making him her Consort. And she knows very well that we'll have time— she'll expect to see me." Mother taps the fingers of her free hand on the edge of the throne. "You will take twenty guards with you, as well as your father and his retinue of twenty."

I don't bother arguing, not when she's in this kind of mood. "Yes, Mother."

"What will you gift her?" Dad asks.

Mother sighs. "I won't attack her for the next month."

Dad shakes his head. "Come now, you can do better than that. She has been your closest ally off and on for centuries."

"And when she's not my ally, she has been my most irritating enemy."

Dad stands up and pulls Mother to her feet. He whispers something in her ear and her bad mood evaporates like water thrown on a hot pan.

"Fine, fine. I've got a few ideas."

"That's more like it." Dad takes Mother's arm in his and tugs her toward the door. "Let's go talk them over."

"Be ready at sunrise tomorrow," Mother says. "Go straight to the training barracks and recover your guards. They should be done by now. Select the ones who will accompany you, notify whomever you choose as your formal escort, and pack your things. Larena can help you with clothing selection if you need advice."

I curtsy and jog out the door, not waiting for her and Dad to leave first. I nearly collide with Alora in the hall outside.

"Excuse me," she says, her eyes wide.

"Sorry," I say. "Mother sent me to pack."

Alora's guards, Isaiah and Lennox, take several large steps back to give us space when they realize we'll be speaking for a moment, and they cross their arms over their chests.

"Pack? You're going to the wedding?"

I swallow. "I guess Mother's annoyed at the short notice."

"I'm a little jealous," Alora says. "We haven't had much dancing here lately, and you'll be there to hear exactly what happened and meet this new Consort in person."

"I could ask Mother to send you along to advise me," I say.

Alora tilts her head. "You would do that?"

Gideon's face flashes through my mind—how could she not even notice him? Would he be part of her retinue if she does come? "If you want me to—I mean, I don't mind. You'd bring a few guards along too—making us look more impressive, right?"

"Isn't father going with you for that very reason?" she asks. "To advise you, I mean?"

"He is." My heart sinks.

"Why do you want me to come?" Alora narrows her eyes at me. She's a good sister, and she gracefully accepted being replaced. She has never threatened me in any way, and she has always offered words of encouragement. Even so, we've never been close or overly friendly, though I'm not quite sure why.

"I don't," I say. "I mean, I don't care either way."

"Gideon stuck around to help you out today," she says slowly. "He killed your horse, didn't he?"

My heart beats faster inside my chest, and I calm it purposefully. "He stayed to ensure I returned safely."

"Mother hared off quickly enough."

"I asked her to—I didn't want to have to kill Diablo in front of everyone."

"You didn't want to do it at all." Alora's eyes see far too much. I'm already regretting my offer to ask Mother to send her. "I don't blame you, mind you. I wouldn't want to do it either. I'd rather cut off my own finger than kill Gladiator."

"What are you really asking?" In spite of my concerted effort to keep my voice regulated, my consonants are a little too clipped.

Her lip turns up very slightly. Not a smile, not quite, but a knowing expression nonetheless. "You want me to come so I'll bring Gideon."

My eyes widen alarmingly, and I wipe at one as if I've

got something in it. "That's not even a question." I hate that she always seems so much more put together than I am.

"He is handsome—and I've noticed you looking." Alora's smile is the warmest I've ever seen from her, the most genuine. "I've always found him to be a little too stiff and unyielding, but if you're taken with him, you should ask Mother to reassign him. You'd have my blessing to add him as one of your guards."

I want to sink into the floor and disappear.

"But to answer your question, I'm shamelessly willing to leverage the face of one of my guards into an invite, so yes. I'll take you up on your offer—if Mother approves the request, I'd love to accompany you."

More allies are always a good thing when you're going into enemy territory. I just wish I were positive that Alora's an ally. "Consider it done."

My older sister whispers softly as she brushes past me. "Mother would hate it if you chose someone more than a hundred years older than you, but isn't that part of the attraction?" She winks at me and disappears around the corner.

I hadn't even thought about what Mother would say if I expressed a preference for Gideon. His bloodlines are immaculate—Mother may not think highly of Leamarta's current predicament or the decisions that landed her in it, but as one of her sons, he's eighth generation. Not bad at all.

"Inara?" Eirik's tenor voice snaps me out of my musings.

I should *not* be standing alone in a main hallway, pondering the respectability of my sister's guard's ancestry. I have got to focus better. "All the training is complete?"

Eirik's nearly onyx eyes evaluate my posture, my location, and my general attitude with a hefty amount of skepticism, but finally he nods. "We've been looking for you, actually, for quite some time. Your mother told us she thought you'd be at your rooms, but you weren't."

"I ran into Alora, quite literally in fact, and was detained."

"Allow me to escort you back to your room," Eirik says.

As if I need a guard to keep me safe. I could butcher the entire palace and no one could stop me, except perhaps my uncle. The people around me should be surrounded by guards—the world is a flock of sheep in danger from a terribly famished wolf. I want to tell him to run away. Fast. But instead I say, "Thank you."

My life is such a farce.

By the time we reach the hallway to the Alamecha living quarters, Eirik has been joined by Tarben, Cassius, and Vasil.

"You shouldn't have approved Balthasar's request to train us all at once," Vasil says, his verdant green eyes snapping. "You were left entirely unattended after the race, and I'm at fault." His words claim culpability, but his eyes accuse.

Normally I'd go toe to toe with him—he shouldn't be taking me to task, especially when nothing went wrong. I couldn't ask for a better head of my personal guard, but he challenges me a little more often than he should. Today, though, I could really have used his overbearing presence. He might not have defied my mother to kill Diablo, but one of my other guards might have. I would have had more options, in any case. "Agreed."

Vasil's eyes widen and his Adam's apple bobs as he processes that I'm not arguing with him. I've always assumed he enjoyed our bickering, but I might be a bit obnoxious to guard, now that I think about it. I'm always complaining about them doing their jobs, mostly because I know I'm not nearly as 'at risk' as they believe me to be based on my private training and lack of participation in public demonstrations of fighting.

When we reach my door, I wave Vasil inside. He hesitates to follow at first, but only for a moment. "Be vigilant," he tells Tarben, Cassius, and Eirik, as if they'll wander off entirely or fall asleep without him to watch them.

I almost giggle at the thought of Cassius drooling on Eirik's shoulder, or Tarben's head leaning against the doorframe while he snores.

"You need me for something?" Vasil's always so terribly serious. With his shock of white hair, and his deep, almost black skin, his eyes look almost impossibly green. They practically glow. I can see why Mother prefers him to my other guards. He'd make an excellent partner—very capable. And no empress of Alamecha has ever chosen a scion of Shenoah—it would please Adika to no end to have her nephew as my Consort.

Not that I'm likely to ever ascend Mother's throne.

But I don't thrill when he's around. I don't long for him when he's gone. With parents who can barely keep their hands off one another, even now, after seven hundred years together, I can't even imagine settling for good bloodlines in my match.

I want true love. The kind that rocks you to your core. The kind that transforms your perspective, that fundamentally changes who you are, so that you orient your entire life around that person instead of around yourself. I want what my mother and father have—I want that or nothing.

Balthasar has never married. In fact, as far as I know, he's never even expressed an interest in anyone. Balthasar is the only other berserker I know. Dad's father was only with Reshaka for three decades before he died—did he love her?

What if we're incapable of love? What if I really am broken? Can I doom someone else to a virtual eternity with me—a monster who might snap at any moment—without even *truly* loving them? Without knowing beyond a doubt that they love me back?

"Inara? Are you okay? I heard about Diablo, and I'm so sorry. I'm sure that was a very difficult trial to endure." Vasil reaches toward me.

I stumble backward, involuntarily remembering Diablo's eyes, and his scream when Gideon— "I'm fine," I say. "But I wanted to ask you about your position."

"Excuse me?" Vasil asks.

"How do you feel about it?"

His only reaction is a furrow between his eyebrows. "My position as head of your guard, Your Highness?"

I nod.

"I was surprised when you chose me," he says. "Shocked might be a better word."

"In a good way?" Why didn't I ask him this before? Mother told me to order my guards years ago, when I was not quite seventeen years old, and I just did it. I didn't even talk to them about it.

He clears his throat. "It is a huge honor to be responsible for your safety, Your Highness."

And my selection usually indicates that I'm leaning toward choosing him as my Consort. I sigh. "I'm not asking whether you're honored. I want to know if you like it."

"You're asking whether I like it? What does that matter?"

Liking something isn't typically much of a priority for us, it's true. I can't think of a time that Mother has ever asked me whether I enjoyed doing something. Not eating a certain type of food, not wearing a particular type of clothing, not completing the various tasks assigned to me. 'Like' doesn't enter into our lives very often, but Gideon's words keep coming back to me.

Emotion isn't a weakness, you know. . . If we carved all

43

emotion out of ourselves entirely, I think we'd be a sorry bunch indeed.

It might be the truest thing I've ever heard. "It may not be something that matters to most people, but I find that it matters to me. Do you *enjoy* leading my guards? Does the pleasure of being in charge make up for the added stress and work?"

Muscles work in Vasil's square jaw.

I guess that's my answer. I shouldn't expect him to actually express displeasure out loud, not when he has been trained in the same way that I have—to deny any and all personal expectations and desires, to subvert them for the good of Alamecha. "Never mind," I say. "You may go. I have a lot of preparations to complete before we leave."

Vasil gulps and pivots on his heel, but not before his shoulders relax, and he exhales quickly.

In relief.

He doesn't harbor any feelings for me that I don't share. That's good to know, at least. But I feel a little guilty for unwittingly torturing him all these years. He must have been waiting all this time for the day the axe would fall— for the time I would express some kind of interest in him. I've been so worried about my own problems that I haven't even looked around myself to see the nightmare I've created for the people in my immediate circle of care.

For all I know, Vasil has been in love with someone else without acting—because he was implicitly bound to me.

Gideon opened my eyes to the situation. That's probably why I keep thinking of him. It can't be that I *like* him. After all, he looked at me like I had lost my mind when I told him he was Alora's best looking guard. I didn't even speak the full truth: he's the best-looking man in the entire palace. Alora suggested that I request Mother transfer him to be part of my guard. I think about it—I've thought of little else since she suggested it—but as awful as it was to

44

see that Vasil had no interest in me, I'm not sure I could handle the same from Gideon.

It's better that I keep my distance.

By sunrise, I deeply regret my decision to invite Alora. She's already mounted when I reach the stable. She's chatting with Dad easily, comfortably, as though they don't share any horrific secrets. Honestly, she looks like she doesn't have a care in the world.

I wish, and not for the first time, that this stupid curse hadn't passed to me. I wish it had gone to Alora, or Dad, or anyone else. But wishes don't change a thing, so I try not to waste much time on them.

"Who would you like to ride?" Jocelyn asks.

"Diablo," I snap, knowing that's impossible.

Jocelyn flinches, and guilt strikes me deeply. It's wrong to make others suffer just because I am, and yet, I couldn't help myself.

"She'll ride Verian," a deep voice behind me says. "He's not quite as fast as Diablo, but he's close, and he has the smoothest gallop you've ever felt in your life."

My heart stutters embarrassingly, and I turn around to face Gideon. "I couldn't possibly take your horse."

His eyebrows lift. "Oh, I'm not offering to give him to you."

He's done it again—made me feel utterly idiotic—and somehow it only makes me like him more. "I didn't mean take, as in take forever. I meant—"

A deep laugh rumbles through his chest. "I knew what you meant," he says, his voice pitched low, just for me. "I'm teasing you, Your Royal Highness, but I gather that's not a common occurrence."

Alora thought he was too stiff? I wish he were a little more formal. Then maybe my stomach would stop acting like I ate something questionable and settle down.

"Your Highness," Vasil says from inside the stable. "I

took the liberty of saddling Kimball for you." He's holding the reins for his white gelding in his right hand.

Gideon scrunches his nose slightly. "I think she's a little better suited to a stallion, don't you?"

Before the two of them can come to blows, I say, "I appreciate the gesture, Vasil, more than you can know. But I just told Gideon I'd borrow his horse, Verian."

Vasil doesn't scowl at Gideon. He simply bows and leads his horse out of the stable, mounts, and waits. Thank goodness for that.

"Who will you ride?" I ask.

"Oh, I've got Verian's sister, you know. She's one of the feistiest mares I've ever bred."

"Can you handle her?" I look up at him through my lashes.

"I'm not sure yet, but I'm always eager for a challenge."

"Let's go," Dad says. "We have a long way to go yet."

Once we leave, Gideon falls in with Alora's nine other guards, but almost every time I glance his direction, he's looking at me. It almost redeems me from my stupid comment yesterday. Not quite, perhaps, but almost. The day's ride is boring and grueling, as it always is to travel sixty miles by horseback in one day. By the time we reach Brighton, I'm more than ready to fall into a bath and then bed in our sea cottage.

But I need to at least thank Gideon for the use of his horse.

"Thanks for lending Verian," I say. "He was as wonderful as you promised."

Gideon smiles at me, his eyes lightening to amber. "I'm glad he was a gentleman for you."

"And how was his sister? It looks like you managed."

"She's not as accustomed to long rides as he is, but she's more stubborn. It's an undervalued trait. She and I got along just fine."

"I'm glad to hear it," I say.

"I'm not surprised," he says. "I've known she had extraordinary fire inside of her since the first time I saw her let loose."

"Why didn't you ride her much before now?"

"Someone else was always in the way," he says softly. "Her sibling, in fact."

"Her brother Verian, you mean?"

He shrugs. "What else could I mean?"

What else, indeed?

As exhausted as I am, I barely sleep that night. The next morning, Dad commands nearly all my attention on the channel crossing. He walks me through what to expect, and how to present Mother's gift—a beachside estate in Brighton, actually, a few miles from the one we slept at the night before, in case Senah's current property prompts unwanted memories. It's not a bad idea, as far as wedding gifts go. It's supportive and it has some value, but nothing that will sway the balance of power between our families.

"We need the alliance between our families," Dad says. "Or your mother could be in a very precarious position. Based on Senah's support, we have extended ourselves quite far in Europe and beyond."

"Mother has advanced the position of the family more than anyone thought possible," I say.

"But it was a gamble," Dad says. "We are in a. . . delicate position right now. Your mother doesn't see it, but our empire is a house of cards, and one wrong move could topple our control in several places at once. The other families are jealous of our progress and they'd like to tear us down—more than I care to contemplate."

"Your brother thinks we should pounce, now," I say. "Take out the other families one by one."

"Balthasar has always been too ambitious, and not nearly cautious enough."

"He's a brilliant strategist," I say. "Everyone says so."

Dad places his hand over mine on the edge of the barge, his eyes watching the approaching coastline of France. "He is brilliant, but he plays a different game than you or I."

"How so?"

"Balthasar has never had much to lose."

No wife, no children, and no family he values, other than his brother and his nieces. Is it because he's a berserker? I want to ask, but Dad's already upset about the whole issue. What I really need is to ask Balthasar these questions himself. "I don't get why I can't tell him."

Dad doesn't look at me, but his hand stiffens. "No one else can know, but especially not him. Don't you think he hates being the only one? Don't you think he's tired of being used? All the weight resting on his shoulders is taxing —he would love to share it with someone else. I know you feel like you're connected in some way, and that you would benefit from his knowledge, but trust me. He would benefit far more."

"Maybe I *should* share some of the responsibility that falls on him. Maybe that's why—"

"No," Dad says. "I've seen what it has done to him, and no—not to my daughter." He turns toward me then, his eyes full to the brim with love, with hope, and with plans for my future. "You have a millennium of living rolling out before you—and I want it to be everything you deserve. This will not ruin another member of my family."

"Fine." But I have questions, so many unanswered questions. Dad's right though—information can't be unshared once it's out. If I tell Balthasar who I am, or if I tell Mother, they can't ever un-know.

We don't arrive until nearly ten p.m. the night before the wedding. It leaves Joanne working nearly all night to prepare our creased and rumpled gowns, but by sunrise, they're ready.

48

Without even planning it, we look like a coordinated set. Dad's wearing all white—except for his double-breasted black silk coat and a crimson cravat, tied Osbaldeston style. Alora's gown is such a rich indigo that it's practically black, with faint crimson accents. The neckline is low and narrow, hugging her shoulder blades and scooping dangerously low in the back. As if to dare someone to challenge her, she piled her cinnamon colored hair high on her head, drawing attention to it.

My crimson gown is made of a silk so shimmery that it almost feels wrong to simply call it satin. Where Alora's dips low in the back, mine is nearly too low in the front. Unlike her, I don't have the confidence to accentuate the gown, so I made Joanne leave my hair down, only plaiting enough around my crown to secure the deep pigeon blood ruby tiara Mother sent.

We walk together toward the seats reserved for us, Alora on one side of Dad, me on the other. Our guards are arrayed both in front of and behind us, but I notice that Gideon is behind me, not Alora, and his cravat matches my dress. I shouldn't react at all, but it makes me smile into my fan.

For a wedding that caused so much gossip, this one is remarkably smooth. Lainina performs the ceremony, presumably because Mother chose not to come. She doesn't pause in any strange places or imply in any way that she resents the death of her brother—Senah's former Consort. No one protests, no one scowls, and no one even looks upset.

Of course, knowing Senah, she may have already eliminated anyone who might cause issues. She's not exactly known for tolerance or forgiveness. And no one ever claimed that Hessiah and Lainina were close, so it's no surprise she's willing to perform the ceremony between Senah and a random nobody from Shenoah as a show of good faith—the new Consort, Ekon, is the wildcard. No one really knows anything about him.

"That wasn't nearly as fun as I had hoped," Alora whispers.

"The day has barely begun," Dad says. "Be patient."

The banquet goes just as smoothly, but perhaps it's for the best. I've had enough drama in the past week already. When I present Senah with Mother's gift, she smiles broadly. "She couldn't quite bring herself to come, but at least she's sending me a thoughtful gift."

I open my mouth to defend Mother, but no words form.

"It's alright, child. I knew your Mother would struggle with the ugliness of the past few weeks." She takes my hand in hers and squeezes. "May you be as lucky in love as your mother has been. That is my prayer for you, you know. Not many of us find what she has found. If you do, never let go."

For a moment, I'm worried she'll never release my hand. I know she's eight hundred and twenty years old, but it's hard to really conceive of what that means when she looks barely older than me. "Thank you for the advice," I say, finally.

"Pah, you don't care about my advice," she says, her generous lips curling upward. "You're far too young to be interested in what I have to say, but maybe one day, you'll remember what I said. Maybe it'll help you make the right decision instead of the wrong one."

"Have you made the wrong decision?" I ask.

"Too many times to count," she says. "But if you quote me on that, I'll call you a liar."

Again, I have no idea what to say.

"Pardon my candor, child. My wedding day has me in an uncommonly good humor."

"I'm glad that you're in a good mood," I say. "You should be today."

"You too," she says. "Promise me you'll dance to every song."

"Of course I will," I say.

But when Senah dances her first song, a two-step, I realize that I might break that promise. No one has asked me to dance, and Dad is talking to Alora, which surely means he'll dance with her first. How embarrassing.

"Are you already engaged for the first song?" Gideon asks, his hand at my elbow.

"Is it pathetic if I say no?"

"Nothing you do is pathetic," he says.

He has no idea how wrong he is. I shake my head. "Not engaged."

"Well, you certainly are now. And although it might create a fuss, I'm happy to fill in on any dance in which you aren't otherwise engaged, all night long."

"Almost like you were my escort here tonight."

"Do you have an escort?" He lifts his left eyebrow.

"I didn't select one, so I think technically my father is my escort."

"He's never been very attentive to anyone other than your mother."

"Which is probably just as it should be," I say.

"I'm happy to fill in for him." When Gideon smiles broadly, a dimple appears on the left side, but not on the right. His smile has always been absolutely breathtaking, but now it's also endearing. And it feels as if I know a secret—which is absurd. Everyone who has seen him smile this big has seen that dimple.

When the music begins and his arm circles my waist, I look away from him in desperation. I can't do or say anything else as idiotic as that first conversation we had. My eyes lock with Alora's, and her knowing smile is almost more humiliating than my stupid declaration.

"Your guard is glaring at me," Gideon whispers.

"Who?" I glance around, scanning the crowd as we spin. Vasil's standing at attention, as always. Conner looks bored. Eirik and Cassius are dancing with two of Dad's guards.

"Vasil, of course. I've usurped him again."

I can't keep from giggling. "Vasil? He looks like he always looks."

"He needs to find a new expression then. His glare looks practically constipated."

"Stop," I say. "Poor Vasil doesn't mind that you're dancing with me. In fact, if I had to guess, I'd say he's relieved."

Gideon nearly stumbles, but he recovers quickly. "How could he possibly be relieved?"

I squeeze his hand. "He sort of told me the other day that he doesn't much like leading my guards." I drop my voice. "I think he might actually have a crush on someone else."

Gideon's eyes burn into mine. "He's a fool."

"It didn't upset me."

"It didn't?"

I shake my head. "I was relieved. He might be Mother's pick for me, but it's not like she chose Dad for his pedigree."

"He's eighth generation," Gideon observes. "Not a bad pedigree."

I laugh. "He wasn't one of her guards at all. She met him on the battlefield."

"I heard that rumor, but I hadn't heard it confirmed."

"He says that her beauty caused him to betray his own family," I say. "Although I'm sure it's more complicated than that. I mean, we're evian. We're all beautiful."

"Even so, some of us shine a little brighter." Gideon bows over my hand, and I realize the song has ended.

Before I can say another word, I'm claimed by Dad, and then a sequence of other royals attending the ball. I don't pay much attention to any of them. I keep hoping for a break, keep glancing at where Gideon is standing, smiling at me, but it doesn't happen.

Finally, I've had enough. "I'm sorry," I say to the tall young man approaching me. "I need to take a short break."

I make a beeline for the refreshment table and fill a plate with every savory treat I can manage. I grab a glass of something honey colored and dart toward the veranda. I need air and space to clear my mind of the golden eyes that haunt me.

Or so that I can think about them without having to make small talk. One or the other.

But I've barely reached a stone bench in the garden when someone knocks my plate to the ground, pins my arms behind my back, and presses a blade to my throat. *Here? Really?*

Fury bubbles up inside of me. Where's Vasil when I need him?

"We have a score to settle, Your Highness," an unfamiliar female voice behind me hisses.

"I have no idea who you are or what you want," I whisper. No sense calling anyone else out here, not when I might have to kill this woman and go ballistic.

"My name is Iris, and you killed my mother," she says. "It had to be you. Twelve years ago, our queen sent her to kill your father, and I've confirmed that he admitted to killing several members of the party. But he said he was out training his daughter, and that she killed two women. Other than the woman your father killed, there were only two women. One of them was my mother."

"So you're going to get yourself killed now, too?"

The knife blade presses more tightly. "Oh, I don't think so."

"Even if you kill me," I say. "You'll never escape this party with your life."

53

"A price I am more than willing to pay."

When I sigh heavily in response, the blade presses further, slicing the skin of my neck. Blood trickles down my neck, running into my cleavage. "You value your own life too low. I may have killed your mother, but only because she forced me. I'd really prefer not to kill you as well, and so far you haven't done anything that can't be undone. Release me, and I'll never speak a word of this to anyone."

My captor grunts loudly, her heart rate accelerating rapidly, and drops the blade. I spin around in time to see Gideon's bloody blade receding from where it protrudes beneath her ribcage. A severed spine.

I groan.

"You didn't want me to kill her?" Gideon asks.

I didn't want to end her life at all. I'm sick of all the death. But as party guests gather to see what's going on, I have no choice. Whether we end her life now or not, she'll be executed. May as well make it quick. "No, of course I did. I appreciate you saving me."

Gideon's next stroke slices her heart in two—she can't heal both major injuries. It's done, and I didn't have to do it. I didn't destroy anyone at the wedding for Mother's ally. It's a real win—for me and for the family. Why, then, does it feel like such a loss?

5

1842

In the end, I don't even have to suggest that Gideon join my guard. After his save, Dad insists upon it. "That Vasil was so distracted by the festivities that he didn't do his job, and he didn't make sure any of the other guards did theirs either."

"Dad, I'm fine."

"You could have died," he says.

I laugh.

"Fine, you could have killed a *lot* of people."

Which would probably have been much, much worse. Ironically, if I wasn't the berserker who puts everyone around me at risk at all times, I'd have died at the hand of Iris' mother years before—and none of this would even be happening.

"One day you'll meet someone," Dad says. "Someone who makes your heart soar, someone who is your reason for existing."

"Maybe," I say.

"But until then, I think you need someone like Gideon, someone who will ensure you live long enough for that to happen."

I don't mention that I think about Gideon constantly. I don't mention that I wanted to kiss him almost as badly as I wanted to slap him after his earlier help. "You think I should replace Vasil, just like that?"

Dad crosses the room, wrapping his hands around my upper arms. "I'm not saying you have to cast Vasil off forever, but maybe give him to Alora to deal with, at least until he's been properly trained. She knows what to do with green guards. Gideon can train your others, and he knows how to run a tight ship. Then later, maybe, you can—"

"Fine," I say. "Okay."

Dad drops his hands and stares at me. "Fine?"

"Sure. I'll take Gideon, if Alora's okay with it, and give her Vasil."

"His fighting skills are competent enough," Dad says. "But he's not attentive."

"If Alora doesn't want him, maybe we release him," I say.

"We can't give him back to Shenoah," Dad says. "That's not how it works."

I laugh again. "I'm not even suggesting that. He's one of us, but Dad, I think he might be distracted by someone else." I think about his glare last night. I'm almost positive it wasn't aimed at me. "I think he might be in love with one of your guards."

Dad's mouth dangles open in a very satisfying way.

"And I wish them the best, if he is."

Dad shakes his head. "Well, alright. Should I talk to Alora, or do you want to?"

"I can handle it," I say. "But I won't force him. If Gideon wants to remain in her service. . ."

Dad shrugs. "If he does, that's alright, but you need a new head of your guard."

"Agreed."

Alora doesn't laugh, and she doesn't say *I told you so*, either. But her self-satisfied grin is almost worse. Even so, I'd rather tell her a dozen times in a row than approach Gideon about the whole thing. He's in the stables feeding Verian a handful of oats I'm pretty sure he stole from the kitchen when I find him. I instruct Cassiel and Eirik to wait just around the corner. Within hearing distance, if I shouted anyway.

"Does the Chef know you swiped those?"

Gideon jumps and turns. When he realizes it's me, that dimple comes out. "She gave me a whole bucket, if you must know."

"It was your dimple that did it, right?"

"What?" His brow furrows.

"Nothing, never mind."

"You didn't bring him a treat too, did you? Because he loves apples, but Chef insisted they didn't have any left."

"Uh, no, I didn't actually come out to see the horses."

"Are we leaving earlier than I thought?" Gideon looks down at my riding habit.

"No, it's not that."

He cocks his head slightly. "Is everything okay?"

"Yes, I'm fine, truly, but I have something to ask you."

He steps closer, his eyes intent. "What?"

"Dad didn't like that Vasil wasn't there, when Iris—last night I mean."

"He was derelict," Gideon says.

"Dad wants him removed."

"At a minimum." His eyes flash like hammered gold in the sunlight.

"He suggested, since you were there last night when Vasil." I clear my throat. This is not going well. No matter how I say it, he's going to think it's strange. People don't simply change from guarding one princess to another. They just don't. "Well, he said that I should—"

"You're going to have to say it." Gideon's voice is raspy. "You'll have to be crystal clear."

I look up and meet his eyes. My heart speeds up in a way it hasn't before. Is this how my mother felt when she saw Dad across the battlefield? Did her heart race? Did her breath catch? "I already spoke to Alora, and she doesn't mind, that is, if it's alright with you."

Gideon lifts his eyebrows.

"Would you be interested in being the head of my guard? Changing from guarding my sister to guarding me?"

"Yes." He's utterly still, his gaze still intent on mine.

"Yes, you'll do it?"

"Yes."

"You can say no. You know that, right?"

Gideon smiles. "Yes."

"Okay. But is it something you *want* to do?"

"I'm a hundred and thirty-seven years old, Inara. I stopped doing things I didn't want to do about a hundred years ago."

I swallow.

His eyes drop to my mouth.

I want him to kiss me.

But he doesn't.

Finally, I nod and step back. "I'll inform the guards, but it'll be effective immediately."

"Good." He smiles, but not enough for the dimple to appear.

"Are you nervous?"

"The best things in life always make me nervous," he says.

I'm halfway back to my room to make sure my things are packed and ready to go when I realize that he didn't answer my question. With as nervous as I am, you'd think this was the best thing to happen in my life.

And maybe it is.

Everything is exactly the same on the ride home as it was on the trip to Paris. And everything is totally different. Gideon never leaves my side. He smiles a lot, but I have to work to see that dimple. When we stop for the night, prepared for the channel voyage tomorrow, I pass Verian off to the stable manager with relief.

"He's not the same with you," Alora says softly.

My head snaps to the left. "What?"

"He was always so formal with me," she says. "I almost never saw him smile. He's happy around you—like a totally different person. I feel a little bad about it, honestly." Her words make something in my chest lift. The sun's rays seem to shine a little brighter, too.

"You did nothing wrong," I assure her.

"I'm happy for you." She jogs ahead to catch up with Dad.

We met because he killed my horse. It's not exactly the most romantic of stories, if I cared about that sort of thing. Luckily I don't.

"We may have ridden nearly fifty miles today," Gideon says behind me. "But I haven't used my normal muscles in days. I'd like to take a walk."

I'm absolutely starving, and I want a bath. "Me too," I lie. Does love make you a liar? Is that what happens?

Gideon holds out his arm and I slide mine through it. The sea breeze is actually fairly refreshing, with the sun setting on the horizon.

"Your men don't seem to mind my promotion," he says. "Even Vasil seems happier."

"I might suggest to Mother that she always assign someone geriatric to manage the young recruits," I say.

Ah, that one earned me a glance at the dimple. "Geriatric, huh?"

"Your term, I thought," I say.

He bumps my hip with his, which is only possible

because my riding habit has split skirts and no hoops. "I'm quite sure that I've never described myself as geriatric."

"No?" I ask. "My mistake, then." A dolphin jumps in the channel, and I turn to watch for more, leaning against the handrail along the pier.

"And are you happier?" Gideon asks.

I shrug. "Does it matter?"

"It does to me."

Forget the dolphins. I turn to face him, and my heart leaps into my throat. His eyes meet mine, and his body turns, his hands bracing the handrail on either side of me. "I'm nervous." My eyes flutter at my boldness.

A smile curves across his full lips and his head dips toward mine. "Me too." His mouth meets mine, his lips covering my mouth and slanting sideways, his arms wrapping around my back and pulling me closer, closer.

Not close enough.

My hands reach up to cup his jaw and he groans.

I love it, all of it. The waves lapping gently behind us, the cool breeze, the way my hair sticks to the back of my neck, the way his arms squeeze me just a little tighter than they should.

The feel of his mouth on mine, his breath mixing with my own.

By the time the sun sets, I realize I want more. More than kissing on a pier. I want everything, all of it, with him. Is this how my dad feels? Is this how Mother feels?

I bunch my hands on Gideon's collar and pull him even closer. His face is so close to mine that I can barely see it— eyes aren't meant to see things this close. But the idea of moving away from him breaks my heart.

"This," I say. "This makes me happy."

I *feel* his smile against mine. "Me too." He kisses me again, briefly, too briefly, and then he kisses the tip of my nose. "But we need to get back, or everyone will figure it out."

"Let them," I say.

Even in the dark, the sharp beauty of his smile cuts me. But finally, I let him steer me back to the Alamecha chateau. When I close my eyes that night, my dreams are full of shining black hair and bright golden eyes.

The next morning on the barge, Dad leans heavily on the edge of the boat.

"Eager to see Mother again?"

He turns to face me and brushes an errant lock out of my face. "Always. Being parted from her is like. . . a sharp rock in my shoe, but worse. Like a constant ache in my heart. I can't forget it, and nothing eases it, not until I'm with her again."

"I might know what you mean," I say.

Dad's eyes widen. "Excuse me?"

"I—Gideon—"

He splutters. I can't recall ever seeing my dad splutter before.

"You don't like him?"

He swallows. "He's old."

"You're more than seven hundred."

He shrugs. "He's a lot older than you."

"Do you care?"

Dad slumps against the rail. "I suppose not."

"But?"

"But nothing, I guess. I hope he makes you happy."

"So do I."

"If he doesn't, I'll kill him." Dad grins like he's kidding, but I worry he might not be.

"That won't be necessary," I say. "I can assure you."

"Well, you certainly can't kill him yourself." Dad's grin is gone.

And for the first time since Gideon kissed me, the

reality of my situation sinks in. If I truly love Gideon, I shouldn't want him anywhere near me, not until I can figure out this berserker thing. Because right now, I'm a danger to everyone around me. He may be an excellent warrior, one of our strongest, but I would still destroy him if I so much as stepped on a mouse and broke its back. The only person I haven't killed in the middle of an episode is Dad.

"I'm ready," I say. "To begin training again."

6

1843

My arms are wrapped around my knees, my head shoved against my thighs. "My fault, my fault, my fault, my fault, my fault." My mouth speaks the words, but inside, just like the first time, just like every time, the same word runs through my mind on repeat. *Monster monster monster monster monster.*

Something sharp presses against my hip. I shift and realize it's my sword. I leap to my feet and hurl it as hard as I can. It lodges tip first in the narrow birch tree, splitting the trunk all the way to the branches. Even in my anger, my complete abandon, I can't do anything clumsy or uncoordinated. The tree isn't even conscious, and I've killed it too. I drop back to the ground and wrap my arms around my knees again, curling inward as if that might reduce the pain.

Oh, the pain.

His eyes, his unseeing eyes.

I told him I was ready.

I asked him to help me.

Begged.

That's a better word for what I did. I begged my father to help me conquer this—this curse. I pleaded with him to

63

help me overcome what I *am* inside, as if a true monster can ever be declawed. As if a bear could ever eat at the dinner table after a good wash and a hair trim.

Monsters rend.

Monsters destroy.

Monsters lay waste.

Monsters should be put down, not invited to tea.

I stand up and force my feet to move—closer. One step at a time, I walk toward my blade. The hilt shines in the sunlight where it has sunk into the tree. The blood's already drying on it in places, and in those places, it's dull. Ugly. Grotesque.

Just like me.

I grab the hilt and twist it sharply, freeing it from the dead tree. I flip it around so that the tip is facing my chest. I close my eyes and grit my teeth, and I shove it inside my own body, the blade parting skin, muscle, and bone. Pain blossoms inside of me, sharp, hot, *welcome*.

No one else can destroy me. No one. But I can rid the world of myself. I shove harder, blood bubbling up in my throat encouragingly.

A hilarious thought occurs to me: I'm the one person I can kill without triggering an episode.

I draw in a ragged breath, pulling hard on the one lung I haven't collapsed, and shove one more time. But my heart doesn't stop beating.

I swear long and loud. I split the tree trunk with an unthinking toss. How did I miss my own heart? I can't even succeed at ending my own life. Tears roll down my face, splattering on the ground when I yank the sword out. I lean against it while I heal, regaining the strength to do it right. To end things once and for all.

This time, I brace the hilt of my blade against the base of a large oak tree. I check and double check that it will sever my heart if I push it all the way through. The weight of gravity should finish the job if I fail.

"Oh, God, if there is a God, please forgive me. Not for killing myself, if that's even wrong, but for waiting this long to do it. Forgive me for the people whose lives I've cut short." My perfectly healed chest heaves with body-wracking sobs. "But mostly, forgive me for killing my own father. All he ever did was help me."

I close my eyes, Dad's glassy, unseeing eyes swimming in my view. I open my eyes again, because even staring at the weapon that took his life is preferable to remembering how he looked when the red haze finally receded.

The pain tears through me again. The guilt. The horror. And the disgust—the soul-searing, bone-deep disgust for who and what I am, for my weakness in not taking this step when it still could have saved him.

I set my feet and shift my weight, shoving downward against the blade.

But someone's hands grab my shoulders and pull me back. "It's not your fault."

"No!" I scream. "No!" I thrash against the grip. The only thing worse than dying here today, the only thing harder, will be facing my mother. I can't confess to her what I've done. I can't tell her that Dad's death is my fault. I can't admit that I destroyed the best person I've ever known. I can't bear it.

An execution would be so much simpler, but it'll take too long. I can't wait.

The strong arms flip me around and shove my face against a chest, a broad, strong, living chest that encases a beating heart. "Shhh," a familiar voice says.

"It can't be." I shove against him, staring up in baffled confusion.

"You didn't kill me," Dad says. "I'm still here."

I crumple, completely spent, and bawl, hot tears spilling

down my cheeks. I'm not sure how long it takes for my mind to work again. Minutes? Hours? But Dad's still there, comforting the person who very nearly killed him. "It's not your fault." He repeats the words over and over, stroking my hair with his free hand.

He comforts me after I nearly killed him. Again.

"You have to end me," I finally whisper. "You have to see why it must be done."

"You're not a rabid dog," he says.

"I'm so much worse." Oh, God, what were you thinking when you created me? How can you hate me this much?

"You aren't worse. You can't see what I see."

I can't even look at him. I don't deserve the waves of relief rolling over me.

"You are strong, beautiful, fierce, intelligent, and compassionate."

He's deluded. He sees what he wants to see.

"Do you hear me, Inara? Is the haze gone?"

"Of course it is!" For now. Until it grips me again. Until I can't even control my own limbs or my own mind.

"We will overcome this." Dad's voice is sad. "The people you killed today were inmates—sentenced to death. You did nothing wrong—in fact, you gave them a fighting chance of release."

I shove away from him then, stumbling backward, and righting myself, and backing away even faster. "Never again," I say. "I won't so much as kill a flea. If a wild boar attacks me, I'll tear off a chunk of my own arm and feed it to him. Don't you see? I can't overcome this. It has defeated me, and I'm done trying."

Dad nods, and he doesn't stop me as I walk away, barely even remembering to wash up in the stream before returning to Windsor.

I've only just reached the door to my room when

66

Gideon falls into step beside me. "You lied to me." His eyes flash.

Now is really not the time. I can't deal with anything else right now.

"You told me you were—"

"Look." I spin on my heel. "I'm not a china doll. I won't break."

Gideon flinches. "I know that. You're far more precious to me than a doll could ever be."

His eyes, oh, his eyes. But they remind me of Dad's eyes —glassy, dead, and staring into nothing. That could just as easily have been Gideon's eyes. His eyes will be glassy one day, just like dad's, if he stays near me.

Because I'm a monster. Dad may not see it, but I do. The truth is crystal clear. What I love, I destroy. "We need to talk," I say.

Gideon frowns. "That sounds ominous."

I practically run for my room. He follows me inside, barking orders at the guards who fell into step beside us, and then slamming the door.

"This." I gesture between us. "This is over."

Thanks to the disgusting beast that I am, I know exactly how someone looks when their guts have been ripped out of their belly and strewn across the floor. That's how Gideon looks right now. And just like always, it's my fault. More than anything else could, that expression galvanizes me.

I think of our future together. Even if I vow never to kill another being again, given the life we lead, how can I keep that promise? If someone attacks me in the middle of the night and I react with my perfect reflexes, I could go insane in our bed. I could slit his throat before he's even awake.

Or any other of a million ways I could destroy him.

The one certainty is that horror follows in my wake,

and I'm powerless to stop it. I can't even kill myself successfully.

"I'm sorry this pains you." I'm proud that my voice barely wobbles. "But I think it's best if I replace you as head of my guard as well."

"No." Gideon reaches for my hand, but I pull back.

"This is my decision, and I've made it."

"This morning you—"

I hold up my hand. I can't think about this morning. I can't think about how soft his lips were, or how firm his arms. I can't think about how he kissed my nose, like he always kisses my nose. I can't think about any part of the last six months.

I can't.

I'll break.

I wonder, for the first time, if heartbreak can trigger an episode.

I hope it can't, because if it can, we're all dead.

"I know this excuse may not make sense," I whisper. "But it's still true. I want you to know that you did nothing wrong. There's something I can't tell you about myself, a secret, a huge one. I wish I could, but I *can't*, and—" I shake my head. "This has to be over. It's killing me, Gideon. *Killing me*. Is there any part of this you can understand?"

He steps toward me again, and this time I don't have the strength to shove him away. His arms envelop me. "I don't understand any of it, but I know your heart. If you tell me this is how it has to be, I believe you. I know you'd never hurt me, not on purpose. I haven't said this yet, because I didn't want to pressure you, Inara. But I love you. Deeply, utterly, with all that I am. So if you'll allow it, I'll continue as head of your guard. I'll stay by your side in any capacity you'll allow for as long as you allow it."

I choke.

"If you wake up one day, and something changes, and

you can tell me this secret, that's fine. And if you can't ever tell me, that's okay too. No matter what the secret is, no matter what foe you face, you'll face it with me by your side. Even if you don't want me, I'm still your biggest ally. I'll always be your biggest ally."

I wish, so badly, that he could help me.

But no one can help me fight this foe—because I am my only enemy, and I'm not strong enough to defeat myself.

L ainina probably had no idea Dad was in Honolulu on December 7, 1941. I have to assume that if she knew, she'd never have ordered the strike. Flexing your muscles is one thing. Even coordinated military engagements carried out predominantly by humans like this one are within the rules of engagement. But taking out another empress's Consort?

It's not done. Not unless there's an all-out war under-way, and Mother was doing her best to stay out.

Until Pearl Harbor.

To her credit, Mother holds out hope until the bitter end. She shakes her head when Angel tells her she's confirmed that Althuselah didn't survive the attack.

"No," Mother says. "No. You're wrong. Check again."

Angel swallows, her eyes full of broken glass and shat-tered dreams and crumbling hope. "There's been no mistake. I identified the body myself. They're sending it back as quickly as possible."

Balthasar's eyes focus on something far beyond the walls of this room. His body goes taut, and I recognize something horrifying in the tension of his body, in the distraction of his gaze.

"Balthasar," I say.

He doesn't react, but his hand inches toward the hilt of his sword. He hasn't killed anyone—I can attest to that—but he's acting like he's sinking into the haze. Could that be possible? I think about Dad—so close to him they were practically twins—and my heart breaks all over again.

"Enora, we need to discuss the ramifications." Angel takes her hand.

Mother's eyes are vacant, her shoulders slumped, and her eyelashes flutter. For hours now we've all feared the worst—that Dad is gone. But Angel's instinct to get Mother out of here, whether she even realizes what she's doing, is the right one.

My heart races as I rush Mother out the door, nodding reassuringly to a shell-shocked Angel. "I'll keep an eye on Balthasar."

I should be hyperventilating. I should be sinking into despair, or lethargy, or soul-deep in horror and denial. But perhaps my frequent fear that I killed him has uniquely prepared me to withstand the death of the person I love most in this world.

Or perhaps it's the crushing relief that his death wasn't my fault.

I duck back into the war room, ordering my guards to remain outside. If my suspicions are founded, anything could set him off. Anything at all, including my presence. I open the door slowly. Balthasar is still standing frozen, eyes fixed beyond the wall in front of him.

His hand circles the hilt of his sword, but he hasn't drawn it. Not yet, anyway. Dad told me only killing someone or something could trigger the haze. It's the only way I've ever succumbed, but looking at Balthasar right now, lines of grief etched deeply in wrinkles I've never seen before around his eyes, in the set of his mouth, in the slump in his shoulders, I wonder.

Dad has shown me photos of what I look like in the haze. He tells me I don't react to stimuli—excluding everything from my worldview that isn't a threat.

"Balthasar," I say softly.

His head whips toward me, but there's no recognition in his eyes.

"Althuselah is your brother."

"Was." His lip curls and he snarls. "He was killed—by a bunch of *humans*."

Oh, no. All doubt flees my mind. I have no idea how this could have happened, but he's deep in the haze. I have no idea how to control it, and I have no idea how to pull him out. I thought he had a way to control it—that he wasn't a threat. But he certainly seems like a threat right now, as though any move on my part right now could set him off.

"Inara?" Gideon's voice calls from outside the door. He must have found the guards and heard about my father. He'd want to see how I'm doing, to know why I'm in the war room, to make sure I'm not grieving alone.

Balthasar's eyes widen, his nostrils flaring.

I back into the door, and whisper loudly. "I'm fine. Please let me be." I can imagine the look on Gideon's shocked face, but I can't worry about that now.

Because my uncle draws his sword. "He died." His words are low, urgent.

Something that the simplicity of the statement slices through the shield around my heart. My dad is gone. A sob tears through my chest. "He did, yes."

Balthasar flies toward me, faster than anyone else I've ever seen. I pull my sword, the sword Dad gave me himself, the sword that almost killed him a hundred years ago. The sword I still can't control. The one I always hoped Balthasar could help me handle.

Any hope of that drains away.

The same sword that has plagued my life saves it a split second later as I block the rain of blows from Balthasar. Again, again, and again. Every time I block one of his blows, Balthasar's eyes widen. He bites his lip and flips the desk over.

I leap behind it, and he slashes at it with his sword, carving chunks from the dark wood. I use the distraction to scuttle away, sliding behind the drapes.

Do I look this insane when I'm in the haze? I'm afraid I look worse.

What did Dad say or do to pull me out? My name—he said it often—and he reminded me who he was.

"I'm your niece, Balthasar," I say.

He growls and someone starts knocking on the door. Oh, no. No one else can come inside, not right now. The more threats, the more kills, the harder the haze sinks its teeth into me, that part I recall. "Training exercise," I shout. "Come back later." As if anyone will believe that Balthasar and I are training moments after we found out Dad died.

But they leave—almost inexplicably.

Unfortunately, nothing else I try works. Reminding Balthasar who I am does nothing to stave off his fury. I can barely get my sword up in time to keep him from severing my limbs from my body. The lamps go first, sparks shooting from the severed wires. I try shocking him awake, but the electric jolt only enrages him more.

Until it finally hits me—why people have left us alone. Why this is happening at all.

I begged God to save me from myself. When I thought

I killed my father, I prayed and cursed God for making me this way. I wanted to take my own life and failed. But this is my solution. Dad is gone, the only one who could control me, and now I need a way out more than ever. Nothing could possibly drive home the dangerous risk my life is for everyone around me quite like Balthasar's reaction today.

The one person who could actually end me, once and for all, is trying his best to do it.

I think about Dad's eyes—glassy and unfocused. I might not have killed him this time, but I easily could have. And now he's gone. The best person I ever knew, the person I loved more than anyone else in the world.

Snuffed out.

He was the one person who knew who I really am—who thought I was worth saving. And now he's gone. What's the point in struggling any longer? In that moment of clarity, I wonder whether this was always how I was meant to end. It's poetic, in its way—that my uncle, the one person like me in this world, but also the one who can control what I can't—should cleanse the world of the monstrous threat I pose.

So I drop my sword. "Do it," I say simply. "Kill me. Dad would understand."

Balthasar's blade slams into my neck, separating skin and muscle. But somehow, impossibly, he pulls up short, not even severing my carotid. He blinks rapidly. He steps back, dropping the hilt of his sword.

"Enora?" He shakes his head. "Enora? Is that you?"

For more than a century now, I've heard stable boys and scullery maids and, well, basically everyone in between, gush about how much I look exactly like my mother. But Balthasar seems to believe I actually *am* her.

I knock his blade out of my neck and it clatters to the ground. "I'm Inara, actually, but close enough."

He swallows slowly and drops to his knees.

Ah, the crushing guilt. This part I know well.

"I am so sorry. I don't know what happened."

Sure he does, and so do I. A burning desire to tell him grips me. I could finally be honest with someone else—with Dad gone I have no one. That's the selfish part that hurts worst about Dad's death. I'm so alone—utterly alone in a way that most people will never experience.

But his voice comes to me, ringing through my mind.

"You just lost your brother, your best friend, your only real family."

A tear wells up and runs down the right side of his face. "Althuselah."

I yank him back up to his feet. "I know." Great, heaving sobs grip me, too, and I don't stop him when my uncle pulls me against his chest.

"I'm so, so sorry."

I open my mouth to do the very thing Dad forbade me to do. But Dad's gone. He left me, and he's never coming back, never again. He promised he'd always help me, but now he can't.

I'm all alone.

So alone.

But the man right in front of me, the man who almost ended me a moment ago, he would understand. All Dad's warnings and reasons feel fuzzy and intangible. I need his help, and maybe I've always needed his help. Without Dad, though, I'm desperate for it. "Uncle Balthasar, there's something—"

When he looks up and into my eyes, I know that I can trust him. He will understand. He'll be able to help me.

But a persistent banging on the door collapses the moment and we both leap to our feet. I almost told him—I almost confessed who I am to another living soul. *He's a predator in his heart of hearts.* Dad is screaming at me from up in heaven, if it exists. He's shaking his fist for sure, but part of me is devastated. Part of me dies a little bit inside, longing for someone to understand.

I ignore that tiny complaint and open the door.

Gideon's eyebrows draw together sharply. His eyes skate from the upended and smashed desk to the slashes in the wall and finally stop on my blood-soaked neck and shoulder. He swears and draws his sword.

I'm so tired. Far too tired for this nonsense. "Everything's okay now," I say. "We were both drowning in rage, that's all."

Gideon swears and stomps toward Balthasar.

"Stop." My voice cracks. "Please, stop. Balthasar lost touch with reality for a moment—his grief overcame him, but I understood the sentiment, and there's no permanent harm done."

Gideon changes course and pulls me close for a hug, his breath blowing warm and insistent against my ear. I let him hug me, and if I'm being honest, I revel in the contact. He's been true to his word, year after year, with very little encouragement from me. He guards and protects, but he never demands more.

Except with sideways glances. Soulful longing is hard to disguise.

I do better than he does, but even I can't suppress it entirely.

Balthasar clears his throat.

"We have a lot to discuss right now," I whisper. "I'm sure I'm safe. Can you give us a minute?"

Gideon's arms release me, but he glares at my uncle. "I'll be right outside."

Balthasar laughs. "Noted."

Gideon closes the door a little harder than strictly necessary, but I don't blame him.

"There's something about me you should probably know." Balthasar's voice is gravely.

"Dad told me," I say. "It's why I knew to defend and not engage."

"That was risky," Balthasar says. "Stupid and dangerous and risky."

"It worked." I can't even imagine his control, to pull out of the haze like that, before he killed me, before he even mortally wounded me.

"It did, as did your ploy at the end, to make yourself a victim, not a combatant. You got very, very lucky, Inara. I love you, more than you may understand, but that doesn't much matter when. . ." He clears his throat again.

"When you're in the haze."

He blinks. "Yes. That's a good way to describe it." He frowns. "A surprisingly good way to describe it. The haze." He narrows his eyes at me.

"Dad said you described it like that once," I say, hedging.

"Why did he tell you about it?" Balthasar frowns. "It's a closely guarded secret."

"I was crying," I lie. "You had left for a battle and I was worried you'd be injured and Mother laughed. I couldn't let it go, and finally Dad explained."

Balthasar smiles. "Your mother laughed at your concern?" His chest swells at that, inexplicably, as if he's proud that Mother laughed at the thought of him being injured. Perhaps he's proud that a few people know he's practically invincible.

I nod. "Speaking of—I think Mother needs us right now, so it's time for us to pull it together. Can you do that?"

Balthasar's eyes are sad. "You have no idea how right you are. You've heard of Atlas?"

"The Titan who was sentenced to hold up the heavens

after the Olympians defeated their progenitors?" I arch my eyebrow. "That Atlas?"

Balthasar nods. "The very same. Of course you know that those legends are based on the feats humans saw evians perform. They had to find ways to explain the similar appearance but the vast difference in capability. But never mind all that. My point was that my brother has been Atlas for eight hundred years."

I don't understand.

My uncle's smile is sad. "He has held up this entire family. He kept me together, took care of your mother, and softened all the sharp edges that jab together in this place. He has singlehandedly kept Alamecha at the top of its game." Another tear rolls down his cheek. "I don't think we'll survive his loss. The cracks may take some time to show, but they're starting even now. Mark me."

I realize in the days that follow that he's right. Dad was my only confidante. He was mother's foundation and buffer. In a quiet moment, Mother falls asleep, her head on the tabletop of the new workstation in the war room.

"You were right," I admit to Balthasar. "Dad's death may very well spell our entire downfall."

Balthasar taps his chin. "I've been looking for the right word to epitomize our plan—your mother's and mine. Lainina will pay for this. What began as a spat between Senah and your mother snowballed far larger than it ever should have, but Adora." He clenches his hands until the pencil he's holding shatters. "We'll call it Operation Downfall. It won't end until we've shattered everything that matters to her."

The anger in his eyes convinces me that Dad was right. As much as I want to trust Balthasar—and in my fear, I really, really do—he's a predator in his heart.

I watch in awe as he crushes everything that matters to Lainina, just as he vowed.

Hiroshima.

Nagasaki.

I'm not the only Alamecha monster by the time Balthasar and Mother are done extracting their pound of flesh, but nothing we do brings Dad back. Because once Atlas is gone, nothing can restore him, and the world never sits quite right again.

8

1962

With Dad gone, I have no one to keep me from exposing my secret, no one to talk me down from the ledge if I stumble toward it. *So I just don't kill anyone.* That seems like an easy enough task—but when you're evian, it's not always that simple. Assassinations, challenges, dangerous activities all around.

As if he can sense the vacuum left after my father's death, Gideon steps in further. From the moment Balthasar nearly ends my life, Gideon becomes my shadow. If I go somewhere, he's there. If I stay in, he's at my door. If I take a walk, he's a step behind.

And every attack, every threat, he deflects. It's like he knows the stakes without knowing them, protecting me from myself day in and day out. Twenty-one years without a single error. Dad was right when he substituted Gideon in for Vasil so many years ago.

Dad was always right, and every time an emergency crops up, I miss him fiercely. Like right now.

Mother throws a stack of images down on the desk in her room and resumes her pacing.

I flip through them. "So Russia could hit Florida? Are we sure?"

She stops and closes her eyes. "As you see."

"Photos can be faked," I say.

She collapses into a leather armchair and stares out the window at the ocean. "These aren't. The pilot confirmed he saw exactly what's represented in those images."

"Which pilot?"

"Filomeno."

I swear under my breath. Filomeno doesn't make mistakes. "Fine. So then what's our play?"

"It's time," Mother says.

I stand up. "No, it's not."

"The other families have been playing with this ever since we repaid Lainina. We should have gone all the way then."

"By 'all the way,' to clarify, you mean that we should have destroyed the empresses of all the families other than our own. That's what 'all the way' means."

Mother scowls at me. "Of course that's what I mean. Our family is destined to rule again, as was our right from the beginning. Your father knew that, but we were waiting for the right time. When they killed him, my patience dried up."

More like, her will to live disappeared with him. Had we been in a position to do it, she'd have taken the world down with her. But we've muddled through two decades now; she should be better. This is the threat of a rash, uncaring, unmoored individual. The human collateral alone would be staggering, but the evian death toll would also be quite high. Not that she'd much care about either, from what I've seen. "Before we destroy the existing world order, maybe we consider some less dramatic options."

"I'm listening."

"As a preliminary step, I'll go to negotiate with

Melamecha's chosen representative. If they agree to remove the missiles, we stand down too. In the meantime, perhaps you travel to Quebec, or Dublin, or maybe rural Idaho. Someplace safer than here, which most anywhere else we control would be."

"They can't touch us in Hawaii."

"Mother, think about it. They can, and you know that. You're not invincible." Mother became obsessed with Hawaii after Dad died here, and she's made a nice, relatively inaccessible palace on an otherwise mostly deserted island. "Ni'ihau would make a lousy tomb. It's way too hard to visit."

"Hilarious. You're always so very funny." Mother paces. "You think I should just send you, my Heir, so that Melamecha can destroy you too?"

"She knows you'd defeat her if it comes down to an all-out war, but only if you have a *right* to attack. The other families will align with whoever *hasn't* wronged the other party. It's the only reason they didn't join together to take you out after Nagasaki. You had been wronged, and they saw the truth of it."

"They didn't attack because they were scared of me," she says. "Attributing them with any nobler motives is naive."

She might be right. "But also the justice thing." At least a little bit.

"Aren't you sick of all the back and forth and the threats?"

She's been constantly sick of everything since Dad died. *Everything.* Nothing that brought her joy does anymore. I get it—I feel almost as bad as she does. But I haven't lain down to die like she has. Since that didn't work, she's picking fights and hoping they'll take away the pain.

"I am, Mother. I really am."

"Fine," she says. "I'll give you a week."

I breathe a sigh of relief.

"But you aren't going to Cuba, because if this falls apart, there won't be a Cuba, and I won't risk you that senselessly."

"Where, then?" I ask.

"Neutral ground—it can be close to Cuba so you can confirm the dismantling. You can take Filomeno and a handful of guards. I'm sure Gideon will be glued to your hip as always."

Probably. I suppress a smile.

It takes two days to arrange the details. Eventually Melamecha agrees to send a representative to George Town, on Grand Cayman Island. I'm somewhat relieved she agreed to one of our holdings, but seeing as she's the aggressor, it was the obvious move.

"You'll be meeting with a nephew of hers, Mikhail. He looks like this." She slides me a photograph, which is almost too fuzzy to be helpful.

"So he has two eyes *and* a nose?" I lift my eyebrows.

"I didn't say Melamecha was being overly helpful." Mother purses her lips. "But you're the one who begged for this chance to defuse things, so you're the one who can deal with it."

"And?"

"And what?" she asks.

"I'm sure there's some kind of code word that only Mikhail will know, to confirm I'm not wasting my time with some imposter or whatever. Isn't that how this usually goes when I'm meeting someone I've never before seen?"

"He has a birthmark just here." Enora pats a spot just below her right hipbone.

"Are you kidding me right now?" I ask.

She shrugs. "That's the information I was given. It's a reddish spot, shaped like a star."

I groan. "Fine."

"You have four days," Mother says.

"You said a week."

"It took two days to set up this meet," she says.

"At least don't start the timer until tomorrow," I say. "I'll be flying for all of today."

"Done."

"And Inara," she says.

"You're going to tell me how he'll know it's me?"

Mother frowns. "He'll know it's you because you'll be at the location I designate. No, I wanted to tell you that I haven't told Melamecha the name of my representative. Mikhail might not recognize you as my daughter, so maybe use a fake name."

"I've always felt like a Claudia," I say.

She rolls her eyes.

"What's wrong with Claudia?"

"It's too pedestrian." Mother doesn't even hug me good-bye. She just turns back to her desk.

"Maybe I could use a little boring in my life."

Mother's laugh follows me out her bedroom door. "You're many things, Inara, but boring isn't one of them. Try not to get blown up."

I'm not sure whether her lack of concern for my welfare is a compliment—that she finds me competent—or an insult—that she doesn't care.

"It's nice to hear her laughing," Gideon says in the hallway.

"It would be nice if it wasn't ironic," I say.

Gideon has two bags slung over his shoulders—mine and his. "Where are we headed?"

"Grand Cayman," I say. "To meet with someone named Mikhail, and get this. We'll know it's him after we examine a birthmark like an inch above his. . ." I lift my eyebrows.

"You're kidding me."

I shake my head. "You can't make this stuff up."

He pulls a face. "At least we're going somewhere nice for a change."

"Umm, I've never been, but from what I hear, George Town basically sports some offshore fishing and one nice beach. It's literally the worst island in the Caribbean. And newsflash. We live in *Hawaii*."

"Right, but we're always here. We *work* here, we're always being watched and weighed and measured here. I'm excited to get away for once."

Actually, now that he mentions it, so am I. Maybe, if we can get this missile standoff defused, we'll enjoy a few days of rest and relaxation. "I could really go for a massage and some piña coladas," I say.

"Now you're talking," Gideon says.

I fall asleep halfway through the flight. When I wake up, I'm leaning on Gideon's shoulder. "Sorry." I straighten and wipe my eyes.

"Anytime," Gideon says. "Your snoring is so cute that I didn't even mind."

"You're kidding." There's no way I snore. It's caused by a nasal defect.

He shrugs. "You'll never know."

The horrible part is that he's right. Unless I could somehow record it.

He taps the side of my head. "Let it go. I was kidding."

"No, I mean, I know you were." Obviously.

"It's your fault," he says. "You wouldn't have fallen asleep if you'd brought a better book."

My copy of *Advanced Russian through History* has fallen on the floor of the plane and slid into the aisle. "We're meeting Melamecha's nephew, and if he's anything like her, he's bound to be wretched. I figured I should brush up on my Russian in case he insists on communicating in his preferred language."

"It makes sense," Gideon says. "Your logic is always

flawless—it's just kind of the antithesis of a massage and relaxation."

"Mother wants to bomb the other five families out of existence. We're going in a last-ditch effort to prevent total catastrophe."

"When you put it that way, this whole trip sounds like a real drag."

"Did you know that Alora told me you were too stiff and formal?" I lift my eyebrows. "That's why she was shocked that first day."

"Wait, do you mean the *first* first day? The day I beheaded your horse for you?"

I swallow, still a little upset whenever I think about Diablo. "That's the one I mean."

Gideon leans toward me and drops his voice. "You're telling me that you talked to Alora about me that very day?"

Heat rises in my cheeks. I hate that he can still do that to me. "Answer the allegations at your feet. Were you stiff and formal with her?"

Gideon leans back in his seat and sighs. "Guilty, of course."

"Why?"

"Why what?" he counters.

I pin him with a glare. "Why are you not stiff and formal with me?"

"Everything is different when you're here," he says. "You want me to explain love? Because I can't."

I can't breathe. We haven't talked about this in decades. We fell into a safe, steady, friendly relationship and he hasn't revisited anything in so long that I've wondered whether his feelings just disappeared.

"How's that for defusing a situation? Maybe you should have left me home." He sounds like he's kidding, but his eyes are intent. Earnest, even.

"Gideon, I—"

"I know, I know, it's not me, it's you, yada yada."

Except, the threat of the haze feels less horrifying than it did back then. It almost feels like fate was trying to drive a wedge between us back then. In the weeks before I fell for Gideon, I was endangered over and over. But now, I haven't killed anyone or anything. Not since Dad's death more than twenty-one years ago.

Because Gideon has always been at my side. He's dispatched every single threat before I had to do anything about it. Unlike my dad, he was never called away by my mother, or by state matters, or, well, by anything. Gideon has been true to his word. He has stood by my side, impenetrable, constant, steady, keeping me safe—keeping my secret just that—a secret.

I've been stupid.

I should have told him the truth years ago and let him decide whether to face the threat I pose—or whether to walk away. I trust him enough to know he'd keep my secret, even if it's too much for him. The years have taught me that much, at least.

"When this is over," I say, "I think we should get that massage."

I haven't seen his dimple in a long time—in too long. But now, with his broad smile directed right at me, it feels like I've been punishing myself for no reason. "I'd like that. More than you can possibly know." His hand reaches for mine, slowly, cautiously, leaving me plenty of opportunity to pull away.

I don't.

His fingers cover mine, and pivot smoothly, interlacing with mine. I close my eyes and sigh, and for the first time since Dad died, I feel safe, and loved, and whole.

Until the plane lands, anyway, and we rush off to make our meeting on time. Gideon has a spring in his step I'm not sure I've ever seen before, and idiotic or not, I'm taking credit for it. He may be nearly two-hundred and fifty to my hundred and change, but it feels like I'm a twenty-something again—the flush and excitement of a future full of potential in front of me.

The hundred and twenty wasted years don't even bother me, as our arms swing back and forth on the walk from the jet to the waiting car. Eirik, Cassius, and Tarben follow us without making a comment.

But they all want to—they take turns trying to catch my eye. None of them said a word back in 1842 when everything fell apart. What would they have said? But now, a hundred and twenty years later, of course they haven't forgotten.

When I glance back to make sure we're on the right path—I don't know this drive very well, but there are only a handful of significant roads in George Town according to Mother's maps—Eirik smiles and tosses me a thumbs up.

For the love.

But I'm not even mad. How could I be? It feels like I hit the pause button way back then, and my life is finally moving forward again. My heart hasn't been this light in a very long time.

"We're here." Bellatrius stops the car and looks at the enormous blue house sitting on the edge of the only nice beach. A few hundred yards beyond, the land degrades into what appears to be swampland. I groan. I despise mosquitos.

"We better figure this out quickly," Eirik says. "Because this island is significantly less impressive than I was led to believe."

"No one tried to sell us," I say. "It was chosen for its proximity to Cuba, and its relative claim to neutrality. Clearly it's no military power, so Melamecha was willing to risk sending an agent here to negotiate."

"How much power does this person even have to negotiate?" Gideon asks. "Does anyone know?"

I shrug. "I hope it's enough to defuse this whole thing, because if not. . ."

Cassius makes a sound mimicking an explosion.

"Right."

Bellatrius' expression is grim.

"Is something wrong?"

"Was Melamecha's agent supposed to come alone?"

"I have no idea," I say. "Is someone here?"

She nods. "Before I left to pick you up, someone else arrived. Ilyena let him in, but I got a somewhat decent look."

"And?" I can't believe she's only now mentioning this.

"He's. . ." She looks down at her hands. "Well, he was alone."

He's what? What was she going to say? Is he huge? Eight plus feet tall? Does he have a lot of piercings? He has an eye patch? Spit it out, lady! "Is there any relevant information I need before I march into that beach house?"

She opens her mouth again, but then shuts it. She shakes her head. "No, Your Highness, nothing relevant."

I glance around the car, wearing my severest glare. "From here on out, not a single one of you may call me Your Highness. I am simply Claudia, whom Her Majesty sent here with a small amount of latitude to avert a disaster. Are we clear?"

Everyone nods, but only Gideon meets my eye.

"This is serious," I say.

"Absolutely," his words say. But his eyes are still smiling.

I shove the door open and brace myself for whatever oddity about this Mikhail that has Bellatrius all ruffled. All I know about him is that he has longish, somewhat shaggy hair, and he's tall. Or at least, he looked tall, standing next to the car in the photo. Melamecha's information was basi-

89

cally useless. I'm sure she didn't want us doing research on how to manipulate him—or leverage his weaknesses, but she should have wanted us to at least verify he is who he says he is.

"You will all wait here," I say. "I'll signal when I need you."

"Nice try," Gideon says. "I'm not letting you go anywhere alone, *Claudia.*"

I expected that, at least. "Fine. Just Gideon, then." This is exactly why he's kept me free of any incidents. Dogged determination.

On the short walk up the path to the house, and while scaling the steps, I consider all the things that might have flustered Bellatrius. Could he be bristling with weapons? Maybe he's already holding Ilyena hostage. I pause momentarily. Could he have told Bellatrius to come and get us, or he'd kill her? What would Bellatrius do to save her sister?

Surely her loyalty would be to the family before saving one person. Right? I glance back at Bellatrius. She looks curious, but not guilty or afraid. If he's not a threat, what did she almost tell me? No way to know, I suppose, not without pushing my way inside. Before I can open the door, Ilyena opens it for me. Her white blonde hair is pulled up into a very high, very severe ponytail. She has such severe cheekbones already that it's not her best look.

Not that it matters.

"Welcome, Your—"

"My room is ready?" I ask pointedly. "It's a pleasure to meet you. My name is Claudia. I was sent by Her Majesty, Enora Alamecha."

"Right." Ilyena's eyes widen.

"You're finally here," a smooth voice with no trace of an accent intones from the back of the house.

I can't help myself. I'm drawn to it, my curiosity insatiably piqued. I close the distance between us quickly, my eyes hungry to unlock this puzzle. I envisioned dozens of scenarios, all of them intended to protect myself and my guards. The one thing that never occurred to me was that Bellatrius *liked* him.

But looking at the man I assume is Mikhail in front of me, I completely understand her reticence to articulate, in a car full of confident evian men, her feelings at seeing Melamecha's agent.

He's wearing nothing but a pair of black swim trunks, and he's lying on a chair watching the waves crash against the beach a few dozen feet away. "My aunt did not mention what an amazing view we'd have for these negotiations," he says. "Or I wouldn't have complained about coming nearly as much as I did."

He meets my gaze and heat coils in my belly. My throat goes dry. My heart would be racing, no, sprinting, right now if I wasn't utterly focused on keeping it steady.

"You can call me Mikhail, but I don't believe anyone told me your name." His voice is deep, intimate, inviting, as if he knows exactly how I'm reacting inside right now. Which he likely does.

"Her name is Claudia." Gideon's tone could frost the windowpanes, even in this heat.

Mikhail leaps to his feet, his perfect washboard abs contracting in a way I can't help but watch, and extends his hand. "It's a pleasure to meet you, Claudia, and you too, of course, er, I didn't get your name."

Gideon makes no move to take his hand, so I hold out mine. "Gideon is—"

"Claudia's closest friend," he says. "And her guard for these negotiations."

Mikhail licks his lips. "All good information to have, but I assure you that I'm not a threat in that regard at all. In fact, I'll confess to an ulterior motive with my sunbathing. I figured if I was wearing this—" he gestures to his swimsuit, "when we met, you wouldn't worry that I meant you any harm. I genuinely have every intention of working with you fully to defuse this. . . touchy and dangerous situation."

"I think an amicable resolution is best for all parties," I say.

"Agreed, entirely." Mikhail's eyes light up. "I almost forgot. Aunt M told me I was supposed to prove that I'm me by showing you—" He reaches for the waistband of his trunks, presumably to pull it down far enough for us to see the star birthmark.

Gideon's hand shoots out faster than I realized it could and grabs Mikhail's wrist. "That won't be necessary."

"I have a little star," he says, "right here. I was told—"

"That's fine," Gideon says. "We believe you."

Mikhail pulls his hand away and shrugs. "Your call."

"I think we should all get dressed," Gideon says, "and we can talk details over dinner."

"You two *are* dressed," Mikhail says, "so I think that's my cue. If you aren't worried about my posing any imminent danger to either of you, I'll head to my room for a shirt."

"Just wanted to reassure us, my—" Gideon's muttering becomes impossible to understand, but his obvious dislike for Melamecha's agent doesn't stop me from watching Mikhail all the way up the stairs. I can't seem to look away.

Once he's entirely out of my view, I motion the others to come inside.

"So," Bellatrius says.

"What?" Eirik asks. "What is it?"

"The guy was lounging in here practically naked," Gideon says. "It's ridiculous. Is he posing for a human magazine selling beach vacations, or is he here to try and save our holdings from the devastation of nuclear weapons?"

"Yeah," Bellatrius says. "That's what I was trying to say." She clears her throat.

"Why do I feel like I'm missing something?" Eirik asks.

"He's probably the most gorgeous and self-assured evian I've ever met," Ilyena says. "And I've met a lot of evians. Either Gideon didn't notice, or more likely, he did, and it annoys him."

I don't even agree with her, not out loud anyway, but Gideon still stomps outside like a two-hundred-year-old baby. I don't have the energy to follow him out. I'm too busy glancing upstairs.

"Where's my room?" I ask Ilyena.

She points at the third room on the right at the top of the stairs and offers me a key.

"Thanks."

When I open the door, prepared to dump my bag and lay flat on the bed for a moment after a long trip, I pull up short. "Oh," I say.

Mikhail Shamecha has pulled a shirt on, which I'm sure Gideon would be grateful for, but he's also sitting on my bed.

I doubt Gideon would be pleased to discover that.

"What are you doing in my room?" I glance over my shoulder. "And wasn't it locked?"

His sheepish smile shouldn't be so attractive. It just shouldn't, but my belly and my brain and my heart don't seem to have gotten that memo. "It's a talent of mine. Locks don't phase me much." He stands up. "Say the word and I'll leave. But I thought we might make more progress if we had a few minutes together without your watchdog."

My watchdog? I'm not sure I've ever heard a better description of Gideon in my life. No one has ever been more constant in his devotion. "What exactly are you authorized to do?"

"As I see it, the situation is like this. A few years ago, your family crossed a line. Your empress bombed civilians, killing hundreds of thousands."

"I think—"

He holds up his hand. "I'm not trying to lay blame, I promise. I lived through it too, and I'm very clear on what happened at Pearl Harbor to precipitate that radical move. I'm not attacking your monarch, but when that happened, it set in motion a sequence of inevitable events. The other families, existing in a delicate balance at the best of times, began a race toward a new kind of power. It has opened up an option for destruction on a scale we'd never before considered."

"An arms race," I say. "Yes. Weapons that might not kill all evians, but would certainly wipe out our human labor effectively and quickly."

He blinks twice when I say human labor, but he doesn't miss a beat otherwise. "My aunt is at the front of that charge. She's developed several viable weapons to rival your empress's bombs, limited only by her methods of effective distribution."

"Most notably, she built a launch site in Cuba." My tone is flat.

"And that makes your ruler understandably nervous, as her strongest holding is now in my aunt's crosshairs."

"Yes. We're agreed on the issue."

"And you want those weapons removed," he says.

"We do," I agree.

"We have a problem," he says. "Because you also have regionally localized weapons poised to attack my aunt."

I shake my head. "We don't—we have allies in the region, sure, but nothing close enough to threaten you."

He frowns. "Come, now. Don't act stupid. It's unbecoming, even for someone as lovely as you."

Unbecoming? I hate how flustered his words leave me. "I am *never* stupid," I say. "And that's a lie."

"Then we're at an impasse," he says. "For the time being."

He lets go that easily? He's bluffing, then. He must be. I shrug. "I suppose so."

"Come now. Your. . . what did he call himself?" He takes two steps toward me, which should feel threatening, but instead, something bizarre happens.

The ends of my fingers tingle. A thrill races up my spine, and the hair on my arms rises, involuntarily.

"Are you cold?" he whispers.

I shake my head.

"Me either." He looks down at his own arms—the blonde hairs on his powerful forearms are also raised. "Strange, no?"

I can't argue with him, or at least, not about that. "If I can prove to you—"

He presses a finger to my lips, and a shiver runs from my mouth all the way down to my toes. "Shh." His voice is so soft I can barely hear him. "He'll be here any minute."

I lean closer, somehow desperate not to miss a word. "Who?"

"Your. . . your *closest friend* is the phrase he used." He lifts his eyebrows.

Although he hasn't said anything negative, I know he's mocking Gideon and it makes me vaguely uneasy. "Gideon is—"

"No reason to explain anything to me," he says. "Believe me. It's none of my business. But do your homework—quickly." He slides past me to exit before his presence is noticed, but as he does, his arm brushes against my side, and the same exact pull tugs on me again. A thrill runs from my side up and down my body at the same time.

"What *is* that?" I ask.

His eyes lock on mine. He doesn't ask me what I mean. He doesn't protest that he doesn't feel it too. His nostrils flare and he leans toward me slowly. "Once we're past this, once we've done our jobs, it would be my distinct pleasure to find out."

When he shoves out the door and away from me, it's as if my strings have been cut. I sink onto my bed, unmoored, untethered, unordered. Eventually, Gideon comes to check on me, just like Mikhail said he would.

"Are you alright?" His eyes are full of worry.

"I'm fine," I say. "It was a long flight."

"I totally understand."

"Hey, have you heard anything about us having missiles within striking distance of Russia or Mongolia? Or anywhere that Melamecha calls hers?"

Gideon shrugs. "That's a question for your mother, isn't it?"

I nod. "I guess it is. Tell everyone dinner in thirty minutes. I'll be down then, prepared to be as diplomatic as I can possibly muster."

"That guy is a piece of work, isn't he?"

"On that we definitely agree," I say.

Mother picks up on the second ring. "Tell me you made it," she says.

"I did." And my heart swells a little, knowing that she worried about me. "And Melamecha's agent was waiting for me, early for a change."

"That's odd," Mother says. "Usually she makes everyone else wait. She loves to make an entrance."

"But this is an agent, not her."

"I suppose."

"Mother, I need the truth here. Do you have missiles that could reach Melamecha? Is that why you were so eager to respond immediately? Have you been spoiling for this fight?"

"Our intel shows that the Cuban missiles aren't yet ready to deploy." She's evading. Not good.

"Mother."

"Of course we don't. We aren't planning on bombing her. Yet."

I wish I could see her eyes. It's hard to gauge the truthfulness of a skilled evian at the best of times, but without heartbeat, perspiration, and expression, it's impossible.

"You wouldn't have sent me here without all the relevant information, right?"

"Of course not." Is that guilt in her voice? Or perhaps nervousness?

"That's almost a shame. I could use the theoretical missiles, if they existed, to negotiate a coordinated step down."

"Aren't you sick of the stupid bickering and posturing?" she asks.

"I wouldn't be fine with killing millions to end it, if that's what you're asking."

"Humans," Mother says. "Mostly humans would be at risk."

They're not evian, but they're still people. "You can't just play the human card, not when you're talking about catastrophic action like this. Hiroshima and Nagasaki still haunt me."

She doesn't respond.

"They haunt you too," I say. "I know they do."

"Your father's death haunts me more."

I can't argue with her about that. His death haunts me too, and sometimes I still deal with flares of rage over it. "But he wouldn't want you to start hurling more nuclear warheads around, and certainly not as part of some shouting match with his little sister."

"His psychopathic sister."

"Mother, you know that he—"

"We'll never know what he wants," she snaps. "Since he's not here to tell us anymore."

"Mother."

"Fine," she says finally. "He wouldn't want this."

"So you admit we have missiles ready to deploy."

"We absolutely do not, but I would consider reasonable measures to convince Melamecha to step down."

"Fine." I hang up, but I don't give up. Something is off

about the way she replied. Something troubling. Well, she's not the only one with spies. I may not have as extensive a network, but I've been Heir for a hundred and forty years.

I call the head of my spy network, Lionel. He answers on the first ring. "I need to know what types of missiles we have that could target Shamecha, and where they're located. I suspect Turkey."

"I thought your mother denied—"

"She's lying." I'm virtually certain of it.

"Any ideas where they might be located? Turkey's large —and if that's only a guess, then they could be anywhere."

I think back on the conversations we've had, and what I know of Russian geography and rattle off a few ideas. "Push on Oswald. I think he's our best angle."

"Or maybe Gregori," Lionel says. "I'll call you back as quickly as possible."

Gideon will be annoyed that I'm making everyone wait, but I sit by the phone for almost an hour. I lift the receiver three times, about to call Mother and Lionel in turns. But I always put it back down. Calling again, without any extra information, is pointless.

I finally change clothes, ready to go downstairs. I'm headed for the door when the phone finally rings. I snatch it off the receiver and jam it against my ear. "Yes?"

"You were right," Lionel says.

I knew it.

He gives me the details, and I depress the plungers to end the call. I call Mother back so fast, I practically give my fingers whiplash.

"Hello?"

"It's me."

"Lionel works fast."

I laugh. "What was the point of that?"

"A test?"

"Please. You know my network is skilled and comprehensive. Did you really think I wouldn't correct the information you withheld?"

"It was safer for you not to know any locations," Mother says. "I'd actually prefer that you come home, you know."

"Oh, I've been aware of that all along. I'm trying to avert disaster. You've been rushing toward it ever since Dad died, but we still need you."

She pauses so long that I worry about our connection. "If they dismantle the Cuban missiles, then yes."

"Yes, you'll dismantle the Turkish ones? That sounds fair all around—because you have to know that Melamecha would use this to take you down."

"I'd like to see her try."

"You wouldn't," I say. "That's the hurt talking—even now, twenty years later. You know that if you strike first, the others will side with her. Alamecha is strong, but we can't stand up to all of them. Not without destroying everything and everyone, and that cost is too high, even for you."

"I already said I agree." Mother hangs up.

When I go down for dinner, Mikhail isn't there. I look around the room. "Is he coming?"

Eirik shrugs. "I'd really like to meet this guy, but he hasn't come out once."

"Well, we can't wait on him all night," Gideon says.

"Especially after waiting for me for so long?" I smirk. "I'm sorry that took forever. Mother decided to play coy on some of the basics for our operation. But now I'm here, so let's eat."

We're just finishing up when Mikhail finally jogs down the stairs, his jeans hanging way too low on his hips. I swallow and force myself to look away, no matter how badly I'd like a look at that star.

"Good news," he says. "I have evidence of what I asked you about earlier." He's holding a scrap of paper in his hand. I assume it's some kind of coded message they caught. I'll have to make sure to grab it later, so Mother can pass it to Angel and plug any leaks.

"The missiles in Turkey?" I ask.

His jaw drops.

"I talked to my—er, to some contacts." After yelling at everyone else, I almost called her my mother. "I was able to confirm that we do in fact have fully operational nukes in Turkey with a range that would threaten Shamecha's holdings."

He nods. "So our cards are all on the table."

"What do you propose?" I ask.

"Probably the same thing as you."

"You dismantle Cuba, and we dismantle Turkey?"

"Shortest negotiation ever," Gideon says.

"It appears your monarch is a little more willing to empower you than mine is with me." Mikhail frowns. "I'll need some time to convince her that this very reasonable course of action is her only acceptable option."

"Wait," Gideon says. "You came here without the power to do anything?" He stands up with such force that his chair clatters against the ground behind him.

"Melamecha didn't have a lot of faith in Enora's good intentions," he says. "But once I've conveyed her sincerity, I'm sure we'll come around to the same conclusion."

"What can we do to help?" I ask. "Because from our standpoint, this seems pretty straightforward."

"Surely you have a timeframe?" he asks. "Knowing the Cuban missiles are still several days away from being fully operational, whereas yours are currently already active."

I nod. "Three days."

He grins. "I'm confident we'll be able to come to terms by the end of the day tomorrow."

"Great," I say. "I can work with that."

I don't sleep well that night, and the sun isn't even up

yet when I finally give up on sleep and sling my feet out of bed. I pad down the stairs barefoot and walk out on the beach. The moonlight is bright enough that it casts long shadows behind me.

A faint sound behind me alerts me that I'm not the only one awake. I'm not sure who else it is, but I suspect. I spin around and notice a flickering coming from Mikhail's window. I creep back toward the house until I'm just below his window.

Apparently I'm not above espionage—but really, he's using *our* telephone in the middle of night. He should expect to be caught. The audacity.

"No," he says in Russian. Good thing I brushed up. "I know that's what you said. But he would have been a disaster. You know that as well as I do. They deserved to have someone here who actually wanted to solve the problem."

Squeaking from the receiver that I can't make out from this far away.

"Because I think you're wrong. You keep me around because I always tell you the truth, and the truth here is that no matter how much you think you can destroy her, I think it would be a nearly even fight. You'd succeed only in leveling the entire human population."

Squeaking.

"I am well aware that you don't care about them. You've been crystal clear on that point. But even knowing that you don't see things the same way that I do, you *do* care about evian life. And you could end that, too. This is a very dangerous, even stupidly dangerous game. Set aside your irritation with me and do the right thing."

Squeaking.

"No, but she has a lot of latitude. She called Enora right after she arrived and immediately got through to her, so it's someone relatively important."

A pause.

"I told you. Claudia."

Another pause.

"She's blonde, but of course that proves nothing."

Another pause.

"She's tall—as tall as I am. And yes, she's commanding. She'd give you a run for your money."

Squeaking.

"I've never met her, so I don't know. But she has a boyfriend—Gideon something?"

I swear softly. Why didn't we think to give fake names for my guards? It probably doesn't matter, but this whole conversation makes me uneasy.

"Absolutely not. If she *is* Enora's daughter, the last thing you want to do is kill her."

My blood runs cold.

"Fine, you're right. I'm not in charge of what you want, but I'll tell you what I am in charge of—my own actions. There's nothing you can do or threaten that will induce me to *kill* someone who came here to negotiate in good faith."

A longer pause.

"You may be the most idiotic empress in the history of time."

I laugh.

All noise from the room ceases. Then I hear a whispered, "I need to go. No, I'm not afraid of you. I just need to go."

When Mikhail's head pokes out the window, I figure there's no point in hiding my presence, so I wave.

I don't expect him to leap out of the window, landing on the balls of his feet next to me in the sand.

"Whoa," I say.

"You were listening in on my conversation." He frowns.

I shrug.

"You're Inara."

I shrug again. "Your aunt wants me dead."

He rolls his eyes. "Only in the theoretical, grudge-holding sense. She didn't really think I'd kill you."

"Well, that's a huge relief."

"And I'd never do it, in any case."

"I did hear that part." I'm suddenly very aware that I'm standing in the sand wearing nothing more than a long t-shirt.

He's wearing shorts and nothing more. His eyes practically shine in the moonlight, his eyelashes absurdly long, the stubble on his chin drawing my attention in a strange way.

I lift my hand to reach for it, but I stop myself. I'm not insane enough to touch strangers' faces yet, thankfully.

"Well, I suppose this is where I should apologize for spying," I say. "But you'd know I was lying."

When he smiles, my heart soars.

When he takes a step forward, my knees wobble.

When he reaches a hand toward my face, my body curls toward him, yearning pathetically.

If I saw him across a battlefield, would our eyes lock? I lift my face toward his, finally meeting his gaze. "You," he says softly.

I sway toward him.

His breath blows across my face, the scent of him over-powering, compelling in a way I can't pinpoint. Like he's every delicious thing I never knew I wanted. "There's a pull between us, something I've never felt before, not with anyone, ever."

I can't think of a single thing to say, but I know just what he means.

"I'm going to do something stupid right now." Before I can stop him, not that I ever would, he shifts forward, closing the remaining space between us. His breath on my face, the scent of fresh leather and something minty, the tugging from his heart to mine, none of it makes sense, but

I can't imagine being without it. I don't know how long we stand like that, less than an inch separating our bodies, but eventually the delicious agony is too much, and we move together in unison, our hands meeting, our hips bumping, our mouths colliding perfectly.

And the world shifts on its axis in a way I wouldn't have thought possible if I hadn't endured something inversely horrific when my dad passed away. Somehow, the world around me *changes*. The air is heavier. The sand under my feet has more texture. The moon smiles down on me, whereas before it merely provided light.

I thought I loved Gideon, and I did in my way, but this is something else. Something more. A gravitational pull, if that can exist between two people. His hands slide from my shoulders down my arms, and then jump to my hips, searing me as they move, and somehow also leaving me *undone*.

As the first rays of sunlight part the darkness, somehow, in a move I can't quite comprehend, Mikhail stumbles backward. "Can we table this momentarily?" His eyes plead with mine.

I can't deny him anything. I nod wordlessly.

"Let's get this hammered out, let's save both our countries, and then. . ." He shivers. "I'll follow you anywhere."

"You'd leave Shamecha?"

He laughs. "At the first opportunity. But if you want to leave Alamecha, I'll carve out a place for us anywhere you choose."

"That fast?" I lift one eyebrow. "One kiss and you'll follow me anywhere? Take me anywhere?"

His fingers gently brush my jaw. "That was more than one kiss."

I know exactly what he means. "Yes." It was so much more than that, but how could I ever explain it in a way that makes sense?

"Umm," a voice behind us says.

I spin around.

Bellatrius glances from Mikhail to me and back again. "Gideon's looking for you."

I swear under my breath. "He cannot find me here, not like this."

"How high can you jump?" Mikhail asks.

I shrug. "How high can you jump?"

By way of response, he leaps, vertically, to the windowsill above our heads, and pulls himself back into his room. His head pokes back out one second later, a hand extended.

It takes me three tries, and any hope I might have had of being remembered for my grace dies a sad death, but I scramble inside Mikhail's room before Gideon rounds the corner. Mikhail checks the hall and waves me past in time for me to change my clothes and jog downstairs.

"Where have you been?" Gideon's eyes are wide when he flies through the back door.

"I went for a jog," I say. "We must have crossed paths." The lie stings, but not as badly as it would hurt him to know what I was really doing.

I really am a monster.

When Mikhail offered to carve out a place for us anywhere, I thought he was being ridiculous, but looking at Gideon, I consider it. Once I've saved the world from imminent destruction, could I do it? Could I run away? It would hurt Gideon, my mother, Alora, Balthasar, everyone I care about.

But when I think about that kiss, or whatever it was—if it was the only way I could be with Mikhail, I'd do it. I shove that concern away for now. Plenty of time to deal with it later. When Mikhail jogs down the stairs again, which I'm sensing is his way of being in the world—always rushing—I don't meet his eyes. If I do, Gideon will sense whatever it is that hangs between us. I'm sure of it.

We spend the next few hours hashing out the details of disarming the missiles—a coordinated plan that would provide accountability and verification. Once that's done, I catch Gideon's eye and toss my head toward the back porch. He stands up without hesitation and follows me out. He stands a little closer than he would have last week, his features more relaxed now that the end is in sight. The massage, I recall, was supposed to happen once we were done.

"We need to talk," I say.

Gideon beams at me. "Yes."

"Only." I inhale and exhale.

"What's wrong?" He sits down and pats the seat next to him.

I sit across from him instead. "I know what you thought we'd be talking about."

He frowns. "What I *thought* we'd be talking about?"

"The thing is." I swallow.

He straightens, his gaze shuttering. "What is the thing?"

"I thought I loved you," I say. "I want you to know that."

"You thought?" He swallows. "You *thought* you loved me."

I can't meet his eyes. "But when I met Mikhail yesterday—"

He explodes off of the sofa. "You met him yesterday. Yesterday! Can you hear yourself?"

I shake my head. "No, I do hear it. I know it sounds insane. I would be mocking anyone else I heard saying something this stupid, and I love you, Gideon, I really do, and I have for a long time, but I love you like I loved my dad, or my sister—"

"No." He shakes his head vehemently. He shakes it so hard, I can't even catch his eye. "No, you don't know what you're saying. Maybe you've been poisoned. Maybe, I don't know. But this isn't right. We're finally going to talk. We're finally—"

I grab his arm. "Gideon, listen to me. This isn't even about Mikhail. He only helped me realize how I feel about you, and how I've been okay to live alongside you for so long without ever. . . This is coming out all wrong."

"Oh I think you've made your point." Gideon lifts his chin, his head held high. "I understand how you feel."

"I would never, ever want to hurt you."

He nods. "Got it."

"Look, Gideon, I—"

"You know, I think it's my turn to take a 'jog.'" He makes air quotes around the word jog, as if I didn't know he realized I wasn't jogging. As if I didn't know that he knows I lied to him. Then, for the first time in a hundred and twenty years, Gideon leaves my side. Sprints away from me, in fact.

I'm wondering whether he'll ever be back when Mikhail saunters onto the back porch. He doesn't sit next to me. He doesn't touch me. He doesn't have to—he gets it, the agony that I'm enduring. I can tell from his expression that he understands.

"He'll be back."

"You don't know that."

His smile this time is wry. "Actually, I think I do. If he feels anything like how I feel, nothing could prevent his return."

"I hurt him," I say. "It's complicated."

"Oh, I have no doubt about that."

"He has never done a single thing to harm me, never."

"He's a smart guy, then."

"He is," I say. "He really is—smart, good, kind, strong, brave. I could go on. I'm a horrible person."

"Not being right for someone who cares about you doesn't make you a bad person."

"I would have been happy with him, you know," I say.

"If you hadn't met me."

I sigh.

He finally sits next me and slings an arm around my shoulders.

I sink against him, resting my head against his chest. I close my eyes and wonder if there's any way for me to make things right with Gideon. Not choosing him now that I've met Mikhail—it feels strangely out of my control—but guilt eats at me anyway.

A black tarp flung over us from behind shocks me, and I try to leap to my feet. Strong arms shove us to the ground. After a heavy blow to my head, the world goes entirely dark.

❧ 10 ❧

1962

A sharp pain in my belly wakes me up. I can't see. I blink and blink—black fabric over my eyes. I'm lying on my side, my hands secured behind my back. We're indoors, based on air quality and the lack of immediate sounds from the surrounding area. It's too humid and hot to be climate controlled.

A heavy boot slams into my stomach, and then again. I groan involuntarily.

"Finally awake." A female voice says, gravelly, low, but definitely female. It's too far behind me to be my assailant. "Step back."

Bootfalls indicate someone large is moving away from me.

"Get her up and secure her in the restraints."

Large hands grab my shoulders, and I inhale and exhale and start to utilize all my senses. Finally. Heartbeat that must be from the woman I assume is in charge. Four or five feet behind me. Heartbeat of large handed enforcer, just behind me. Two more heartbeats—one in front of me, to the left. Another next to the woman barking commands.

Me and four attackers, I imagine. They either killed Mikhail or they're holding him, too.

Big Hands shoves me forward, my face slamming against the concrete floor, knocking my front tooth loose. Blood blossoms in my mouth, but on the upside, the internal damage from the kicking has healed. I push the tooth back into place with my tongue.

The same large hands slide under my armpits and toss me up and onto a stool, forcing my upper body forward into what must be some kind of torture device. He slams my right wrist down against something smooth and cold—a manacle, I imagine. It'll be titanium, which means it's now or never. If I've ever been grateful to be a berserker before in my life, it's right now. For once, I don't care whether I kill everyone in the room. They can burn for all I care.

"No, Havrel. What are you doing? Right next to him— it'll be easier that way."

Him? My heart sinks.

Big hands shoves me to the left, barking my knee against a hard wooden stool. I inhale deeply and want to string together every swear word I've ever learned. There's a very, very slow heartbeat I failed to notice.

Mikhail is right next to me.

I should be glad he's alive, but I've never felt more help-less in my life. I'm fairly certain I can save myself, but if I kill one of them, I'll kill every single person in this room. And if I can't kill any of them, this just got a lot harder. Big Hands' fingers encircle my wrist.

Decision time.

Do I struggle? Try to escape? Or assume they won't kill us and wait for more information? I've never been very patient. And if they stick me in titanium and I can't ever break free. . .

But if I attack and kill one of them, I'll snap and kill Mikhail, too. It's ironic, really. For the first time, I *want* to fight—I *want* to kill, but if I do, I'll kill the main reason I have to want to live through this. If there is a God, He has one wicked sense of humor.

I agonize too long, and the manacle snaps over my wrist. I bite off a whimper. It didn't hurt but knowing my options have narrowed does. I don't resist as Big Hands forces my other wrist into the same enclosure. He twists something to ratchet it down smaller.

Stupid.

That means there's a hinge, and hinges are weaknesses. They should have had large and small restraints, even if they're side by side. They shackle my legs—the chains jangling as they secure the cuffs around my ankles. Again, any weakness in their system helps me.

The belt strap they secure next isn't even metal. Some kind of stiff fabric.

"Pull off the hood." The female voice has circled around and is standing in front of me.

The first thing I see is Havrel, aka Big Hands, whose hands look fairly normal sized, now that I can actually see them, for a seven foot warrior anyway. His red hair is cut relatively short, but it flies out in every direction from his head. His grin makes me uneasy. He's too happy for someone who spent the last few moments kicking and then restraining the daughter of an empress.

I blink my eyes several times to adjust to the fluorescent lights, and then I glance left. Mikhail isn't conscious, slumped next to me in similar restraints. I wonder why they waited for me to waken, but not him. But his slow, clearly tranqed heartbeat is at least steady, and there are no signs of torture, which means he's either healed already, or they haven't started on him yet.

Most of the boss's features are obscured by Big Hands, er, Havrel, but I can make out enough to know she's smaller than me—Alora's size, maybe, with dark hair and burnished golden skin. Something about her is familiar, but I won't be able to pinpoint what until I see her.

I wrack my brain to try and match the voice I heard with one I know. Twinges, but my brain feels sluggish.

"Did you give me something?" My voice is slurred, my tongue heavy and thick.

"You're smarter than Mother said." The toasted-honey-skinned woman steps closer and Big Hands moves out of her way.

It's Paruka, Melamecha's Heir. I should have guessed. My brain is definitely moving more slowly than it should. "A truckload of ketamine?"

"Very good." Paruka's boots clomp, clomp, clomp, until they stop right in front of my face. "I think it might be time for the neck restraint, before it all wears off entirely. You should not be awake yet, you know. Your mother may be a disgrace, but her blood is strong. I gave you enough to tranquilize a draft horse. My cousin here is still drooling." She laughs. "Havrel. Her neck, idiot."

He shoves my face down so I can't see anything but the rounded black toes of her boots, practically new, but scuffed—probably from kicking me at some point, even if it was Havrel who woke me up. The neck manacle is made of two pieces of solid iron, the top one latching in two places into the bottom half moon. It'll be much, much harder to remove—not that I even have my hands free to work on it. I don't swear or whine or groan, no matter how horrified I am. I won't give her that satisfaction.

"Ultimately, I've been tasked to get some information from you." Paruka sits next to me, dipping her head slightly so that I can see her face. "But I think we're also going to have some fun. I mean, never waste an opportunity, right?"

Her mother is one of the most famous sadists of all time. Looks like her mini-me inherited the same tendencies.

"No small fluffy animals left in Russia? I thought you guys were like, the world's leading exporter of rabbits."

A slap across my cheek. "Yes. I like it. Let's get started."

Paruka stands. Clomp, clomp, clomp, she crosses the room, and a sliding whoosh tells me she's opened a case and laid it flat. "I never leave home without my bag of toys, and when I'm lucky, I get to use all of them."

"My mother won't be pleased," I say softly. "And as you mentioned, her blood is good. Even if you kill me, you're going to die for this. I hope you enjoy experiencing pain as much as you enjoy inflicting it."

Her laugh warbles like a songbird—far too beautiful for someone this ugly inside. "You are just too much. I can't believe we haven't spent any time together before now. A real oversight."

"You've clearly been practicing your English for a while." It occurs to me that homosexuals are not at all accepted in Russia. "How long have you had a crush on me? You can admit it. We're all friends here."

Her black boot slams into my face, and this time two teeth dislodge entirely. Maybe ticking her off wasn't my best plan. Teeth take *forever* to regrow, and it requires a lot of focus. I consider trying to use my tongue to shove the roots back into place, but I can barely breathe, between my split lip and busted tongue. Mouth wounds bleed.

I spit them on the floor.

"Always have to be the prettiest one in the room?" I taunt. What's wrong with me? Why can't I just shut up?

"You're not going to survive this," Paruka purrs at my shoulder. "You have to know that. But, you do have a chance, albeit a small one with as annoyed as I already am, to make this relatively painless. As you may know, my mother is a bit of an artist. I've been studying under her for quite some time. I don't mean to brag, but I can make the next few days quite miserable for you, if you refuse to cooperate."

"What do you want?" I ask. "I mean, I would have given you Angel's famous soufflé recipe if you just asked."

"Ha. Your sense of humor worsens as you lose teeth, it appears." She stands up. "I need the location and launch codes of the missiles in Turkey, obviously."

"I didn't even know the missiles were there until yesterday," I say. "I certainly don't have launch codes. Your mother must trust you more than mine does."

"We can start with the location." Paruka crouches down again, her hand slowly petting my head. "If I believe you're trying, I can be merciful. I do so enjoy sincere begging."

"Paruka?" Mikhail's voice next to me is groggy. "Is that you?"

"Cousin. You should have stayed asleep." She pivots to face him. "I don't even know where to begin with you. Mother is so upset she won't even let me kill you."

"Upset?" He clears his throat. "About what?"

"You were canoodling with this one when I found you. Do you deny it?"

He laughs, low and rich, as though waking in restraints isn't the least concerning. "Let me out already. This is ridiculous."

Paruka kicks him and rage simmers at the edges of my vision. Someone needs to remove her feet until she's been taught what not to do with them. I suppress the threatening haze with an effort. I've never had it hover without being called out by a death. What's going on with me?

"Since when has Aunt M ever cared what we did on a mission, as long as we get the job done?" He swears under his breath. "I got the agreement she needed. They'll dismantle if we will."

"That was never her goal, that was her worst-case scenario." It sounds like Paruka yanks his head back, stopped only by the bands around his neck. "Did you even try to extricate the information on where the Turkey missiles are?"

He spits on her.

I can't turn my head enough to see exactly what's happening, but it's not good. She's pulled some kind of blade and is slicing some kind of design into the gorgeous skin of his belly.

He doesn't make any more jokes.

Livid fury rises up inside of me that feels an awful lot like the haze. I know that only killing something can cause it, but. . .on the day Dad died, Balthasar didn't kill anyone. He was just standing in the war room processing the bad news. I close my eyes and imagine my dad's face. I think about loyal Gideon. I think about always calm Mother. I need to find my own inner peace to navigate this. Stuck in shackles, the haze won't help me at all. I'd struggle like a beast in a trap, frothing and pitiful. No, I need to stay present. I need my brain to work.

"Fine," I say.

Paruka shifts. "What?"

"Fine," I say. "What exactly do you want to know about the location?"

She drops something and it clatters against the floor. Probably the knife. "Why?" Her face appears next to mine. "Why would you give me that?"

"I can't even look at you with this stupid manacle around my neck." I compress my lips.

She rolls her eyes. "Oh, fine. Havrel."

He grunts, then in Russian, says, "Newt has the keys."

Paruka swears. "Then, Newt! Release her head. You two need to take some initiative. Honestly."

Well-worn brown loafers step in front of me. Loafers? Really? A small click and my head is free, at least. I lift it and lock eyes with a much shorter man. His hair is combed neatly, and he's wearing slacks and a button down shirt. His eyes are cunning—calculating. Paruka's wrong if she thinks he's unintelligent. But he doesn't like taking orders from her. That much is clear.

Havrel is nothing but tightly corded muscle, but this guy, he's working for Melamecha directly. I'd stake my life on it, which means Mommy doesn't entirely trust her Heir. He wants to be overlooked, in his unassuming loafers, but he's probably the biggest threat in the room.

"Thank you," I say. "And to answer your question, I've had time to consider the details of your offer."

"You'll tell me where they're located, if I promise not to hurt you badly?" Paruka almost looks disappointed.

"Wrong," Newt says. "She offered to share information when you were slicing—"

Paruka shoves Newt out of the way. "I'm not a moron. I wanted to hear her excuse." She smiles slowly, her head tilting sideways like an eager falcon. "Clearly she likes my cousin as much as he likes her."

"Do you want the location or not?" I lift one eyebrow, aiming for nonchalant, which is hard to do with two teeth missing and my arms and legs stuck in constraints. Probably impossible, actually.

"I think we need to talk." Newt gestures behind me, at a door, I assume, since I can't see one.

"We can say anything you want in front of them," Paruka says, unable to keep a slight whine out of her voice. "They're both dying anyway. Mother said I can."

She's seventy-six years old, but she sounds like an eleven-year-old lunatic. Killing us is the equivalent of demanding her favorite blankie. I wonder whether she even realizes it.

"Outside, now." Newt walks past me without even glancing my way.

She scowls and stomps, but Paruka follows him eventually. Clearly no one taught her that behaving in that way, but following someone's orders, simply surrenders more of your power. Her only play, if he really can order her around, is to act like she wants to do whatever he demands.

A few seconds after the door closes, Mikhail asks, "You weren't really going to give them the location, right?"

I think about his grunts, about the torture I know he's enduring next to me. "If Melamecha isn't going to deal, and if we're dying anyway, what does it matter?" I ask.

"She won't kill me," he says. "This isn't the first time I've ticked her off, and it's not even the first time my dear cousin has threatened to kill me and claimed she had permission. Melamecha values family, she's just big on teaching lessons—and she gives Paruka little tastes of power to keep her on the hook."

"Your aunt sucks."

"No argument from me," he says. "But even if she really does mean to kill us, you can't give her those locations."

Excuse me? "I think you're committing treason right now."

"Treason is just a spoiled ruler crying foul—a word to legitimize their revenge on anyone who didn't blindly follow their lead."

"You honestly don't want me to give them the codes if it would get you out of here?"

"I do not," he says. "Honestly. In fact, I'm begging you not to do it."

"Why?"

"The only thing keeping my insane aunt from firing nuclear weapons on Florida right now is the fear that you could immediately retaliate."

"You really want to avert this," I say. "Maybe more than I do."

"I really do."

"Why?" I ask, genuinely curious.

"This is when you decide that I'm as crazy as my aunt," he says softly.

"We may not have much time. May as well level with me."

"In 1905, I was only ten years old." His voice is faint, so quiet that I have to strain to hear him. "Aunt M assigned my parents to put down a worker revolution. It was supposed to be supervision only, but, well, I don't really know exactly how it happened. My dad told me to wait inside a shed, and then a few minutes later, he yanked me back out. He was wounded—bleeding."

He pauses.

"And?" I have no idea what some worker strike back in 1905 has to do with these bombs, but I don't even care—I want to know about anything that shaped him.

"I've never told anyone else this story."

"Okay," I say, afraid to break the spell.

"Do you know what happens when an evian body is forced, repeatedly, to heal without being able to consume calories?"

I swallow.

"It can't do it, eventually. At a certain point, our reserves are too depleted to heal ourselves anymore. My father was bleeding from several places. He dragged me toward a larger building where my mother struggled against numerous attackers."

I close my eyes. I know what happens next.

"The humans, they killed them." His voice cracks. "I should have fought for them. I think that's why my dad got me, you know. I realized it later. I thought he was trying to save me, but I think he was dragging me there to help defend them, or at least distract their attackers enough that they might survive. I was the sacrificial lamb, but I failed them. Instead, I clung to my father, sobbing."

"That's horrible."

"Is it?" he asks. "I mean, I sure thought so at the time. But looking back as an adult, I know that my parents were slaughtering the people there—workers who were revolting because they were starving." He inhales and exhales. "The humans didn't kill me, you know. And one of them even apologized to me. I didn't pay much attention to it then, but there were hundreds of dead humans, just to take out two evians. Melamecha didn't address any of the reasons for the upheaval. She just wanted them dead—because that would end the unrest. She didn't even consider the reasons behind it."

"As a ten-year-old, you cared why they killed your parents?"

His laugh is bitter. "Not at all. In fact, I was so angry, so full of hatred and rage that I joined with someone named Rasputin. He was one of Melamecha's closest advisors, but he also led a group known as the Ararat. They hated humans, almost as much as I did. They wanted all humans eliminated; they wanted the world cleansed of humans. They saw them as a degraded abomination—and it was our responsibility to clean it up, since we created them."

"Wait," I say. "You joined—"

"Your mother, inadvertently, changed my life, you know."

Huh?

"Her freedom model was doing so well that Aunt M nearly lost her mind. She was sick of everyone singing Enora's praises, and she decided to eliminate all the monarchs ruling in our place. 'Fine—give them freedom at the edge of a blade,' she said. The Russian monarchy, our partners for a long time, was destroyed in 1918. I was sent to help with their slaughter, the Romanovs, I mean. It was sickening, the way we were ordered to treat them. They ordered me to kill the children. Even the humans wouldn't do that to me, after my parents killed everyone who approached them."

He pauses for a moment. "That opened my eyes," he says. "And I killed Rasputin instead. I've never admitted that, not to anyone."

"Melamecha would be furious."

He snorts. "She really would. I've been doing everything I possibly can to spare the humans under her control for the past forty-five years."

"Like siding with the enemy to try and prevent a nuclear war that would kill predominantly humans."

"Exactly," he says. "You know, the families spend a lot of time and resources arguing over who owns what and who names what and who controls what. No one advocates for the humans, and they're *just like us*. No, that's wrong. They *are* us. We're all descended from Eve, after all."

As if some kind of clouds have parted, I realize that he's speaking the most truthful thing I've ever heard. For maybe the first time in my life, I'm talking to someone who sees the world as it *is*, not as he's been *told it is*. I knew I was drawn to this man, but I had no idea why. Now that I've gotten a glimpse of his soul, I can hardly credit that this strength came from the same background as me—was fed the same stories I was. That we're better than humans, that they should serve us.

"So you can see that, whatever you do, you can't give them the location. If they disable your mother's missiles, there will be nothing stopping Melamecha from killing countless humans. She'll do it, too, anything to wound your mother. Think of all the innocent lives snuffed out to further her agenda."

"What do we do, then?" I ask. "If I can't give them codes?"

The door opens behind us.

Paruka walks through first, scowling at me furiously. She

doesn't pause, or kick, or slap me. She walks to the corner and folds her arms. Havrel follows her quietly, crossing his arms over his chest, his eyes shifting from me to Mikhail slowly.

Newt walks through next, but the nice guy façade is gone. His eyes are sharp, his command clear. "You will give me the location?"

"About that," I say. "I know that I said I would."

He frowns.

"And the thing is, I really would like to, but I don't actually know the location. I figured I'd make something up, but while you were gone, your friend convinced me that lying would be a monumentally bad idea."

Newt's nostrils flare.

Paruka rubs her hand together. "If she's not giving us information—"

Newt tosses his hand in the air. "The problem is, I do not believe her." He crouches down next to me. His whisper is so soft that it barely reaches my ears. "Do you know how much pain we with pure blood can endure?"

I shake my head.

He speaks normally this time, his tone matter-of-fact, as though he's teaching a class of eager students. "A human body passes out after the infliction of a very small amount of pain. You can barely do anything to them at all before their receptors overload their system and they black out."

He holds his hand back toward Paruka and says a word I don't understand.

Her lip curls, but she crosses the room and hands him a long, metal utensil. It's not sharp on the end, but then I see it. Holes interspersed across the end, with razor sharp edges. "The Russians call this a terka. I think in English the word is grater." He lifts his eyebrows as though he expects a response.

"Alright."

"Have you ever eaten ice cream?" he asks.

Huh?

"That first bite of ice cream is euphoric. It's bliss. You can't imagine anything better, so you quickly shove another bite in your mouth." His fingers trail across my jaw, and I hear struggling sounds coming from Mikhail.

He wants to protect me. It should make me feel better, but since Newt is only brushing his fingers against my jaw, it makes me nervous. What does Mikhail fear?

"That second bite—it's not as good. Not by a wide margin. In fact, it's only so-so. You shovel more ice cream into your mouth, and more, but you can't get that same rush of excitement, no matter how much you eat."

"I don't understand your point exactly, but I would like some ice cream, if you're offering. I don't even mind about the diminishing returns that seem to so upset you."

He chuckles. "Paruka hates you, you know. But not me, no, I appreciate you, as I would appreciate any fine instrument on which I intend to play. You see, with most torture, the first cut is the worst."

I swallow.

"You endure the first few, and then..." He shrugs. "Diminishing returns. Like ice cream."

"But?"

"But I have developed a method that circumvents this tragedy."

"Oh goody," I say. "I can't wait to hear."

He licks his lips. "I think I'd rather show you."

He rakes the grater across my arm, peeling long furrows of skin away. The pain is exquisite—even through the fiery, piercing shards of it, I'm aware that it's a good comparison —that first bite of ice cream. Distinctly horrific, the very first massive destruction of my skin, the first sublimation of my control over my body.

He sets the bloody grater down and smiles. "You see,

your body has almost healed already. The expenditure of healing energy is not large, relative to the pain inflicted, allowing you to heal this type of injury for a very long time before dying."

"You're saying I won't grow inured to that?" I ask.

"Oh, you would," he says. "Yes. I don't deny that."

Okay. I don't get this guy. Like, at all.

"Spray bottle." He glances back at Paruka.

She chucks it at him. He catches it gracefully. "You're lucky that didn't spill," he says. "Or I'd be forced to try the melter on you first."

The melter? I shudder involuntarily, hating that he's watching my reaction. It's exactly the kind of thing he surely relishes.

"This is a spray, as you can see," he says. "It's a mixture I make myself. Have you heard of the Moruga Scorpion pepper?"

"No one has heard of that. I think you need more hobbies and less free time," I say.

He purses his lips. "Again with the jokes. Your mother must have neglected you as a child, or perhaps you're lashing out since your father died."

I roll my eyes.

"The Moruga originates in Trinidad, but I grow it quite successfully in my greenhouse."

"I'm very impressed," I say. "You're clearly quite the accomplished botanist."

"The thing about that ice cream is that repetition never breeds success. We adapt too well."

"So you're going to rotate me, like a rotisserie chicken?"

He beams at me. "A wonderful analogy, yes. Paruka, you can come closer now."

"You need her help?"

He shrugs. "Need is a strong word, but the torture works better when several people can alternate methods.

She's more of a blunt tool right now, so I let her do the garden variety slicing and dicing."

Paruka scowls.

He lifts the grater again, and a spray bottle. "See, when I do this now, instead of your arm, I do the side of your face. The skin is more sensitive." He yanks it down the side of my face, and he's right.

It's far, far worse.

The haze rises inside of me, flexing and bucking, pulsing and raging.

"But even that, you could ignore, eventually," he says. "The key is to rotate the pain in an irregular manner so you can't prepare. I think a small demonstration is in order."

Paruka removes my boot and carves the bottom of my foot with what I assume is a serrated knife. I inhale quickly, but before I can exhale, Newt is grating my arm again. I strain against the bindings, but before I can heal from either, Paruka stabs my calf and Newt sprays the wounds on my arm with his pepper spray.

This time, the haze slams against me—threatening and beckoning both. I fought it off before, horrified that I might kill Mikhail. But after our conversation, I realize he'd rather die than let them force the location of Mother's missiles out of me.

And stupid Newt forgot to replace the neck manacle.

They're still carving and stabbing and slicing, but when Havrel hands Newt a handheld torch, I flex against the bindings. The lap belt snaps, and Newt leaps back.

"Secure her," Newt says.

Havrel leans near me, his hands reaching toward my head to shove me back into the neck binding. I bite an enormous chunk from his palm.

He leaps back and shouts.

At the taste of blood in my mouth, the haze broadens. My muscles vibrate and I slam against the titanium again. I doubt I could snap two inches of titanium, but the chain links holding my feet in place break, first the left, then the right.

And then the hinge on my right hand gives.

I'm only held by one thing.

"Secure her!" Newt screams.

Paruka and Havrel circle me.

"She has no weapons, and she's still bound on the left," Newt says. "What are you afraid of?"

Paruka has a six-inch knife and a razor blade. I'll happily take either option.

But she's too afraid to come near me. Havrel approaches first from the left side, where I'm still bound, a sword in his right hand, a knife in the left. He shoves the sword in my direction, and I smile. I don't resist as it pierces my side. In fact, I slide toward him, and then I bring my right hand down on the blade, tearing the gash in my skin open wider, but dislodging the hilt from his hand.

Steel might not cut titanium, but slamming the hilt against the hinge frees my left hand.

And I'm armed.

The next few minutes are a blur of shouts and cries, but the best part is when Newt tries to flee. I leap across the room, landing on his back, shoving his face against the concrete floor. "Now where's that spray when you need it?" I growl in his ear, right before cutting it off.

I take my time on him, but the haze presses and eventually I kill them all. I swing around toward the other heartbeat, but the face that looks up at me is one I know.

My eyes widen.

The haze recedes.

I blink.

Mikhail.

The haze disappears, as quickly as morning fog dissipates in the heat of midday.

126

I hardly know him, but I know this. The haze disappears because *I love him.*

As I loved my father, but more deeply, in a way that permeates my entire being. Balthasar was wrong, or at least, what works for him doesn't work for me. The only thing that pulls me out of the haze is love. And as much as I loved my dad, I love Mikhail more.

I drop into a crouch on the floor, because now I realize that Mikhail just saw me feral, incoherent, and crazed. There is no way the saintly champion of life in front of me will possibly understand. He can never accept what I really am.

The fear and stress and horror of the past hours slams into me at the same time, and I bawl like a baby, my face cupped in my bloody hands.

"Inara? Are you there?" Mikhail doesn't sound repulsed.

I wipe my face off on my shirt as quickly as I can, and I realize my teeth are nearly regrown, thankfully. "Uh, I am."

"You're alive?"

He must not have been able to see much. He doesn't know what happened.

"I am."

"How?"

I cross the room as if walking toward my own execution. I use the knife I took from Paruka to pry his restraints open, slicing the lap belt with the wrench of one hand. "It's kind of a long story."

He sits up, rubbing his wrists as he does. "I think we have more time now." He laughs, and then he looks around the room, his eyes widening in alarm.

"We may not need that much time." I've wanted to tell so many people the truth. Mother, Uncle Balthasar, Gideon. My heart twinges at the thought of dear, sweet Gideon sprinting away from me. I was always scared to tell them, but not because I worried how they'd take it. I knew they would accept me, and some of them would welcome the news. No, I kept my secret out of fear that it would ruin my life.

But today I'm terrified that if I tell this man in front of me, possibly the best person I've ever met, that he'll recoil. I'm scared he won't accept it—that he won't be able to accept me.

That he won't love me once he knows the truth.

"I'm a berserker," I say.

His forehead furrows. "A what?"

I sit down cross-legged in front of him.

He does the same, reaching out to take my hand. "I think maybe it's a word I haven't learned in English yet. Does it mean you're trained as, like, a super fighter?"

I snort. "Trained? No."

"I don't understand."

I explain—including trying to describe the haze. He listens patiently, pulling me against him to sob on his chest when I tell him how I discovered it, and how many times I nearly killed my own father.

"But you didn't ever scare me," he says. "Maybe you've figured it out—gained the control you said your dad talked about."

I don't tell him about Balthasar. I told him my dad had heard from his own father that it was about self-control. It didn't feel right to out my uncle's secret, not when I've so closely guarded my own. "My grandfather was wrong," I say softly. "The reason my dad could help me come out of it was that I loved him, deeply."

"Oh," he says. "Well, alright."

"But I didn't realize that until right now."

"How?" His eyes widen.

"I snapped out of the haze the second I looked at you," I whisper, more nervous now than I was to reveal my secret.

"You did?" His eyes brighten.

"I know I've only known you for a day, Mikhail, but I am quite sure that I'm in love with you."

He closes his eyes.

My heart stops dead in my chest. I struggle to breathe. "You don't—"

He shakes his head, and I want to disappear. He grabs my hand. "No, I mean I do, I love you too. I can't explain it, and it sounds insane, but I do. I know exactly how you feel."

I draw in a ragged breath. "You do?"

He smiles at me, and the world shifts on its axis again. "I do, truly. Nothing you've said sounds crazy to me."

"Oh." My heart hammers in my chest like it might punch through my skin. "But you—"

"The thing is, I do love you, and that means I have a secret to share too."

My hands tremble.

"Nothing like yours," he says, "and it has nothing to do with you. But the thing is, my name isn't actually Mikhail."

"Huh?" I ask. "It's not?"

He shakes his head. Aunt M didn't send me, you see. She meant to send my cousin, Mikhail. He's a moron, but she knew he'd do what Paruka was doing—torture you for information on the missiles in Turkey. Her plan all along has always been to destroy Florida—to devastate your mother and encourage the other families to join with her and bring Alamecha down, once and for all."

I swallow.

"You can understand that while I didn't know you or your mother, I couldn't let that happen. I knew if I negotiated a better option, her Consort and her Council would make her take it. None of them are quite as sure the other empresses will follow her lead."

"Where is the real Mikhail?" I ask.

He smiles. "Oh, I gave up quite a large property in Moscow to reroute him, but the pilot took him to Iceland. He won't be here for quite some time yet."

"So the birthmark?"

He bites his lip and inches the waistband of his shorts down. Nothing but smooth skin.

Deliciously smooth skin.

"That was quite a gamble."

He grins a chagrined smile. "When I saw how possessive your Gideon was, I felt confident he wouldn't really want me to prove it."

I shake my head—he was right on the mark there. "What *is* your name, then?"

"I didn't lie about my parents. My mother was Melamecha's older sister, not that they were especially close or anything. But I think at this point in our relationship, we probably ought to know one another's real names."

"That seems like a good idea." Although, I'll call him anything at all. I can't imagine a name I wouldn't like, if it was his.

He extends his hand so we can shake—just like the first time we met. "It's nice to meet you, Inara. My name is Eamon Shamecha."

My hands are tacky against his. . .because the blood is drying. Eww. I yank my hand away, horrified. I can guess how I look—I've seen a version of this in the reflections from rivers and streams after coming out of the haze far too many times. I duck my head, wishing I hadn't just told Eamon that *I loved him* while covered in gore.

I am still a monster—I need to remember that. Always.

"You really busted out of the restraints, unarmed, and then took out three of Shamecha's toughest warriors?"

I nod, but I can't bring myself to look at him, even with the note of awe in his tone.

"I wish I had been able to watch—like really watch. I'm sure it was a thing of beauty."

My face snaps up. "Beauty?"

"I didn't have the strength to break those restraints," he says in deadly earnest. "I tried. Several times. They didn't budge, and I know that I'm strong. Like, as strong as any other ninth gen I've trained alongside."

"That's part of it," I say. "Extra strength, super agility, unparalleled speed."

"You looked shocked, but I meant it when I said beauty."

I've spent a lot of time thinking about being a berserker —I've felt cursed, unloved, more beast than person. But in more than a hundred and thirty years, I have never once thought it was beautiful.

Until now.

"Think about it. We don't know why, but God made you this way. He gave you this gift—it must have been for a reason."

"You really believe there's a God?" I lift both eyebrows. "With all the ugliness in the world? All the greed, and anger, and hatred? With the. . ." I glance around and swallow. "With the murder and destruction?"

"I think things exist in a balance that's always shifting. Beauty and horror. Joy and sorrow. Hatred and love. Peace and war. Rage and comfort. I think that you can't have one without the other—and so of course there is pain and anguish and regret. But thanks to those things, we also experience healing and forgiveness and the calm that comes from repairing our wrongs."

"I can't possibly ever repair all the wrong I've done," I whisper. "Not if I tried for centuries."

He takes my hand, seemingly unbothered by the drying blood coating it. "I don't believe that you've done as much bad as you might think—but even if you have, you can set things right."

The key to my absolution is sitting right in front of me. Eamon himself pulled me out of the haze, unwittingly, just by *being*. Suddenly, like the first rays of sun in the morning, like the first lightning strike in a summer storm, like the first ray of hope in my life since Dad's death, I realize that what was taken from me on that day we were attacked by the Thames, my *future,* has been restored. I have the ability to move ahead with my life without a curse hanging over me.

"Maybe we should get out of here," Eamon says. "In case Aunt M sent anyone else."

"Right," I say. "Good call."

Thanks to one of those humans who likes to inhale burning smoke, we find a few matches in a small cardboard box on the ground amidst some other detritus. The shed where we were being held, constructed of crude cinder blocks, burns much better than I expect. We head for the beach once the fire has caught well, hopefully destroying the evidence of my crimes. "Melamecha will not be pleased that I killed Paruka."

"And why should we tell her?" Eamon asks.

My jaw drops. "I assumed you would tell her."

"I already told you—I only came to try and prevent massive destruction. Melamecha is a mad dog, and I think she needs to be put down, but for now, I've been doing my best to counter her most awful plans. I'm certainly not about to call her and out the person I love as the murderer of her psychotic daughter."

Right. Okay, then. "I think I hear the ocean."

"Me too," Eamon says. "We better get you washed off and then head straight for that beach house. Hopefully your people are still there."

I'm rubbing the last of the obvious bloodstains when I hear him.

"Inara!" Gideon's sprinting toward me, sword strapped to his back, sand flying behind him. His eyes are haunted, his mouth still open.

I smile. "You have no idea how happy I am to see you."

He splashes into the water, pulls me into a hug, and swings me around before releasing me. "You're alive."

I catch him up on what happened while my other guards catch up.

"We followed the trail until it went into the ocean and disappeared."

"I'm sure they brought us to that horrid shack on a boat," Eamon says.

"I'm sorry," Gideon whispers. "This was all my fault. My stupid pride—you almost died."

"I didn't," I say. "And I'm fine."

He isn't satisfied until I'm back at the Alamecha beach house, freshly showered, and inhaling half the food on the island. "What kind of fish is this, exactly?" I peer at it, scraping a little at the batter.

"The kind that swims and can be cooked," Gideon says. "Now is not the time to be picky. Eat."

I shovel food fast enough to satisfy even him. Eamon eats nearly as much as I do.

"Melamecha knows we have active missiles in Turkey," I say, "but we didn't tell her where or any specifics, not that I knew a lot even had I wanted to share. Eamon wanted to leverage that threat to get both sides to dismantle, removing the threat of someone pulling that trigger."

Gideon grunts. "I'm guessing that ship has sailed?"

"I have an idea," Eamon says.

"What?" My hands and legs are jittery, and it's no longer from lack of sustenance. I don't like the sound of his 'idea.'

"I'll call Aunt M, and I'll tell her we're holding Paruka hostage."

I shake my head. "No way."

"Hear him out," Gideon says.

"I tell her you have Paruka, and that the only way to save her daughter is to agree to the dismantling. She loves feeling like she's getting the better deal, and she'd jump on that. She gets her Heir back *and* an equal dismantle?"

"But we can't return her daughter. We can't even return her body. We burned it, remember?"

"It's hard to hold an evian hostage," Eamon says. "But it

can be done. We simply need to convince her long enough to get the missiles removed from Cuba."

"If she wanted to blow us up before, how will she feel if she finds out we double-crossed her?" I shake my head. "I think that's a non-starter. She could even use it to convince the others to side against us. Better if we don't even admit that we ever saw Paruka."

Eamon smiles. "You don't understand her at all. For Melamecha, what's acceptable is what you *can* do, not what is *right*. She would respect you more for tricking her, and it will work precisely *because* it's not something you'd ever do —so she won't imagine it's your play."

"He might be right," Gideon says grudgingly. "And I doubt she can use this as grounds for riling up the other families. What would she say? My Heir took Enora's Heir hostage, and Inara broke free and killed mine? Now grab your pitchforks?"

"Even if this is a good plan, Melamecha will want some evidence that we have Paruka," I say. "How will we provide that?"

"You saw what she was wearing, and her hair, her skin color." He eyes me up and down slowly. "How good are you with your modifications?"

Is he kidding?

"You want me to pretend to be Melamecha's daughter?"

"Not to truly fool Aunt M, no. But we'd gag you, and we'd stick you in restraints. With a little careful manipulation, for a photo, yes, I think it would work. And then once we reach Cuba—"

"Hold on, Comrade," Gideon says. "We aren't going anywhere near Cuba."

"That's where the missiles are. Did you plan to take my aunt's word that she'd dismantle? I mean, I bet she'd promise very prettily, if that helps you feel better, but me? I want to see those nuclear weapons destroyed with my own eyes."

Gideon scowls. "It's too dangerous. Let Bellatrius pose as Paruka or her sister."

"How are their modifications?" Eamon glances back at them. "If they're good enough—"

Ilyena frowns.

"We're thirteenth gen," Bellatrius says. "I can darken my skin reasonably well, but I've never been able to speed my hair growth, much less control the color."

"They have hair dye for that," Gideon mutters.

"It's fine," I say. "I'm willing to do it, and I have met Paruka, so if I have to talk like her or walk in the stompy way she does, I'm the most prepared to do it." I hold Gideon's gaze, but my words are for Eamon. "Make the call."

Eamon is a master manipulator. He starts off panicked. Paruka was *torturing him*, Melamecha's own nephew! And then the Alamecha contingent shows up, and bam, suddenly Paruka's the one being tortured instead. "Although in retrospect," he whispers, "if she hadn't been mistreating me badly, they'd never have freed me at all, and I wouldn't be able to call you. They think I'm on their side."

It takes him a few more moments of planting careful seeds, but eventually, he convinces Melamecha that he has worked the impossible. In spite of Paruka's catastrophic mistake in capturing and abusing Inara Alamecha, and thanks to his outrageous charm, this can be salvaged.

"Inara likes me." Eamon winks at me when he says it. "And she believed me when I told her that the only way you'll back down is if they surrender your Heir *and* dismantle the missiles in Turkey."

It's faint, but I'm standing close enough to hear

Melamecha when she yells. "Which is exactly what you were pushing yesterday."

"Yesterday it was the expedient move," Eamon says. "Today it's a bloody miracle that you have this option at all. You would have slit Inara's throat for capturing and torturing Paruka. You should be offering up your sincere thanks to your maker right now that there's not a bomb headed for Russia already."

"Enora wouldn't dare," she says.

"Oh? And who was the only leader brave enough to deploy a nuclear weapon to date? I think you know she'd do it again. You have an hour to decide before the offer to save your daughter is removed from the table."

She doesn't call back for an hour and five minutes. Clearly testing me. Eamon smiles, and answers the phone. "I told you one hour."

"What's your point?" Melamecha asks. "It took me some time, but I've decided to take it."

"That's good—but of course you're too late to save your Heir."

Melamecha is wintry. "What did you say?"

"I told you one hour," Eamon hisses. "One hour. It's the same in Russia as here, and you pushed it. Your daughter is dead, and you have no one to thank but yourself. The missiles are about to launch for Russia, and I have no idea where they'll hit. Are you ready to prevent this? Or did you want a dead daughter *and* a bombed wasteland?" Eamon drops his voice. "Because between you and me, your missiles aren't yet operational. *They* don't know that, but I do. Which means you're going to have a dead daughter *and* a blasted country and nothing to show for it."

"Fine. Do it." She hangs up.

"Guess I don't have to change my hair after all." I can't believe he told her that we called her bluff and made it look like her fault. What a stroke of luck.

Eamon smiles. "Thanks to Aunt M's power plays, no, you don't. That worked out well."

The next two days in Cuba are miserably hot, but the vast majority of the dismantling is done, and I'm ready to leave Eirik to supervise the remaining tasks.

"It's time to go home." I collapse onto the campstool next to Gideon in the tent we set up. Accommodations in Cuba are sadly lacking—especially when you're not exactly a welcomed guest. Three miserably small tents without adequate air flow, but then this entire country lacks airflow. For an island, the breezes have been practically non-existent. And I can't even discuss the mosquitoes.

"I'll let Filomeno know," Gideon says.

"Eamon is coming with us," I say.

Gideon shakes his head. "That's a terrible idea."

"He can't go home," I say. "Melamecha will kill him for this—she has to punish someone for her daughter, even if the whole thing was no one's fault but her own."

He fumes. "You want to take a refugee home and what? Tell your mother that you've chosen your consort? A kid who's what? A hundred years younger than you, and whom Melamecha can't wait to kill? He brings exactly nothing to the table, and is skilled at... smiling at women? Flexing his perfectly sculpted abdominal muscles?"

I close my eyes and inhale and exhale. Yelling at him won't help. "I love him, Gideon. I know you think it's idiotic, and I know you think he's too young, which I think is a little hypocritical, but the point is that I do love him."

"Your mother will never accept him."

Gideon is absolutely right. I see the entire thing playing out in my head. We arrive, we describe what happened, and Eamon shakes her hand. Mother will hate him on sight—both for his connection to Melamecha, and for his lack of clout and experience. She'll hate his youthful optimism, and his radical views on humans. She will hate everything about him.

I'm one hundred percent positive.

"That's why I won't be presenting him as my boyfriend," I say. "I'm going to take him back as a refugee and let him slowly, without any preconceived notions or irritation over his affection for her heir, win her over."

Gideon blinks. "And if she never comes around?"

"Then I won't choose him as my consort," I lie. "Mother will never remarry. You know that—everyone in the world knows that. Which means whomever I choose *will* rule. Mother would make my life an utter misery if she thought I chose someone unsuitable."

"She would, yes."

"She might even have me removed from the line of succession and name Alora instead."

Gideon snorts.

"Or maybe not," I say.

"Maybe not, since your sister is currently in New York City performing for humans."

"Dancing." I laugh.

Gideon joins me.

"I know this sucks," I say. "I know it's not fair, and I know you're angry with Eamon and probably with me too."

My oldest friend, my best friend, my most faithful supporter, grabs my hand. He stills entirely, and his eyes lock on mine. "When I thought you were dead." He chokes. "I abandoned you. I swore never, ever to do that, under any circumstance, and I broke that promise like a spoiled toddler throwing a tantrum."

I shake my head. "No, you—"

He places one finger on my lips, and I remember the moment we shared, when I thought maybe we— but then after Eamon, it all paled. It was a facsimile of love, not the real thing, not the burning, boiling passion Eamon causes.

"You told me your truth—how you felt—what you needed. I didn't listen. I tried to tell you that you were wrong. I didn't have faith in you, and I failed you because of my own selfishness. That will never happen again, I swear it. I know my word doesn't mean much, but before anything else and beyond everything else, I am your guard and your protector. If you want Eamon, I will help you get him. I don't trust him, and I think he's going to betray you. Now or in a few hundred years, I don't know, but if it happens, I'll be there to slit his throat, I swear that too."

"He loves me," I say.

"I don't doubt that," Gideon says. "How could he not?"

I roll my eyes. "Two men, out of hundreds and hundreds of my acquaintance, feel that way about me. I'm hardly some siren."

Gideon's smile is wry. "Two that you know of. Look, the point is that I'm not angry with you. I'm angry with myself, and I will move on from that. What I can't have is you worrying about what you say or do around me."

"You know I love Eamon, and I am asking a huge favor right now."

"Okay," he says. "Anything."

"Don't tell a soul."

"But Cassius and—"

"None of them know. Bellatrius is the only one who saw anything, and she's staying here for now. All she saw was the two of us standing close together. Only you know how I feel, the details of my plan to introduce him to mother. Is this a secret you can keep for me?"

Gideon nods, reluctantly. "Of course."

"It won't be for long," I say. "Only until we've won her over. Then I'll come clean, I swear."

"I would do far, far more if you asked me," Gideon says. "But I beg one boon of you."

I lift my eyebrows.

"Please, if you haven't already told Eamon what has passed between us, that I proclaimed my love for you, that I begged you to. . ." He cuts off, closes his eyes, then reopens them. "Can you not tell him that I told you I love you? Can you not tell him what passed between us—I know to you it was almost nothing anyway."

Ah, Gideon. It wasn't nothing to me until Eamon eclipsed everything, but telling him that would only hurt more. "Yes, I promise. I haven't told Eamon anything about us, other than that we're friends, and I won't speak of it. Will that leave you more at ease?"

"He's seen that I'm jealous," Gideon says. "He's not an idiot, but I'd like to slowly let this go. That won't be possible if we make this a big ordeal."

I rest one hand on his arm. "Consider it done."

"Thank you."

"One last thing," Gideon says. "I'll support your ridiculous plan, and I'll guard you and protect you, and I won't roll my eyes or groan or argue about Eamon, ever, but—"

Oh, no.

"I won't ever stop loving you, either. If, at any point, you change your mind. If your feelings shift, I will be here. And if he hurts you."

"I know," I say. "You'll—"

"It's not a turn of phrase for me," Gideon says. "If he hurts you, I will end him."

I laugh, because I am absolutely sure of one thing in this world: Eamon would never, ever hurt me.

12

1962

Mother won't be waiting to greet me when our jet lands. The first forty years I was alive, sure, but not now. Even so, I'm fidgety on the final descent.

"So remember to make eye contact," I say.

Eamon reaches across the armrest to hold my hand.

I flinch and bat his hand away, hoping no one else on the plane noticed. "You *can't* do that, or this will never work. If I show up with a refugee from Melamecha, Mother won't mind. She hates Melamecha and an enemy of her enemy is at least given a fair shot. But it won't recommend you to her. She respects power, and command, and control."

Eamon laughs.

"What about this is funny?"

He shrugs. "Mothers always love me."

I fume. "She's hardly a typical mother."

He shrugs again. "I'm not worried."

"No?"

"Not even a little bit." He scrunches up his nose. "Look, we have plenty of time. She'll come around." He leans an inch closer. "And if she doesn't, the last time I checked, you're old enough to make your own decisions. Or are you not an adult yet for a few more decades?"

"It destroyed my mother when she lost my dad," I say. "And she will never remarry, which means I'm not her current heir, I am *it* for Alamecha. She's eight hundred and forty-two, so she has plenty of time, but my mother hasn't even glanced at another man."

"And?"

"She will insist on me marrying someone she approves of—or she will make my life a misery for defying her."

"Our life?" He lifts his eyebrows.

"Yes," I whisper, "but we can't let on right now. Not until she comes around. First, she loves—"

"To be involved," Eamon says. "It'll go best if she comes up with the idea that you and I should—" He waves a hand between himself and me and wiggles his eyebrows.

"I know, I've already told you. You know all this. I'm sorry. It's just that we only get one chance to make a first impression and—"

The plane sets down and my heart floats up into my throat.

A few quick inhale exhales and I am ready. I grab my bag and throw my hair behind my back, Gideon falling in step behind me, and I walk down the steps to the ground. . .where my mother is, shockingly, waiting. Her eyes lock on mine, and the second my feet touch the ground, she yanks me close.

"You should not have gone." Her voice even wavers. Was she. . . frightened?

"I'm fine," I say.

She squeezes me harder, until my ribs creak.

"I'm here, and I'm healthy, and we stopped the nuclear war, so it was the right call."

"Don't you know that I'd burn the entire world to the

ground to spare you?" She finally releases me, unshed tears in her eyes.

A frog rises in my throat. Tears drop straight from my eyes to the ground below, circumventing my cheeks entirely in their size and weight. I open my mouth to tell her that I met someone, because maybe I was wrong. Maybe she'll accept me—the real me—my real choice, just as simply.

Mother's eyes dart around, taking in the guards around the jet, and the other passengers waiting to come down the steps. "Now that you're here, you'd better explain why I shouldn't beat you soundly." She steps backward, her eyes flashing.

Ah, there it is.

"You should have called me the very second you realized Melamecha's agent wanted more information. As it is, you escaped and then negotiated a deal, and then dismantled the missiles and only afterward did you actually reach out to *inform me* of what you had done."

"The reason is that—"

She shakes her head. "I am still the monarch. In case you have forgotten what that means, it means *I* make the decisions about Alamecha and our policies, strategies, and plans. You would do well to recall that I have ten other daughters." She spins on her heel and marches away without a backward glance.

I don't even have time to tell her I brought a refugee, much less introduce her to Eamon. I blink several times, finally moving out of the way so the other passengers can also escape the plane. I notice, out of the corner of my eye, that Gideon is suppressing a smirk.

I clench my hand, and then forcibly release my fist. A minor setback maybe, but I never expected her to hug Eamon, so it's exactly as I expected. I'll stick to the plan.

"You survived." Alora jogs toward me. "Sorry, I just heard you landed." She hugs me too.

"I thought you were in New York."

"I flew home when I heard you were in trouble." Her eyes widen. "I can't believe Paruka tortured you."

"Maybe I should be captured and nearly killed by our enemies more often," I say.

She laughs. "We're not the most overtly caring family, but what we lack in displays of affection, we make up for in plots for vengeance after the fact."

"So if I'd died, you'd have—"

"Oh, Mother would have razed half of Asia to the ground without a second glance. And Balthasar and I would probably have had to hunt Melamecha down to kill her ourselves, slowly. Death by slug consumption, maybe, or some kind of violently aggressive bacteria that would turn her into goo, one painful inch at a time. While Balthasar saws on her, of course."

She's probably right.

"Umm, who's this?" Alora asks.

Eamon has finally reached the ground. He offers his hand with an easy flourish. "You must be Inara's older sister."

Alora half-smiles. "I am."

"Pleasure to meet any family member of the woman who saved my unworthy neck in George Town."

Alora lifts her eyebrows. "Inara saved you?"

Eamon bobs his head. "She destroyed Paruka, Havrel, and Newt."

My sister swallows slowly. "Newt? Melamecha's notorious assassin?" Her head swivels slowly in my direction. "Is he kidding?"

"I may not be known for being the most adept fighter in the family," I say, "but I know the pointy end of the blade from the hilt."

Eamon's eyes widen. I should really have explained that Dad insisted that I fly under the radar, lest I draw undesirable attention. "Uh, yes, you do know your way around a blade."

"We'll have to set up a few practice rounds soon," Alora says. "I crave a good challenge, you know."

Great. I'll spend the next few weeks dodging her invites now. "Eamon is being far, far too modest. He distracted and disarmed Newt, and that's what allowed me to get the better of Paruka, who was improperly arrogant and careless. I only succeeded thanks to a perfect combination of luck and solid back-up support from their own agent."

"Well, whatever happened over there," Alora says, "I am entirely relieved at your return."

The sincerity in her voice surprises me. She's never acted as if she resented my birth, but I always assumed she was disappointed not to be the Heir. Perhaps she isn't. It bears additional consideration. If she's not interested in taking my position, she could make a very powerful ally.

"I'm sure you're all exhausted." Alora tilts her head at Gideon. "And sweet Gideon. I owe you another debt of gratitude for keeping my sister safe."

He bows. Even now, he's still so stiff around her.

We all head for our respective rooms, Larena showing up to take Eamon to a guest accommodation. When I finally reach my own door, Gideon takes up a position outside, relieving Lucivar, who's waiting when we arrive.

"Surely Lucivar can stay," I say. "You need to rest as much as I do."

Gideon frowns. "I'm not tired."

I step closer, putting a hand on his forearm. "You must be exhausted. I know I am."

He doesn't meet my eye. He doesn't argue. He merely bows. "As you wish," he says.

And for the first time, he's Formal Gideon with me. It slices like a blade to my heart. My dear, hilarious, devoted friend is clearly hurting, and it's all my fault. I want to reach for him and soothe him, apologize and make things right. But the only reason I feel totally comfortable doing that is because of Eamon. Without him, I'd still, in the recesses of my heart, be terrified that I would harm him.

Comforting Gideon now would be a cruelty. Extending him hope, offering a salve to his heart, is only prolonging the healing he needs to do and only can do. . . without me.

So I go inside, and I close my door. The next morning when I wake, my resolve is renewed. My plan is a good one. If I stick to it, things will improve steadily, day by day. I'm not in a rush. I have plenty of time.

I slice my boiled egg precisely, taking pleasure in the perfectly divided portions, and spear a bite. "Did you hear, after you flounced away from me in a fit yesterday, that I returned with one of Melamecha's commanders?"

"I never flounce." Mother purses her lips. "Do you mean the refugee? Her wild-card nephew whose parents died when he was quite young?"

"He's perfectly trained, brilliant, and gutsy. Your kind of operative." I force myself to continue eating, my heartbeat impressively steady.

Mother sighs. "Another cog for whom we must find a wheel to turn." She sets her fork on the table and folds her hands in her lap. "You're quite sure he's not a counteragent? Melamecha plays a long game."

I don't roll my eyes. I don't scowl. I don't tell her, sarcastically, that I'm an utter moron. No, my face is entirely serene, just as she taught me. "If he were a counter-operative, he could have helped them torture the truth about the Turkish missile location from me. Instead he flipped on them, and came up with the idea of dismantling before any further action. He's the one who managed Melamecha and her daughter's death. He could have returned home to her, having done nothing but diffused the situation elegantly, but he chose to join us here."

"He's a regular angel, I suppose." Mother lifts one eyebrow.

I laid it on a little too heavily, but she is so entirely infuriating. "He's a womanizer, I think, and far too self-assured. And he struggles against leadership."

She bobs her head. "I can work with that. I'll think on a few placement options and confer with Balthasar."

"Angel might be a better fit," I say. "I don't think his strengths are as much tactical as strategic."

"Noted," Mother says.

I open my mouth to see whether she'd like to go for a ride today—which of course, Eamon will be invited to take as well, but Mother stands up abruptly, cutting me off.

"You're a hundred and forty-five years old," she says.

"A hundred and forty-four," I mutter.

"In three weeks, you'll be a hundred and forty-five," Mother continues. "And I've been quite patient. I've never pressured you, but it's time for you to stand up tall and finally excel for once."

I swallow.

"My patience has worn thin, but beyond that, the other Empresses are beginning to ask."

I look up and meet her eyes. Steely is the best description for her expression.

"Let them ask. It's none of their business."

"They're starting rumors." Her lips compress in a flat line.

"As if I'd have any ilicit—"

"They are not flattering." Mother's eyes widen. "They involve—" She clears her throat. "They involve *females*."

"Of all the ridiculous. . ." I roll my eyes.

"*Are* the rumors ridiculous?" Mother pins me with a stare.

I splutter. "Yes, okay?"

"I will never love another man, Inara, and I will never

have any more children. That makes your personal life of critical importance to the continuation of our family. Surely you understand your duty to me, to the family, and to the world. You will name a Consort by your birthday, or I'll name Gideon for you. He, at least, seems more than willing to do his duty."

"We're on a bit of a timeline," I whisper as I check the girth on Heracles.

Eamon's eyebrows draw together. "Excuse me?"

"My birthday in three weeks."

"You're giving me fair warning so I can find the perfect gift?" Eamon asks. "That's considerate, but I already have a few ideas."

"You do?"

He lifts his eyebrows.

Heat rises in my cheeks. "Oh. But that's not actually the timeline I mean."

Eamon steps closer, causing my heart to hammer. "No?"

"No," I whisper. "Mother says I must name a Consort by then."

"That's great, too."

I huff. "I need to get her to come around to your side by then." Of course, in light of the rumors, she might be happy to hear that I'm interested in a man—any man. But I don't just want her happy. I want her to love and support us. I can't handle a hundred or more years of digs and complaints and undermining.

"Am I that repulsive?" Eamon smiles at me, and my heart skips a beat. Or maybe two.

"You're wonderful," I say, "as you well know. But you need to be aiming that charm at her."

"Well, at least we get a few moments alone," he says. "Before the arduous task of taming the shrew begins."

"Who are we taming?" Gideon strides up, already wearing riding boots and leading Odysseus behind him.

"I didn't realize anyone else was coming along," Eamon says.

"Nor did I," I say.

"I heard it had been a while for your mother," Gideon says.

Over his shoulder, I see her coming toward us, already astride—this is his doing, convincing Mother to come for a ride too. Bless him, Gideon may object, but he's still helping.

"Are we racing?" She gathers the reins for Demeter, her palomino mare. "Because I think we're spoiling for one."

"Why not?" Eamon asks. "Competition is always invigorating."

Enora smiles at him. "You must be Melamecha's nephew."

He executes a perfect half bow, holding his reins steady, and he meets Mother's eyes directly when he stands again. "I prefer the sound of Eamon ex'Alamecha."

"So I hear." Mother's eyes narrow slightly, but her head tilts consideringly.

Not entirely bad. Gideon, Eamon, and I all mount our horses and we turn to follow Mother. We take the path from the stable down to the beach slowly, walking the horses calmly, but Heracles knows what's coming and he tosses his head several times.

"How comfortable do you feel on him?" Gideon asks.

"He's settled in quite well," I say. "Especially for only being four years old."

Gideon smiles. "So you think he can finally take Odysseus?"

"Only one way to find out," I say.

"Are we thinking a long or a short race?" Gideon asks loudly enough for Mother and Eamon to hear. "I'm thinking short, so Inara's poor little adolescent horse won't tire out. Perhaps from the palm trees to that ridge up there?"

His descriptions are entirely for Eamon's benefit. We almost always race from the treeline, around the edge of Mount Pānīau, and up to the ridge that overlooks the north shore. It's not as great a view today—the fog means that Lehua is barely visible. Frequently, we loop around and come back, but for Eamon's first race, a straight shot might be best.

"Is my horse much of a racer?" Eamon asks. "She doesn't seem to be very energetic."

"You're riding Hestia, Demeter's sister." Mother arches one eyebrow.

"Who's Demeter?" Eamon asks.

"Other than a Greek Goddess?" Gideon asks. "It's Her Majesty's mare."

"Ah," Eamon says. "Well, I'm assuming I'm riding the older sister."

"Only by one year," Mother says. "And I've won plenty of races on her, thank you very much. A little extra age isn't always a bad thing. Experience is generally undervalued."

Eamon should back down, but he doesn't, not even a hair. "So you're saying when we defeat you, I won't even get credit since I'm borrowing your horse?"

Instead of scowling, Mother smiles. Well, at least something's going right.

"Trees are coming up fast," Gideon says. "Are we doing this?"

"What's the prize for the winner?" Eamon asks.

"A boon from me," Mother says with a sardonic smile.

"What if you win?" Eamon asks.

"For a reward worth winning, there's always a price to pay. If I win, you each owe me something that I will choose at a later time," Mother says.

"Better not let her win, then," Gideon says as Odysseus reaches the trees. "H'yah!" With one solid kick from Gideon, his coal black stallion's haunches bunch and he leaps forward, Gideon leaning over his neck, urging him forward.

I don't even have to encourage Heracles—he's always down for a good sprint. One kiss from me, and he's off, churning sandy loam behind us and narrowing the advantage Gideon has. I hear Eamon and Mother behind us, the hooves of their mounts pounding the loamy ground.

The wind in my hair, the movement of Heracles, the ocean waves crashing to the right, my mother, my best friend, and my love. Things couldn't be more perfect—no matter who wins. Eamon edges toward me on my right side, a little nearer the surf than I'd venture. It's a careful balance. Too wet, and the footing is hard and slippery. Too dry and the sand churns, slowing the horse terribly.

But to pass, you have to pick one side or the other.

Mother's coming around on the dry side, and Gideon's a frustrating length ahead, galloping across the perfect in-between ground directly in front of me.

"It's alright boy," I whisper. "We'll catch him once he tires, around the cove. He always flags there."

Except before the cove, Mother and Eamon both make their moves, urging their mares ahead on either side of me. I want Eamon to make a good impression, so I make a split second decision. I shift a little toward the sand, crowding

Mother. She hates that, and she's sure to drop back, giving Eamon the chance to pull ahead.

He takes it, but Mother doesn't back off. Her right eyebrow rises in annoyance and she whips *my* mount instead.

Heracles hates whips. *Hates* them. I've been meaning to work on it, but he's so young and I haven't had much time lately—and he's eager to run without one, so I've been lazy.

Which makes it my fault when he rears back angrily, forcing me to lean forward to counterbalance his tantrum. I keep my seat as his hooves slam back into the ground, but he's not quite done. He surges forward, head tossing, eyes wild, his shoulder slamming into the haunches of Demeter, Mother's mare.

Demeter stumbles and Mother tumbles over her head.

I urge Heracles forward, and he leaps over Mother and races toward Gideon, who has taken advantage of all the nonsense to pull several lengths ahead. No matter what we do, it's unlikely we can defeat him at this point. Heracles makes a valiant effort to close the gap, but as I suspected, I'm still nearly a full length behind Gideon when we reach the ridge.

Gideon lets off a whoop of victory, and I slow Heracles with a tug and a pat on his neck. "Nice run, boy." I swing him around to see how far behind us Eamon fell.

He's nowhere to be seen.

"Uh, where's your boyfriend?" Gideon pulls up at my side, his eyes glinting.

"Hush," I hiss.

"Worried the seagulls will hear me?"

I roll my eyes. "That's not the point. If you keep being so cavalier, eventually someone will overhear."

"Oh calm down. I'd be more worried that your mother was eating him right now, like an irritated praying mantis."

I gag. "They eat their mates. Can you even imagine

Mother with someone eight hundred years younger than her? Gross."

He laughs. "But seriously, where are they?"

"Mother fell," I say.

"But Eamon?" Gideon's nose scrunches as if saying his name was distasteful. "What happened to him?"

I shrug and click to Heracles, who trots ahead easily. "One way to find out, I guess."

As we round the bend, we nearly collide with Mother and Eamon.

"I was worried you'd fallen into a portal or something," I say.

Mother scowls. "This idiot stopped to check on me when I fell."

"As the monarch, I felt an obligation to ensure you weren't badly injured," Eamon says.

I can't defend him, or Mother will immediately know something is wrong. "Even if she was, she'd have healed immediately." I arch one eyebrow. "Do you doubt her abilities?"

Eamon's jaw drops. "I—You two ran off and left her unattended."

"Unattended?" I toss my head behind them at the dozen guards lagging behind. "Any of them could have helped."

"Which he surely knew," Mother says. "Must have been a clever ploy to mitigate the realization he couldn't have won."

Mother hates ineptitude and excuses, which means today was a complete failure. "I think I'll keep riding," I say. "Heracles needs a good workout."

"Suit yourself," Mother says. "I'm heading back. I have petitions to hear."

Gideon wheels Odysseus around to follow me.

"Would it be an imposition if I asked to follow you and

watch?" Eamon asks. "I've only seen my aunt handle peti-tions. I'd dearly love to see how you handle them."

Mother rolls her eyes, but doesn't stop him.

"You find that attractive?" Gideon asks, the second they've ridden out of earshot. "The boot licking and forced compliments?"

"He didn't compliment her at all—he's showing interest in her management and leadership. It's smart." Secretly, it annoys me that he'd rather spend the day watching her than riding with me, but it *is* exactly what I asked him to do. I'm certainly not going to admit to Gideon that I'm annoyed.

"Where did you want to ride?"

"Heracles here just told me that he wants a chance to redeem himself."

Gideon smiles. "Back to the treeline?"

"We should walk them down to the ridge first, just to let them cool down a bit."

He spins Odysseus and begins walking back. "That'll give me time to think, in any case."

"About what?" I ask.

"What to request as my boon." He smiles. "Your mother owes me, now."

I laugh. "What are you considering?"

"You know exactly what I'll do with it." Gideon stares straight ahead, his eyes focused between Odysseus' ears.

I swallow. It's a boon from my mother. What does he mean?

His voice is quiet, calm, resolved. "It's yours, like every-thing I have is yours."

My heart contracts. Ah, Gideon. Even cast aside, wounded and rejected, he's still doing everything he can for me. "I wouldn't dare—"

"You should use it," he says. "I'll ask for something that will help her see something good about him."

I realize that I don't even know what that is—I haven't

spent enough time around him to know what he excels in yet. "Thank you," I say.

The ridge looms.

"Ready?" Gideon's eyes flash this time, devoid of injury, pity, or anger. They're too full of excitement.

At least we still have this—the activities we've always enjoyed doing together. "I am."

This time I beat him, and it almost restores the morning. Even if a small part of me wonders whether he let me win.

"Get back to me as soon as you know what you want me to ask for," Gideon says. "I don't relish the thought of putting your mother off if she presses me for an answer."

Right. "I will."

I surrender Heracles' reins to a stable girl. "Cool him down well," I say. "I worked him pretty hard." I shower before heading for Mother's throne room, two of my guards, Pauline and Korin, in tow. I figure it'll be a good chance to stare at Eamon, who is hopefully gaining some insight into my mother and how her brain works.

As I walk through the doors and up the aisle toward my throne at the front, I hear a strong, articulate voice that sends chills down my arms.

"—a monumental mistake. Don't you think that banishing half evians is an outdated practice?" Eamon asks.

Mother's eyes flash.

Oh, no. Did he listen to nothing I said?

"Explain." She folds her hands across her lap.

"I mean, in the past few weeks, Sean Connery *and* John Lennon have both made headlines in England, have they not?"

Mother's lip curls. "I don't follow human publications."

"You mean you don't follow human news. Surely you own the publications."

"Of course we do," Mother says. "But I don't read them.

I don't need to—the news that matters comes to me first, and then we filter what messages to spread."

"Fine, even if you haven't noticed, I'll tell you what I've noticed. Humans love the half evians we kick out—and they're able to use that adoration to shift public perception and make statements. If you kept them here, if you didn't banish them, they'd be another tool in your arsenal toward easily controlling the humans, if nothing more."

"Another weapon? When you have a thousand bazookas, you don't need a few handguns," Mother says with a wry smile.

The onlookers snicker.

"That depends on what you want to accomplish, surely." Eamon bites his lip. Too late for that.

"What does that mean?" Her tone is sharp, irritated.

"If I want to kill someone quietly, efficiently, a handgun is a better option than a bazooka, which would destroy the entire room and alert everyone to his or her death. Every tool has benefits, and it's a mistake to cast any of them away."

Mother stands abruptly. "I think that's quite enough for today. I need a word with my daughter, in any case." She marches down the aisle, passing me without stopping.

I pivot on my heel and follow her out, tossing a glare at Eamon on my way out. What is he thinking, arguing with her during the petitions on his first day here?

Frederick follows Mother inside, and the moment we reach her antechamber, she slams her door shut. "What are you up to, bringing a radical human-loving lunatic to our court?"

I splutter.

"He deviled my every interaction, advocating for mercy and asking me to have pity on the humans. He acts as though Melamecha and I institute the same policies."

I open my mouth, but I don't even have time to say a word.

"He's the single most obnoxious, irritating, subversive. . ." She throws her hands up in the air. "I can't even think what to call him."

I gulp.

"Be honest." She pins me with a glare.

I blink.

"Are you in love with him?"

I choke.

"He's good-looking, perhaps the best looking man in all of Alamecha. Eve knows no one could argue with that, and he's well spoken, for all his liberal notions."

I shake my head. "No, I mean, I wouldn't have brought him here to trick you."

She lifts one eyebrow. "You certainly would."

Oh, no. What a snarl. "I can't believe you think—"

"Fine." She waves her hand. "I needed to make sure."

Well this isn't going well at all, and now I'll look doubly idiotic when I tell her I did bring him here to try and convince her to like him before declaring how I feel.

"How did the petitions go?" I'm desperate to change the subject.

Thirty minutes later, I race down the hall so quickly that Pauline and Korin can barely keep up. I glance right and left, ensuring no one has followed me, before banging on Eamon's door.

He opens it, and his eyes widen when he sees me. "I thought—"

Before he can object, I place my hand on his chest and shove backward, pushing past him and slamming the door.

"Your guards," he says. "What will they think?"

I shrug. "I don't care." Now that I'm here, standing less than a foot away from him, my fear, frustration, and anxiety melts away. My hand reaches for his chest again, but this time I don't want to shove him away. "I need you."

His mouth covers mine before I can say another word. His lips on mine are ocean spray on a parched face, they're victory over a foe, they're sunlight after a long night. My arms twine around his shoulders, my fingers curling against the muscles of his back.

He lifts me up and carries me across the room, setting me on the edge of his bed. Yes. Yes, this is what I need. Eamon. He fixes everything that's wrong, fills all the holes in my life. He's the light to my darkness, holding the abyss that yawns inside me at bay. He fixes the red haze and he repairs my broken pieces.

"Why?" he finally asks against my mouth. "Why are you here?"

I shake my head.

"I made your mother mad."

I groan, and pull away. I don't want to think about my mother, not right now, but she's the reason I lost my head and raced over. The fact that he knows it should irritate me —his job was to cause her to like him, to approve of him, not to tick her off. But my irritation won't hold, not with him right in front of me. It melts away like butter on a hot pan, leaving nothing but a delicious sizzle.

"She's quite a woman." He gives me my space, not resisting when I flop backward across the bottom of his bed.

"She hates you."

He sighs. "I always choose the wrong thing with her. When she fell, I figured I'd stop, since you and Gideon kept racing. I clearly wasn't going to beat either of you."

"But she saw that as sycophantic," I say.

"Or maybe as too empathetic," he says. "She seemed to believe in my genuine concern. It was a pretty bad fall."

I shove away an unwelcome pang of guilt. "I knew she'd

heal, but I've made that mistake before. She always sees sacrificing a win as weak."

"She did—she accused me of stopping because I knew I'd lose, so at least I might curry favor from it." He shakes his head. "I'm afraid I'm not a very good actor."

"What *are* you good at?" I ask. "Mother always respects skill, in any arena. I need to know your strengths so we can make a plan to play to them."

"I'd say I'm a decent strategist," he says. "I had no power in Aunt M's court and managed to foil her plans often enough, without losing my head."

"I'm glad you never lost that." My hand reaches up and brushes the hair at his temple. "I'm fond of it."

He smirks. "Me too."

"Then apply some strategy here. How do you convince my mother that you're a catch for me?"

He tilts his head, leaning toward my hand. "Melamecha meant to send me to compete in Sovereignty at the next games."

"You're good, I assume?"

"No one in the family could beat me."

I tap my lip.

"That's distracting," he whispers, leaning toward me.

I suppress a smile. "I'll arrange a Sovereignty tournament. Mother's always impressed by any victory and all dominance."

His mouth brushes against my temple. "And what about you?"

Thoughts and words and plans jumble in my brain. "What about me?"

His breath is warm against my face. "What impresses you?" He presses a kiss to my jaw.

I close my eyes. "Not much."

"That's not encouraging." He kisses a line down my jaw, pausing above my mouth.

I whimper.

"But that noise is," he whispers.

His mouth finally closes over mine, his hands sliding up the side of my body.

A banging on the door outside stalls my heart. Eamon leaps to his feet, his eyes wide and questioning.

For a split second, I consider just owning it. I'm not doing anything wrong—just something Mother won't appreciate. I'm sick of trying to convince her that my decisions are worthy. *It's time for you to stand up tall and finally excel for once.* Her words reverberate through my brain.

I will earn her approval for Eamon. We have time yet. I slip across the bed and lever the window open.

"Your guards?" Eamon mouths.

"Be creative," I mouth back before slipping out the window and crouching in the bushes on the back side of the palace.

More banging.

Eamon answers the door.

"You're Eamon Shamecha?" Balthasar asks gruffly.

"I am," he says. "Although I prefer not to use Shamecha. It was never a surname I chose."

I don't even need to see Balthasar to know he's using his patented 'I'm scary—fear my might and glory' scowl. "That's why I'm here—Enora sent me to determine whether you're trustworthy."

"I don't imagine this is going to be a very comfortable conversation," Eamon says, his usual boyish humor edging its way in—which Balthasar won't appreciate.

"Is that one of your primary concerns?" Balthasar asks. "Comfort, I mean."

"Of course not," Eamon says.

"Well, then sit down." Balthasar steps nearer the window and I shrink backward. "I noticed Inara's guards outside." He pauses. "Inara?"

Eamon clears his throat. "She came flying through here half an hour or so ago—but she shot through my window."

"Why would she do that?"

"I have no idea—I barely know her. She muttered something about never being alone?"

Balthasar grunts. I hear the door open. "She isn't here. Go find her, and tell Gideon she's evading his people again."

All the years Dad and I routinely evaded my guards so that we could trigger an episode are coming in handy for once. Even so, I probably can't hang around and listen in on the interview. It's only a matter of time before Balthasar notices a shift or a snap of a branch. Or if he walks close enough to the window, my heartbeat.

"Tell me why you left Shamecha?" Balthasar asks.

It almost hurts to tear myself away from Eamon's lyrical voice, but I do it quietly. I'm sneaking in the window to my own room when Gideon hops the fence to my courtyard.

"Hey," I wave.

He rolls his eyes. "I assume this had something to do with your new boyfriend, but one of these days you're going to need your guards, and you'll wish you hadn't abandoned us."

I smile. "You're always there for me."

He doesn't argue, because we both know it's true.

14

1962

"Remind me again why I used my boon so that I could look idiotic?" Gideon mutters.

I can't quite suppress a smile as I decimate his royal guard and advance on his queen. "You did it to make *me* smile."

He drops his voice so low I can barely hear him. "I'd do most anything for that."

I squash the guilt. "What about lose gracefully?"

"Doubtful—grace isn't part of my nature." He smirks as I take out his queen. "But I will wish you luck in spite of my irritation."

His wish of luck for me holds through the rest of this match, but I lose in the second round of the next.

Gideon offers me a drink. "Sovereignty always feels a little... washed out to me."

"You're just saying that because we both lost."

"And because he's still blazing his way upward." His eyes narrow.

Eamon's fighting a pitched battle against Angel. They've defeated the other four competitors already. "You think he'll beat her?"

"I don't mind his winning," Gideon mutters. "It's that everyone he beats *thanks him* for it. Why does everyone like him so much?"

I jab his beefy arm. "You could try smiling a little more. That might help."

Gideon rolls his eyes. "I'll never whore myself out like that, thanks."

"You're just jealous."

He frowns.

I forget sometimes, with as well as Gideon has handled all this, how much it must hurt him. He's been covering for me so I can see Eamon every night, and setting up horse races, and then using his boon to request things that will help me win Mother's approval. "I'm sorry."

He wraps an arm around me. "I am jealous, but I'm sorry about the times I act obnoxious about it."

Eamon's queen and his heir reach the Throne, and I watch, enthralled, as he dispatches even Angel.

"Nicely played, young man." She stands up and offers him a hand, her eyes shining at him.

"You play quite well too." Eamon meets her eye and grins.

Angel keeps hold of his hand too long. Gideon's not wrong about one thing. Eamon's ungodly gorgeous and he uses it to his advantage as easily as he breathes. If I didn't love looking at him so much, it might irritate me—all the other women who notice.

"And he moves to the final round," Gideon says. "So far, he's doing as well as he said he would."

I turn toward Mother. She's watching him intently, tapping her lower lip with her index finger.

"It's not easy to impress Angel," I say. "She's almost as hard to win over as Mother."

"She's only been beaten in Sovereignty a handful of

times." Gideon grunts. "This was definitely the right thing to have me request."

Finally something's going right. "Now if he can keep from saying anything that upsets her. . ."

"He does like to run his mouth," Gideon says. "But at least he's consistent."

"When he was younger, some humans showed him a kindness," I say.

Gideon raises his eyebrows. "Is that why he loves them so much?"

I don't feel comfortable sharing more of Eamon's story than that. "He feels *called* to help them," I say. "And if you think about it, it makes sense. They're genetically descended from the same place as us—and we don't really treat them like they matter."

"Do they matter?"

My jaw drops.

"I'm not saying they don't matter, to other humans, in their place. But. . . look around. Do they matter to us? They're a tool. A useful tool, but a tool nonetheless."

I roll my eyes. "You don't really believe that."

Gideon shrugs. "They're weak. They're slow—mentally and physically—and they're short-lived. Any way you look at it, they may be descended from the same place, but we've diverged substantially enough that we aren't the same —no more than chimps and humans are the same."

I cross my arms. "I agree with Eamon, actually. We should be caring for them, not disregarding them."

"Your mother has already done more for them than any other evian monarch in history," Gideon says. "They're freer, richer, and safer than any other time or place in history. And with that same model in place, they're healthier too. Their innovations in healthcare are impressive, even to me."

"Her freedom model was impressive," I say. "And

Eamon admires that greatly. It's her motivations he questions. I mean, did she do it for them or for herself?"

"Does it matter why she did it if she's helping them?"

I sniff. "I think it does matter—her motivations. That's what will govern how much aid they receive in the future."

"If he loves humans so much, why is he here?" Gideon raises both eyebrows.

"What does that mean?" I ask.

"He could be out there among them, helping, educating, and elevating them. Or he could go a step further and marry one of them."

"Did you really just ask me, 'If he loves them, why doesn't he marry one?'" I snort.

Gideon smiles. "I guess I did."

"Because he loves me," I whisper. "And we can do so much more here—once I ascend Mother's throne, think how we could revolutionize the way they're treated, the world they live in, all of it."

"So he's cool to wait a hundred years before he does anything for them? Or a hundred and fifty?" Gideon mock cringes. "Because he didn't seem super patient or willing to wait when he was arguing with her the day after he arrived."

"He'll wait," I say. "In the grand scheme of things, it's a drop in the bucket."

"Not to them it isn't," Gideon points out.

"Which is why we'll work to convince Mother of some policy changes now, hopefully."

"Right," Gideon says. "Your mother's pretty swayable, so that's a good call."

"If there weren't so many people here, I would punch you in the nose."

Gideon holds up his hands. "When did people being here ever stop your violent urges before?"

He's so irritating. I slug him in the shoulder, and he laughs about it.

When I glance back at Mother, she's smiling broadly. Oh, for the love, she probably thinks I'm flirting with Gideon. Only a week until my birthday, and I still haven't gotten her to come around on Eamon. Making her think I've softened toward Gideon isn't helping. I stiffen and fold my arms. "We'd better grab something to eat before the next round starts."

"Right," Gideon says. "I'll go grab you something. Maybe you can get a quick word in with loverboy before I return."

Eamon heads my direction almost the second Gideon disappears. "I saw you were eliminated," he says.

I smirk. "I didn't want you to cry when I beat you."

He bites his lip. "That might not impress your mother."

I shake my head. "Maybe not so much."

Mother taps her glass. Everyone gathered quiets and looks toward her. "As we have now narrowed the field to only four competitors, I thought I'd announce the prize for the winner. You've probably heard that my daughter Inara's one-hundred and forty-fifth birthday party is one week from today." Mother glances from me to Gideon and back again with a sly smile. As if she believes she's going to finally force me to do what I've been too shy to do. "Normally, the prize for today's winner would be a fête in the next week or so, but to keep from interfering with that, we'll hold a celebration in honor of today's winner the first week of December. We'll even invite a few select members from the other families to that celebration."

"My prize if I win today is. . . a party?" Eamon whispers.

"Mother likes her parties, but it's more about the honor and attention that bestows. That's the whole reason you need to win—as I told you, she appreciates people who are good at something."

Eamon arches his eyebrow. "Speaking of trying to make

an impression—I think your Mother quite fancies the idea of you and Gideon together."

"He's an excellent captain of my guard, and we spend a lot of time together. A lot of people have made assumptions over the years."

He sips his drink. "It makes sense. You two are inseparable."

Is he jealous of Gideon? "He's been captain of my guard for over a century."

"And you never?" He lifts his eyebrows.

I shrug. "I might have chosen him."

"If you hadn't met me."

"Maybe."

"I don't like him much," Eamon says. "But I'm glad he's so attentive to keeping you safe."

"He's not your biggest fan, either."

Eamon faces me straight on then, his eyes commanding my attention. "I hadn't noticed." They sparkle.

"Shut up."

His voice drops. "Make me."

"Later," I promise. "When this is over today, if you win, maybe we can tell Mother." I imagine walking down the hall with his hand in mine, and strolling right into my room. And closing the door. I swallow.

"I'll do my best," he says.

"I think you can pull this off," I say. "You already defeated Angel."

"Who are my competitors?" he asks.

"Job—Mother's executioner. I didn't expect him to make it to the final round, honestly. He's not very devious. Frederick, Mother's Captain of the Guard, and Lyssa, Mother's best friend for centuries. No one to worry about."

Eamon chuckles. "Sure, just three of the scariest people here."

I suppose technically they are. "But Job is pretty

straightforward. Expect him to take the obvious moves. And Lyssa is the opposite. If you think she'll go up, expect her to tunnel under."

"What about Frederick?"

I open my mouth and then close it. "I mean, I don't really know. He's always been there. He loves Mother, in the way that, like, a Golden Retriever loves its owner. He's solid. He always seems to spot the danger before it happens. He was one of the men she purchased for Avina, my older sister, but Avina moved to Canada to run things there and didn't take him with her. He sort of. . . attached himself to Mother after that, from what I understand."

Eamon narrows his eyes. "You're sure he loves her like a golden retriever?"

"What does that mean?"

"He doesn't look dopey. To maintain his position for. . . what? A few hundred years?"

"At least five hundred," I admit.

"He must have a good handle on political intrigue, and somehow he never upset either Balthasar or your father."

True.

"And he kept your mother safe."

Maybe I never gave Frederick enough credit.

"Are you nervous?" Eamon asks softly.

"It's a game," I say. "Of course not."

"It's really all about strategy," Eamon says. "I am guessing that Job and Lyssa are brilliant strategists, and that Frederick is probably the better tactician. Either way, don't worry. I've got this."

"You don't even know them—how can you possibly play against their weaknesses?"

"Have you ever watched a casual game between friends —cards, or dice?"

I shake my head. Things are rarely casual with evians.

"Do you know who wins, luck aside?"

I shrug.

"People tend to be nicer to people they perceive as weak, or nonthreatening. And barring those issues, they help their friends."

"So your affable demeanor?"

"It's got a purpose. I spent ten minutes talking to Lyssa earlier, and she's already predisposed to like me, and to trust me. And we have zero baggage from the past to deal with."

"But surely men won't like you automatically."

"You'd be surprised," Eamon winks.

What?

"Not that," Eamon says. "Usually." He laughs. "But men and women aren't so different. We all just want to be seen."

He's so smart with people.

"For instance, did you know Frederick has chickens?" He shrugs. "He loves them."

"Excuse me?"

His eyes cut toward me sideways. "He has a dozen chickens in his personal courtyard."

"Chickens." I can't quite get my brain around it.

"He thinks they're hilarious. Angel and I were discussing that when I defeated her. She's known about his hobby for a while. He eats their eggs, or your mother does, but when there are extra. . ."

"Angel takes them." He knows the people surrounding me better than I do, and he's been here for a week and a half.

"You don't need to worry," Eamon says. "I didn't mention this as a talent lightly."

I want to hold his hand. I want to sink against his chest and run my fingers down to his hips, drawing him near. I long to sink into his smell, his smile, and his security. But I can't—not quite yet. Soon though, so soon.

"It's time," Larena says. "The board has been set. Come and draw positions."

Eamon, Frederick, Lyssa, and Job approach the throne. Mother holds out her hand, four golden chains trailing from the end of it. Each of the contestants grasps one of them, and Mother lets go.

Frederick draws the diamond—sparkling beautifully in the afternoon sunlight. From Job's hand dangles the emerald, his eyes reflecting his disappointment. Lyssa holds the sapphire aloft with a barely concealed smirk. And Eamon, poor Eamon, draws the bottom opposite Job—the blood red ruby.

He would have to draw the one person who he doesn't know and that doesn't already like him to face off against. Even so, he looks unfazed.

The four of them take their seats casually, as if there aren't over two hundred spectators gathered to watch. I'm lucky that I have a front row seat reserved. I walk up to the raised dais to sit next to mother. Gideon's already there, waiting for me like always. He offers me a new drink.

"Thanks," I say.

"Who are you cheering for?" Mother asks.

"I haven't decided," I say. "Maybe Job."

Mother lifts her left eyebrow. "Job?"

I shrug. "Lyssa?"

"I find myself pulling for the colt," Mother says.

"Eamon?" I ask, my heart lifting.

"He's overeager, and he's brash, but he's also charming. I'm shocked he's made it this far, if I'm being honest. Perhaps it was a tremendous fluke."

Finally! Progress. "He is charming," I admit.

"My money's on Lyssa," Gideon says.

The game drags, all four of them playing slow, methodical games. "We should have thrown a few time bonuses in there," Mother mutters. "This game is boring."

I focus on the pieces, watching as Eamon sacrifices his heir to take Job's warlord. But then I see it. He's in position now for a double strike. I almost laugh, but I don't want to warn anyone else.

Within three more moves, they all see it.

Too late.

He takes Job's king, making a new heir for himself, and then eliminates his queen, converting all his remaining pieces into his own. And then he rises, already poised to strike—so much for boring. He was hiding in plain view, but no one paid enough attention to realize it.

Lyssa and Frederick are still at a standoff when Eamon moves upward from both sides at once, his pieces pouring into the gaps he was preparing to infiltrate below.

In a century, I've never seen anyone defeat their opponent in a way that sets them up perfectly to rise—he had to have been predicting Lyssa and Frederick's moves several ahead—on top of Job's.

I swallow. How could he follow all of that while carrying on a steady stream of conversation? My pride in him soars, and I wish everyone knew already that he's mine.

Everyone in the room has fallen silent, but he presses, his heir from the right, his queen from the left, shoving Lyssa and Frederick together, forcing them to cannibalize their own pieces and fall against one another to escape.

In the end, he takes Frederick's queen two moves after taking Lyssa's.

Mother stands up and claps before anyone else, but a beat later, the entire room is clapping.

"Not so boring after all," Gideon mutters.

"It appears that we have a winner," Mother says. "And probably not the one any of us expected. I had intended to send Eamon ne'Shamecha ex'Alamecha out into the field next week, but as we'll be hosting a party for him in a few weeks, it appears those plans will have to be delayed."

Eamon stands up and half bows, turning to meet Mother's eyes. "Thank you, Your Majesty. It's a wonderful honor."

"Would you like to choose the theme for your party?"

An engagement party. I'm about to stand up and announce it, but then I remember that Mother said there would be an announcement at my birthday party. She'll be frustrated if I spoil that. I bite my tongue, contenting myself with the knowledge that I've made great strides toward showing her the wonderful things about my choice.

"Actually," Eamon says. "I do have a request."

"Name it," Mother says. "As lavish as you'd like."

"It makes me happy to hear that," he says. "Because I'd actually love if it you would take the money and resources you'd normally spend for a celebration of that sort and instead dedicate them to the families of the humans who died in the Columbus Day Storm."

Mother blinks.

"I'm sure you heard about it. Some called it the Big Blow or Typhoon Freda, but it was a windstorm that killed forty-seven and took out the entire power grid in northwest Oregon."

Oh, Eamon. You idiot.

"You don't want a celebration?" Mother's lips tighten into a flat line.

"I can't wait to attend the birthday party for Inara next week," he says. "And I'm sure you have holiday celebrations planned for the month of December, which I'd be delighted to attend as well. But for myself, I wouldn't enjoy being the center of any kind of special accolades when all I've done is win a silly game."

Silly? I want to pinch the bridge of my nose. I want to tighten my hands into fists. Why couldn't he simply accept gracefully?

Mother's laughter is almost as big a shock as Eamon's

brilliant win. "Fine. If that's what you want, that's what we'll do. I'll send funds to the families of the deceased, and I'll bail out the flailing insurance companies. Maximillian has been badgering me about that for weeks, in any case."

"You will?" Eamon beams.

My heart lightens. Life with him will never be simple, but maybe that's what I love most about him. He takes all the big risks—swings at every opportunity, as if the fear of failure never occurs to him.

"You gambled today and won," Mother says. "Twice."

He bows. "Thank you, Your Majesty."

"I'd suggest you play it safe." Her eyes sparkle. "At least for the rest of the day."

"Of course, Your Majesty."

I barely have the chance to congratulate him, for all the evians falling over themselves to meet him, but it barely bothers me. After the party is over, Gideon walks me to my room, indicates to Eirik and Vasil that they'll be taking up guard outside my door, and follows me inside.

"Your feet barely touched the floor on the way back," he says.

I sigh. "Finally, after all these attempts, we made solid progress today."

"When will you tell her?" he asks.

"Tomorrow morning over breakfast, maybe," I say. "She's always happy in the morning. I should suggest to Angel that she serve omelets."

"I'm pleased for you," Gideon says. "You know I want you to be happy."

I beam up at him. "I am happy."

He bobs his head at the door to the patio outside. "You're going to go see him, I assume."

I clap my hands. "You don't mind?"

"Go."

I hug him, and then sneak out my patio and through

the shrubs. I reach the hibiscus beneath Eamon's window, my fingers gripping the windowsill lightly. I've barely shifted it an inch when I hear voices. I freeze, my eyes peering through the gap. I can't see much—just that Eamon's standing next to someone else, someone in a blue gown. A woman.

I can't quite make out who she is, but surely he's ushering her out. We didn't have plans to see one another tonight, but he's always happy to see me.

I wait. And I wait.

But then, the wind shifts and even through the small crack in the window, a voice carries. A voice I recognize. My breathing hitches. My heart floods with ice. My fingers tremble. What is Mother doing in his room? *In his room.* My ears strain and strain, but I don't hear another word. But I do hear another sound—like a sigh, like an inhalation of air. A small movement. What's going on?

I shift to the balls of my feet and lift up, up, up. If I can see them, they can see me. This is stupid. What am I doing? But I can't help myself.

My eyes finally reach the point where I can make out their faces, and I wish I had simply run away.

Because Eamon and my mother are kissing.

❧ 15 ❧

1962

I can't—my brain can't wrap around it. I— it's too much. I blink and blink and blink. I inhale and exhale. I should be worried they'll hear me. I should be worried that anyone will see me.

But I can't think about anything.

Except Mother kissing Eamon. Eamon kissing Mother. His hand cupping her jaw. Her arms around his back.

I stand up, unconcerned who might see me, and race down toward the beach, still wearing the cocktail dress I was wearing to the competition and to dinner afterward.

I'm not sure when I lose my high heels. I'm not sure when I wade into the ocean.

I'm not sure when I collapse to my knees, sobbing.

I'm not sure when Gideon finds me.

But that finally pulls me out of my trance. His sword is drawn. Fury battles rage in the lines of his face. His jaw is carved of iron. His brow is wrought of steel.

He spins on his heel and heads back in the direction from which I ran.

He's going to kill Eamon, I know it in my bones. The

only thing worse than Eamon kissing someone else is Eamon dead.

I stand up and race after him. I don't call his name, but as if he can feel me, he turns.

"Don't ask me not to go." His voice is flat.

"You can't." I shake my head, tears still dripping from my chin, sliding down the runnels carved into my cheeks.

"I must." Every line in his body is taut, as if carved of stone—or smelted from iron.

"You don't even know what he did."

"I made him a promise," Gideon says. "And he may be prettier than anyone else alive, but I'm positive I can carve him up like a holiday chicken."

I choke on a sob. "He didn't hurt me."

"You want to tell me that again when you're not sobbing?"

"It's not—he didn't—I don't even know what's going on."

"You went to see him." His voice is as cold as I've ever heard it.

"I did, and Mother was—"

I can't say it.

Gideon frowns. "Is he alright? Did she take him? Did she discover something? Is he working for Melamecha? A plant?"

I shake my head, but I can't even get the words out. He's as clueless as me.

"What's going on?" He softens then, his shoulders wilting, and he slides his sword back into the sheath on his back. He reaches for me.

I tumble into his arms, sobbing against his chest. "He was kissing—" I hiccup and bawl harder.

He stiffens next to me. "You're going to have to say it. He was kissing. . . whom?"

"I can't say it," I wail.

"Your mother?" Gideon's hands tighten on my back. "He was kissing *the empress?*"

I nod jerkily, like a marionette with her strings yanked by a toddler.

Gideon swears. "That can't be right." He grabs my forearms with his hands and shoves me backward far enough that he can see my face. "What did he say?"

I shrug.

"You saw it, but they didn't see you?"

I nod.

"And you ran."

I hiccup again.

He yanks me against him. "It's a misunderstanding, I'm sure. Your mother. . ." He laughs. "He did his job a little too well. No one thought that after Althuselah. . ." He shakes his head, his hand caressing my hair. "It will be fine. She's probably looking for a fling. He'll shut her down, and if she doesn't know you ever know. . . Well, she can hardly object to someone for you who she had an interest in herself, can she?"

My stomach twists.

"It is unfortunate."

I bend over double and vomit on the sand. I straighten up and wipe my mouth. "Unfortunate. Yes."

"You need to go back," Gideon says. "And you know how badly I'd like to kill him instead of telling you to do this, but if you go see him, I'm sure he'll clear it up. He loves you—I'm sure of that from the way he looks at you, the way his eyes follow you, and the way he glares at me when no one is watching."

Of course. He couldn't very well shove Mother away when she showed up. He would have had to let her kiss him, and Mother doesn't know I like him. In fact, when she asked, I denied it, vehemently. And tonight, I said I was pulling for Lyssa. "I'm an idiot."

"Sometimes, yes." Gideon lifts my chin with his hand. "But you're also brilliant, hilarious, kind, generous, and stunning. Now, go see him and let him tell you how horrifying that interchange was. In a few years, you two will laugh endlessly about it, I'm sure. Poor Enora."

I inhale and exhale slowly, ragged breaths full of ocean air calming me. "I'm a mess," I say. "I can't go like this."

"You can tell him what you saw, and trust me. He won't care that you're tear-streaked, wet, or salty." Gideon's sad eyes urge me down the path toward the back side of the palace.

"Thanks," I say, tripping over the unsteady sand. I find my shoes about halfway back, the first a dozen paces away from the second. By the time I've put them back on, I realize Gideon's surely right. Why did I panic? Eamon loves *me*. No matter how awkward, this isn't an impediment. The earth practically shook the first time we touched, and he felt it too, I know he did.

We're meant to be together.

By the time I reach his window again, I'm calm—my hands steady, my heart beating regularly. The whole thing doesn't seem humorous yet, but it's not the nightmare I imagined. Not even close. Just another roadblock, and I'm a veteran of handling roadblocks.

I slide the window up the rest of the way and pause. I set my shoes at the base of the bush. Not a sound coming from the room, other than one single, steady heartbeat. I vault over the windowsill and into the room, landing softly on the balls of my sandy feet.

"Eamon?"

I can barely make him out in the darkness, his eyes shining dimly. He sits up. "I'm here."

My feet make no noise against the carpet as I pad across the room and sit next to him. "Are you alright?"

He inhales deeply. He's surely traumatized.

My family is pretty twisted—how embarrassing. "I'm sorry."

He flinches next to me.

Why would he flinch? Why hasn't he turned on a lamp, at least? I lean across him to switch it on, and he leaps away from me as if my touch burns. I click it on, flooding the room with soft yellow light.

Eamon doesn't meet my eye.

"What's going on?"

He twists his hands, his strong, beautiful hands, in his lap, his eyes trained on them.

"Do you love me?" The words come out as a plea. I asked a question, but really I'm begging him. *Love me. Want me. Care for me as I care for you.*

"It's complicated," he says.

My heart shatters into as many pieces as grains of sand on the beach, as many shards as stars in the sky, as many daggers as exist in the Alamecha armory. And each one pierces my mind and my soul and my life-force, causing eternal suffering.

"How is it complicated?" My voice breaks at the end, and I wish I had never come back. I wish I had never met him. The haze would end this—Balthasar would put me down. But now, I could never hurl myself into that again. Not now that I know him.

Because I still love him.

Knowing something has changed, knowing he won't meet my eye, knowing I'm alone in my feelings somehow, unbearably alone, I still would do anything, slay anyone, destroy everything, if he asked.

"Tell me." I swallow and it's like shards of glass sliding down my throat. Like my own body has turned on me. Like the world has stumbled and fallen and broken and will never spin properly again.

"I do love you," Eamon says slowly.

I close my eyes and the world stops spinning. "Thank the—"

"But."

I open them again and force myself to look at him. "But what?"

"You already know," he says. "The window was cracked. When your mother left, I noticed that the window was cracked." His eyes are the ocean, brimming with dark depths and quiet sorrow.

"I know," I say. "But I don't understand. Two hours ago, you loved me."

"I love you still," he says. "But what you can't understand is the one thing that matters more than two people in love."

"Then tell me," I cry. "Tell me and I'll understand. We can fix it."

He stands up and turns away, facing the open window. "You won't understand. No one ever does," he whispers. "But after my parents died, something broke inside of me. I had no purpose, no family, no love in my life. I joined Rasputin because he promised *meaning*."

"And he lied to you," I say.

"He did. He was a butcher—and he had no insight, no empathy, no real goal other than power and control and destruction."

"But the humans saved you, and you've been working to help them ever since."

When he spins to face me, a single tear trails down his cheek. "The humans didn't save me. They can't even save themselves."

He's right. I don't understand.

"God saved me that day."

My lips part, and I have no idea what to say.

"I'm surrounded by God's people, and yet not a single one of you believe in Him. I didn't believe in Him either.

Believe me, I am well aware of the irony. He gave us this *gift*, these bodies that can do miraculous things with ease. He tasked us to protect his children, *all* of his children, and that day, I realized that He gave each of us a spark of the divine. All of us have the capacity for greatness, to be like Him, to do His will, and we are all failing."

I shake my head. "I don't understand—"

"I meant to serve Him at your side," he says. "I could see it, the future rolling out before us. It was clear, it made sense, and it was in line with my calling. Your mother wouldn't remarry, and you and I would have children, and we'd make policy, and you'd treat me as your equal. We'd restore balance to the genders; we'd set things right among the humans." He closes his eyes and inhales, his face peaceful. "The world we could create together." He opens his eyes and smiles ruefully. "But that future is a lie."

"It's not!" I step toward him. "I'm right here. I want that, too."

"Your mother will remarry," he whispers. "In fact, she wants to marry me."

A fling. That's what Gideon and I assumed she wanted. She hasn't even glanced at another male since Dad's death. I close my eyes and recall my mother with Dad. She was different with him, brighter and lighter. She had a spring in her steps and a flash in her eyes. She had joy in her heart. She has been a shell of herself since he died.

And now she wants to marry Eamon. *My Eamon.*

I can't think about it. I back up, my feet shuffling backward on their own, until my back bumps into a dresser and things tumble to the ground. A bottle, some kind of vase. Flowers. "No."

"No?" Eamon tilts his head. "If I tell her no, she'll marry someone else."

I shake my head. "Let her."

"You think I don't want to turn her down?" He lifts his

hands toward me, pleading with me. "Of course I do—I love you as much as you love me, but if she remarries and they have an heir. . ." He drops his hands and sinks to the ground, running his fingers through his hair. "You and I couldn't change a thing, then. I'd just be a lunatic shouting at her from the corner, and you'd resent me for it. You'd grow to hate me and my obsession. You and I would be packed off to Canada, or Cuba, or I don't know where. I would accomplish nothing."

"No," I say. "This can't be happening."

"Except it is," he says.

"You love me, and I love you." I step toward him. "And not in the way that most people do. We have a connection I can't even explain."

He closes his eyes.

"You can't deny it."

When he opens them, his eyes are sad. "I can't. I feel different around you— better, stronger, more alive. I would do anything for you—anything except give up the unparalleled chance to forever improve the world in the way that God has placed in my path."

"Don't you believe God made us who we are?" I ask. "You and me, this connection. You deny it?"

He shrugs. "Did God intend my parents to die? I don't know. Did he create this connection? Maybe. But that doesn't mean we aren't supposed to overcome it to fulfill our destinies, to do the things He wants us to do. And right now, I can't turn down this chance."

I told him my secret—the one Dad forbade me to tell *anyone*. He's seen me—he knows.

"You're afraid." He steps closer. "Of what?"

"You know about me," I say. "About what I am—what I can do."

His eyes soften. "I would never, ever disclose that, not to anyone."

My lips curl up. "Until you think God wants you too."

He shakes his head. "Don't do that. Don't act like I'm doing this lightly. I know that was shared in confidence and it saved my life. No matter what happens, I will never tell another soul. That's your secret and I'll keep it until my dying day."

"You said you'd love me forever too," I say, my tone unintentionally sharp.

"Your mother. . .I misread the signs before tonight. If I had known before, I would have come to the same conclusion, and I would have prepared better."

He would have prepared me. . . to dump me? He must not feel a tenth of what I do. "I could tell her about us. She would never marry you, not once she knows how I feel about you."

He straightens, his eyes rapt. "You could, but that would kill any love I have for you. If you shred any hope I have of accomplishing—" He spins in a circle and flings his arms wide. "As a Consort, with the ear of an empress, nay, the world's most powerful empress, I could finally fulfill the promise I made to God, to do His work, to save his children. Don't you see how much bigger this is than our happiness? This has always been my calling."

"*You're* my calling," I whisper.

"You brought me here," he says. "And I'll always be grateful for that. I do care for you—and I always will—but you have to understand that things must have happened the way they did for a reason. I know that's true."

His eyes are shining even brighter now than they ever did when he looked at me. He can say we feel the same things, but clearly we never did. I would sooner cut my heart out and toss it into a fire than marry anyone but him.

This time when I spring out of his window and race across the beach, no one tells me what I want to hear. This time, Gideon doesn't draw his sword or threaten to kill Eamon.

In fact, he doesn't say a word. Finally, when I'm cried out, I stumble into my room. That's when I realize I left my shoes outside of Eamon's window. Somehow, the image makes me laugh. Just like me, they've been abandoned, never to be reclaimed.

❦ 16 ❦

1962 & 1980

"I don't recommend turning one-hundred and forty-five. I give it two thumbs down."

"It's too late for that advice to help me," Gideon reminds me. "I'm two-hundred and fifty-eight."

I roll my eyes. "You think I'm senile? I know that."

"You'll get through this."

I collapse against his chest. "I don't even want to survive."

His hand against my back is strong. "You will, eventually."

I doubt he's right. "How am I even supposed to survive tonight?"

"What does that mean?"

I realize I never told him about Mother's threat. "I should have warned you before, but I didn't think I needed too, since I was going to name Eamon." My shoulders slump. "Mother told me that I had to choose a Consort by today. She said if I didn't—"

"If you didn't?"

I step back from him. "She said she'd name you." Part of me wants her to do it. It might hurt Eamon, and I want to hurt him. But I also want to keep him safe, and I want to fling myself into his arms and beg, and I want to run away, and I want to swim into the ocean and never stop swimming.

Eventually I'd have to drown, or a shark would eat me and this would all be over.

"A little more warning might have been nice." Gideon backs away from me slowly.

"It's been a weird week," I say.

"This is a big deal," he says.

"I guess I figured—"

"You figured I'd be giddy." Gideon's words are bitter.

My eyes snap toward his. "No, not giddy, I'm not—"

"You figured, why bother warning Gideon, since that's all he's ever wanted, to marry me, so you know, if everything else falls apart, and my heart is totally broken, and I'm borderline suicidal, no reason to worry. There's always good old Gideon."

"No," I say. "I don't think that—I mean, yes, you're good, and I know you're always there for me."

"I don't want to be a consolation prize." He straightens and I take a good look, for the first time in a long time. His face is rugged. It's severe. It's sharp angles and flashing eyes and warrior scowls. He's not beautiful like Eamon. He's not smooth, or polished, or effortlessly charming.

But he's fierce, he's brave, and he's solid. I do care for him, so much. "You would never be—"

"You are—" He chokes. "You have no idea what you are to me. You're air. You're sunlight. You're baby animals and chocolate cake and birdsong and everything beautiful in the world. You're—" He cuts off and shakes his head. "I deserve to be that to someone. I deserve not to be your fallback."

He's right. "I'll tell my mother this morning that I can't choose anyone, and she can't name you," I say. "I'll figure out something."

"And even now, what I want more than anything in the world is to tell you never mind. To beg you to name me, to want me, to look at me like you look at him." His voice breaks. "But I can't do that. It would shatter me—you must see that it would unmake me—change something fundamental about who I am that could never be repaired."

"I do see that."

He nods, straightens his tux, and ducks out the door.

When I meet Mother for breakfast, she's lit from the inside, smiling at the surf as she watches it crash against the beach through the window. She's been that way every morning this week. "Happy birthday, darling!" She stands up and crosses the room, pulling me close for a hug.

"Uh, thanks," I say.

"Sit, sit. I had Angel make Eggs Benedict."

"Oh," I say. "Great."

"Your favorite."

Yep. It sure is. "Are these from Frederick's eggs?" I ask.

Her eyebrows rise. "He told you about his chickens?" She beams. "He never talks about them. If I hadn't accidentally stumbled over one that hopped the fence, I'd never know he kept them as pets. He must really like you."

"Er, actually, he told Eamon."

"Ah, I'm so glad that you and Eamon get along so well."

A memory of Eamon's lips pressed to mine flashes through my brain. I shake my head to clear it and curse evian recall. "Right."

"Well, sit."

I do, and I force myself to shovel bite after sawdust-flavored bite. "Thanks," I say.

"Angel has a few last minute things to ask you about the party menu," she says. "If you have time."

I nod.

"And Inara, I'm sure you're stressing. I feel terrible."

I look up at her. "Huh?"

"I issued you an ultimatum a few weeks ago," Mother says. "It wasn't kind, and I insinuated things. . . I wanted to apologize. I never should have done that."

"Wait, what are you saying?"

Mother sighs. "You know how very much I loved your father."

My throat closes off, because for the first time, I really do understand just how much she loved him. I nod.

"After he died, I thought I'd never be happy again."

"But you are now?" My brow furrows.

"Not quite the same as that," she says, "but I am. . . bright again. I've found that even if I won't have another epic love, I'm tired of being so alone, so mopey."

"How wonderful." I can't quite inject any meaningful emotion into the words, but she doesn't seem to notice.

"And I have you to thank for it," she says. "If you hadn't saved his life and insisted on bringing him back here, I'd never have met Eamon."

I expect to bawl in front of her, or stand up and shout hysterically, or to crack right down the middle, since that's happening inside my brain. But I simply sit still, a forced smile on my face.

"I know it's ironic—Melamecha's nephew, which makes him Althuselah's nephew too, I suppose—but she abhors him, and I find that he makes me laugh."

"And he's gorgeous," I say.

"That doesn't hurt." She takes my hand in hers. "I'm going to announce that I've selected him as my next Consort tonight at your party—so you won't need to announce a Consort of your own—not until you *want* to choose someone. I promise not to pressure you again."

Because I'm now entirely irrelevant to Mother, soon to her line of succession, to Eamon, and to the world—which is exactly how I feel. I stand up. "Thanks."

"Are you alright?" Mother stands up, her eyes searching mine. "You seem sad."

I shake my head.

"Do you feel alright?" She frowns.

"Everything is fine." But in that moment, I want to hurt her. I want her to feel as bad as I do. "I miss Dad, that's all."

Her face falls, and her hands twist together. "Of course you do. I don't expect you to be excited for me—believe me, I feel it too—a guilt, like I'm betraying him. In fact, when I first met Eamon and wanted to drag him across the floor to kiss him, I was a little rude to him because of it. Being around him made me feel disloyal to your father, and I unfairly took that out on him."

Oh, no. I can't listen to any more.

"But now, I've spent quite a bit of time thinking about it." She sighs. "I think Althuselah would want me to find any joy that I can."

I nod.

"There's no pressure for you to be excited," Mother says. "In fact, if you don't want to attend the ceremony, well, I'd be sad, but I'd understand."

Ah, Mother. She's been so *broken* since Dad died. She's been a shell of herself, really. How can I begrudge her this joy? She doesn't even know she's hurting me—she thinks her news will be a relief. The pain I'm enduring is really all on Eamon—and on me, for lying to her from the start because of my own cowardice.

And I know why he's doing what he's doing, and I love him for his passion and his certainty and his purpose, which makes it hard to hold on to my righteous indignation. I want to hate them both, but when Mother announces their engagement that night, as the culminating pinnacle of my birthday celebration, I can't summon rage at either of them.

After all, I love the two of them more than any other people on earth.

So in the end, when the day of their wedding dawns, I put on the champagne and pink dress Mother chose. When Varvara tugs and yanks and pulls on my hair, I don't protest, and I don't even offer suggestions or requests. I'm going for them, not for me, so I may as well look exactly as they want me to look.

I grit my teeth outside the door to the breakfast room —now that Eamon joins Mother too, breakfast has become an agony—and I push through the heavy double doors. I brace myself to see them holding hands, or leaning heads together or some other horrifying display of affection.

But Mother isn't here.

Eamon's eyes meet mine and electricity sizzles between us, even from across the room. I spin on my heel to leave.

"Wait," he says.

"What?" I can't keep my tone even. "Did you have some daggers you needed to test and you need a target? I'm afraid this one's not available, not today, not ever."

Eamon flinches. "No, nothing like that." He walks toward me.

I close the door behind me and walk toward him, circling around the table. For a moment, a brief moment, I wonder whether he's rethinking things. Could he be regretting his decision? Could he be willing to tell Mother the truth and shut down the wedding? Do I matter more than his *calling*?

But when he freezes in front of the open window, a few steps away from me, the ocean air ruffling his perfect mahogany hair, I know. It's not what I've hoped for—what I've longed for. Eamon has no good news, or at least, not the kind I want to hear. "Inara," he says.

It's almost enough—to hear him say my name. My heart accelerates. My lips tremble. "Yes?" I will not cry. I will not crack—not now. Not after everything I've endured, I will not give in this late in the game. The birds fall silent outside, and a tiny alert goes off in my head. Nightingales rarely stop trilling all at the same time, especially on a beautiful morning like this.

"I've been worried about something," he says. "You told me—"

I shake my head and hold up my hand.

His eyes widen.

And that's when I hear it. I'm not sure whether a normal evian would have heard it—the slight shuffling sound. But I'm not normal, never have been. I'm a berserker. Sometimes I forget, sometimes I intentionally pretend I'm not, but it doesn't alter reality.

I shove Eamon under the table and unsheathe my sword. I use its blade to deflect the dart meant to incapacitate me, and I leap through the window. An assassin snuck through with the wedding visitors—pretty common. I should have expected it.

Not one, I realize, but two—they run separate directions, knowing I can only follow one. But I'm not a normal warrior. I hurl my sword at one and don't watch its trajectory, spinning to chase the other brown-clad runner, but I do hear it. The blade spins round and round, striking exactly as I knew it would—severing the man's head from his neck cleanly. I hear the thump when the body hits the ground, and the whump when the head follows suit, a small clang signaling my sword clattered against the cobblestone path.

I don't slow down as the red haze snaps across my field of vision. If anything, I speed up. I can't help my feral cry as I leap onto the back of the one who shot that dart, my full ball gown skirts impeding my agility enough to be a nuisance, and I claw at them with one hand, wrapping my other arm around the neck of the woman who almost hit me. The woman who would have killed Eamon. The monster inside of me snarls and froths at the mouth. My arm tightens, but the assassin doesn't give up. Her arm whips toward me, a dagger glinting in the early sunlight.

I laugh, but it doesn't sound quite right, even to my ears. I release her neck and strike her wrist. She drops the dagger and I snatch it up—I needed something sharp.

She draws her sword, and pleasure floods me. A real fight. I need a fight, badly. The fury this time is bad—stronger than ever before. It wells within me—and I bounce from one foot to the other.

"I have no quarrel with you, Inara," the brown-clad woman says. "I'm here for Eamon. His aunt is displeased with his swift and steep ascension."

Eamon. The word vibrates through my brain somehow. Eamon.

I shake my head.

The red descends stronger—harder. I want this, no, I need this. To plunge this dagger into something.

"I don't want to kill you," the woman says, "especially since you're not armed with anything other than my dagger."

She must not have seen me throw my sword at the man. I smile. "But I want to kill you."

The brown-clad woman stumbles back.

That motion was all the encouragement I need. I race toward her, deflecting her strikes and blows easily, playing with her. I slice the side of her face and watch as the blood spatter hits the cobblestones below our feet. She swings for my left, and I sidestep easily, opening a gash in her thigh. The blood spurts in a very satisfying way—and I want more.

I cut off her ear.

And her thumb.

She howls.

"Inara, stop," a voice says.

A voice I know, one I long to hear. I freeze.

"You're going to draw attention soon," he whispers urgently. "You must stop."

Stop? Why would I stop? I'm having fun—the most fun I've had in a long time. The blood, the whimpers, the thrill of the kill beckons me.

"Inara, please." My eyes follow the voice, locking on the face of an angel. A face I know. A face I love.

I blink. I lick my lips and taste the salty tang of blood. I spit it out. "Eamon."

He nods at me. "Yes, it's me. You saved my life, and I appreciate that, but it's time to stop. Your mother will want to interrogate—" He glances down. "Um, once she's been healed a little and regrown. . ."

I follow his gaze. The poor woman at our feet writhes. Fingers and an entire hand, an ear, a nose and three toes litter the ground around us.

"Maybe you should hand me that." He points at the dagger in my hand.

Did you have some daggers you needed to test? Need a target? My earlier words ring in my ears. I was hurting then, about something. I shake my head and the haze dissipates.

But with it, my pain returns. I drop the dagger and spin on my heel, glancing down at my dress. It's streaked liberally with blood and the skirts are torn and spattered. "Tell my mother the dress she chose for me was, sadly, ruined."

"I'll tell her you saved me, and that when I found you struggling, I kind of lost it."

He'll take credit for the horrible torture I inflicted on the woman Melamecha sent. "She works for your aunt."

Several people stop dead in their tracks when they see me striding toward my room, but no one says a word. I toss the dress in my incinerator. They weren't my colors, but it's still a shame to waste a brand new gown. At least I know that, whether he loves me or not, Eamon still has the power to pull me out of my haze. Now I just need to figure out how to use his memory, without his physical presence, to free myself.

I focus on that one positive byproduct while I shower and dress to go to the wedding. And even if I'm not in the dress she chose, I walk Mother down the aisle to marry the man of my dreams without scowling or flinching or bawling.

Every single day thereafter, I grit my teeth and endure, and with every day that passes, I breathe a little easier. After the agony of the first cut, the pain dulls infinitesimally with time. Newt really was right about the ice cream. And as a tiny blessing, a grace I didn't expect, even though Eamon has married my mother, he still allows me to control the haze, whether he's present or not. I'm able to think of his face, and it recedes—no longer controlling me.

With the passage of enough time, eventually I don't daydream my every waking moment about falling on a sword, or swimming out into the ocean, or every other way an evian might successfully commit suicide. Even so, I can't manage a genuine smile, not unless Gideon's around. Luckily, he rarely leaves my side. Somehow, with him close, the pain isn't quite as unbearable. The two of us muddle through, both hurting, both surviving, both moving ahead, one day at a time.

Until Mother greets me at breakfast with a smile one morning, her left hand over her belly. It's been years and years and years. Almost two decades should be enough time for me to prepare, but it's still too soon. I'm still not ready. I want to turn and run. I want to pretend it's not true. I want to stick my fingers in my ears and shout, 'lalalalala!'

But I am Inara, daughter of Enora and Althuselah Alamecha. I do not hide, I do not run, I do not bawl. I face things head on, now and always.

"Guess what?" Her eyes lighten, the sides of them crinkling with her smile. "I'm pregnant!"

I can't think about how that could have happened—and I can't think of anything else, either. The images bombard me, flaying me anew.

"Thanks to a technology called an ultrasound," Eamon says, "we're pretty sure it's a girl."

When I meet his eyes, I see the sympathy lurking there. I'm finally free. I can finally leave this place, my home that became a prison seventeen years ago. "Congratulations."

Instead of relief, instead of relishing the freedom that has *finally* come, the pain is sharp and fresh and every bit as horrible as it was the day I discovered Eamon and my mother were. . . I still can't think the actual words, and they've been married since 1963. But thanks to twenty years of practice, I fake a smile without trouble. I gush and congratulate and beam at them both, mouthing the right words, going through the expected motions.

The second I walk through the doorway of my room, Gideon on my heels, I say, "I'm leaving. I'm going somewhere far, far away."

He closes his eyes and inhales deeply, slowly. He exhales and opens his eyes. "Why?"

"Mother's having a baby—a girl. I'll finally be free."

His eyes widen. "It's about time."

I nod.

"We can leave court." The smile spreads slowly, so slowly across his face.

I beam at him, because I know what he knows. Without the constant reminder, without the never-ending farce our lives have become, maybe my heart can heal. Maybe his can, too. Maybe maybe maybe.

Gideon crushes me against his chest, his arms squeezing me almost too tightly. "Finally."

Mother's not feeling up to petitions in the afternoon, so

I do them for her. When I reach her room to report, she waves me in with a half smile from where she's crouched over her desk.

"Are you alright?" I ask.

She waves me off. "Of course, of course. I'm just tired, that's all. I took a nap—which was much more invigorating than mediating between squabbling brats."

"Wow, do you feel ready to start all over?" I smile. "With this new Heir?"

"Are you upset?" She stands and crosses the room. "Do you feel angry about being displaced?"

I think about the baby inside of my mother, a child of the man I love and a mother I respect and love. "I'm not upset." Not any more than I am every time I think about the fact that he married her, anyway.

"Are you sure?"

I nod. "But even so, I think it would be better for me and for her if I took a position elsewhere."

Mother stiffens. "You're leaving?"

"It's not that—"

She grabs my hand. "Please stay, at least for the pregnancy. Please."

I don't grit my teeth. I don't bawl. I don't scream. If nothing else, I've learned to act like the perfect dead-eyed robot over the past seventeen years, no matter the provocation. Not even Angel can tell when I'm upset, not anymore. I doubt anyone in the palace can lie as well as I can. "Of course. I'd be happy to."

I'm not happy, but I do it. As I always do everything I'm asked to do. I hear petitions with Lyssa, I negotiate trade deals with Katherine, I work out details of the nursery and the baby's training regimen with Larena, I plot strategy with Balthasar, and I review guard rotations with Frederick. I am the model older sister. I am the perfect daughter. I am the ideal Heir, even preparing for when I won't be anymore.

And then the day finally arrives. "Are you ready to meet your little sister?" Job asks, as he wheels a cart into Mother's room.

"Giddy," I say, but I don't go inside. I lean against the wall. On the other side of this door, Eamon will be holding my mother's hand, whispering soothing words into her ear or some other nonsense. And I'll have to pretend that I'm delighted to be there, a part of this special moment. A part of the magical moment when my birthright is stolen by a mewling baby.

"You okay?" Gideon whispers.

I don't answer, but he doesn't really expect a response. He leans against the wall so close that his heat radiates outward, warming me from my shoulder to my toes. As always, he demands nothing and offers everything. I want, more than anything, to love him. To pine for him. To forget about Eamon and the draw I feel, even now, toward his smile, toward his laugh, toward his burning passion for life and change and reform.

"Mother promised me a spot in Washington D.C. Apparently Alora hates being liaison—bless her—and I can take that spot. We'd only need to spend two weeks a year here in Hawaii."

Gideon smiles.

And I go inside, to meet the sister I never wanted. Mother is swearing, and Eamon's eyes are wide, and Job is huffing.

"You've done this so many times, I shouldn't need to tell you this."

"And in all those times, you're as useless as always," Mother says.

"I could cut you open again," Job says. "Would you prefer I do that?"

"At least I'd be done with all the stupid exams and questions."

"It's better for the baby if it—"

Mother screams, and I stumble backward, bumping into Gideon. "Horrifying," I whisper.

He nods mutely.

Moments later, Mother pushes my new sister out, and Job wraps her in a towel. She's coated in white gunk, under which she's a bright purplish red, her tiny hands shaking and her face scrunched up. She begins belting screams quite loudly almost the second she's out in the world.

"I should have tried harder to get out of this," I whisper.

Gideon bobs his head.

Wait. I spin around to face him. "Were you here for my birth?"

He chuckles. "First of all, we weren't in Hawaii yet. The palace was in England when you were born if you'll recall, and. . .no. I was not present for any of this."

"Thank goodness."

"I was a lowly attendant for your sister, not even favored by her, when you came into the world." He leans closer. "But I'm sure you were much prettier, and less vehement in your screeching."

"What's so funny?" Eamon walks toward us, the baby wrapped and in his arms.

"Nothing," Gideon says, the same time that I say, "Nothing at all."

Eamon looks from Gideon to me and back again. "Well, if there's nothing wrong, would you like to meet your sister?"

I suppress my irritation at being kept here until her birth, and my fury at her very existence. I paste a smile on my face. "Of course I would."

He hands the white-wrapped bundle to me, and I look

down into her eyes. She looks up at me, the same deep bronze eyes I've watched in her father's face a million times. The same eyes that haunt my dreams. The second she sees me, she smiles, her toothless grin unbelievably endearing. A single mahogany curl falls into her eye and she blinks and blinks until I gently shift it out of the way.

She grins again, and this time, I know it's her way of saying thank you.

I hated her just for existing, for ruining my life, for destroying my dreams, for taking everything I ever wanted effortlessly. But now, staring into her eyes, I realize that she could have been my daughter just as easily.

She *should* have been mine.

I should have been in that bed, screaming. I should have given birth to this tiny, perfect angel. I should be the one protecting her from the world. I should be teaching her to fight. I should be explaining to her how to fairly judge others, how to negotiate the best deal, and how to throw a beautiful party.

She should be my daughter, mine and Eamon's.

While I'm having this epiphany, angry voices are shouting behind me. Her eyes widen and her lip trembles, clearly already comprehending the strife in the room.

"—the most ridiculous name I've ever heard." Mother throws the covers back and climbs out of bed, her hands clenched at her side. "So it's a good thing that you have absolutely no say in what we name her."

"I *made* half of her," Eamon says. "I don't get a say on anything in this entire palace. Why should I think I might have input on the name of our *daughter?* I must have lost my mind."

"You made half of her?" Mother laughs bitterly. "Excuse me while I go to wash all the blood from my body—the one that created that baby all on my own. Perhaps you can make her a brother while I'm gone."

Eamon's nostrils widen and he paces in front of the window.

Mother stops at the door. "When I come out, I'll name my daughter, and if you can't be civil, Eamon, Frederick will escort you to your rooms." She slams the door behind her.

Neither of them notice the distress on the face of their newborn daughter. In fact, neither of them seem to be concerned about her at all. Eamon's still glaring at the door to the bathroom.

They've always had a tempestuous relationship, but it hasn't improved at all over the years. If anything, it has worsened. I try to avoid being present for any of their actual shouting matches, but in this case, I could hardly duck out with their baby, no matter how badly I'd like to do that.

A moment later, Mother emerges, clean and strong, eyes flashing, ready for battle.

Before Eamon can bait her, I suggest, "How about Melina? It's a pretty name that honors the M for Mahalesh and Melamecha and the 'ina' from—"

"From Cainina, my mother," Mother says softly, approaching me with her arms held out wide.

"And Meridalina," I say. "Your great-grandmother."

"I like it," Mother says.

"So do I." Eamon approaches from the other side. "It's a good thing you're here to broker a peace agreement." His smile is lopsided.

Mother brushes my hair away from my face. "True."

"Melina," I whisper. I don't tell her that she could have been my tiny angel, but I wish I could.

She coos at me.

I didn't think newborns could really make noises, but she coos at me purposefully. That's when I change my mind about leaving. I spend the next few hours holding her every single second that I can, and mediating between the fights that crop up every few moments between Eamon and Enora. They really need a good shaking. Or a marriage counselor.

Probably both.

By the time I finally announce that I'm heading back to my room, I'm exhausted. I press a kiss to Melina's tiny forehead and wish her a good night. I stumble down the hall to my door, the door into a room from which I'll be removed before too long, since it's the Heir's room.

"We aren't going to Washington, are we?" Gideon asks softly.

"Do you hate me?"

Gideon's head leans, face first, against the wall. "I could never hate you. Never."

"I'm sorry. I wanted to go as badly as you did, but I think she needs me."

Gideon straightens and nods. "I wish desperately that it wasn't so, but you're not wrong. That little girl will need you quite a lot, I think."

So we stay.

The rhythmic movement of the canter, the pounding sound of Loki's hooves, the familiar smell of horse perspiration, they all ease my mind when I'm agitated. Gideon knows, which is exactly why he suggested a ride to begin with—the Millennial Games and the pre-game summit have Mother wound tighter than a quartz watch. If I have to intervene in any more fights between Eamon and my mother, I'll explode. Or carve something up.

Seagulls wheel overhead, the waves crash, and my heart untwists, one mile at a time.

"You ever going to give Loki a break?" Gideon asks.

When we reach the ridge at the north end of the island, I finally ease up. "He likes running too."

Gideon smiles. "We all do, but you shouldn't cause a heart attack in the one horse that loves to run as much as you do."

"Fine."

"I've got a meeting with Balthasar," he says. "In less than half an hour."

I look behind us, and sure enough, Eirik and Pauline are headed our way. "So you're about to ditch me."

Gideon shrugs. "Only to review last minute details for the summit."

"Why don't you take the horses back," I say. "I'll walk back to the palace."

"Good idea," he says. "Take your time. When you're gone, your mother has to deal with her problems herself."

I swing off Loki, noticing that he's lathered and his sides are heaving. Gideon may be the one person left who really tries to keep my life happy. I hand my reins up to him. "Thanks— make sure you don't press him on the way back, and tell them to cool him down really well. And turn him out right away."

He rolls his eyes. "Thanks for the specific instructions. I get so confused about the proper care for horses. I've only been doing it better than you for close than three hundred years." He ties the reins onto a loop on the back of Hermes' saddle.

I can't even swat his arm when he's sitting up there. "Get out of here." I settle for slapping Hermes on the rear.

Gideon wheels around, but doesn't take off—he trots both of the boys back the same way we came. He's not even out of view yet when my guards catch up. Always a seamless transition. I really ought to tell Gideon the truth—I need guards less than most anyone on the entire island, other than maybe Balthasar.

I don't rush back, scanning the beach for shells as I walk, kicking driftwood and rocks back toward the incoming tide.

A familiar figure is up ahead, alone, hurling shells into the waves.

I consider turning around and taking the long way back, but something catches his eye and Eamon sees me. Too late now.

"Inara," he says.

And even now, a tiny thrill runs up my spine when I hear my name on his lips. I hate how much I still love him, but it's a familiar pain now, like recertifying in Modern Torture Practices, or enduring a training session with Balthasar. "Eamon."

The flutter in his eyelashes tells me he isn't immune to hearing his name from me either.

I wish I hadn't noticed, because I know it won't change anything. When I reach where he's standing, he starts to walk, too. "I'm headed back," I say.

"I should be as well."

I glance back at my guards—they've already fallen back a dozen paces, giving us the freedom to speak without being heard. "What are you even doing out here? Isn't there a Council meeting?"

"Last I checked, you were on the Council too."

I shrug. "Honorary. It's time for Melina to take over and do the tasks of the Heir herself."

"She hates it," he says.

"I know," I say. "I hated it too. You get used to it."

"I hope so," he says. "Because there's so much work for us to do."

"I've been thinking," I say.

He stops walking, so I stop too. He turns toward the ocean. "I never stop thinking."

I shake my head. "No, not like, in general. I've been thinking about what's best for Melina. She needed me, for a long time, I believe she needed someone in her life who wasn't—" I cut off. I almost said someone who isn't always fighting like a fishwife. But that seems. . . unnecessarily judgmental.

"She needed you—yes. Her mother and I can't even spend five minutes in the same room without screaming at one another."

It has worsened in past years, but I don't point that out.

"You've been thinking about Melina," he says. "Of course you have. You're always thinking about someone else. I admit my thoughts have been more selfish, more morose."

It's not like Eamon to talk like this. He's always sunshine and rainbows and grand plans, or else he's predicting the end of the world.

"I think we're headed for something. . . cataclysmic."

Ah, there it is. "So what's new?" I joke.

He doesn't meet my eye. "It has been *two thousand* years since the human's savior was born. That has significance, you know. Even if you don't buy into their bible, or their religion, they worship the same God we do."

To be fair, most evians don't strictly believe in God—not in the sense of a great and loving creator who will love and watch over us—but I don't argue. "What do you think is coming?"

He shakes his head. "Solar flare? Earthquakes? Possibly a new ice age."

I don't laugh. Nothing he says surprises me anymore. "I almost hope you get your apocalyptic event."

He frowns. "I think we have a chance to avert it, you know."

"You and your wife do," I say. "Yes, I'm aware."

"No, not me and Enora." He sighs. "There is no Enora and anyone else, certainly not me. I can finally admit that I made a terrible mistake. My pride blinded me to the truth."

The waves crash in front of us, the birds swoop overhead, and the guards keep watch a few paces back, but it all disappears in the space between one heartbeat and the next. The entire world drops away. I turn toward him slowly, disbelieving. "What?"

"I should never have put my ambition ahead of what we

shared," he whispers. "It was prideful, it was weak, and I was wrong. I'm sorry."

I close my eyes, and the life we might have shared flashes in front of my eyes. Melina, a toddler beneath my feet, clinging to my leg. "Momma," she would have said. I would have picked her up and held her tightly against my hip, her curls soft against my face.

But he ruined all of that, long ago. Nothing he says now can change the reality.

"It's too late." I can barely speak the words.

"Your mother won't live much longer."

I laugh, but the sound is bitter. "She could live a hundred years, yet."

Eamon grabs my arm. "What's a hundred years to you and me?"

His fingers brand my skin, and I want to pull him against me. I want his mouth against mine, our breath tangling, our bodies pressed together. The memories are sweet, sharp, and tantalizing, in spite of the age that rests on them. "You chose her." The words wrench their way out, against my will, against my desperate desires. And even as I say them, my heart longs as it hasn't in decades. Longs for him to argue with me, to deny the truth, as if anything can change what has been, what is broken.

"I didn't ever choose Enora—I chose my desire to do something great—to be remembered for all time as an instrument of God. I wanted to leave a legacy. I wanted—" He drops my arm and steps back. "I was wrong, and I've tortured us both, and I've accomplished nothing."

The ocean breeze lifts my hair off the nape of my neck, kissing my skin. It's the reason I'm flushed. It's the reason I'm breathing too heavily. "I'll wait." Again, the words are foreign, as if I didn't actually say them myself.

Eamon steps toward me, his eyes pinning mine. "Say it again."

I don't want to speak right now. I want his arms around me. I want him to declare his love for me. I want to leave this place and never return.

But Melina—daughter of my heart, if not my body—I could never leave her. Our place is by her side.

"I'll wait." Tears wells in my eyes, but they don't fall. They can't. Not today, not the first time I have dared to hope in nearly forty years. "I'll wait forever."

"You'd forgive me?" he whispers the question, but the caress of his voice, the sensation of a private conversation with him, it lingers, it soothes.

"Of anything, always."

His face breaks into the most heartbreaking smile I've ever seen.

"I can't ever tell you how sorry I am," Eamon says. "Truly. For the pain I've caused, for the misery. All I can do is tell you that if there was anything I could do right now, I would do it."

"Leave her." The words are so quiet, the wind whisks them away immediately.

He opens his mouth, but before he can reply, I press my hand to his mouth.

"No, don't. I could never do that to her, or to you, or to Melina. Forget I said it."

His eyes burn, shining bronze against the cerulean blue of the ocean beyond his head. "I—"

"Don't," I say. "I never said it."

He swallows. "We'll wait."

"We have time," I say. "Centuries and centuries."

"Assuming the world doesn't end this year," he says.

I laugh, but this time the bitterness has been carried away by the wind, and the apologies, and my hope for a future. This time, for the first time in a long time, my laugh is filled with joy. I worry, when we walk back together, that everyone will notice.

But the guards look bored.

Melina simply smiles and hugs us both.

Enora brushes Eamon off and pelts me with questions about our demands for the summit.

And even Gideon, sweet, insightful Gideon, doesn't seem to notice a thing. It's a little deflating to realize that something that seemed so monumental is like vapor—like mist—but I'm also relieved.

Over the next few days, every time Eamon catches my eye, I duck my head, hiding my smile. When I bump into him in the hall or at breakfast, a shiver shoots down my spine. It's like I'm in my first century again, or even my first few decades. The world is washed new, and the sun shines brighter than it ever has. I breeze through the pre-game summit, and even the trip to Brazil, nervous at every moment that someone will discover our secret.

Not that there's anything to discover.

It's funny that a few words can change nothing at all, and also completely alter my entire world. *I made a terrible mistake.* I didn't realize that I'd been waiting to hear them for almost four decades. But I can't be distracted—not now. Poor Melina needs me.

When Melisania takes great pains to point out that Melina is the first Heir to enter more than one competition, ensuring all eyes will be firmly fixed on her, I want to carve her up in a way a sister never would. I don't even feel bad about being proprietary. Once Mother is gone, Melina will need my help and guidance. I realize that for the first time ever, an empress will have an advisor she can trust absolutely, someone who would never betray her. Someone who loves her just like a mother would.

I hope she doesn't freak out at being singled out. Her skin is so golden that it's hard to tell, but she looks pale, nervous even.

Once the welcome has passed, I stand up, Gideon

taking a place on my left. Melina and Lucas approach from the right, and I move purposefully toward the training fields. The rest of Melina's guards trail behind us —I don't miss having so many people tailing me all the time.

"How exciting to have Melisania make sure all eyes are on you," I say.

Her nostrils flare. "Right? What's her problem?"

I laugh. "Her heir is thirteen years old. That means she's too young to have any hope of winning—which means she has no opportunity for upside here. But if she can draw attention to any mistakes you make, or better yet, force you into errors by stressing you out, she mitigates her rival's progress, which is nearly as good."

"Evians suck," Melina says. "I mean, really. Why can't we be less. . ."

I know exactly what she means. "Less like a pack of wolves in the middle of winter, ready to eat a wounded packmate? Because, it's a kill or be killed world, goose. That's how it works."

"I don't want to kill," she whispers. "I hate this world."

I want to tuck her under my arm and fight every single battle for her. I want to surround her in bubble wrap and keep her safe, pristine and perfect, forever.

I look across the field where two teams are engaged in a mock battle, preparing for tomorrow. It's ironic that as she describes the kind of world we live in, we're faced with a tangible demonstration of just how feral we can be—slicing one another up as sport.

I catch Gideon's eye and toss my head. He knows instantly that I need space to speak to her and backs off, tugging Lucas and the rest of Melina's guard dogs along with him. She hates our world—and I don't blame her in the slightest for it. "I'm sorry to hear that."

Her face falls, her lips turning downward, her shoulders

dropping. There's not a shred of dead-eyed robot in Melina. I doubt she could fool a human.

I clear my throat. "But not for the reasons you probably imagine."

"What?" Her head spins upward, meeting my eyes eagerly.

"I've noticed that you don't seem to enjoy fighting."

Her large, expressive eyes well with tears.

"I had hoped I was imagining it."

"No."

"You hate the negotiations, too. You hate asking for more and more and more."

She bites her lip and nods.

"You hate the heart of who we are."

A tear rolls down her cheek before she can duck her head.

I can't hug her like I want to, but I grab her hand. "You can always abdicate, you know. There's no reason to spend your entire life hating the core of who you are. The rest of the world isn't like this. I've thought about leaving a million times."

Her quick exhalation is precious. I suppress a smile. "Why didn't you?"

"I think you know why," I say. "You freed me, and you shackled me, too. I love you, Melina, like a sister should, more than any of mine ever did by a long shot. I stayed to help you. Mother isn't. . . the most effusive parent."

"But you could have children of your own," she offers feebly. "So why haven't you?" For twenty years, I've dreaded the moment she would ask me why I never married. I worried she'd realize the truth—that she'd see through any lie I told. I worried that the daughter of my heart would realize that I loved her father—and her—far too much to ever replace them with a facsimile of any kind.

But now that she asks, my heart swells, knowing Eamon and I will be together one day. Things will eventually be right again. I encircle her in my arms, needing to feel the tangible proof that she's here, that she's safe, that she's mine. And one day, Eamon and I will have another child, hopefully another girl, and Melina will be free, as she freed me. But for now, since she knows none of that, she worries. I try to soothe her fears, eliminate her stress, and set her heart at ease. "You're as much a daughter to me as any blood child ever could be, and it kills me to see you miserable."

"Mother would be furious if I abdicated."

Mother. Her mother—my mother. I don't flinch, but I do release her. She thinks I mean that she should abdicate so that I can step in. She has no idea I mean to have children who can step into her place instead. "Wait to do it until she dies, then."

She stiffens, like I'm suggesting she should expedite Mother's death.

I laugh—I can't help it. The whole idea of Melina taking someone's life is ludicrous. She could train until her hair turns grey, but she'll never be a killer, not her. She's a beautiful-eyed dreamer like her father, not made for shouldering the hardest, filthiest, ugliest parts of our world. "I don't mean *kill her*, goose. I love Mother as much as I love you. But here's my promise to you. The second she dies, I'll be there to hug you, to wipe your tears, and to step into your place if you still don't want it. You don't have to do anything you don't want to. You can escape all of it simply by telling me you wish to."

Her entire countenance brightens. "Thank you."

That night, I dream of a future I gave up on decades before—Melina on my left, Eamon on my right, children playing at our feet, and the world bowing to us.

A day and a half after our return, a commotion from

Mother's rooms draws attention from all quarters. "What did you say you heard?" I ask.

"Whooping," Vasil says. "I'm not sure what else to call it."

"And then?"

"Melina, Her Majesty, and the Consort left. They took a walk along the beach."

"Together?" I quirk my eyebrow.

Vasil nods, his expression as puzzled as I'm sure mine is.

I don't have the chance to interrogate Eamon until the next day. Mother's meeting with human heads of state, and Melina's training with Balthasar. He reaches Gideon and me just outside the stable, looking up at me with eager impatience. "I thought you might be out here. It's a beautiful day."

"You just missed the ride," Gideon says.

"Enora wanted me to talk to you about the upcoming human election for the American president," Eamon says.

"I better make sure the horses are cooled down properly," Gideon jokes. "You two go ahead."

Korin and Tarben fall in behind us as we walk back toward the palace. "Do you really need my thoughts on the elections?" I lift both eyebrows.

Eamon shakes his head. "Not unless you have strong ones."

"Not really," I say. "I mean, I think the younger Bush is a little bumbly, but Americans seem to like that. It gives them someone to laugh at, and a lot of them find him relatable. His father listened well and was a wonderful whipping boy when we needed to raise revenue. He's a good choice to let them feel like they're making changes, and that they're generally in control of things."

"Glad to have a soundbite," Eamon says.

I slow down. "What do you really need to say? It's nothing good, or you wouldn't be delaying."

Eamon's brow furrows. "I hate that you know me so well."

"Do you? I like that you know me." I look at my feet. "Sometimes I wish you knew me better. I wish you could tell my smiles apart, for instance."

His hand lifts my chin gently, and I spring back, glancing nervously at the guards.

They're laughing about something, and I relax. "What's wrong?"

"It's not that something is wrong, per se," he says. "You love Melina, right? She's a blessing."

I know, in that moment, what the problem is. "Mother is pregnant again." I don't expect the pain that blossoms beneath my chest, sharp and hot and fresh. I'm not a naive child. I know he's married.

He reaches for my hand, but I block him. "No."

"It happened before we spoke, obviously."

My nostrils flare. "I don't expect you to—"

"It was a strange circumstance," he whispers. "And I swear, Inara, it's not like that between us, not for a long time."

I swallow. I didn't ask him to tell me that, I didn't beg for him to make me any promises.

"This won't change how I feel about you—it won't change what I said, I swear."

I finally allow myself to meet his eyes. They're burning, afire, intent. "It won't?"

He shakes his head.

"If it's a girl, she'll displace Melina." I frown. "And if it's a boy—you haven't seen how hard that is."

"Enora wants to keep him." He gulps. "And so do I, unless that will hurt you."

"It won't," I say, surprised that it's true. "I love you, and I'll love all your children, just as I love Melina."

He beams then.

I cling to those words over the weeks that follow, but I realize, slowly at first, that they were a lie. The way he looks at Enora shifts, slowly, but it changes steadily. As the baby grows in my mother's belly, the way he feels for her shifts too, softening, improving.

And the guilt he feels looking at me deepens.

I'm afraid this child will destroy us, more soundly than his bad choices ever did. And I can't even blame him or her or it. Even so, the pain that had receded is sharp again, and I begin to wonder whether love is worth the risk and the pain.

Always pain. So much pain.

We might be better off without it entirely.

❧ 18 ❧

2001

"Jered is the cutest baby in the world," I say.

And I mean it. He really is—maybe even more adorable than Melina was. But it's all I can do to hold it together for the fifteen minutes I spend in Mother's room with him, Melina, and Eamon.

I hardly reach the safety of my room before I break down sobbing. I've never felt like a worse person in my entire life—not when I almost killed my father, not when I couldn't control the haze, not even when Eamon and Mother married. At least then I was only hurting.

Now I'm angry about something that brings joy to the three people I love most in the world, because their boundless joy leaves me feeling more alone than ever before.

Watching their tiny, joyful family. . .I've never felt so lonely in my entire life.

Gideon bangs on my door—I know it's him. It can't be anyone else. I ignore him. I'm not up to faking right now, and I can't let him see how upset Jered makes me—or more correctly, how jealous I am that they're the family I wish I had.

More banging. "Inara."

"Go away, Gideon."

The banging stops, thankfully. But instead of relief, somehow, the fact that even Gideon left me alone sends me into a renewed fit. I collapse against my bed, leaning into it, when a sound outside my patio yanks me out of it.

Gideon's standing in the doorway, his head tilted, his arms out.

I rush toward him and leap into his arms. "I'm sorry I'm such a mess," I manage to croak.

"You still love him." His voice is gruff, his words unbearably sad. "Seeing them happy—it has to hurt. You want that, but you're happy for them, and their happiness means your own lack of a place."

He gets it. Every single bit of it, and he doesn't hold it against me. "Oh, Gideon, I'm so unfair to you. You should walk out that door and never come back."

"But just like you, I still love someone who doesn't love me." His voice cracks and my heart, which I thought was already irretrievably broken, cracks a little more.

"I do love you, too."

"Not the way I wish you did," he says. "But how could you? When he's shoved into your face every single day?"

He lifts me up easily, and carries me across the room. He sets me gently on my bed and sits next to me, wrapping a strong arm around my shoulders. "Let me take you away." His voice is shredded, torn, destroyed. "Please."

"I can't leave," I say. "They need me."

"They'll always need you." His free hand brushes the hair back from my face. "They'll never be okay without you until they're forced to figure it out. You don't owe them anything, not anymore."

"They're the three people I love more than anyone else in the world," I say.

"They are." Gideon doesn't look upset at all. "But they

also hurt you more than anyone else, and at some point you have to staunch the flow of blood or die yourself."

"Melina—"

"That girl's existence is pain for you," he says. "You're such a good person that you don't even realize it. Did you know that you can place a razor blade in the center of a tree, and it will grow around it? It will survive, with this terrible foreign object at its core, ruining its strength, damaging its structural integrity, preventing proper nutrient uptake—it'll grow and grow, but the damage at its core is permanent." He squeezes my shoulders. "A windstorm, irregular rain, any of those things could split the trunk down the middle, killing the tree immediately."

"But the deformity is at the heart of the tree." I hang my head. "It can't be repaired."

"Wrong." His voice is low, urgent. "That razor can be removed, carefully, and the tree will heal around it. Let me remove it so you can finally heal. Come with me—anywhere."

"Mother would be furious," I say. "She'd make me come back."

He snorts. "She might, at that. She's a stubborn woman, but. . ." He clears his throat. "I've never told you this before, because, well, you'll see. But I'm a leader, near the very top, of a group of evians. I have resources, Inara."

I scoot away from him, even though losing his arm around me hurts. I need to watch his face. "What are you talking about?"

"Eamon's a zealot," he says. "You admit that at least, right?"

I think about his eyes blazing when he talks about saving the humans, how he calls them God's children. I think about him saying God led him to me, and to my mother. I think about his certainty about everything. . . until he changes his mind. Grudgingly, I nod.

"Well, you might think I'm a zealot too. I've kept a secret from you, and I'm sorry for that. But before I ever met you, I met a. . . Let's call her a warrior."

"A warrior?" I raise my eyebrows. "Who is she?" Irrationally, I'm jealous.

"I was young then, and I was chafing against the rules overlaying my life."

"What does that mean?"

Gideon sighs. "I was *purchased* as a child, Inara. I'm technically still property of the Alamecha family, and giving me a name didn't exactly remove the injustice. Golden shackles are still shackles."

For the first time, I see things as he must have seen them. Before he could even speak or walk, he was sold like a. . . well, like a dog. . .or some other commodity. . . or like the human slaves. "You wanted to leave before now?" I swallow. I hate the thought that I was his slave master.

He shoves me lightly. "I never wanted to leave after I met you, and you've never acted as though I was anything other than a friend, or maybe a valued employee."

That's a relief, at least.

"Your sister Alora wasn't awful, but we didn't get along. And the captain of her guard. . . didn't like me."

"Sometimes I forget that you had an entire lifetime before I was ever born."

He grins. "Evian life is strange, that's for sure."

"What's this group?" I gasp. "Wait, do you conspire against my mother?"

"Absolutely not," he says, so vehemently I can't doubt his sincerity. "We have the utmost respect for Enora. We in no way advocate rebellions or coups or anything of the sort, at least not against her."

"Against her?"

"The overall leader. . .has great respect for Enora. In fact, one of the reasons the group began initially was to redirect rebels within the evian community, to give them a purpose and ensure they'd remain loyal."

"Wait," I say. "How big is this group?"

Gideon sighs. "It's large, and as I mentioned, I'm very near the top. You'll be disappointed to discover that we oppose most everything Eamon stands for."

Actually, a perverse part of me likes that. He has kept me on the hook, wittingly or not, for decades. I've hung around here, harming myself just as Gideon said, hoping, wishing, imagining. Punishing myself, and I've done nothing wrong. And Eamon's ignoring that the humans are nothing like us—I didn't choose the biological difference between us, and they're not my fault. But they're a fact.

"What does this group do exactly?" I ask. "If you support the empresses?"

"We support *Enora*," he says. "But the Sons of Gilgamesh began here, with Alamecha. In fact, I'm fairly certain your mother knows about the entire organization."

"But what are your goals? What do you *do?*"

"We nudge things, sometimes, and encourage policy shifts."

"Human ones?"

"Human, evian, everywhere. For instance, we'd like to eliminate the sale of empress' sons. We've been working on the idea for a long time, so we take a little credit for Enora's decision to keep Jered." He beams.

"A secret group that works behind the scenes to influence evian policy?" No matter what he says, I can't imagine that Mother would approve of this at all.

"I know it's problematic," he says. "And you'll like this even less. It crosses family lines. There are members in all six families—but we began recruiting across lines for a very particular purpose. At some point, we believe that Alamecha will be required to take over the other families, resuming its rightful place as ruler of the world. When that happens, we'll already have an extensive support system in place."

I'm quiet for a moment, processing. "Mother has no idea?"

He shrugs. "I'm not entirely certain what she knows, but certainly not the breadth or depth of the network."

I wonder whether I ought to tell my mother everything I know about this.

"You can't tell Enora what I've told you," Gideon says sharply. "I'd be executed immediately, for one thing."

"I would never tell her you're part of it," I say. "Have a little faith."

He shakes his head. "You misunderstand. They would execute me."

I blink repeatedly. "The Sons of Gilgamesh?" I frown. "How long has this group been around? Are we talking Akkadian Gilgamesh?"

"We are. Some form of this group has been around far longer than you or I, that's for sure. I'm not entirely certain it's true, but they claim to have precipitated the flood, anciently."

I scoff. "Oh come on, the biblical flood? The one that supposedly wiped out everyone but Noah?"

"You and I both know there was a huge influx of regional flooding then, and that a plague took out the rest of the human population."

"The records are unclear—"

"Believe me or not, the point is that I have resources. If your mother refuses to allow you to leave, we can escape. I could keep us hidden for as long as we wanted. Certainly long enough for Enora to calm down and realize she can't reasonably keep you here forever, treading water at her bidding."

And long enough to remove that razor so that I could love someone else, like him. He's certainly been patient enough. "And if I agreed to this, your group would just say, 'Where to, Gideon?' and then they'd take us wherever we want?"

He laughs. "I have a code name, of course, and I only know a few dozen members personally—my lieutenants and the others I've met over the years."

"You have a code name?" I lean a little closer and drop my voice. "You *have* to tell me the code name now."

"In for a penny, in for a pound," he mutters. "Fine. I'm known as Nereus."

"Nereus." The name has a good sound. It rolls around in my mouth in an interesting way. "I like it."

He grabs my hand. "I've made all my lieutenants swear to serve you as they would serve me. That's usually only allowed for spouses, but—" His mouth twists. "I convinced them to make an exception."

I wonder what that cost.

"But please promise me that you won't ever tell a soul about any of this." His words are light, but his eyes are as intense as I've ever seen them. He's not kidding—he's taken a huge risk sharing this with me.

"Never," I say. "I swear it."

His shoulders relax slightly, and I realize that he was scared that I would betray him, again. Let him down, again. Choose someone else, again. Oh, my poor Gideon. "You know that other than my mother and Eamon and Melina, you're the person I love most in all the world."

He leans toward me, our foreheads touching. "I do. Of course I do. I wish that was enough, for either of us."

"Me too." So much of my strength comes from knowing Gideon is always behind me. Unfailingly. "I will think about it, alright?"

"Thank you."

For now, his presence, his trust, and his support are enough to pull me out of my nosedive. By the next day, I'm able to fake joy with much more believability. I still can't spend too much time with the happy little family, but I muddle along, much as I always have. Good old reliable Inara, dependable as the tides, solid and supportive and only a little bit of a dead-eyed robot, and only if you really know to look.

Not that anyone is looking. They don't even notice when I skip a string of family breakfasts in a row.

When I finally show up two weeks after Jered's birth, I'm the only one there. I sit alone for a few minutes before I go hunting for the others. I round the bend to the kitchen and poke my head through the swinging door. Dozens of people cross the room, carrying pans, dirty dishes, and platters.

When I do spot Angel, she's berating a pale-faced girl who can't be more than fifteen.

"Angel?" I practically shout in my zeal to spare that poor girl. "A word?"

She brushes her hands off on her apron and crosses the room, veering off toward her office at the last moment. I duck inside behind her. It's a much larger office than most chefs probably need, but then, she's not only a chef. It's hard to believe that she runs the entire Alamecha network out of this room, its shelves stacked high with spices, cook-books, and handwritten notes.

Now that I think of it, I doubt I'd rely on any of these recipes. They're as likely to be ciphers as anything else. The only reason we need to write down recipes is so that others can use them—with our perfect recall we never require a recipe for something we've made ourselves.

"What's wrong?" She stares.

"I hoped you could tell me. I just came from an empty breakfast room."

Her eyes soften. "You haven't heard?"

"Heard what?" My heart contracts. What now?

"Your mother—" She drops into her chair, her breath whooshing out of her. "You've never had a baby, so this might be hard to understand."

I sit on the hard wooden chair she keeps to intimidate her staff. "Is Mother sick?" My heart accelerates and I calm it.

"After a manner of speaking." Angel leans toward me, her brow furrowed, her posture entreating. "Your mother is heartsick. She has given up seventy sons, you know, every one she's ever had. She made the brave decision to keep this one, but in his tiny face, she saw every single baby she had sold over the years. It caused her more pain than joy— and nightmares, waking and sleeping."

I don't understand. "She's sad because he. . . Wait, you said he *caused*. Past tense."

Angel leans back slowly. "She sold him—to Adika."

She *sold him?* After keeping him for weeks? I've tried not to form a bond to him, not like the one I have with Melina, but even for me it stings. I can only imagine how Eamon and Melina are taking it. Oh, they'll both be hurting, and Mother too of course. "It was a pretty unilateral move, then," I say.

Angel purses her lips. "Enora has had eight hundred years of only worrying about herself and Althuselah. She's not accustomed to doing things that cause harm to herself in order to spare others."

That's a diplomatic way of saying she's a selfish jerk. "Well, thanks for telling me." I stand up woodenly, my legs doing as they're told, but only just.

"If you think of something I can do, for any of them," Angel says. "Please tell me."

"Right." I nearly plow into Pauline when I fly out of the kitchen door. "Excuse me."

She doesn't meet my eye, which means she already

knows. Was I the last one to find out? "I need a ride." She and Cassius follow me outside without comment.

Before I can even tell the groom which horse I want, I smell him behind me. No one else in Ni'ihau smells quite like Eamon. I square my shoulders, wracking my brain for something I could say to help him.

But when I turn around, he rushes toward me, pulling me against him in a bear hug. "I can't," he whispers. "Not anymore."

When he finally releases me, I ask, "Can't what?"

His eyes are dry, but his cheeks are red, the skin under his eyes puffy. It takes a lot of crying for an evian to look like that. "I can't do it anymore. Not for another second."

"Can't do what?" I ask.

"I'm going to leave Enora," he says. "I can't wait until she dies. I won't survive it. I'll kill her, or she'll kill me."

I should pity him. I should be heartbroken for my mother and for him. Or I could talk him down like a good daughter would do. Leaving the empress—it's a death sentence. But Gideon told me his people could help us escape—I hope they can help three of us escape. The thought of asking Gideon for this favor, it slays me. I shouldn't do it. I shouldn't do any of it.

There are a million appropriate ways I could respond to Eamon in this moment, but I don't do any of them.

"Finally," I whisper.

Eamon's in such a fog over Jered's loss and Enora's betrayal that he can barely string together words for the first few days, much less make any other plans. He falls into a bizarre rut, acting in a way I recognize: his movements are rote and stiff. He's become a dead-eyed robot.

But slowly, so slowly, he comes out of it.

He asks me questions, and we begin to make a plan. By the time Mother celebrates her birthday, I start to believe it might happen. We might actually leave here.

Talking to Gideon is hard. I'm essentially doing what he suggested, but with Eamon.

"I'll help you," he says. "Of course I will. My men will help you, protect you, safeguard your departure."

"Your men?"

Gideon can't meet my eye. "I can't come, Inara. I hope you can understand that. I've always been there for you, and if it were ordinary circumstances, if I had a role to play as head of your guard." He swallows. "I can't go on the run with the two of you. Can you understand why not?"

I look at my feet, sparing him the pain of seeing the loss on my face. "Of course I do."

Even so, it hurts, thinking of losing him in my life. But it's a price I'll pay to finally be with Eamon. I hardly think there's any price I wouldn't pay.

"I think we've been looking at this wrong," Eamon says one night. He's shredding flowers from a bush growing just above the high tide line.

"I'm sick of meeting you a few times a week after sunset," I complain. "And I frequently have to wait here alone forever before you actually come."

He takes my hand and my irritation evaporates. "I think we'll need to die."

My heart stutters.

"Not *really* die, of course," he says. "We'll have to fake our deaths."

"Wait, are you kidding?" I look into his eyes. "Gideon will help us. He promised."

"I know he will, and I'm unbelievably grateful for that. But think this through," he says. "Melina and Enora won't ever have closure if we simply sneak away. I'm not sure about me, but I know for sure that Enora won't just quit looking for you."

I'm not sure he's right. "She has an Heir," I say. "She doesn't need me."

"You're her clone," he whispers. "You know that. She'd ransack the world to find you—and punish whoever took you from her. We have to give her an alternate narrative, or we'll never be free to live without fear and anxiety. And it's the kinder thing to do."

I wish he was wrong, but he's not. Only Gideon would remain with the truth. I wish I could give him closure, too. I wish I didn't need him so much, even in my escape.

"It's so hard not to kiss you."

My heart accelerates, but I shift away from him. "We

can't. Not while we're here, not until we've actually left. I can't do that, not to Mother, not to you, not to myself." I bite my lip coyly. "Not until we're dead."

"I'll still be married after we leave," he says.

"But once we're declared dead," I say. "At least to the ones we love, things will be over. It will still be a betrayal, but not in the same way, not right under their noses."

"A bright line," he says. "I get it."

It's hard for me too, but after waiting all this time, what's a few more weeks? "Alright, so how would that work?"

A sentry comes around the bend and we split. It takes us several more weeks to develop a plan, but finally, we have one in place. "October feels too far," I whine.

"It's only two months away," he says. "It'll pass in a blink."

And the days do race past. I soak in every minute I have with Mother, with Melina, and with Gideon. I'll miss them all so much in different ways.

Not enough that I waver, not in the slightest.

But when banging at the door wakes me up in the early morning hours of September 11, I realize that our plans might be delayed yet again. It's almost as though the world's conspiring against us. Not that I can complain, not in the face of such terrible tragedy. My complaints seem suddenly small.

Eamon takes the attack harder than the rest of us—his heart breaks over the loss of human life.

"I can't—we can't move ahead," he says that night. "Obviously."

"What can you possibly do about it now?" I ask. "I actually think the chaos will make our departure even easier. We could request to be assigned to one of the crews that goes in to investigate. Then, boom."

Eamon's face falls, incredulity spreading across his

features. "We have an obligation to mitigate this. Don't you see that?"

Guilt washes over me. "Of course I do, I mean, yes. But how will we actually do anything to help?"

"The empresses have all been quick to deny any involvement, and Enora believes them. That means that humans, or at best, a rebel evian group perpetrated this attack. We're going to find out exactly what happened soon, and Enora will be livid. She'll punish whoever did this, harshly, and you know what that means—the impact in New York will be minuscule compared to the horror she'll rain down on the perpetrators."

The humans will bear the brunt of it, as usual. I sigh. "Fine. So we delay again—until this is resolved."

He stands up. "Indefinitely."

I remind myself that indefinitely is not forever. It's just an undetermined period. "Fine."

When I turn to leave, his fingers brush against my hand. "This isn't about you," he says softly. "I haven't changed my mind."

My heart eases, a bit. "I know that."

"You do?"

I sit again, my hands flattening against the cool sand.

He sits next to me, facing the opposite way, his eyes finding mine, glowing lightly, reflecting the moonlight on the waves beyond us.

"I'm not sure whether this will make sense," I say. "But. . .you have your faith in God, and it sustains you."

He nods.

"I guess that I've never had that."

"You don't believe in God?" His eyebrows rise sharply.

I shrug. "When I was small, just thirteen, I killed my first person, a warrior sent to kill my dad and me. And you know what happened next."

He grunts, but his hand moves across my calf, his fingers caressing the skin there, sending tiny thrills of pleasure up my leg and on toward my spine.

"I had a hard time believing that any benevolent being might have made me. . . like I am." I can't even meet his eyes, not right now. "I felt cursed. Even that word feels. . . insufficient to describe how I felt." Finally, it hits me. "Forsaken."

"But now?"

He's jumping ahead, and it's not the whole picture. "Losing my dad—I don't talk about him much, but he was larger than life. He was the greatest person in my life—right up until the moment I met you."

Eamon leans against me, our bodies connecting at our shoulders, our arms, and our hips.

I can't see his eyes anymore, not leaning against him like this, but that makes this easier, somehow. "When he died, I can't describe it. As bad as I felt before, as *other*, as disconnected to the rest of the world, his death just tore me further from everything. I felt. . .alien. And I feared all of it—what I could do, the lack of control, the hunger of the monster inside of me."

"You would never truly do anything bad. You've only attacked when provoked."

My laugh is mirthless, my body shaking involuntarily. "Since I met you, that's true. But before—" I shudder. "It snapped down over my brain." I close my eyes. "It took over my free will, my desires, everything that makes me *me*."

"That sounds terrifying."

"It was, but meeting you, somehow, it gave me my life back. The day Paruka abducted us and I realized that thanks to you, I could control myself, it was as if I climbed out of a bottomless pit. I had a life, for the first time ever. I had choices, and control, and I knew my own abilities wouldn't cause people around me to recoil."

"So that's the first time you believed God loved you?"

"When I'm near you, I believe, but it's more like I've just latched on to your faith. Mine is simpler. I think that, even in my lowest moments, like the morning of your wedding, I knew that somehow, like a boomerang, like the salmon returning upstream, you would fight your way back to me."

His hand tightens on my ankle, and I know that he's telling me that he will. He feels it too.

"It's like, no matter what, no matter how bleak things become, you and I will eventually find one another. That's my hope, that's my light in the darkness." I turn to face him in the moonlight. "You are my strength. You are my home."

He kisses me then, lightly, gently, soulfully. And it's enough. I stand up and walk away from him.

The next morning, when we meet for the War Council, he meets my eyes across the Council table and my heart swells with peace, comfort, and joy.

There may be another delay in a sequence of delays since we met, but I can endure it as I have endured all the others that came before.

"We have been able to identify that the attacks were coordinated and planned by a man named Osama bin Laden," Balthasar says. "He's currently in Afghanistan, as we suspected. He works closely with the local leadership there, the Taliban."

That effectively snaps us both to attention.

"We're going to bomb them out of existence," Mother says.

Eamon's eyes snap. "I think we should offer the local government the opportunity to surrender all the individuals involved."

"Why does that not surprise me?" Mother asks.

Eamon frowns. "We should demand they hand over all the terrorists—leaders and supporters alike. We'll also demand they dismantle all training camps. Require them to release every imprisoned foreign national, and give us full access to verify that they have complied. But at least allow the innocent humans the chance to avoid the fallout on this, or we're as bad as they are."

Mother's nostrils flare. "Adriana, Katalina, Richard, Wallace—"

"I lost people I care for, too," Eamon says. "But it doesn't justify the wholesale destruction of an entire country."

Mother turns toward me, of all people. "And do you agree?"

I can't very well argue with him, no matter how badly Mother wants me to. I nod tightly.

"And what about you?" Mother glares at Melina, whose face is already pale. "Are you worried that I'm turning into a despot, hurling the lives of these people away for no reason?"

Melina sighs. "We should at least give them the chance to do the right thing. You and I both know they're unlikely to comply with all of those demands."

"Fine," Mother says. "Do it. Send your little list. But Balthasar?"

He grunts.

"Prepare a plan to pulverize the entire country."

"I would like to fly over myself," Eamon says. "I'd like to talk to them as a show of good faith. You can send me as the American ambassador—not letting on who I really am, if that makes you feel better, but this happened because those people feel disenfranchised and angry. They know someone powerful is pulling the strings, and they're lashing out in the only way they can. I'd like to broker a peace agreement that will make this type of attack less likely in the future. Security measures help, especially to dissuade the weaponization of commercial travel in the future, but there are too many ways for them to harm the innocent. Sending a sweeping ultimatum isn't the same thing as letting them feel *heard*."

"You want to fly across the world and negotiate with the people who attacked us?" Mother lifts one eyebrow. "Right now?"

"The entire country didn't attack us," Eamon says. "It was a very small group of dissidents who felt they had no other choice."

"Fine," Mother says. "Go." She turns away from him, contempt etched in every line of her body.

"Enora." The way he says her name sends a sense of uneasy foreboding through my entire body. "Talk to me first. Let's discuss this without everyone else and come to a decision." It's been years and years since Eamon addressed her as a husband, as a Consort, as a *lover.* The words slice into me like a whip, like a lash across my back, rending my soul bare.

"Get out." Mother's as cold as I've ever heard her.

Eamon glares at her for a moment, but quickly enough he spins on his heel and marches out the door. The rest of us follow closely, leaving Mother to hash out details with Balthasar, Frederick, and Miles. From the snippets of discussion I hear on my way out, it appears she's planning the attack that will take place after Eamon's planned attempt to elicit a surrender fails. Not a lot of faith in his skill set on her part.

"You really ticked her off in there," I say. "Was that wise?"

"She's not being rational right now," Eamon says. "She'll realize that I was trying to spare us and them. I'm just trying to work this out in the best way possible. A surgical extraction is always a better option than fifty pounds of C4."

"I think that's the right call." Surprisingly, Gideon agrees with him.

"You would think that," Melina practically spits.

My eyes widen, and I realize I'm not the only one staring at her in shock. We all are.

"I'm sorry. I'm stressed out, I think," she says.

I pat her arm. "We all are."

"I'd like to go with you," Gideon says to Eamon. "It might be nice for you to have someone else with the same goal. You're only one person. You can't be everywhere at once."

Gideon can barely stand him, but he's offering to protect him, to guard his back in enemy territory—for my sake. "That's a good idea," I say quickly. "It's always good to have someone to watch the angles you can't."

Eamon smiles at me, relief plain across his face. "Yes, although I've nearly forgotten what that feels like. Thank you."

"You two be safe, okay?" I wrap an arm around each of their shoulders.

"We will," Eamon says.

They both pack more quickly than I imagined possible. Mother refuses to leave her room, intent on planning the utter destruction of anyone affiliated with anyone who propagated the attack, but Melina and I watch the jet take off together. Gideon's face, over Eamon's shoulder, when Eamon throws Melina and me a double thumbs up, is priceless.

In that moment, I'm at peace, excited for the future—and if Eamon succeeds, that only hastens our final departure.

A few days later, I'm reviewing the proposal Eamon

sent, thinking of ways to make it more palatable to Mother, when urgent rapping at my door startles me. I cross the room wearily. What now? I do not expect Job to be standing in the hallway, his hands clenched into tight fists at his side.

My voice comes out strange, all strangled and high. "What's wrong?"

He pushes past me and slams the door behind him. "I have news."

"And not good news," I say. "What is it?"

"Enora has known for some time, but she asked for my . . . discretion."

"Okay." Why won't he meet my eye? "Job? What's going on?"

His face finally lifts, his eyes as wide as silver dollars. "Enora is pregnant again."

My brain struggles to process his words. How can that be? Eamon couldn't have. . .could he? My mind blanks, my heart stalls, and my fingernails dig into my palms, slicing the skin open. The last time Enora was pregnant, Eamon rushed to my side to explain. He told me it happened before we spoke, before he told me that marrying her was a mistake. He told me that it wouldn't change a thing.

It changed everything, but even after that we found our way to back to one another.

But that was a boy, and he is gone. What if she has another girl? Will that rekindle whatever bizarre connection my mother and my soulmate share? I can't quite suppress the shudder that wracks my body.

"Inara?"

"What?" I force myself to meet his eyes.

"She's pregnant with twins."

Twins? I blink. Twins is very bad. But maybe. . . "Twin boys?" I ask, hating the hope that permeates my question, the desperate, sickening hope that the love of my life and my mother created two *boys*. The alternative is too ghastly.

He shakes his head.

Oh, no. No, no, no. As if we don't have enough going on right now already, enough tearing us all apart. "Well." Fury pulses through me, sending heat to my cheeks and energy shooting through my sluggish limbs. I'd like nothing more than to tear into something or someone. To drag a blade across someone's throat and watch the blood spurt out. To lose myself in destruction and rage.

I drag in a deep breath. I'll need to revisit my feelings about this—I at least owe Eamon the chance to defend himself before I assume the worst about him. There are methods now, by which people create children without. . . It's possible he hasn't betrayed my trust. The way he entreated Mother before he left. I close my eyes again and force out the question I must ask. "How long has she known?"

Job's lips tighten, the words practically spit out as if they're poison. "She just found out, and she made Melina promise to kill one of them."

Melina? No. I choke. "She did what?"

"She's worried she won't be able to do it herself, and apparently the Charter holds that the Heir won't be displaced until the newborn has survived for more than twenty-four hours."

"So Melina would still have the capacity to legally challenge her, if Mother balks."

He nods mutely.

She can't ask it of her, she can't. I need to talk to Eamon, and Melina, and Enora. I need—I wish I knew what I needed. "Thanks," I say, shooing him toward the door with open arms as I walk that direction. "I'll figure something out, I swear."

Job stumbles backward, clearly still processing the ramifications of this newest bombshell himself. "Right. I guess I'll be going."

"Good idea." The second the door closes, I call Eamon. It goes straight to voicemail. I call again. Same. I call Gideon. Same. Voicemail. I swear and throw my phone across the room. It bounces on my bed once, then again, coming to rest against a fluffy pillow.

Poor Melina. She has struggled since Jered, but to find out she's finally free of the burden of ruling, only to be told that she'll have to kill her own sister. I can barely swallow past the frog in my throat, thinking about how hard this must be hitting her. Her dad's not even here, so the task falls to me to comfort her, to reassure her that she won't be asked to do it, not really. That's a task I'd rather not complete, but it's better than fretting about whose children Mother is having.

And for the first time since Job's knock at my door, I wonder whether it's possible that the children aren't Eamon's. Could Mother have a lover? While Eamon has been sneaking out to visit me. . .has Mother been meeting someone else? Frederick, maybe? I can't think about this, not right now.

I sprint down the hall, Laverne and Tarben's heavy footfalls behind me comforting in this moment. Familiar is good right now, with the world spinning more out of control every moment.

Tears already streak Melina's face when I reach her door. I throw my arms around her, taking as much comfort from her arms as I give with mine. We cling to one another, as if somehow our love can heal the broken world around us.

Part of me sobs at the thought that in a few months, once this new mess has been cleaned up, I won't see her anymore. *Sufficient unto the day is the evil thereof*, one of Eamon's sayings, springs to mind. "I am sorry, Melina. Job told me what she made you promise, and it's not fair. She shouldn't put that on you."

I am not expecting Melina to tell me the whole thing is her fault, but her explanation of how Mother's pregnancy could possibly have anything to do with her is even a bigger shock. "I think I'm gay."

What? "You *think* you're gay?"

She explains that she fell for a girl at the Games, and that she's been struggling ever since. And oh boy, do I understand how it feels to love the wrong person.

I sit down on her floor, weighed down by the waves of madness that seem to crash over me non-stop lately. "I don't understand." How could any of this be her fault, even if Mother will never accept Aline?

"I was confused at first," she says. "I thought maybe I only liked Aline. Of course, I do like her, but what I mean—"

I shake my head. Oh, Melina. "No, no, not about all that. I should have seen all of that before." Now that I think about it, it's clear as day. If I hadn't been struggling with so much of my own garbage, I'd have been a better guardian to her—I'd have noticed. I'm a terrible mother, as it turns out—not as bad as our actual mother—but still terrible. "I'm sorry that I didn't, and I'm sorry that you've been so alone with all of this." I sigh. "But I've been wracking my brain, and I can't think of an explanation for what that possibly has to do with Mother's pregnancy and twins."

When she tells me she *prayed* for a solution, and God gave Enora twins in response, well. I can't help thinking of how immaculate conception would actually solve all my horror at this pregnancy too, although I know the whole concept is rubbish. Enora absolutely created those twins with some man or other. Laughter bubbles up from deep inside, a combination of relief that Melina will be alright once she gets herself out of this bizarre religious pretzel she has contorted herself into, and hilarity over the ridiculousness of her fears. Especially compared to the real danger we're facing, between the terrorists and the twins, and my imminent departure.

I pull her against me for a hug, but after a brief moment, she shoves me off. "What's so funny?"

She looks so angry that I almost collapse in another fit of laughter, but she needs me right now. I need to be on my game. "Oh, sweet Melina, I'm sure your father would be touched by your faith, but you can't *pray* twins into existence." No matter how much I wish you could. "It's a biological phenomenon. This is no more your fault than the terrorist attack. Sometimes things happen and we don't have any control over them. In fact, I think that's the strongest argument against Eamon's fanatical faith. What kind of God would punish a child he loved by putting her through something like this?" Although, clear as a bell, I question my most basic assumption. I have zero evidence that God loves me, or any of us, really. Maybe this is all a big joke to him. That would explain a lot—maybe we're all being tortured.

"I feel it in my bones," she says. "This is because I begged for something wicked." By the end she's whispering.

And how many wicked things have I begged for in my life? Maybe there's something to her guilt after all. "Oh Melina." She is the sweetest, the best, the brightest, the kindest person I've ever known. Any God that would punish her—I want nothing to do with him or her. That much I know. "I can't convince you in this moment, but maybe one day you'll see that it isn't so. This isn't a punishment, I promise you that. It's just something that happened." Because Eamon, the love of my life, lied to me. He's been meeting me at night and kissing my mother as soon as he leaves my side. Does he even mean to leave her at all? I need to hold it together, at least until I can escape this room.

Poor Melina still isn't convinced, but when she starts suggesting that this is penance, I can't handle it.

"Not everything is about you," I snap.

Her eyes fall.

I'm such a terrible person. I soften my voice. "Not everything is a message, and sometimes all we can do is survive until things improve."

Finally, she inhales and exhales, her eyes brightening a bit. "Accept the world as it is."

"You're doing things to change it, and you're making great strides in the right direction," I say.

"I'll think about it."

"I'm beginning to dread waking up in the morning, but take cheer. Things can't get much worse."

Melina forces a smile, and I wonder whether I can duck out. I want to stay by her side, but I have my own demons to vanquish. I can't help her if I'm sobbing on her shoulder myself.

A banging on the door saves me—I hope I can use whoever this is as an excuse to escape. Melina yanks the door open and we both have to drop our eyes a good two feet to the tiny fellow standing in the doorway, his hands raised over his head like a beggar asking for change for dinner. I only absently notice he's holding a slip of paper.

"Well," I say. "I had better—"

But Melina has taken the paper, and as her eyes scan its contents, her heart rate spikes. Not like, uh oh, Balthasar wants to see me. Not even like, darn, Mother's angry with me. No, her heart is sprinting away from a lion chasing it at a dead run. What could be on the paper that would freak her out this badly?

"Why didn't you take this to the empress?" she asks.

The little boy doesn't look up. "She won't answer the

door. Balthasar told me to fetch you, and I wasn't supposed to bring this, but I thought you needed to know." His features are beautiful, almost as stunning as those of Eamon, but fairer, brighter somehow. The rays of the sun at midday, to Eamon's moonlit beauty.

Melina's frozen in place, her heart still hammering in her chest.

"He didn't notice I took it," the boy stammers. "Maybe you could not mention that."

This little boy knows what the paper says, and a desperate desire to read it grips me. As if she can sense it, the paper slips from Melina's fingers and flutters to the floor. My limbs move involuntarily, snatching the paper up and holding it in front of my face, even as something inside of me warns me to run and hide.

The proposed meeting was a trap. Gideon and Eamon both killed along with fourteen humans. Remains to ship immediately. Condolences. -M

Perhaps Melamecha is wrong. Eamon can't be dead. Gideon will yet come home. Both of them will, I know it. They're evian, they're larger than life, they're the bedrock of my entire existence—my best friend and my soulmate, both eliminated with one line of text. It can't be true.

But Melina believes it—I can tell.

And the words were so final. Killed. *Remains* to ship. As in, what's left of them. My hands tremble at the thought, my head shakes, my lungs fill with cotton, and my mind disconnects. What happens to a building when the support beams are destroyed? I recently watched as two enormous skyscrapers melted to the ground—hundreds of thousands of tons of concrete, wood, and metal collapsed. I survived Atlas' destruction when Dad died. I survived Eamon marrying my mother—and God somehow replaced Dad's support with Melina's, but now.

I won't survive this—losing the twin support beams of

my entire life. No one could withstand it. My knees wobble and give out entirely. I collapse to the ground, everything around me fraying at the edges, and I stop trying to process what anyone around me is saying or doing.

Because if this is all true, nothing matters anymore.

Nothing.

❧ 20 ❧

2001 & 2002

The tiny bundle of ashes Melamecha sends contain a genetic match for both of the samples we take from Eamon and Gideon's hairbrushes and the saliva we find on their toothbrushes. It makes it a lot harder to hold out hope, but not impossible. The ashes could have been created from a severed hand or foot from each man—something an evian could regrow.

Or maybe the ashes are a rare mercy from Melamecha. Perhaps she gathered as many of the chunks of them as she could find, and burned them so we wouldn't have to contemplate the exact nature of the explosion and the way they died.

It's hard to know whether to hold out hope—or whether to surrender to despair. Especially since Eamon and I discussed just this possibility—faking our deaths. Could Gideon have decided this was the time? Perhaps they are waiting a proper amount of time to send me a message. Certainly that's my dream at least half of the times I'm able to sleep.

The other half aren't nearly as encouraging.

But the question that plagues me, the one I need

answers to—only Mother can answer it. She keeps to her rooms, denying entry to most everyone.

That has never stopped me before.

I shove my way through a week and a half after the news, ignoring Frederick, and Lyssa, and everyone else who tries to stop me. "I'll speak with my mother. Right now."

She's lying on her side in bed when I stride through the door. Her expression is vacant, her body slack. I almost regret shoving past. Almost.

I crouch down in front of her. "I know you're hurting," I say softly.

If she'd look around like a mother ought, she'd notice that she's not the only one.

"I hate to bother you." That's just a lie. I'm disgusted by her utter apathy, her apparent lack of care for anyone or anything but herself. "But I need to know something."

"Yes," she nearly croaks.

"Yes?" I lift my right eyebrow. "Yes what? I haven't asked yet."

Her eyes finally focus on mine. "Yes, I really am having twins."

My hand itches to slap her. It's as though she only cares about one thing in the world: herself. Does the rest of the universe really not matter to her? "Gideon is dead," I say flatly. "Eamon is dead."

Her lips turn downward. "I told him not to go."

She did. That's the truth. "He couldn't have done any differently than he did," I say. "If you knew him at all, you'd have known that."

Her eyes snap. I clearly hit a nerve. "You barged into my room and accosted a grieving widow to tell me that I didn't know my husband? Or are you accusing me of causing his death by sending him?"

"Did you?" The question I need to know pops out.

Mother and Eamon fought a lot, violently, vocally, physically, and everyone knew it. "Are you relieved?"

She slumps against the mattress. "What if I am?"

"Are the twins his children?"

Her breath catches in her throat. "How dare you ask me that?"

She didn't answer the question. "Wouldn't he have known you were pregnant if they were his?" I ask. "And wouldn't he have stayed here with you?"

Mother shoves up to a sitting position. "If you think my husband cared enough about me to stay behind because I was pregnant if human lives were on the line, then you're the one who didn't know him at all." She swings out of bed and walks stiffly to the bathroom. "I'll give you a pass for your wretched behavior, because I know how much Gideon meant to you. But you'd better be gone by the time I get back out." She doesn't slam the door, but she closes it with much more force than necessary.

Could she be carrying someone else's children? And if so, could she have killed Eamon to keep that secret? How many things do we now keep from one another? Do we have any common ground at all anymore? To the world, I'm her clone. Yet, no matter how much we resemble one another physically, we're nothing alike.

I lie awake that night, tossing and turning, wrestling with the questions that still lie before me, unanswered. Is Eamon really dead or could this have been a setup? And if he is gone, could Mother have done it?

On my best days, I've wondered whether my entire existence was a mistake. I argued with Dad regularly over the years about whether I was too large a liability. I was never sure whether the value I added in serving Mother could possibly offset the damage I've done as a berserker. Eamon healed that part of me, allowing me to control the uncontrollable within myself, limiting the damage I might cause.

And if I believe anything at all, it's that Eamon loved me. He wouldn't have done anything to cause me this kind of pain. Which means he'd have immediately sent me some kind of message, any kind of message, letting me know that he wasn't really dead.

This wasn't part of our plan. This was a risk he knew he took, and the very reason Gideon went with him—to protect him from the danger of flying into a hostile area and pleading with humans to make the rational call.

Which means he's dead.

And I choose to believe that if Mother is carrying his twins, he didn't betray me in the creation of them. Because there's enough pain in the world. I don't need to manufacture any more. But once I've come to those conclusions, I don't find the peace I sought.

No, with those concerns resolved, I find myself drowning in anger. Boundless, limitless rage.

For possibly the first time, I want to harm something— no, I *need* to destroy something the way the world is trying to destroy me. I smash a vase in my room and stare numbly at the shards scattered across my floor. It helps, but it's not enough. Not nearly enough. I punch the huge, pristine pane of glass covering my window next, captivated by the blood that pours from my knuckles to drip on the windowsill.

I climb through the window, slicing my knees and the palms of my hands to ribbons.

The pain dissipates too quickly, and I curse my stupid body for its efficiency. My feet begin to pound the ground without much thought, and I leap the low walls around my private courtyard and head for Mt. Pānī'au. The burning in my thighs helps, but it's not enough. I push harder, my lungs screaming before too much longer. As I burst through the brambles and into a clearing, a squeal distracts me.

A wild boar.

It charges me, and I let it gore me, its powerful tusks flaying the skin and muscle in my thigh to reveal a shining white bone.

I sink to my knees, smiling.

Finally the pain in my body matches that of my heart. But when it comes at me again, joined by another dark, bristly-bodied hog companion, something kicks in, against my will, rising up against the pain, and I draw my sword. Seconds later, both hogs are dead, and the haze descends, dark and rich.

At first I welcome my old friend, and I race back toward the palace. If my own pain helped, how much more will the destruction battle back the horrible pain of losing Eamon? The clear, savage release of destruction beckons me.

Until Eamon's rueful face swims before my mind's eye.

I stumble, and slow, and then stop to lean against a tree. *Eamon!* My heart cries out, my mind aches, and my fists clench, my right hand gripping my sword like a lifeline.

No, I can't rend and tear and shred. No matter how much I'd like it. I drop my sword to the ground, because I realize that no pain—inflicted or received—will ever be enough. Nothing will erase this soul-sucking ache. Nothing will fill the gaping hole.

It's time—for my wretched, star-crossed, cursed life to end. Finally. No more haze. No more suffering. No more. . . anything.

I look around enough to orient myself—I'm on the far west side of the island, which is perfect. I race toward the sea and dive in headfirst. My arms and legs pump rapidly, swimming against the waves, diving down and resurfacing until I can't see Ni'ihau any longer. I have no idea how long it takes to swim until it disappears entirely from view, but even then, I don't stop. There's nothing between here and the Philippines—plenty of space to drown myself, even an evian. And every time a shark eats my hand or my foot, or my leg, that's another wound to heal, more energy to tap, until finally my body won't be able to heal any more.

I swim until the sun fades and the moon glows in the sky, my tears mixing with the surf, and then I keep going. Eventually, I'm not quite sure when, the world around me goes black.

Arms wrap around me, and voices shout. "Yes, right now, it's her. Hurry up."

The sound of waves slapping against the side of a boat.

I blink against the sun. I'm dragged onto the boat.

"No," I groan, coughing. I curse and lunge for the water again.

"Oh no you don't," Eirik says.

"She's a slippery thing," Pauline says.

My scream sounds so pathetic—ragged, half-hearted—that I cut off quickly.

"What were you thinking?" Pauline asks.

"She wasn't," Eirik says. "She was *feeling*."

I slump down against the smooth wood of the boat deck. "You can't take me back."

"Oh, I absolutely have to take you back," Eirik says. "If you're not back soon, someone is **bound** to notice. I can only put them off for so long."

What do I care who knows that I left?

"Inara of Alamecha is entitled to throw a tantrum when her best friend of a century dies." Eirik's voice is flat, emotionless. "She's allowed to grieve, but she's not allowed to commit suicide. Not that it would have worked, in any case, barring consumption by an orca."

I sit up then, scowling. "What are you talking about?"

"I assume you've been swimming for quite some time," Eirik says, "seeing as you've been gone for two days."

I blink repeatedly.

"But we're less than a three hour push from Ni'ihau." Eirik puts one hand on his hip. "Currents trump even evian strength."

I swear.

"You are coming back with us," Eirik says. "In fact, I found something you might like to see."

The next three hours stretch into an eternity. I refuse food and water, and I ignore Pauline and Eirik's well-intentioned attempts to interact. I hate them both. They should be grateful I don't wring their necks.

When they deposit me inside my room via the back patio sliding door, I notice that the window has already been replaced, and the vase shards cleaned up. My room looks exactly as it did before Gideon and Eamon died. In fact, there's nothing at all to indicate that anything in my life has changed.

My room should be blackened—smoking cinders. That would be fitting. But this? Immaculate, polished, pristine? This is a slap to the face. They're gone, and I'm supposed to just march right along. No, it can't be.

I stomp toward the door, noticing my sword resting on my bed. I stop. Eirik found my blade and tracked me, the disloyal moron. He's far too good at his job.

"I'll leave you to clean up on your own," he says softly. "I know I'm not a replacement for him, but Gideon—" His voice cracks. "I was tasked to clean out his things."

Fury floods my entire body, stiffening my limbs, curling my lip. Clean out his things? Toss them in the trash? I turn slowly.

"I packed most of it up, unsure what you'd want to keep. But I found a box of. . ." He trails off when he gets a good look at my face. "I left the box on your desk."

The fury drains as quickly as it came, and my gaze continues to slew sideways. A large brown box rests on the top of my well-ordered desk. How did I not notice it before?

I nod, and wave absently, and Eirik bows and leaves, closing the sliding door behind him. He doesn't go far, since he's still presumably on suicide watch, but it's enough. I cross the room and stand in front of the box. What's inside? My fingers tremble as I reach out slowly, barely brushing the top of the cardboard, and finally I flip it open.

Paper. It's full of paper.

What did I think it would contain? His head? A Gideon blow-up doll? Some kind of treasure? Tapes of him talking to me, telling me what to do? Magical armor? A summoning potion? I feel idiotic for being disappointed.

But then I look more closely.

Inara.

Sheaths of paper are folded and clipped, with my name inscribed in Gideon's beautiful curling script on the top of each one.

He wrote me. . . letters? A great many of them, it appears. My heart twists inside of my chest, and I reach out and snap one up. When I flip it over, I realize it's several pages long and was sealed with wax, the impression of his insignia pressed into it before the wax cooled, adhering it to the pages.

I slide my finger underneath the seal and press until it opens, the seal crumbling slightly. It smells faintly of him, and a frog creeps into my throat.

Dearest Inara,

I'm not sure why I still write to you—at first I figured you might want to read them—look back and laugh at how I reacted differently to things than you did. Then I wondered whether maybe our kids would want to read them one day. I continued after George Town because it felt more personal than writing a sterile journal entry to record my thoughts and feelings. Aren't we, all of us, really just looking for someone to listen, anyway?

You've always been that person for me, even when I knew you didn't want me. You were still the person who got me, the person I wanted to talk to—to share things with. So I share them here, instead of telling you everything I think and feel.

As I think about your impending trip—I'm more conflicted than I've ever been. I know you've reconciled with Eamon, and I'm happy for you. As hard as it is to see you with him, it was harder to see you pining. I would never commit treason against Alamecha or your mother, but I'd do most everything else, if I knew it would bring you peace and joy.

If I'm totally honest, even treason isn't out for me. You already know I run an organization—I gave you the name. You also know one of my lieutenants. He's my second in command in normal life as well. I don't know why I'm telling you this, except that I worry about what will happen to you if something ever happens to me.

Gideon worried he might die. And Eirik is one of the sons of Gilgamesh. It's a lot of information in one hand-scrawled letter.

Your boyfriend is wrong. He wants to save a bunch of humans who don't know who we are, who don't understand the world. He's wrong that they're worth saving. No matter how much he wishes they were, humans aren't like us. They aren't logical, or intelligent, or skilled. And their lives are so short, they have completely different perspectives, which gives them entirely different motives and impulses and desires.

And now I'm rambling, which is fine, since you'll likely never see this anyway. But I guess I wanted to document somewhere that I did something selfless. I'm leaving your side for maybe the first time in years, because I know you'll be in relative safety, to watch over the person you love, so that when we return you can leave me forever.

I still wish it were me.

But in case anything does go wrong, in case this nagging feeling isn't wrong, I'll still care for you from this side of the grave. I've told my second-in-command that if anything ever happens to me, you'll inherit my entire network, my position, and my control. You are not alone—even without me by your side, you're never alone.

It cuts off there. No signature, no sign-off of any kind. I drop the letter into the box, and rummage around. It appears to be an entire box full to the brim of letters.

I'm looking at my own personal lingchi right here in front of me—death by a thousand cuts. Even so, I can't quite help myself. I start reading, shuffling around so that some of the letters are much older than others. Eirik returns to drop off a plate of food, and I take a break.

"Thank you," I say softly.

"You're welcome," Eirik says, executing a perfect half bow.

"You've read these?" I lift one eyebrow.

He shakes his head. "Of course not. They were all addressed to you."

"But Gideon gave you some instructions." I'm not sure what else to say. "He told you that he was giving me more than these letters, should he ever die."

Eirik smiles then. "He did."

"He considered you to be like family," I say softly. "Like a son to him?" I lift both eyebrows.

His smile widens. "Indeed. And I've got a lot to teach you about Gideon's *family,* Your Highness."

I pat the seat next to me. "Why don't you eat with me?"

"I'd like that," Eirik says. "But I need to know who I'm eating with?"

Gideon told me his name—as if it mattered. I scan my memories for the name. It was a strange one. "You can call me Nereus," I say.

Eirik spends the next few hours teaching me about the operatives within Alamecha, and the code words, the protocols, and Gideon's current plans.

And then he tells me something Gideon never did. "Did he tell you his position?" he asks as he stands to leave.

I shake my head. "You mean within the sons?"

Eirik nods.

"No. I know he's near the top, but if there's a certain phrase or title, then no."

"He always insisted there was someone he reported too," Eirik says. "But in all the time I've known Gideon, I never heard or saw any evidence of that."

I lift my eyebrows. "And?"

"We all believe he's the leader of the entire organization."

My mouth hangs open. "Which means that now. . ."

I'll never be alone. More than two hundred and fifty members right here in Ni'ihau. All of them pledged to do anything I ask—no questions. All of them trained to kill themselves before revealing the smallest piece of information. All of them dedicated to support Alamecha, but also to uplift evians and maintain the purity of the six families. Above all else.

Mother would have executed Gideon on the spot if she knew.

I should probably hand all of this information over to her right now, but for some reason, I don't. Maybe I only keep the secret because it feels like a tie to Gideon. Maybe I want to lead something, even if I'll be two times displaced from Mother's throne. Or maybe I like having some power, after so many years feeling powerless.

I spend the next day and a half filtering through the rest of Gideon's letters.

They're full of tiny pieces of information that I can use to manage the sons, to grow and expand their power. But those aren't the things that I keep returning to in my mind. No, the piece of information that keeps running through my head over and over is the identity of a procurer of rare poison. He provides the poison pills that kill the sons if they're ever caught. A poison that's undetectable and impossible to trace.

I ask Eirik about it, but he insists that Gideon handed those out and that each member has only one. "I'm not sure where he kept them, or whether he has more."

"I'd like yours."

Eirik narrows his eyes at me, clearly remembering my attempts to swim myself to death. "I respectfully refuse."

"I'll order another son," I say.

Eirik crosses his arms. "They'll also refuse you—I'll explain that it's the only thing we can do right now. We'll serve you best by refusing you this."

But after he leaves, I close my eyes and imagine the shop Gideon described—and what I can purchase there. No impaling myself on a sword, where if I'm off by a quarter inch, I'll simply heal. No swimming for hours on end to no purpose. No picking a fight with someone who will kill me—as if anyone on the island could do it. No, finding this shop is the solution I've been searching for since Eamon died. And again, Gideon has given me this solution.

Simple.

Clean.

Expedient.

The timing is difficult, what with Mother declaring war on, well, basically an entire region, but finally I find a perfect moment. Melina is preoccupied with days of back-logged petitions, and both Angel and Lyssa are stuck managing details of the stupid human Olympics, hosted in Salt Lake City.

The hardest person to evade is Eirik, who practically never leaves my side. But when I tell him I need a sabbatical, a rock climb somewhere remote, he practically sighs in relief. "I'm not going to tell Mother or Melina," I say. "It's not as if they'll notice I'm gone."

Eirik says, "Since you never leave your room?"

I can't even argue. He's right. "I know I need to live my life again. I think I need a day or two away from here to get back on track."

"Fine," he says. "When do we leave?"

I knew he was going to be hard to shake. "Tomorrow," I say. "Sunrise."

David is waiting for me an hour before sunrise, and it's a profound relief to go somewhere without a group of people following me around. If they knew where I was going and why, they might realize their services will not be required much longer.

All in all, it's relatively easy to convince David that I need to stop in Vegas on the way home. Turns out he likes slot machines—which I find hilarious. He's certainly aware of the abysmal nature of the payout.

"It's soothing," he says. "Like the world is on pause and chaos reigns."

"But you just lose money," I say.

He shrugs. "What do we need money for?"

I leave him, flushing coins down a machine in a stinky room with no windows and too much sound, and walk out the door and around the corner. My anxiety eases slightly away from the flashing lights and the blinging, clinking sounds. I dart between people and cars, several blocks out of the way.

I pass a Chevron station, and then I see it—a tiny shop with an image of a fortuneteller, her head covered in a scarf. 'Apothecary,' the signage says, just like Gideon said it would. Outside, the lines for the parking spaces are painted in a rainbow of colors, as if a child determined the decor. The curtains in the windows are red velvet, and blue check, and green corduroy, and white slubbed linen. Could it possibly look more quackpot? I wonder whether perhaps Gideon's information was wrong.

Only one way to know for sure.

I push the glass door open, triggering a chime that sounds more like modulated duck quacks. Really? I struggle to keep my head held high as I stride toward the counter at the back where a tall man has turned my direction.

His heartbeat is too slow to be human, which means he's at least half evian. His dark eyes widen when they meet mine and he gulps.

He knows who I am.

"I'm here for something." I can do this. "I'm here for poison. Something that will kill. . . someone like me."

His jaw drops and his mouth dangles open for a split second. Then he licks his lips. "I'll need the name for the account."

I smile. "Even if I pay in full?"

"It's protocol," he says.

"I go by Nereus," I say.

His face falls. "I'm very sorry for your loss."

He knew Gideon. Of course he did, and he heard that he died, which means he's connected. "Thank you."

"I'll only be a moment." He ducks through a door into the back of the shop and my heart rate spikes. Where is he going? Could he be calling someone? I listen carefully.

Less than a minute later, his head pops through the doorway, followed by his narrow shoulders. "How many doses do you need?"

If I tell him one, is that more or less suspicious? I have no idea, but if he's connected, then he knows what's going on with Alamecha. It's probably better to throw him off the truth. "Five."

His lips move without words emerging. His hands carefully measure a light green powder into a bag. "You have exactly enough here—and it's flavorless, scentless, and quick acting."

I blink. "Alright. How long will it take, then?"

"Half an hour?" He lifts his eyebrows. "If you take twice as much, it will act much faster. Moments at most." He clears his throat. "I believe Nereus typically combined doses into a single pill to make them fast acting."

"Is it painful?"

He shrugs. "I've never had the chance to ask any victims."

Of course. "Okay."

"I'll send a bill as I usually do?"

I nod. "That's great." Dave and Eirik are probably looking for me right now.

"Thank you." I hold out my hand.

When he places the small brown bag in my palm, his fingers grip mine. "Make sure you're positive before you use these. Death isn't reversible."

I nod. "Right." He can't know quite how long I've had to make this decision.

"A pleasure."

I rush back as quickly as I can, and I'm relieved when Dave is right where I left him. "Are you up or down?" I ask.

He tears his eyes away and meets mine. "Up. You?"

I laugh. "I'm broke now. Thanks a lot."

He holds out a handful of coins. "You can have some of mine."

I roll my eyes. "I think we better go."

"Oh, fine."

When we find him, Eirik is smiling too. Apparently he's quite adept at blackjack. "How was your hike?"

"Just what we needed, right David?" I ask.

David smirks. "Absolutely."

I wish Lyssa was in as good of a mood when I return. "You took a vacation?" Her eyes flash. I sit in one of my wingbacks while she scolds me, scowling like a recalcitrant child. "Your Mother isn't doing well, and neither is Melina. I've been helping as much as possible, but Melina has been stuck doing everything alone. I know Gideon's death has been hard on you, but your family needs you to engage—pay attention. We need the old Inara back."

The old Inara. I almost laugh. The one who used to slaughter indiscriminately? Or the one who felt so alone, she nearly married her best friend? Or does she mean the one who suffered quietly while her soulmate married her mother? Which old Inara am I supposed to imitate for this dead-eyed robot impression?

"Are you listening?" Lyssa throws her hands on her hips. "Right now, Melina is hearing petitions. She hates that, as you well know. And she's done it without complaining for months while you and Enora hide in your bedrooms—or take little vacations to who knows where, apparently."

Guilt flares up inside me for the first time since Eamon and Gideon's deaths. Is taking this poison the coward's way out? Anger quickly takes its place. After all, I haven't been Heir for a long time. None of this is my job. Let her yell at Mother, not me.

I waffle back and forth for days, alternating between guilt and anger, but eventually, the guilt dissipates and the familiar throbbing pain of loss settles back in to replace it. One day in early March, I wake up to the sound of a nightingale singing by my window, and waves crashing a few dozen yards beyond. When I walk outside, the sun is shining brightly, the breeze blowing gently past my hair and face.

I realize that it's the perfect day to die.

I haven't made it to breakfast with Mother or Melina in month, but it seems like a fitting place to tell them good-bye. I measure out the exact amount of a single dose in my room before I leave, and as instructed, when no one is looking, I blend it right into a spinach and strawberry smoothie in the kitchen—then I fill a glass and walk with it down the hall and into the breakfast room.

No one is there.

I pivot on my heel, irrationally irritated that my last-minute plan to say goodbye and then drink poison elegantly, simply, has been spoiled by something as prosaic as them not showing up for their typical breakfast. "Lionel, where are Mother and Melina?"

"They take breakfast in your mother's room now." He doesn't meet my eyes, probably embarrassed for me that I know nothing about what my family is doing.

I march out the door and down the hall, hesitating briefly before pushing past Mother's guards and into her room. Melina's sitting in a chair by the bed, and Mother is sitting up but leaning against her headboard.

She looks awful. Her hair is greasy. Her eyes have circles under them. Her expression is sullen. "What are you doing here?"

I drag her desk chair across the thick carpet, careful not to slosh any of my smoothie over the side. "I came to have breakfast with you."

Mother looks out the window, probably remembering our last conversation in which I accused her of killing Eamon and having someone else's children.

"I'm late already," Melina says. "I'd better go." She stands and opens her arms to me. She wants a hug. The reality of the situation hits me like a hammer in the chest. This will be the last time I see her—my almost-daughter. I set the smoothie on Mother's nightstand and wrap my arms around Melina.

Is this the first time I've hugged her since Eamon died? Her arms tighten, her face dropping into my hair and inhaling deeply. "I've missed you." Her whispered words cut like a serrated blade.

Can I do this to her? Can I leave her to face everything alone? My poor, sweet Melina. Scared, kind, generous, and so very alone. But how can I stay? I can't really help her, not with as damaged and broken as I am now. She finally releases me and I straighten, my eyes following her out, hungry for one last look at the person I love more than anyone else alive.

When I turn back, Mother's drinking my smoothie.

I snatch it out of her hands reflexively and it spills, dripping across her blankets and down onto her pristine carpet.

"Why would you do that?" She scowls at me and reaches for the half-empty glass.

I open my mouth, but I can't think of a single thing to say that would explain my actions. "I—" I swallow. "I'm sorry it made such a mess. I haven't eaten yet today, and I guess I wasn't thinking."

She blinks. "I thought you brought that for me."

I glance at the tray of food sitting next to her, utterly untouched. "What about all of that?"

She leans back against the pillows, her head resting against her headboard, her face far too pale. "None of that looks good. You can take whatever you want."

I stare at her.

"Go ahead." She shoves it toward me.

I force myself to eat a croissant, probably a delicious one. It tastes like everything else I've eaten in the past few months: cardboard. Dry, crumbly, stiff cardboard.

Mother reaches for my smoothie. "Do you mind?"

I dump it out, the entire glass, on her carpet.

She swings her legs out of the bed and stands on her feet, her eyes flashing. "What is wrong with you? You weren't even drinking it."

"It had. . . alcohol in it," I say. "That's bad for babies."

Mother's eyes widen. "Not for evians. It does nothing to us."

"Um, are you sure?"

Mother walks toward the bathroom. "Positive. If it was that easy to get rid of these babies, don't you think I'd already have done it?"

My mouth gapes.

Mother ducks inside, flushes the toilet, and then I hear her washing her hands. Then I hear a slam on the ground, and a wham against the bathroom door.

I rush toward her and fling it open. Mother's lying on the ground, her hands grasping her belly.

"What's wrong?" I ask.

But I already know.

I've killed my own sisters. It was a mistake, but it's still my fault. I can't even get my own suicide right. I lift Mother up, cradling her against my chest. I stroke her hair. "I'll go get Job. He'll know what to do."

She shakes her head. "No. Don't. Stay here."

"I really think—"

"No." Her eyes burn into mine. "God has finally answered a prayer—after nine hundred years of ignoring me. I've begged and begged him to take this burden from me."

Oh, Mother.

"I can't do it." Tears stream down her face. "Every time I close my eyes, I kill a baby. Every single time. I wake in a cold sweat, panicking. I can't do it, Inara. Don't make me do it. Let God kill them for me, the babies who never should have been born to begin with."

I want to ask her how, I want to know the truth, even if it hurts. Eamon swore to me he wouldn't—but I can't even think about it. "You don't really want them to die."

"I can't have twins." Her voice is sad. "You know what happens. It has happened one hundred percent of the times that an empress has spared them both." She clutches her belly again and screams, biting down on her own sleeve to keep from making too much noise and alerting her guards. "You can't tell anyone," she whispers. "Please."

But the cramps recede, and it seems the babies are fine. I help her up and back to her bed. "You seem quite unwell," I say. "Please let me grab Job."

She shakes her head. "I want another smoothie tomorrow, exactly like that one you gave me today. Promise me."

I want to take my dose back in my room and be done with it, but I can't, not now, not after watching Mother. Not after hugging Melina. I can't abandon them.

But am I helping Mother to keep the babies alive? Or would she really be better if they were to die? For the first time in a very long time, I drop to my knees and pray. I beg God to tell me what to do. I know I can't dose Mother with a full dose—it would kill her. But would a sequence of half doses allow Mother to live and the babies die? I should have asked the guy in Vegas for a phone number.

Maybe he would know.

I wrestle with it all day, unsure what to do, unsure how to proceed. In the end, I decide to leave it in God's hands. I make another smoothie, just like the last, but this time with only a half dose, and I take it to Mother's room. She drinks the entire thing, and again, the cramps incapacitate her.

But the babies survive.

"Please bring me the same thing tomorrow," Mother begs.

I tell her no over and over, but the next day, I bring another.

Again and again, God spares the babes. In what shape, I don't know, but they don't die as Mother wishes.

But after a week of smoothies, I flat out refuse to bring anymore. Clearly God wants these babies to survive, if he exists at all, and I am down to only one more dose.

And this one is mine.

I know that if I meet Mother or Melina for a meal, or if I go to say goodbye, I'll lose my resolve again. I don't make a smoothie, I don't prepare something special. I simply dump it into a glass of water and stir it up. I bring the glass to my mouth when Frederick bursts through my door, shouting.

"Come quick! Enora needs you!"

I drop the glass and it shatters on the ground.

When I turn to face him, he stumbles backward. "How dare you barge into my room like that?"

"Enora is dying," he whispers. "She needs you right now."

I go, and I stand with Mother, defending the babies even when it breaks Melina's heart, because I realize it's the only way to give Melina what I've never been able to do for myself: freedom. From court, from Mother's iron grasp, and the freedom to love.

It's also the only way to keep her from hating herself. And since I'm the queen of hating myself, I know just how that feels. I could never allow that to happen to Melina, never. So I side with my mother, against my sister, and I set her free.

I hope that she finds all the joy I never had.

21

2020

I've been summoned, which always annoys me, but if Judica and Chancery are in another of their stupid fights. . . I swear, a swift kick to Judica's backside and a little extra torture training for Chancery would solve most of their issues. Mother acts like it's an unknowable problem, but she caused it by coddling one and neglecting the other. I'm not sure how much longer I can bite my tongue.

Mother's guard opens the door for me before I even need to knock, and I breeze through. I scan the room quickly, from the sitting area that also serves as a convenient office, to the bedroom. Mother isn't on the bed, or at the desk, or at one of the chairs.

Where could she be?

My heart accelerates for a moment, and I consider shouting for the guards. But then it occurs to me. . .could she be in the vault? Why would she call for me to come when she's inside her vault? I walk around the corner, noticing that the vault is cracked open. I step toward it and stumble over a book.

It's brown leather, finely bound. When I pick it up, it

265

flips open to the last page written naturally—which makes sense. It's the place where the pages have recently been forced apart. I don't mean to read Mother's journal, but a word catches my eye and I can't look away.

Baby.

My breath catches in my throat. Why is she writing about a baby? Whose baby? I really hope that Judica and that heart-stoppingly handsome boyfriend of hers. . . My eyes shift to the date—yesterday—and I begin reading almost involuntarily.

I'm not being poisoned after all. My fatigue, my appetite shifts and my body aches have an explanation. A happy one, in fact. Against all odds, something strange and wonderful has happened.

I'm pregnant.

I want to tell the father, but I don't know how he'll take it, and then I'll have to explain too many other things. I might be better off letting him assume it isn't his, like I did the last time. Either way, I'm more optimistic about the future of Alamecha than I have been for a long time.

It sounds terrible, but I'm most excited about this baby for the hope that it might heal things between Judica and Chancery. Their anger and inability to get along pains me more deeply than any other wound of my long life, including Althuselah's death. I would give almost anything to repair their relationship. A new Heir would free them both and clean up the fallout from my decision to spare Chancery's life.

If it's a girl, I'm going to name her Sotiris, because she could be their salvation.

The page ends, and my mouth goes utterly dry.

I should close this journal right now. I shouldn't know any of this, not until Mother tells me. But when I lower it, the page turns over and I realize it wasn't the last page. It was the second to last.

My biggest concern is that if I tell him about this baby, he'll figure out that the twins were his too. He might forgive me for

266

that, but I doubt Inara would. She suspected eighteen years ago—I can't face the prospect of telling her what I've done.

The guilt, oh, the guilt. It eats at me still.

The guilt? It eats at her still?

Mother wouldn't suffer from guilt about being unfaithful to Eamon. It's not in her nature. But. . .if she had him killed—if she fell in love with someone else. The guilt over that kind of decision might prevent her from marrying whomever fathered Judica and Chancery.

It wasn't Eamon.

Relief washes over me. For nearly twenty years I've harbored so much anger at Eamon for betraying me, again, for telling me he was going to leave my mother and then fathering more children with her.

Except he didn't.

I wish, even more than usual, that I could hold him close, that I could apologize for all the anger I've felt, all the blame I've heaped on him that he never deserved. If only he hadn't died, he could have told me. . .

If he hadn't died. Just as Mother discovered that she was carrying the children of another man. I swallow. I need to calm down—it's all conjecture, wild, unfounded conjecture.

The guilt eats at her still.

I suspected back then, with far, far less to go on—but now. Could Mother have killed Eamon? My hands begin to tremble, my fingers clench, anger I long since released raising its ugly head. Did Mother murder Eamon to keep him from decrying her children as not his? Did she eliminate him because he had become a nuisance? Or because she loved someone else?

I realize I've crumpled the last page and the ones that follow beyond repair. In fact, they've torn away from the binding near the top. Oh, no. No, no, no. Mother's going to notice that for sure.

I hear a rustling from the nearby vault—I'm lucky I didn't bring Brutus with me this morning. He would have rounded the corner and woken her up already with his wet nose. But surely Mother has heard me now—she knows I'm here. I tear the crumpled pages out and stuff them in my pocket. I'll burn them. If she asks, I'll deny any knowledge of it. I tuck the book behind my back.

I round the corner, my features schooled to calm, my heartbeat steady as the tide.

The noise I heard must have been her shifting—she's asleep, her head pillowed on her bent arm, a parchment beneath her. I carefully place her journal in the center of the table.

And I clear my throat.

She jumps, sits up, and wipes her eyes. "Inara."

"You asked for me," I say.

She nods. "Yes, I'm so sorry. I didn't sleep well last night, and it's catching up to me."

She's lying again. She's exhausted. . . from being pregnant. Oh, how I wish she'd tell me the truth. I want to shake it out of her. *Did you kill Eamon?* I want to apply pressure until she confesses.

I step backward. "I'm sorry I came in. I was concerned when I couldn't find you."

She stands up and brushes off her pants. "Of course you were, but I'm fine." She smiles at me, but it's forced.

"Well, did you need something?"

"Right," she says. "Yes, I wanted to talk to you about the guest list for my party, and how to mitigate the risk that our guests will attack one another with a brilliant seating chart."

We move into her office, and within half an hour, we've hammered out the skeleton of the seating chart. "I think Larena and I can drop in buffer guests around this," she says.

268

I stand up too abruptly and her eyes widen. "I've got a meeting. . ."

"Right," she says. "Go right ahead. We can talk later."

The rest of the day passes in a blur—robotic responses, only half-hearing what anyone says. Mother killed Eamon—any way I look at it, she must have. Or at least, it's a very real possibility that she ordered his death. I stood aside when she married him. I looked the other way when she treated him badly, belittled him, cut him down, and diminished him in every way possible. I sent Gideon to protect him—and that means her plans killed him too.

I gave her everything that ever mattered to me, and she burned it all down.

Wrath.

That's what I'm feeling right now. Rage, fury, seething anger. How could she have done it? And the man she betrayed him with is still here—still creating more children in her belly. Her life keeps right on turning, and I stand by her side, supporting her, buoying her up, like the world's most pathetic dupe.

"I've got to go to Vegas tomorrow to pick up the new ovens," Angel says, "but I won't be gone long."

My head snaps toward her. Vegas. The Apothecary. The last time she was pregnant, she begged me for smoothies. Could I really make her one with purpose this time? Could I kill my own mother?

"I need to go," I say. "I wanted to talk to Varnier about a few modifications to my dress, and he says he's in Vegas opening a new store there. I could have him come here, but it might be nice to get away."

"I'd be happy to share a jet," Angel says. "There are about four others coming along too, for various things. Who knew Vegas would be so popular a destination?"

I nod, unable to say anything else.

Can I really kill Mother? The words run through my

269

head over and over for the entire time I pack, and the entire time I sit frozen on the flight. I stare out the window blankly. Every time I decide that I can't, Eamon's face flashes in my mind. His hand brushing against my jaw. The smell of his hair. The beauty of his smile.

Or when I shove those memories away, others crowd in to fill the void. Gideon's dimpled smile. The saucy look on his face when he turns to look at me over his shoulder from the back of one of his beloved stallions.

Mother never pays, not for any of her decisions. It's time she pays, for once.

But when I close my eyes, I remember other things too.

Mother tucking me in as a child, kissing my head. Teaching me how to fight at hand to hand. Teaching me how to play sovereignty. Dancing with Dad. Swimming with me in the ocean. Kissing my nose. Swinging me around in circles. Holding me when I couldn't stop sobbing after Dad died. I recall how often she stared out the window, broken-hearted, only half alive.

Can I kill someone I love with all my heart? Someone who has given her entire life for Alamecha, for our family and for me? She didn't realize Eamon was my heart's desire. If she had, would it have changed her actions?

By the time we land, I know what I need to do. I meet with Varnier to preserve my cover, and then I duck out and head for the Apothecary. Only, he's gone. There's a gourmet pet food store where his shop previously stood. Who in the world buys gourmet pet food? My feet move ahead of their own volition, and a little bell jangles when I enter. Surreal. The frame of the building is the same, burned perfectly into my memory in every particular, but the interior couldn't be less similar.

"Would you like to take home a bag of custom dog treat samples?" A perky redhead with bright blue eye shadow holds a bag toward me.

"Samples?"

"Yes, we make them all here on site. Duck, turkey, beef, and lamb."

My lip curls.

Her frozen smile wavers. A cat rubs against my leg.

"Or maybe you'd like to check out our selection of cat toys. They're all locally sourced."

I shove the cat away, and the smile slides right off her face. "What I need," I say, "is to know to where the store that used to be here has relocated."

"Um, I've only been here for two years. I'm not sure what store was here before that."

I grit my teeth.

She perks up. "Do you recall the name?"

"Apothecary," I say flatly.

"That's it?" She frowns. "Well, it's worth a try." She whips out her phone and starts tapping away. Then she flips it around to face me. "Look, could this be it?"

The image in front of me looks entirely different than the place I visited. It's tasteful and bright. It looks more like an Apple store than the horrible, seedy shop I visited twenty years ago. "Uh, probably not, but thanks."

"Alright, well, if you decide to check it out, it's only seven blocks that way." She points.

It's not like I have any other leads. Rat poison won't do a thing to an evian. Eirik took over managing the procurement of the poison doses for the Sons, and I can't very well ask him for poison right before Enora. . . This is my only option. Gideon was right that one of the main tenets of the Sons is loyalty to the monarch. If I poison my mother, they won't follow me—not after that.

The stupid cat practically chases me to the door, and if I let the door close on its tail, well, at least I didn't bring my mastiff Brutus. He'd have eaten it in one snap.

I move quickly toward the shiny, bright Apothecary

shop that can't possibly be the right place. Once I reach the front, a growing certainty that I'm in the wrong place steals over me, but I force myself to step inside anyway.

And at the back of the light and bright store, set up more like a modern pharmacy, is the same man from before. Narrow shoulders, pinched face. He hasn't changed at all—which tells me he's likely full evian. Banished from somewhere, if I had to guess.

He swallows, his Adam's apple bobbing, when he sees me. "You're back."

I stride quickly to the back of the store. "I am."

"You were satisfied last time." He doesn't ask a question, but his eyebrows rise at the end, as if he's asking for confirmation.

Not really, but it wasn't his fault. "I was." Well enough, anyway.

"And what can I do for you today?" he asks. "We have a very nice paralytic in that you would not believe—"

As if I'd ever need a paralytic, with as fast as I move. "I'd like something that will kill a baby without killing the mother, and another dose of poison—a full adult dose. I want them both sourced from somewhere strange— untraceable. Nothing that we've ever used before." I glare pointedly. "For the Sons."

He opens his mouth as if to argue.

My hand shifts to the hilt of my sword. "You know what I love about Vegas? There aren't many places left in America where you can wear a sword anymore. But here everyone assumes it's ornamental, and that I'm working for some kind of Medieval performing group."

"I have something new that might work. It's pricey—"

I glare harder.

"Right, well, let me get those for you."

He disappears into the back again, and I draw my sword

272

and pretend to examine it while he's gone. When he returns with two separate containers, he freezes.

I sheathe my sword again. "It's hard to find time to clean the blade these days. Life moves at a mile a minute, doesn't it?"

"Yes, Your Highness," he says.

"Oh, I think you're mistaken," I say. "I'm not royal. My name is Nereus."

He gulps. "Of course." When he names his price, a quick inhale from me has him backpedaling. "Costs are only going up, you know." He grabs a box from under the counter. "But look, I'll throw in one of these paralytics for free. It's quite effective, really. Once you try it, you'll be back, I assure you. Just light the fuse and it'll fill the entire room, paralyzing anyone who inhales it. The antidote is in the box as well, clearly marked. It'll prevent the paralytic from impacting you as long as you take it twenty minutes before. Or it'll release the victims from the effects, but that's slower."

He spends another few moments going through the minutiae of the other two poisons as well.

"Where did you even find these?" I lift one eyebrow. "Is there an entire industry for this stuff?"

He shakes his head. "Very, very few of us have the skill required to harvest and prepare anything that will be effective, and all of these poisons come from deep in the ocean. They're extremely difficult to locate. You don't need to worry—I only sell to legitimate members of the royal families."

Very reassuring.

I spin on my boot heel and march out. I reach the Varnier shop just as Angel turns the corner. She waves at me and smiles, and I walk through the door and meet her on the sidewalk. "Oven details all in order?"

"Oh, yes. These are real beauties."

"If I ever get excited about an oven," I say, "you have my permission to slap me."

She rolls her eyes. "Once you've eaten the soufflés I have planned, you'll slap your mama."

"What does that phrase even mean?" I ask.

"Oh you know, it's a Cajun phrase, I think, from Louisiana. They say it to indicate that something is so good, it makes you go berserk and do something like slapping your own mother."

My mother, for whom I just purchased poison. And the word berserk is an odd coincidence, too. I eye Angel carefully for a moment, but she moves along so quickly, it seems that neither phrase held a double meaning. In fact, when we return, it appears that no one suspects a thing.

Including my mother, whose baby I'm about to kill.

🦋 22 🦋

2020

Mother, understandably, plans to spend the entire morning training Chancery. I'm still shocked that she reacted to Mother's ring. I never put much faith in any part of the old prophecy rumors being true—and now that I've heard it, I really wouldn't have. It's so vague that it could mean most anything. I always assumed, when I heard rumors about 'one queen to reunite the families,' that Mahalesh or one of her daughters made it up, to keep all the other families on their toes. I mean, every rabbit runs faster with a carrot dangled in front of its face, right?

But I wait just outside the bunker for her. "Hey—last minute party questions."

She waves Chancery ahead. "I'll meet you in the courtyard."

"Okay." Chancy smiles at me as she leaves.

"That girl is far too kind to rule," I say. "The piranhas will consume her immediately."

"That's where you come in," Mother says.

If she actually rules. I want to ask about the baby. I want to accuse her and have it out, but I can't quite bring myself to do that. "I'll do anything I can to help her, of course."

"You always do," Mother says. "Some days I can't believe I've been so lucky—you never grew bitter after being displaced. You stayed, keeping your finger in the holes in the dike as they appeared. I can't even count the number of times you've saved us."

As if being displaced was the greatest wrong I ever endured. I want to laugh out loud. For someone who knows everything, Mother sees nothing. "I am pretty amazing."

"I don't tell you enough." Mother's eyes well with tears.

Pregnancy hormones are beastly, it seems. "I know you appreciate me," I say.

"What did you need to ask me?"

"It's about the jets," I say.

Mother sighs. "What now?"

"We allowed each family two," I say.

"Let me guess. More than two are hailing from each family?"

I snort. "Of course."

"Okay, well, the third jet in each family, no matter which guests are on it, will land on the far landing strip. They can hike to the palace."

"Three miles?" I lift my eyebrows.

She frowns. "Fine, ask Larena to arrange for transportation. But if Melamecha's jet could be *accidentally* diverted over there. . ."

I laugh. "I'll see what I can do."

"Thanks."

"Speaking of Melamecha," I say. "I was reviewing some of Gideon's things the other day, and I realized that she never sent over signet rings from either of them."

"She did," Mother says. "Or I've got Eamon's, anyway."

My nostrils flare. "I didn't realize you cared enough to keep it." Too bitter, far, far too bitter. I force a smile.

"We fought a lot, but I did care for him." Mother pins me with her patented stare. "Where is this coming from?"

"Melina was asking me about him the other day," I lie, "and I realized you never talk about him. Don't you miss him?"

I haven't talked to Melina in far too long—it hurts too much as she becomes more like her father every day—but Mother doesn't know that.

Her eyebrows draw together. "I do. Of course I do, but. . ." She looks at the ground. "I dreaded this conversation for years, and you never asked me about it."

"About what?" My breath catches in my throat.

She finally looks up at me. "There's a reason that you and Gideon never—" She turns away again.

"Never what?"

I've never seen Mother this nervous. Never. "Eamon loved someone other than me."

My heart stalls out. Did she know?

"I kept trying to think of a way to tell you, and at first I wasn't sure, but it grew unbearably obvious with time."

Oh, no.

Mother takes my hand. "Eamon and Gideon were. . ."

Wait, what? She can't be serious.

"Uh, I don't think so."

Her face is grim. "Can you imagine if that ever got out? I thought when you left for that whole Cuban missile debacle that you and Gideon might. . . But when he came back, he was in love with someone else. Once I realized that's when the changes in him began, I figured out that there was something between them, but it was too late. I'd already married Eamon."

I have no idea how to respond. Mother attributed all Eamon's and Gideon's strangeness about our situation as *their* being in love with one another. No wonder she never realized that Eamon and I. . .

"I think they made each other happy, but I found that it made my life almost unbearable. When they left together, on such a dangerous mission. . ." Mother's eyes meet mine, and there's so much guilt in them—guilt I never realized the depth of until now.

When they left together.

"It was an opportunity you couldn't pass up," I say, frozen in place. I can't look at her, but I can't look away. I stand, transfixed, hoping she confesses. Desperately hoping there's nothing to confess.

"In so many ways, their deaths made my life simpler, but I know losing Gideon caused you almost unbearable pain." Her face falls, and she squeezes my hand and lets it go. "I've never seen you more. . . broken, but I think it was the best thing that could have happened to us. Truly."

"You'd prefer that Eamon *died* than that he loved someone else? Really?" I hold my breath. Deny it. Deny it. Say you'd have let him go.

Mother's eyes widen. "Think of the damage it would have done to the family for him to leave. Think about how much it would have hurt Melina."

"Less than his death," I say. "Surely."

"My greatest regret was the pain Gideon's loss caused you," Mother whispers. "I truly believe Melina is better off without the unrest and conflict he caused us." The guilt in her eyes is so deep and so raw that I finally see the truth. She had Eamon and Gideon killed. It removed a problem—their insistence on delaying her revenge on the terrorists—and it freed her at the same time. How did I ignore this for so long? How much did my love for her blind me?

"I actually think that you and I have done the best anyone could do for Judica and Chancery. Don't you think so?"

Not Eamon's children—which he would have surely objected to, had he known about them. I nod, mute.

"Of course I'm sad when I think of Eamon," she says.

"Are you?" This time, I'm the one glaring.

Mother looks away, but not before I see the guilt, still plain on her face. Judging from her tone, she doesn't even regret it. My only question is whether the lover had anything to do with it.

When I go by the kitchen to pick up my breakfast, galvanized by our conversation, I don't hesitate. I sprinkle the ocean-derived powder across the fried eggs, knowing they're Mother's favorites and Chancery won't eat any. Luckily, the powder is so fine that it dissolves almost instantly. When she loses the newest baby from this man, whoever he is, hopefully they'll both suffer a fraction of what I've suffered.

A twinge of regret slows me on my way out of the kitchen, but then her words run through my brain. *I truly believe Melina is better off without the unrest and conflict he caused us.* I squash down any feelings of remorse—this is quid pro quo—and it's not as if I'm harming an actual person like she did. That baby is barely a speck at this point—more an idea than a living entity.

Part of me wants to hover—to make sure Mother actually eats the eggs. Or maybe to stop her from doing it. Which is exactly why I can't sit and watch. I'll lose my nerve. I gobble down my breakfast and head over to help Larena with the party details, which are completely unraveling as they always do the day of the event.

We handle canapé snafus, staff squabbles, and storage of exotic gifts. But a few issues require Mother's intervention. It's the excuse I need to check on her.

I bang on the door instead of knocking, and Larena looks at me sideways. I might be a little overly anxious. Is this how Mother felt after she ordered Eamon and Gideon killed? I'm sure she felt far worse—because she can make another baby—but I'll never get them back. I thought this through thoroughly, and now that it's happening, I need to calm down. The decision has already been made.

"Enter," Mother says.

Brutus trots through the door before I do, but Larena and I walk in side by side.

"Is everything alright?" Mother asks.

That's what I want to know, too. I refuse to glance at her still flat belly. I can't let her know that I know anything, but looking at her face—it's almost grey, and her eyes are tired. She must have consumed some of it at least.

"Adika and Venagra are wearing the same color and they're upset," I say. "Shamecha's hiking oil prices and Adika has raised their tariffs, which I suspect has something to do with it. But either way, Adika's insisting you loan something to Venagra. I'd normally pull something from your closet, but it all smells of smoke. If I hand over something that smells, they'll ply me with questions."

"Which we couldn't answer even if we wanted to," Larena mutters. "Since you won't tell us what really happened."

"In due time," Mother says, "but for now, I'd better go. Venagra will fit into something of Chancy's just fine."

Which is our cue to wait for her outside. We duck outside, waiting for her to be ready to address her guests in person. It takes her a moment to pry Chancery-the-koala off her leg, but eventually, she strides out the door.

Her step isn't very energetic, and for the first time, I worry.

When she was pregnant last time and I poisoned her by accident, I kept waiting for the worst. It never came. What if something went wrong here, too? What if I got the dosage confused? What if she didn't eat it all—or worse, ate too much?

It takes a ridiculous amount of time to satisfy Adika and

Venagra, and Larena escorts them out of the small conference room. "

"I need your help," Mother says. "I've decided to change the Heirship documents to name Chancery."

Judica is not going to take this well. "That's a huge decision."

Mother leans forward, her elbows braced on the table. Her heart rate is accelerated.

"Are you okay?"

She swallows. "I had intended to tell Chancery this first, as she'll be the most impacted by it, but I'm concerned and I need your help right now." She looks up and meets my gaze. "I'm pregnant, and I confirmed by blood test this morning that it's a girl."

My jaw drops. "Job knows?"

Mother shakes her head. "No one does. I submitted a blood sample under another name—it's a long story, but this is what matters." Her voice drops to a whisper. "I'm worried there's something very wrong."

Oh, Mother, do you suspect? "What do you mean?"

"You know that Job believes I was poisoned during my pregnancy with the twins."

I shake my head. "I hadn't heard."

"He took blood samples and hair samples and both returned positive readings in my body for trace elements of poison."

"Are you serious?"

"He claims that's the reason the twins are as strong as they are—and as talented. You must have noticed their speed and agility are off the charts. They heal faster than most evians, too, faster than me by a hair as well. That shouldn't happen, given that they're a generation further from Eve."

I blink. I hadn't actually noticed.

"When I found out I was pregnant, I—" She stands up,

her chair screeching across the floor. She begins pacing by the window, but she's clearly not admiring the view.

"What?" My stomach sinks, and I wonder what she's getting at, exactly.

She stops and places one hand over her belly. "I thought that if surviving poison strengthened them. . .I would give this child the same boost."

Oh, no. No, no, no. "Tell me you didn't poison yourself." I stand up and race to where she's standing. "Mother, you've looked tired lately, exhausted even." And more than that, I gave her what amounts to a 2/3 dose of poison. Something an evian could withstand, but a fetus couldn't.

But an evian already weakened by poison? Adrenaline floods my body. I want to run around the palace, or leap to the top of the ceiling, or slice something into small pieces.

I want to take it back—I want to go back in time and unsprinkle those eggs.

"I'm worried that perhaps someone else meant me ill, too," she whispers. "I decided today to discontinue using the poison, but I feel worse, not better. I'm not sure what to do—but I fear that my rash actions combined with an attempt on my life. . ." Her eyes are full of fear.

I swallow. "We need to get you to Job immediately. He can pump your stomach." Or give her an antidote if I confess to what I gave her.

Her hands grip mine tightly. "I'm not afraid of death. I've lived a long life, and in spite of some hard decisions, I've done my best to steer the family in the right direction. No, I'm afraid for Chancery and Judica."

"We need to get to Job right now."

She shakes her head. "I need to assemble the Council to finalize the Heirship papers I drew up and signed. That's all that matters right now."

I practically growl. "What will that accomplish? If you die today, whoever you name—formal or not—will just be challenged by the other. Think, Mother. You mustn't die. Come with me."

Mother scowls. "If this is the end, there's nothing Job can do to stop it. With as smart as we are, the one thing we haven't been able to improve upon is the healing of our perfect bodies." She claws at her stomach and winces, and this time her eyes on mine are desperate. "I've felt a lot of things in nine centuries, but with the prophecy being fulfilled, and this inexplicable pain—I think my time is running out quickly, Inara. Help me accomplish this last task, please."

I wrap one arm around her waist and do the math. It's been hours since she ate those fried eggs, but we have to try. Maybe Job can reverse it. "First we see Job, and then I'll gather the Council in the middle of your party while your guests gossip about where you've gone. Deal?"

Her lips flatten into a line. "Fine, but I have to drop off Chancery's dress first. Perhaps the twins can keep the guests happy while we get this document executed." Duchess, Mother's Great Pyrenees, scrambles to her feet to follow me and Brutus out the door.

I grab the gown on the way out, and we navigate through the halls to her room, and through the adjoining door to drop off Chancery's dress. Mother sets the dress on Chancery's bed carefully and opens the door to the hall, but she freezes when voices pour through the doorway.

"I'm going to challenge you," Chancery says.

"You're challenging me?" Judica laughs, but it's not a happy sound. "Do it, I beg you. I've wanted to challenge you for years, but Mother would never forgive me. If you challenge me, I'll finally be rid of you, and it won't even be my fault."

Mother closes her eyes and shudders, seeming to be suffering from more pain than she was before. I wonder how much of it is physical.

"Fine," Chancery says. "I, Chancery Divinity—"

Mother steps into the hall. "Would you break my heart, Chancy? On my birthday? My two beautiful daughters at one another's throats?"

This is going to take some time. I can't wait, and Mother won't listen. I need to find Job myself. I escape through Mother's room and race down the halls, Brutus' toenails clicking on the marble floor behind me. He's not in his lab. He's not in the kitchen. No one has seen him.

I swear under my breath.

"Is something wrong?" Balthasar asks.

"Mother looks. . . tired," I say. "I'm worried about her. I want Job to take a look before the party."

Balthasar points at the clock. "Since it starts in less than fifteen minutes, I wouldn't count on it. He's likely in the ballroom, though. He's never late to big gatherings. As the only doctor on Ni'ihau, he's usually prepared for any sort of fight that might break out."

Of course he is.

I barely acknowledge Balthasar, nodding my head in thanks, and sprint around him and out the door. But by the time I reach the ballroom, Job has already found Mother.

She's lying on the ground, and Job is slamming his closed fist against her chest repeatedly.

"What's going on?" I race to her side.

Job doesn't stop the rhythmic shoving. "Her heart has stopped." His words are wooden, his movements stiff. "I have no idea why." I've never seen Job look so wrecked, not in the two hundred years I've known him.

I rock back on my heels. "It's poison," I whisper.

His head whips around. "Why do you say that?"

"What else could it be?" I ask. "She was perfectly healthy a few days ago."

"She's looked. . . off to me lately." Job presses his lips to hers and breathes into them.

"What are you doing?"

"It's not usually effective on evians," he says. "It's a human emergency measure, but I don't know what else to do."

I open my mouth to tell him what I gave her and explain that she was also poisoning herself, but I realize how that will sound. They'll execute me, and it won't bring her back. Nothing can, not now, not if he's trying to save her with human medical techniques. What have I done?

I've killed my own mother, that's what.

I stand up and stumble backward. An exhalation next to me reminds me how many people are here, all of them watching in fascinated horror. Mother would hate this—every single thing about it. My eyes scan the room frenetically, pausing to glare at a gloating Analessa and a smug Adika.

"Is there any chance what you're doing might bring her back?" I whisper.

Job stops.

That's my answer.

Job stands and backs up until he's standing shoulder to shoulder with me. "There couldn't have been a worse time for this to happen."

He doesn't know the half of it.

Frederick drops to his knees, his blade drawn, his face a mask of grief. His eyes stare at Mother, as if he's unable to look away. He must blame himself. I know what that feels like, but in my case, it's legitimate. Oh, Mother. Mother! Why would you ingest poison? Why? I wanted her to hurt —I didn't want her to die!

When Chancery walks in, I expect a reaction like Frederick's, or perhaps Job, who's rocking back and forth on his heels soundlessly. But it's worse for her—so much worse. Something inside of her snaps when she sees Mother on the floor. She's utterly unprepared for this, for everything, really. It's never been more clear to me than it is right now, watching her completely insensate, rocking over Mother's body and sobbing hysterically, that she is incapable of ruling our family as she is right now, and yet that was Mother's wish. Mother would have prepared her—of that I am sure—had I not cut her life short unwittingly.

Which means it falls to me to right this wrong and somehow make peace between Judica and Chancery, however unlikely that seems.

The next few hours are horrific, and I deserve every minute of pain. I caused all of this with my anger, my refusal to forgive, and my thirst for revenge. Mother's hubris didn't help, but ultimately, the fault lies with me. It takes every ounce of my strength to keep Judica from beheading poor Chancery on the spot. It makes me wonder whether Judica's emotions don't run nearly as deep as her twin's. She's fierce, but she's not bloodthirsty, whatever Chancery may believe.

When we're hurting, that's when we're at our most dangerous, to ourselves and to others. It's not lost on me that my pain over discovering what Mother unwittingly did to me is what caused me to act, but I'm not at all sure that it excuses my actions—any of them. I advise Chancery, offering to flee with her, but she turns me down.

She wants me to stay here—to take on the impossible task of somehow smoothing things over with Judica—of making peace. Mother would have wanted me to try, so I do, but when I wave goodbye to Chancery's departing jet, my heart is heavy. It feels like we've been on a collision course with utter ruin ever since I read Mother's journal.

I wait all day for a summons from Judica, but it never comes. When I ask around, I discover she has interrogated Angel, spent time with Job and Balthasar, and set her guards to work.

Which means it's only a matter of time before someone

tracks down the poison. I didn't want to have to do this but it seems I have no choice. I call one of Gideon's operatives —located in San Francisco so no one in Vegas will recognize her. The Sons of Gilgamesh boast a surprising number of women.

"This is Nereus," I say softly, knowing my phone number is blocked. Many older evians struggle with technology, but only because they choose to. Most of it is simple science and mathematics, so it's easy enough to stay on the cutting edge, and the entire process has only been made easier by the advent of the Internet.

The slight gasp on the other end of the phone is satisfying.

"I have an order for you."

"I had no idea you were a woman," she whispers.

"Does that please you?"

"I suppose that it shouldn't," she says. "But I find that it does."

Since I took over Gideon's network of zealots, I've contemplated eliminating their defining rhetoric over and over, but it's the reason they all joined. If I remove their defining motivation, the entire network will crumble. "I am as interested as anyone else in the purity of the evian race— and in ensuring that we maintain our world dominance and positions of strength."

"Of course you are," she says. "What do you need me to do?"

"It's a big ask, but I've heard that you're the best at precisely these types of issues."

"I'm devoted to the cause, if that's what you mean, one thousand percent."

For the love. "I need you to kill Vincent Bertram." I give her the address of the apothecary. "There can be no evidence of the hit, and if there is, if anyone finds you, you know how to handle it."

"I carry my pill at all times. No one will ever know the Sons of Gilgamesh had anything to do with his death." I suppose Eirik will have to find a new supplier of the stupid suicide pills after this. I ought to feel guilt over the man's death—he only ever filled the orders exactly as I asked—but I can't mourn someone who knowingly provides methods by which evians can poison others.

It's unfair for me to blame him for Mother's death, and yet, it's easier than accepting the full blame myself. Even so, I don't sleep well. Nightmares of Mother begging for her life, and Vincent protesting that it wasn't his fault plague me every time I successfully drift off.

The next morning, my summons from Judica comes bright and early as if she's also punishing me. Pauline and Tarben insist on escorting me, even though I don't need them. I walk calmly behind Roman, but when we turn the corridor headed for the Heir's chambers, I'm surprised.

"She's meeting me in. . . her room?" I ask.

Roman turns toward me but doesn't slow down. "She should have been left as empress, but she's keeping her word to Chancery—not stepping in to claim the position of empress for a week."

Interesting.

When I walk into Judica's room, she's just finishing her breakfast, stuffing the last bite of a fried egg in her mouth. I will not flinch, and my heart rate will not spike. Surely it's a coincidence. Judica, unlike Chancery, has always loved fried eggs.

"Your Majesty," I say.

The corner of her mouth curls up. "I imagine you say the same thing to Chancery."

"I stayed here," I say, more calmly than I feel.

"But you've always done exactly as Mother wished—and I hear she made Angel swear to serve the family before she died. I imagine she insisted you do something similar—and

288

with her changing the heirship and declaring for Chancery, it's pretty clear she felt at the end that my sister was the better choice. You are one of the few people who knows the truth of what changed her mind."

I sit down on one of the wooden chairs in Judica's receiving room so that we're on eye level. "I do know what changed her mind. I also know that all her reasons for selecting you for the past seventeen years still exist. And you're also my family, you know."

"That's not an answer—which is as clever as always. You're so much like Mother that it almost hurts. I kept meaning to call you to see me yesterday, but I couldn't face you. I find that even now, with all the preparation I did, I'm still not ready to stare at your identical face."

"We're all suffering right now," I say.

"But I killed her, right?" Judica lifts her chin, daring me to argue the point. "Isn't that what everyone thinks? I'm not entitled to my pain, as the perpetrator of her death."

"I'm not Chancery—I don't believe it was you, but even if you *did* kill Mother because you believed she was making catastrophic mistakes, it doesn't mean her death doesn't pain you." Keeping my eyes from welling with tears is one of the hardest things I've ever done. I know for a fact that Judica didn't kill Mother, and I know that even if she had, she'd be hurting—because it's all my fault, and I feel flayed wide open. I decide to tell her, to confess. Of all the people in my life, Judica is the one person who might understand. "Actually—"

"If it were genuine, I would appreciate your support," Judica says, "but I called you here to explain something. It gives me no pleasure to confront you with this, but I know you stayed to spy for Chancery, and I can't allow you to succeed."

"Excuse me?" My eyebrows shoot up my forehead.

"You love me, just as Mother loved me, but I'm not a

fool. I know you both preferred her, and I know that in light of the ring's reaction to her, you stayed to ensure that she takes the throne, not me."

I have no idea what to say.

"Mother was making a huge mistake, and I plan to rectify it. I can't allow you or anyone else, however well intentioned, to stop me. Chancery would destroy Alamecha within a month, no matter what some prophecy from the time of Eve or Mahalesh might say."

"I agree that she's not ready."

Judica frowns. "You do."

"I do."

"But you want to place her on the throne anyway."

I fold my arms. "Mother wanted that, and I won't lie and say that I don't want to honor her wishes, but I'm not Chancery's spy." It's only partially untrue. I'm serving Chancery far more as diplomat than I could as a spy.

"I don't believe you."

"You don't have to believe me," I say. "But you'll be costing yourself the advice I could have given if you lock me up. Even so, it's your decision to make. I won't struggle if you want to send me below with Angel."

Her eyelids tremble slightly. She has outstanding control for someone her age. "What are you offering to do for me?"

"I'll tell you what Mother would have told you when you have questions or need advice. I'll help you find Mother's killer." The last part is a bald-faced lie—one of the boldest I've ever told. I've never felt quite so boxed in over the course of my life. How can I possibly confess now?

How can I not?

She doesn't seem to notice I've said a word out of place. "When Chancery comes back, she'll discover you advised me," Judica says. "Are you at all worried she'll defeat me?"

"I think Chancery's odds of defeating you are very slim

indeed," I confess. "You've always been the stronger fighter, the less distracted combatant, and the more savage contender. But even if she wins, I'm not worried about having advised you, as long as you make it look, convincingly, like you and I were not allies."

"What does that mean?" she asks.

How can I get through to her—and also buy Chancery the slightest hope of reconciliation? Or at least be able to warn Chancery when Judica might attack her. The biggest danger here is that Judica will order a hit while Chancery is vulnerable. "It means that you can listen to me, to the extent you deem it wise, and use me as a resource, and still, before your twin's return, make it clear that I was no friend to you."

"By?"

I sigh. "You could cut off my fingers, or if you think it's required, even my hand. As you know, it's painful but they'll regrow with time."

She gulps. "You'd endure that willingly?"

I shrug. "As you say, I doubt she could defeat you, so it's likely unnecessary. But you never know when her trust of me might help you."

Judica taps her mouth with one finger. "I may have a reputation for savagery. But sometimes, Inara, I worry that you're the scariest member of the Alamecha family."

If she only knew. But after that, she listens to me, and I begin to work on her deep-seated sense of injustice, her ingrained jealousy, and her determined rage against Chancery. It will take a lot of small attempts, but I might convince her that some of the enmity between them isn't Chancery's fault. Perhaps, with a great deal of effort, I can chip away at the wall separating them, drawing them closer to Mother's dream of united sisters standing against the world.

When I reach my room, I feel as though I've been

wrung out. Nearly every negative emotion on the spectrum has pulverized me in the last few days, shifting from fear to anger to rage to regret. I nearly step over the slip of paper on the floor in front of me. But something small catches my eye and pulls me up short—the first letter of my name in Russian, З, is scrawled on the top.

It's the exact symbol Eamon used when he left messages for me near the end.

I want to reach for it, I'm dying to, but I can't move.

For years and years and years, I searched high and low. I dreamt of receiving a note just like this one. As certain as I was that Eamon would never leave me to suffer his death without telling me he'd survived, a kernel of hope persisted.

We planned to fake our deaths.

And then he died.

Could this be. . .?

As though I really am the dead-eyed robot I've pretended to be since his death, I stand transfixed, imagining all the reasons there might be a piece of paper on my floor today, of all days. All the reasons that aren't a message from Eamon. All the reasons that aren't Eamon telling me he survived.

And deep, deep down, I ignore all those reasons, hoping as I haven't in twenty years.

Millions of people use this alphabet, of course. It's about as far from being some special connection to a long dead man as I can imagine. And yet, I stand still, hope clawing at my chest. Once I pick up the note, some training exercise from Judica, or a missive from an old friend. A scrawled note of encouragement from Balthasar. A note about the supplies from Larena, in Cyrillic because she's brushing up.

It could be a billion things, none of them encouraging at all.

The second I read it, the second my brain processes the

boring, mundane words scrawled on that slip of paper, the hope that has sprung up inside of my chest will die, like everything in my life has.

But eventually, I can't delay any longer. I must face the inevitable disappointment of the truth. I lean over and pick it up, the stiff paper rough between my fingers. I open it slowly, my heart in my throat. The entire message is in Russian, but it's printed from a computer, not handwritten. Harder to trace.

Dearest Inara,

I know you have lived the past two decades believing me dead, but I'm alive, held by M. I only got this message out today thanks to the chaos here where I'm being held—chaos caused by Enora's death, if the rumors I hear are to be believed.

I'm not sure what's fact and what's fiction, but if she has truly died, perhaps now you can finally take the throne.

Melina certainly doesn't want it.

If it's possible, do it. Destroy M and save me. The only thing that has kept me alive all this time is regret that we missed our chance—George Town still haunts me. But no matter what torture I've endured, I never shared your secret, and I never will.

Sometimes we have to make our own fate.

It's not signed, but it doesn't need to be. I've been waiting for twenty years for this—any sign that Eamon might have survived. And now, the one compelling emotion I haven't felt today surges in me strong enough to sweep away all the others. Joy. I know exactly what I have to do— play Chancery and Judica against one another until the path to the throne is finally clear.

Eamon and Melina and I will finally be a family. No matter what comes, nothing will stop me, nothing will preempt my happy ending, not this time.

Chancery will never forgive me for what I did to Mother, even if it was inadvertent. Killing a child —she could never countenance it—and that's my *excuse* for killing Mother. Judica, on the other hand, might understand. She might even have done the same thing, albeit for different reasons. My bald-faced lie earlier won't help, but Judica might forgive a lie, if I explain that I wasn't sure whether I could trust her at that point.

I pinch the bridge of my nose and think. *Think, Inara.*

Melina would never accept the truth about what happened to Mother, either. She would never have harmed a defenseless baby—in the end, even when Mother ordered her to, even facing the debacle of twins, she couldn't do it. Melina would also never have used her grief as justification to harm someone else. I'm not entirely certain Eamon can forgive my actions either, even knowing Mother tried to kill him. Even knowing how I've suffered in the past two decades.

Or, since he's presumably been tortured this entire time, maybe he can. I have no idea how he might have changed in all this time.

But I can't play this wrong—not a single, tiny thing can go sideways, not now. Not this time. As much as I want to honor Mother's wishes, she's gone, and Eamon's still alive, no thanks to her. For the first time, I consider a second option—really consider it. Can I confess to Judica and hope she will accept that killing Mother was an accident? Or should I proceed with the only way I saw—eliminating both twins?

Clearly Eamon wants to rule—that's the only way he can finally do what he's always wanted and help all the humans. But would he still want it at the cost of my family's lives? Does he know Mother ordered his death, assuming I'm right and she did? Does he want the twins dead? My half-sisters are young and rash, and both of them are inexperienced—and I have no idea who their father is or what his role in Eamon's capture might have been—but they're still family. The thought of encouraging them to kill one another makes me sick.

After enduring twenty years of torture, I'm sure Eamon will understand that sometimes the right path is the one of the least pain. Besides, as Judica and Chancery's older sister, I'd have a lot of influence over either of them.

When Judica calls me into her study to discuss Alamecha's strategy, I'm prepared. I breeze through the door, ready to bare my soul. Frankly, I'm looking forward to confessing what I've done. It's risky—hoping that she'll forgive me—but I need it; forgiveness. Absolution. It beckons to me.

If savage Judica can't forgive me, how could Eamon ever do it?

My little sister's sitting at her desk, finishing up a letter. She looks up when I enter, her eyes open and bright. "Inara, I wanted to talk to you about Alamecha's current position. I have let too much time pass without taking any action."

"You've been busy."

Judica's knuckles go white around the pen in her hand, and I worry the plastic case will shatter. "That's a wonderful excuse, but I don't make excuses. I do things that need to be done—whatever it takes. I am not my sister."

"No, you're not like her, but both you and Chancery are like your Mother, and you both have positive attributes that you took from her."

"But you're her clone—everyone says so. Whatever she wanted, you wanted. From the day you were born, I hear. In fact, I probably heard that every day of my life."

"Mother and I had our differences. No one agrees on everything."

Judica leaps to her feet. "I fought her every month, every week, every day. I wanted to snatch up China. I wanted to attack our enemies. I wanted to *do something* instead of simply maintaining the peace."

"War is messy," I say. "Mother knew that firsthand, and you're young. You haven't seen it yourself yet."

"Yes, I'm just a child, and I know nothing." There's no bitterness in her tone, no anger, not this time. This time, Judica's words come out more as a sob than a complaint.

"You're not a child," I say slowly. "And I think you were right about some of your suggestions." Perhaps this is a chance for me to nudge her toward taking out Melamecha. I have no idea where Eamon's being held, but we could barter for him if we took something his aunt wanted.

Her eyes spark. "You do?"

I nod. "You've never been someone to shy away from a fight, and you don't struggle to do hard things when you know they're right."

She crosses her arms.

"For example, if someone wronged you, you wouldn't balk at striking back."

"I would not," Judica says.

"Even if it was someone you trusted, someone you loved."

Judica flinches. "You think I killed her."

I shake my head. Now is the moment. I have to tell her right now. "I don't, because—"

She steps closer, her eyes as fierce as I've ever seen them. "I didn't kill her, but I will find out who did. I'm drawing closer every day, and when I find out who took her from me, I will rip them limb from limb and wait for their limbs to regrow so that I can rip them off again." Her entire body trembles with suppressed rage. "And if they let down their guard because they think of me as a child, I'll be happy to disabuse them of that notion, one bloody, protracted beating at a time."

I swallow. Maybe option two is the better call. "I'm happy to hear you're making progress on the investigation." I'm desperate to ask what she's discovered, but I force myself to change the subject. "But you're right to be thinking about the exterior forces at play. Mother would want to make sure that above all things, Alamecha remains strong."

"I've focused most of my attention on discovering the viper in our midst," she says. "But you're right. We need a plan to deal with the five. Chancery's histrionics after Mother's death didn't help, and it was all far too public. They know we're weak right now, and they'll take advantage."

"You should strike," I say. "Take the Philippines back, for example."

Judica taps her lip, staring off at nothing for a very long time.

I'm drawing closer every day.

Does she know it's me? What evidence has she found? The apothecary's dead; that has been confirmed; but what records did he keep? I want to swear under my breath. The second I leave, I'll do a more thorough job cleaning up any evidence of my involvement.

"Not Melamecha," Judica finally says. "She and Mother had a fraught relationship, it's true, made more complicated by Mother's relationship with her siblings—Balthasar has been advising me there. He thinks that we might be able to make some reparations, and I agree. Mother's wars need not be mine, at least not until we're ready to take them down."

I open my mouth to argue, but she plows ahead. So much for my role as her advisor.

"But China is open territory. Why not take it, grow our strength and reduce the debt liability for the United States at the same time." Shrewd, calculating eyes meet mine. "What say you?"

She's dangerous, more dangerous than I realized. "I think we need to plan exactly what steps to take," I say. "You don't want to destroy something you're stealing, after all, but we need to strike them in such a way that they're weakened."

Judica smiles broadly. "I couldn't agree more. Take a seat."

An hour later, I feel even worse about the prospect of taking Judica's life—but there's no other way out. She won't forgive me for what happened with Mother if I confess, that much is clear. And on top of that, Judica isn't interested in picking a fight with Melamecha, and I can't leave Eamon there any longer—I just can't. It leaves me only one option. Undermine Judica, prepare Chancery, and let them kill each other.

It's not easy, but I play both sides against the middle, step by careful step. Melina can never know that I worked against either of them, or she won't forgive me.

Thanks to Gideon, I already had the head of the digital security in my pocket. Chancery gives me the key to destroying her allies when she asks me to send her videos of Judica. When we stumble on the video of Edam talking to someone, likely Analessa, on the phone, it's a stroke of almost unbelievable luck.

And I already have the full-strength dose of poison I intended for the father of Mother's child. I mix it carefully. From what I could discover, it takes about two minutes to work when delivered into the bloodstream, which should give Judica time to defeat Chancery before it kills her.

There's no chance that Chancery would ever agree to use poison on anyone, especially after what happened with Mother, but she also doesn't have a blade of her own. It pains me to give her the blade Dad gave me so many years ago, but it's the only way. I sneak into her room and leave it wrapped in her closet, the poison already coating the blade. At the last minute, I scrawl a message on the package. *Until you have your own.* My sweet, sentimental little sister will be touched that I'm not afraid to declare my support for her, and if Chancery can get in a single swipe, this will all be over, leaving my hands entirely clean to the rest of the world.

I track down the video surveillance for more than a block around the Apothecary and make sure it has been expunged. I make sure none of his paperwork mentions me —but I leave the "N" notation in the ledger. It's suitably confusing. Let them wonder about it.

When Chancery arrives, everything goes perfectly, right up until the two of them face off. Except Chancery isn't using my blade. She chooses one from the unclaimed practice blades. No matter—at least one of them will be eliminated by the end of this, and then I only have to figure out how to kill one of them without implicating myself.

Except, bizarrely, in spite of everything I've done, in spite of what Mother did, in spite of the longstanding enmity between them, in spite of Judica's huge head start on Chancery with her training, Judica yields. And then Chancery spares her life.

And I'm back to square one—further than ever from being able to save Eamon.

The next few weeks are nonstop ups and downs— Melina kidnaps Judica, unwittingly helping both her father and myself with her plan to eliminate her, but then stupid, bullheaded Judica escapes. The first message that Melina sends to Chancery nearly stops my heart. Had I not been present when it arrived. . .

But I am.

Melina believes that her father would be delighted that Chancery is fulfilling the prophecy. She says Chancery will do what Eamon always sought to accomplish: save the world, free the humans, and liberate all the children of Eve.

What if she's right?

I stare at the message for a long time before I burn it and flush the ashes.

Right or not, my path to Eamon requires me to destroy Chancery and Judica. If either of them remains, if I'm discovered, if anything at all goes wrong, I can't save him. But I watch the messages and the phone calls for Chancery and Judica, and when she arrives, for Melina, closely.

Almost too closely.

I'm not sleeping enough, and I'm beginning to feel unraveled, exhausted, impaired. I rub my eyes and blink, combing through the correspondence that has come through for Chancery, before passing it along. I almost ignore the alert on my phone—Chancery will be back very soon, now.

Every time I think something might eliminate her, she conquers it, just barely. By all counts, Adika had her beat, and yet she defeated her and is returning. I flip open my phone and listen, wondering what exactly set off the alert I set. I've listened to some bizarre conversations lately.

The voice on the other end of the phone when the tap clicks in sends chills down my spine. It wasn't a keyword that triggered the notification—it was a voice. Voice triggering technology is so new that as far as I know, only our family has it.

And it's a good thing we do.

The voice on the phone is Angel's—an old friend, a respected teacher, a loyal member of Mother's council. Also, the only person on whom I can pin Mother's death. The scapegoat for my worst mistake, thanks to a bizarre sequence of events on her part that place her in or near Vegas at the same times as me.

"I've left Arizona," she says, "and I'm still safe."

Arizona? What's in Arizona?

"Glad to hear it," Melina says. "Is that why you called?"

Please let that be the reason. Let her just be checking in with Melina. I can send my clean-up crew to check in Arizona—but what part of Arizona, and where is she now?

Angel's laugh causes goosebumps to burst out along my bare arms. "It's not."

"You're being mean," Melina says. "Just tell me."

"I located the video, and it's bad, Melina." Her voice is almost too soft to make out her next words. "Like, I can't tell you anything over the phone, bad."

"Okay." Melina's voice is tense, fear-drenched.

"I'm sending you the video, because you'll need it as evidence. And I'm also sending the record books as verification. You're going to need all of it to pull this off."

"Okay." I wish Melina would say more than 'okay.' I wonder whether she guesses that it's me. I wonder how she'll react when she finds out. "How will you send it?"

"It's the same way I sent you the update that Enora died, but in reverse."

What does that mean? How can I block something if I

don't know how it's being transmitted? Email? Messenger? Smoke signal?

"Absolutely," Melina says. "I remember."

"Stay safe," Angel says. "Predators are at their most dangerous when you're closing in on them. They can sense it."

Or they can hear the conversations, if they're smart. And Angel doesn't know the half of how dangerous I am.

"Accept the world as it is," Melina says.

"Or do something to change it," Angel says.

My hands tremble as I set my phone on the desk in front of me. Melina is in a tiny beach cottage, guarded by my men. If Chancery hadn't taken the Motherless with her, or if I hadn't wanted to be able to go on a ride with Melina and allow her the little privileges that would keep her happy. . .

But my guards do surround her, guards who will turn the other way on my command. Soldiers I control thanks to Gideon's network. My brain races a million miles a minute, looking for a way to handle this other than the obvious one that pulses in front of me.

Kill them all.

They all know that Angel has a video, and Angel is coming—which means that she knows it's me. She's never hidden from a fight. She's coming for me, and I have a very small lead with which to fix this, or I'll lose everything. I'll fail Eamon. I'll forfeit my happy ending.

No.

I will not.

Whatever it takes.

My fingers tremble. What video could she have found? I wiped every video within a mile radius of the Apothecary, and every video around the old shop.

That's when it hits me.

I didn't check for videos from my first visit, back when

I was buying the poison I wanted for *myself*—the poison that inadvertently nearly killed the twins. I swear under my breath. Angel is unbelievably canny. I hate her and I'm impressed simultaneously. That must be it. I place a few calls—someone must be able to find a copy of the video she means—there must be a way to counter this.

Only, I'm running out of time. It will take me days to work out a solution, days to figure out what Angel has and develop some kind of defense that muddies the waters, time I don't have. Any moment, Melina will get that file, and any moment she'll tell Chancery what I did and who I really am.

Then I'll be executed, and Eamon will never be freed. None of which will bring Mother back. None of which will make the world better or brighter or more fair.

None of this is justice.

As much as it pains me, immediate action is required. Eamon will understand—he'll have to—if I don't act right now, all chances for us will go down in flames. I prepare a fake report, and then call Fernando and ask his men to address a disturbance that was reported on the east side of the island. Only Fernando and two others from the inner circle of the Sons of Gilgamesh will remain, and they'll never report me, no matter what I do. Crossing my t's and dotting my i's takes time, too much time. I'm cutting it dangerously close.

While the island is preparing for Chancery's exciting, victorious arrival, I sprint to the bunker. I enter, grab the paralyzing agent and antidote from where I stashed it in the deep storage. I inhale the fumes from the vial marked antidote, breathing it in for the required thirty seconds, and then I use my password and clearance to change the approved persons allowed inside. I remove Judica, and I remove Mother, and then I reset my name to Enora.

Chancery's far too sentimental to remove Mother's

ability to enter, and it will never occur to her that Mother's data might actually be mine. If she thinks to check, she'll believe that only herself and Mother are allowed entry. As far as I know, the first time she came down was a few weeks ago when Mother first discovered her reaction to the staridium. She's extremely unlikely to know about the deep storage, sealed off from the rest of the bunker.

My phone rings the second I reach the surface. It's Fernando. "Aline, Melina's wife, wishes to go for a run."

My hand trembles. Is she going out to get the video? Maybe she's meeting someone, or there will be a drop. I can't risk it. "Go with her. All of you. Knock her out and meet me after dark, at the usual meeting point."

I am going to have to kill all of Melina's people—which is going to devastate her—but I can't kill my sister, and if I kill her wife, she'll never forgive me. And I need her to forgive me—I love her too much to contemplate the alternative. With a cage for them prepared, I race out the door and down to the beach, avoiding the sentry rotations. I move fast—faster than anyone else can, until the cottage comes into view.

My heart hammers in my chest.

Melina, oh my darling, how can I do this? Will you ever forgive me? But I can't trust your people, can I? For a moment, I wonder whether perhaps she took the call in a back room or on the porch. Perhaps none of them heard.

Maybe I can sneak in, take Melina out with me, tell her we're meeting Chancery's returning plane, and then. . . Her people will see her leaving with me, but I can work around that somehow. I can think of something. The door mocks me, with its brightly painted frame. The waves crash behind me, and my heart beats a staccato rhythm. Urging me onward. I'm nearly out of time.

I knock.

"Hey." Melina opens the door with a smile. "I was

wondering if you'd come."

I told her when we rode the other day that I'd come by. I promised her that we'd catch up. She's lost so very much in her life, nearly as much as me. Mother, father, home, family, the throne. My heart sinks. She misses me, and she wanted to see me. But not like this, never like this. I can barely force myself to step inside.

"Come in before you're completely soaked," Melina urges. She even steps aside, as if her proximity was causing my reticence, not my horror at the task before me.

When I pass her, I begin to count faces and heartbeats. Twenty-five, including my sister. Why didn't we give them several places to stay? Why didn't we split their group? I should have insisted. I would have, if I had any idea it would come to this.

Melina notices that I'm taking in how many people are gathered. "Oh, we're a little cramped in here, not that I'm complaining, but you can have a seat at the kitchen table." So much for hoping that no one else heard. If even one of them heard, the news of a video would have whipped through them like wildfire.

"I can't stay," I protest.

Melina's eyes sharpen, focusing on mine intently. "Oh, did things not go well with Chancery?" She coughs. "Tell me she's alright."

"You're still in contact with Angel?" My voice sounds wooden, disconnected.

Her jaw drops. "Yes. She's fine as far as I know."

"She called you earlier," I say, "and you took the call here, where everyone could hear you." I should be subtle, I should be teasing the information out, but there's not time, and I don't have any subtlety in me, not in this moment, not with this horrific task looming before me. My humanity slowly drains away as the realization of what's coming sinks into my brain. The red haze beckons to me.

"What are you asking me about, Inara?" The raw, undisguised fear in her voice nearly crumbles me. Her eyes beg me not to be here about the video. Her people tense, several of them reaching for weapons. They sense the danger, but it's too late for that. Their course is set—was set before I entered this cottage.

If only she hadn't taken the call out here, with them all gathered around. If Angel hadn't dug quite so deep or quite so well. If I had done a better job covering my tracks, if I'd considered the possibility of old video feeds. If if if. But none of the ifs are real, and it's too late to undo what has been done.

Sometimes the only path out is through, and this won't be the first time I drown in regret after the fact. I just hope that Melina can someday understand and somehow forgive. Lucas, Paolo, those two for sure will pain her, badly. Will it turn her against me?

I scramble for any way to save them, to spare them, but I can't haul more than one person out of here. Someone would be bound to notice.

At least Aline went for a run. She'd never forgive Aline, but she's not here. I've dealt with her already. Melina will have to give me some credit for that, right?

"Inara, why are you here?" Melina's voice is raw, demanding, and impressively brave. Because by now, she already knows.

Even so, before I take this last step, I want to confirm there's no way out. "So they all heard?"

"Heard what?" Her head tilts. Her voice trembles. Her eyes plead.

I reach into my pocket and pull out the ball, the curiosity I told the Apothecary I would never need. The ball that I don't need—but this is for Melina, now. I can't control myself in the middle of the haze, and I worry what she might do, and how I might react without thinking.

"What is that?" Melina steps toward me, arm raised as if she might stop me from whatever I'm planning.

"I hate that things have happened this way, but I don't have a choice, not if they all know about Angel's video."

Angel's bloody video.

I hurl the paralytic into the fireplace—the flue that will surely be closed this time of year. Just as I knew it would, smoke billows out. At first they all blink, confused. What in the world am I doing, throwing a smoke bomb into the fireplace? Have I lost my mind? I might think the same, but then, just as he promised they would, everyone freezes. Even sweet, well-intentioned Melina.

"The ocean is full of all kinds of interesting things," I say. Anything to delay doing what I'm so desperate to avoid. "Mother really should have spent a little more time exploring its depths."

Evians are hard to kill. Do enough damage, and their bodies shut down, but most things, if given enough time, can be repaired. Severed spines, sliced hearts, terrible head wounds, these things can all be healed. They can all be undone.

I can't allow that.

And I'm running out of time. Chancery's plane lands in a few moments. I need to be there to greet her, to compliment her, to reassure her that I'm her ally. I need this to be done and in the past. So I do what has to be done the fastest way I can do it—and when the first head rolls, the red haze descends and it all becomes so much easier. My blade arcs, my muscles bunch, my body moves as one fluid unit, ending my opponents one after another.

They don't suffer. They don't agonize. They simply cease to exist.

I'm deep within the haze when I kill the twenty-fourth evian Melina brought with her, and my face reaches hers. Tear-stained, beloved, frozen in place.

But I can't freeze her eyes, and they're shooting daggers. No, not daggers. Broadswords. Crossbows. Poison-tipped darts. Anything and everything she could send my way. In her mind, I murdered Mother to steal the throne, and now I've destroyed everyone she loves.

"Where's your wife?" I ask, to redirect her focus. Her wife isn't dead. Her wife isn't beheaded. Her wife isn't here.

Fear pulses in her eyes.

"Oh. I forgot. You can't talk. You need the antidote." I hold it under her nose, but only for a few seconds. "I've only given you half a dose. Can't have you freaking out on me. It takes ten seconds or so to work."

She begins to quiver, with fury, I imagine, and I know it has begun to work. At least she won't be stiff as a statue when I haul her back. She fumbles forward, catching herself on the back of a kitchen chair.

"Time to go," I say. "I'll have to question you later. Chancery's just arriving. This couldn't have happened at a worse time."

"Sorry to inconvenience you." Her syllables blur together, but I've never been more proud of her. She's not breaking down. She's not giving in. She's fighting me, as much as she can, and she's fiery and fierce. I love her so much. Her eyes fixate on Lucas' blade.

I can't help my laughter. "Really, Melina. Come on." I shove the sword hilt away, shifting Lucas' body disrespectfully. I tug my hood down over my face again, and grab Melina, tugging her toward the door.

She's not making it easy, but I manage to pull us both free. "Stop, stop!"

Her shrieking is not good.

"Why would you do that?" Her tortured question is whispered, at least, but the pain of it slices through me like a real blade.

Oh, Melina, if I had seen any other way. I want to tell

her it's to save her dad. I want to tell her everything, but I can't blurt it out, not right now, not while it's all so fresh in her mind. I need her wound to begin to heal, I need time to smooth it over. I need to give her the peace offering of Aline, and *then* I can explain. Then she'll be in a position to listen.

I pull her forward, toward the steps, but the way she looks at me, with such hatred. I have to at least try to defend myself. "I had no choice. My hand was forced from the first day. It had to happen, and this does too. Stop struggling," I plead. Please, please stop struggling. Don't make me kill you or anyone else.

"You're Nereus," she whispers. "You must be. Which means you killed her."

And that's when I realize that the pain is too fresh, the wound too deep. I won't be able to force her to follow me. She may never trust me again. But I'm out of time. I shove her against the doorframe, clocking her head hard enough to render her unconscious. Then I scoop her up, cradling her in my arms, and sprint back for the bunker.

I'm right around the corner from Mother's courtyard when I hear voices. I slam my back up against the wall and hold my breath, slowing my heart as much as possible, and they pass.

When I finally set Melina down in the dark, cool earth of the bottom of one of the drainage pits, I breathe in and out deeply for the first time. Since I answered that notification and heard that call, I've been on high alert, worried that everything would collapse, plunging me back into the dark.

Ironically, I'm sitting in almost complete darkness right now, but for the first time since that moment, I can breathe.

Eamon, I did it. You and I are going to make it.

W hen I tell Melina that Mikhail is Eamon. . .
Her eyes widen. Her breathing hitches,
shallow, short breaths, and she shakes her
head, ever so slightly. "No, Dad was. . . I knew he didn't
love Mother, not like he. . . But he." She swallows. She and
Aline exchange a glance.

"Eamon was gay," Aline says. "He and Melina talked
about it once."

I can't help my laugh, even if it's fraught with sorrow.
For some reason, Mother thought the same. Perhaps
Mother led her down this path, or even told her it wasn't
her fault, that she inherited this from him. "I can assure
you that Eamon was never in love with Gideon, and he was
most definitely not gay." I stand up. "I can't stay right now,
but I'll be back."

They don't argue when I lock them into the secured
overflow area—but I wonder how well they'll listen to my
instruction. In my experience, reinforcing behavior with an
evian by beating them has the lowest chance of success—
but I'm not sure what else to do. If Melina realizes quite
how much I love her, she'll realize that even if she attempts

to escape, I couldn't possibly hurt her. Even this, keeping her locked away, makes me nervous—what will Eamon say when I rescue him?

He'll understand that I had no choice. He's been held for almost twenty years—I shudder to think what he's endured or what it will have done to him. But whatever the impact, we'll repair it together, however long that takes. I want to tell Melina now—share the joy I felt when I realized Eamon was alive—but I force myself to wait. She'll need to hear it at the right time to understand why I reacted the way I did.

And what I have to do now. . .

It's two days before I can get away again—and I use another recording, Judica's voice for a change. This time, no matter how many times I play it, neither Aline nor Melina make any noise. When I unlock the doorway to the extra space, they're waiting for me, neither one stressed or upset. I toss them a bag full of fresh baked treats from the kitchens.

"We aren't dogs," Aline says. "You can't toss us a bone for being good and expect us to wag our tails and lick your hand."

In spite of the bitterness in her tone, she and Melina gobble up the croissants, the crusty bread, and the kolaches. The bunker rations will keep them alive, but they don't taste good.

"I've been thinking about what you told me, reviewing our interactions in my mind, and I see it." Melina meets my eyes, empathy in her gaze. "But I want to know how Dad could have cast you aside," Melina says. "If you say he loved you too—and you came to the island with a plan. The Dad I knew would never have betrayed someone he loved."

"It wasn't that simple for him. He had to choose between betraying me—and I represented a selfish desire, because our love made him as happy as it did me—and betraying what he felt was *right*, what he felt was his *purpose*."

They both listen quietly as I explain Eamon's history and childhood—the group he joined and the things he did for Rasputin—how they changed his views on humans. How he decided it was his calling and suddenly found peace in his actions.

"We're shaped by so many things," I say. "And Eamon was shaped as much by his childhood as he was by the transformational connection we felt in George Town."

"But he chose wrong," Aline says. "Love isn't selfish—in fact, it's the least selfish thing I've ever done in my life."

"He loved the humans—millions and millions of them, and unlike me, they had no ally, no advocate, and no one to speak for them. I hated Eamon for what he did," I say. "But I also understood him well enough to respect and accept his decision."

"But he changed his mind," Melina says. "Didn't he?"

I swallow. "Twice. Once before, and once after."

"Jered," she says.

I nod. "He told me he made a mistake before your brother was born and that if I'd wait, once Mother passed away, we would be together again. I would have waited too, patiently, but things shifted when Jered was born, for a while, anyway. After Mother gave his son away, Eamon was done in a different way."

"Did Mother find out?" Melina's eyes are haunted—probably a lot like mine were.

"About us?" I shake my head. "No, but she knew that Eamon loved someone else."

"She blamed Gideon too," Melina says. "She said some things."

"I wish I had realized what everyone assumed," I say, "although, I might have just been relieved."

"Did Mother. . ." Melina stands up and begins to pace.

312

"Did Mother what?" I want her to ask it. I want her to go there, too.

She spins around and meets my eyes. "Did she kill him?"

"I'm not one hundred percent sure," I say slowly, "but based on the things she said to me, and the relief she felt that he was gone, yes. I'm virtually certain that she did."

"How could she do that?" Tears trail down her face.

I shrug.

"That's why you killed her?" This time, anger joins the tears. "Killing someone for killing someone doesn't fix it."

I explain what happened with Mother, that I poisoned the twins—on accident, and then in a misguided attempt to help. And then, that I poisoned Mother again—when I discovered she was pregnant. I tell her about the journal entry, and my reaction to it.

And then I explain how I tried to punish her by killing her child.

Melina's eyes. Disappointment mixed with relief that I didn't murder our mother *on purpose*. "I can't believe you meant to kill a baby who did nothing to you."

"You meant to kill Chancery after her birth," I remind her. "And you nearly did kill Judica not long ago."

"That was different," Aline says.

"Not that different," Melina says.

Hope springs inside my chest. Will she understand? Will she forgive me? "I wanted to hurt Mother," I admit. "But I loved her too much to ever plan to do her permanent harm."

"You figured killing a child who never did anything was better?" Aline's lip curls.

"I didn't say it was a good decision—but had I known she was already weakened due to poisoning herself, I never would have done it, and she'd still be alive. So yes, I killed her, but I didn't *mean* to kill her."

313

Melina sobs then, great heaving sobs, tears rolling down her face. "The whole thing is too tragic."

Aline is not similarly afflicted. "Why didn't you just confess all this?" She pins Melina with a glare. "Because while I see the tragedy in it, you *murdered* twenty-four of my friends to cover this up. No matter what drove you, no matter what mistakes did or didn't excuse your mistake, you knew exactly what you were doing when you walked into that house and decapitated my brother, and Lucas, and Horatio, Kira, Douglas, Or—"

"I did." I inhale and exhale. "There's no way that Chancery would ever forgive me for trying to kill Mother's unborn child. If you knew her like I did, you would know that much. But she might not have killed me—she might have banished me, and that might have been good enough. Except for one thing."

"What?" Melina asks.

"Right after Mother died, I received a message—from Eamon."

Melina stops sobbing and sits up straight. "From Dad?" Her eyelashes flutter erratically. I've got her on the hook. Now I need to drag her through—if she just understands, if she even can relate, then with time, maybe. . .

"He's alive. He's been held and tortured by Melamecha this entire time."

"So we save him," Melina says. "Chancery will help us do that. I know she will."

I grimace. "There's no going back for me, not now. It might have been the wrong decision, but when I heard that Angel was bringing you a video, I had to do something. I could have survived execution, had that been my punishment, but not if it meant Eamon wasn't rescued. Not if it meant that we lost our chance. So I did what I had to do— I should have killed everyone that day." I swallow. "I meant what I said. I needed nothing from you, Melina, and I still don't. I should kill you both right now, but I can't bring myself to do that, not if you can forgive me. Not if you'll work on my side to help restore your father."

"Let me understand you," Melina says. "You need me to bring Angel back and keep her from sharing the video of you getting the poison."

I shake my head. "Not exactly. Eliminating your people and hiding you here bought me time. I realized that the only person who could also be guilty of what I did—poisoning Mother—was Angel. When I got the poison the first time, she was in Utah for the Olympics, close to Vegas. When I went back, she was with me, picking up ovens. She had access to the food—access to Mother." I look down at my hands. "And she ran after Mother died."

"To help me!" Melina stands up, her face hardening alarmingly. "What did you do?"

"I realized long ago the value of computer skills. I've always kept mine at the top of the game—and that helped me monitor all information and security footage. It allowed me to make my own video, and plant it as an alternative to the one Angel brought—the one I knew she would have."

"No." Melina looks me in the eye, and I realize she might have forgiven me for what I did that day, rashly, without time to think. She might have forgiven me for killing her people—since I felt it was the only way to ensure her dad would survive.

But not this. Not for shoving Angel in front of a bus, knowingly, with foresight. Not for allowing her to bear the burden of my actions, to atone for my sins.

"Chancery believed me," I say. "She closed the investigation into Mother's murder."

"Angel never came?"

I frown.

"Tell me what happened." My little sister has never looked more furious or more terrified.

"Balthasar executed Angel."

"No." Melina shakes her head. "No, she didn't. You made a mistake with Mother. Why didn't you just tell everyone and beg for mercy?"

I square my shoulders. "A daughter of Alamecha doesn't ask for mercy."

"But you made it worse!" She screams. "You made it so much worse!"

"I had no choice each time," I say. "You must understand that. Eamon is alive, and fate has ripped us apart over and over and over. I'll do *anything*, kill *anyone*, if that's what it takes."

"Dad won't want anything to do with you now."

I'm terrified that she's right. "Angel was no saint. She has done plenty of things she shouldn't have done."

"Balthasar may have beheaded her, but you murdered her, and you murdered my brother-in-law, and you murdered my friends." Melina steps backward, shaking her head. "I can never forgive you, Inara. Dad will never forgive you. Your only hope is to confess to Chancery and beg for a chance for redemption."

Something bashes me across the back of my head, and stars explode in front of my eyes. *Aline.*

There's no way that Melina was unaware of what her wife was doing. In one smooth movement, I spin in a circle and draw my sword. Aline's holding a trash can. *A trash can.* Like she could take me down with something so pathetic.

"Don't make me do this," I whisper. "Don't."

"You're a monster," Aline says. "And you'll never harm me or my wife again." She throws the trash can and lunges at me, swiping at me with something sharp—I realize what it is, as it slices my thigh. A dagger crafted out of a piece of wood. They've been busy in my absence.

Aline is angrier than Melina. She's the one pushing all of this. If I put her life in jeopardy, if Melina realizes that I

316

mean it, she'll listen. She'll consider. I engage with Aline then, letting her score a few hits, but slicing her in return, slowly, methodically, backing her toward the wall. Melina watches it all from the corner in horror, transfixed and trembling. Aline is cornered, stuck, with nowhere to go. Melina must know that the end is coming for her wife—she must realize that I can end them.

Surely she'll listen.

I'll take one final shot, stopping short before I actually kill her.

But when my blade flies through the air, something pops up in front of Aline, far closer than Aline was. Too close. I can't stop in time. My blade parts the obstacle like a dagger through cream cheese, almost no resistance at all.

Melina's head falls to the floor.

Something cracks inside of me, something I can't comprehend. The red haze descends, as always, but I shove it away forcefully. When I kill Aline for what she made me do, I'm entirely aware of my own surroundings, entirely in control of my movements.

Aline doesn't die fast, and she doesn't die easily.

But once she's gone and my adrenaline recedes, I sink to the ground, cradling Melina's body in my arms. My fault, my fault, my fault.

Everything I love, I destroy.

And there's no way Eamon will ever forgive this. Never. The only way I can be with him is to lie to him, and I'm not sure I can do it. I think of a million times that, if things had been slightly different, I wouldn't be here. A million ways fate has spited me, hated me, used me, and destroyed me.

After a very long time, I stand up.

Because I am a daughter of Enora and Althuselah Alamecha. We never give up, we never give in, and we never beg for mercy. This was my fault, but also, this was not. I am who I am—I am who God made me. I didn't ask for this, any of it.

I bury Melina and Aline's bodies deep in the earthen pit, and I clean myself up in the same shower where Melina cleaned herself when I offered her mercy. No matter how much I am hurting, this is not the time to crumble. This is not the time to collapse. I have another fight in front of me, and no matter the pain inside me, no matter the loss, I won't lose this fight.

I'm going to reclaim Eamon.

This will all be worth it when I do.

"She did what?" I ask.

Alora's smile is smug. Irritatingly smug. "Melamecha and Rothgar. . . exploded."

I swallow. Chancery was weak. Chancery was unsure. Chancery was a mess. And now, a few weeks after everyone was sure she would be killed by Judica, she has destroyed Adika, taken down Analessa, made an ally of Melisania, and turned both Melamecha and Lainina's Consort Rothgar into confetti.

"You would have been so proud of her," Alora says. "I mean, it was gross, and for a moment I was terrified she'd die. Melamecha's blade was halfway through—"

"Of course I'm proud of her," I say. "But securing a ring and a few prisoners is only the beginning. Do you think she'll be able to competently rule all these families? Taking this many at once. . ."

"I'm worried," Alora says. "I won't lie about that. She needs us close, to guide and advise her, but she also needs people she can trust to hammer out the bumps and unrest all over the world."

"You think she'll ask me to step in somewhere?" Like, perhaps, Shamecha? That would be too easy.

Alora shrugs. "Probably, but don't you think that she needs you here? I mean, I'm sure Judica's doing her best to filter through whom she can trust, but the list isn't long."

"Anyone acting as her regent will also be on the Council." My brain spins at a million miles a minute, thinking this through. "Has she joined the new stones yet?"

Alora shakes her head. "No. I think she's afraid, honestly."

I don't blame her—she caused a volcano last time, and the time before that, she sheared off a huge chunk of island and almost killed one of her boyfriends. "But she'll have to do it."

"She says it's getting worse—and joining the last two stones. . ." Alora exhales. "I wish I knew what to tell her."

"Do you leave soon?" I ask. "I mean, weren't you supposed to be in Paris right about now?"

Alora laughs. "I'm sure they're scratching their heads, wondering where I am."

"Or they're relieved, thinking maybe you won't show up to whip them into shape. I'm sure they're all surveying that throne, trying to figure out how to snatch it back for themselves."

"Of course they are." She sighs. "I'm not looking forward to this, you know."

"It was time for you to come out of retirement," I say. "You had a nice break, but you said it yourself. It's all hands on deck."

"I guess. I'm leaving in about four hours. I want to make sure Chancery's alright, but once I know she is, I'll go. And this time, I'll actually leave. I sent Isamu ahead to make sure nothing goes awry in my absence."

Chancery's supporters are spread thin. Lark is dead. Alora's leaving. Moses yet holds Shenoah, but he barely knows her. Edam and Chancery have fallen out ever since he challenged his sister and forced Chancery to challenge her. Only Noah, Frederick, and Judica will be by her side by this time tomorrow. Well, Noah and a host of Motherless zealots, trained from birth to fight, and sworn to defend her thanks to her edict of liberty and freedom.

Even so.

I've been waiting, patiently waiting, for the perfect time. Since Chancery has been such a successful conqueror, I'd have been a moron to step in until she completed taking all five families. She's toppled one family after another and gathered their staridium like it's all some straightforward game of sovereignty played against idiots.

But now that she has taken everyone down and collected the stones. . . if I can convince her to join them, it's finally time.

Adrenaline floods my body, enervating my hands, making my feet tap. *Not yet*, I tell myself. Not quite yet. A few more hours. The only thing standing between me and a throne from which Eamon and I could rule the entire world is. . . Chancery, Judica, and Noah. And no one is strong enough to stop me from taking it.

Except possibly Balthasar.

He's one of the three men I suspect of being Chancery and Judica's father, but as far as I can tell, no one knows that Eamon isn't their father, other than perhaps whoever stole Enora's body and incinerated it. It still bothers me that two of the people implicated in that whole ordeal had nothing to do with me—and I have no idea what they were doing or who gave them orders.

Tristan, who worked for Job, killed himself by ingesting a pill. That's standard procedure for the Sons, but I didn't order it. Eirik has no record of him being a member. And according to Judica, Nihils did the same thing when she realized he'd been switching shifts to have access to Mother.

Someone is pulling strings, and it has to be the father of Mother's unborn child. Right? But who is he? Job? Balthasar? Frederick? It has to be one of them—but which of them would have a connection to the Sons? And how would I not know about it?

Job wouldn't have needed to use Tristan—he could have snagged Enora's body himself at any time. He also had access to it to pull a DNA sample from a fetus at any point. Frederick, well. He's the one most likely to have infiltrated the Sons, but would he? I wrack my brain for any interaction he had with Eamon, and I don't recall any that were fraught.

Then again, no one knew I loved Eamon. So maybe I'll never know.

Balthasar's my uncle, and he hated Eamon by all counts —so unless he knows the truth about the twins' paternity and he happens to be their father, he won't be a huge fan of them either. I think if I take the throne before I rescue Eamon and set him next to me on it, Balthasar will prefer to support me over one of the twins. Frederick and Job could be problematic, especially if one of them discovers that I killed Enora, but I can kill either of them easily enough if the situation demands it.

No, any way I look at it, now is the time to strike.

Alora leaves to see to a few details before she checks on Chancery one last time, and I realize that this is my moment. If I wait, Alora will make it to Paris, and it'll be harder than ever to pry her back out. No, it's time to act now.

I call Eirik and tell him it's time. The plan's in motion, and I'm baiting the trap. And then I find Chancery, in Mother's courtyard, alone. And as if providence shines on my enterprise, she's already decided to send Balthasar and

Job as well as all the Motherless to stabilize Shamecha and Adora.

Something is finally going my way.

Once they're gone, I set my other plans in order, deploying my warriors to do the final step: round up Chancery's last remaining supporters. Edam, Alora—who delayed her departure yet again, Judica and Roman, and Noah. And then it's time to spring the trap. I don't have to look long to find her—sitting in her courtyard in the shade of the enormous banyan tree, staring at the staridium she's amassed. It's really the only thing she's done right since taking Mother's place. I'd be staring at them too, looking for reassurance.

"Are you thinking about joining them?" I peek over the gate.

She jumps, and then smiles once she sees that it's *only* me. "Thinking about it."

"Still not the right time?"

"I wish I knew. I'm sick of never having any idea what I'm doing."

"You look like you could use an energizing walk. Maybe toward the water this time." I look over my shoulder somewhat wistfully. If we don't go far enough north, she won't be in the right place to see when it's time.

She hops to her feet, still barefoot. "That's not a bad idea." We're halfway to the ocean when she finally realizes no guards are following us. "We aren't being followed."

I killed them, of course, the ones that weren't part of the Sons of Gilgamesh, but I can hardly admit to that to her while she's wearing the billion-dollar bling that could explode and incinerate me, and then flip my remains upside down and inside out, so I force a laugh instead. "I suppose Edam needs to figure out a new rotation, now that the Motherless have all been shipped away."

Her eyes light up with mischief. "I'm going to have so much fun telling him how much danger I was in."

"You are sort of exposed," I say. "With no one but me to protect you."

"I guess I'm lucky you're such an accomplished fighter."

My heart skips a beat. How could she know that? "You've never even seen me fight."

She frowns, the corners of her mouth turning down. "Why is that? You never fight—not in training, not in matches, not in competitions."

Sometimes the absolute truth is the best shield—no one in their right mind would believe it anyway. "I'm horrifyingly good. In fact, I often wonder whether I could take Balthasar. It just comes naturally to me, and I don't want anyone to feel bad when they watch, so I don't fight in public. Ever."

Disbelief and then exhaustion flash across her face in such quick succession I can't figure out what motivated them. "Sometimes I wish you could take over for me."

She wishes. . .that I could take over? Am I handling this the wrong way? Should I simply offer to step in? But the prophecy—she won't really pass off the control, not if she thinks it would endanger the humans. That utter destruction nonsense is infuriating.

"You know." She taps her lip. "We haven't even tried the stones, not since that first day. Maybe you and Judica could use them."

"I held one when you fought Analessa." And it barely even registered me as Mother's daughter—tiny flashes and soft colors. Nothing like her rings look right now.

"But you didn't *try* to make it react to you, did you?"

I focused on it with every speck of my concentration. I cast about wildly in my mind to see whether I could sense any kind of power and. . .nothing. But if she thinks she might be able to pass off a task she hates. . .would she simply hand the stones to me? She'll still have to die eventually, there's no way around that, but the whole thing could be far less. . .distasteful.

"Would you like to try?"

She wants to hand me the very thing I need. The key to saving Eamon and building the world we always wanted. For all I know, the prophecy means *me*—I am the eldest out of Chancery, Judica, Melina, and myself. Of course, that doesn't make as much sense given that I have ten older sisters, but translations and prophecies are tricky. Who can really tell what they mean? With Eamon's guidance, I might be able to prevent utter destruction more effectively than poor, naive little Chancery.

"I mean, I'm not, like, trying to shove them on you." But she's still holding out her hand—trying to give me the very thing I've been trying to figure out how to take. Providence again?

"Sure," I say. "What can it hurt to try?"

"You have to be careful not to let them all touch," she says. "Unless you fancy melting down the island, that is." She holds out the largest ring, the one that used to be Mom's before she glued it to Adika's, and Melisania's and Analessa's—and when I extend my hand, she slides it on my finger for me.

I stare at the stone for a full breath cycle, and then for another. I cast about inside my brain for *anything* that might indicate that there's something there—power, awareness, anything *other* than the norm. Nothing. Then the same soft play of color that took place when it was a single stone on Mother's finger starts. I don't swear or scream or fume.

"Here, you can try these too." She holds the larger ring toward me casually, as if it doesn't much matter—Melamecha's I think.

The band of this ring is huge—it slides on my pointer

finger easily. "It's a good thing Melamecha had such meaty hands."

"Stop." Chancery smiles, guilty at even the mention of a somewhat negative observation about someone whom she killed. "You're ridiculous."

"Mother hated her." And so do I—especially now that I know what she hid from me all these years. If she hadn't already been blown to bits, I'd relish inflicting the same kind of pain on her that she's caused to Eamon, and through him, to me.

"I didn't like her much myself." I'm surprised to hear that—Chancery loves everyone.

"I wish I'd seen her explode," I confess.

She holds out the last stone, still set into Lainina's black band. "Here, try this one. Maybe with the full set. . ."

I can't act overly eager—she might suspect and this could get nasty fast. My hand trembles a little when I reach for it. If they do react once they're all together. . . I wait again, hoping, almost expectant. But nothing happens.

"That's too bad," she says.

"Do you really think that?" My words are a little too angry—but she can't really be hoping that I would take over everything for her. Deep down she must love the power, the attention, the hero worship, the men falling at her feet.

She walks into the water, painfully unaware of the danger she's in. "I do."

Something about her complacency, her air of being put upon by all this power at her fingertips, her false grief over having destroyed two empresses with the flicker of her hand, it infuriates me. The world has been handed to her on a silver platter, and yet she eschews it. Unbelievably unappreciative. Woefully blind to the truth of the world. In that moment, I want to hurt her—the way I've been hurt. The way the world has thrown daggers at me instead of lobbing me flowers and gemstones and thrones and princi-palities like it does for her. "Would you still pass the throne off to me with such abandon if you discovered that I killed Mother?"

"Excuse me?" She freezes, her heart lurching along erratically. "What are you talking about?"

My words scare her, and I enjoy the fear—like a salve to my misunderstood heart. "I didn't mean to do it, of course. I only meant to punish her for killing him."

She blinks, looking utterly perplexed, like her brain can't make sense of my words. "You killed her?" Ah. She's feeling guilty for executing Angel, I'm sure.

Someone had to take the blame, and it wasn't as if I really meant to murder her anyway. "Mother was poisoning herself, you know. That's why you and Judica and Balthasar failed to figure things out. I had no idea either, not until after I dosed her."

She turns toward me slowly, her eyes eerily wide. "You dosed her."

"She was pregnant, and I was the only one who knew. She said she sent the blood test off under a false name so even Job would have no idea. How she managed that, I'm not sure. Mother was never the most tech-savvy. I've wondered for a while whether he knew more than he let on, of course."

"Wait, if you didn't want her to die—"

"I wanted her to *suffer*—" I say, sick of no one getting it. "I wanted her to feel what I felt, losing something she wanted desperately."

"But why?"

I never should have hid how I felt about Eamon, I know that, but it still rankles that no one has any idea how much I've suffered. "She killed the love of my life, and at the same time, she killed my best friend. Imagine, if you will, discovering that in her jealousy, in her misguided frustration, your mother killed not only one, but both of the men you cared about."

She looks down at the sand, as if she'll find the answers there. Probably wondering why I hurt Mother now, why I acted so far after anyone even remotely related to me died. She may even be wondering whether she knows me at all— and who in the world I loved and lost. She turns to face me slowly, her face so full of pity I want to slap it. "You wanted to kill the baby."

"But she was poisoning herself already." Yes, try to catch up, little ingénue.

"Wait, why?"

"Turns out you're a freak of nature in more ways than one," I explain. "You see, I poisoned Mother another time as well. That's an even longer story, I'm afraid, but again, I meant her no harm. It was an accident."

"That's a lot of accidents." As if her brain has finally kicked into gear, she notices the staridium rings that I'm still wearing. Her voice is strained, like a guitar string wound far too tight. "I'd like the rings back."

Precious. "I'm afraid I can't give these back to you quite yet." I wave my fingers airily.

She glances around, looking for help or weapons, I imagine. "Melina knew? About what you did to Mother?"

Better late than never. "Very good," I say. "She figured it out, with Angel's help of course, and she meant to tell you."

"She meant?" The color drains from her face. "Where is she now?"

"I hoped you might wait a bit longer before asking me that. I'm afraid I had no choice. I didn't mean to kill her either, you must understand."

And now she's thinking about the people I had to kill in order to prevent Melina from confessing that I obtained the poison and having me executed. "All those people, everyone who came with her." She closes her eyes.

"It's pointless for me to deny that, of course. I had no choice—they meant to turn me in to you."

My pitiful little sister looks at me with imploring eyes, begging me to redeem myself in some way. "Why didn't you tell me at the beginning? When it was only Mom? Before you killed anyone else?"

"It hardly seemed likely to help matters then," I admit. "And then things sort of, well, they spiraled out of control."

She pulls a thigh dagger and jumps at me with it.

I evade her easily, like moving out of the way of a clumsy, overeager puppy. "I take it you're not planning to forgive me?"

"Did you really think I could?" Her voice breaks, and I realize how badly she wants to do just that.

With a little encouragement, maybe she'll see things the right way. "I hoped. You forgave Judica."

"You murdered Mom." Her huge doe eyes glisten. "And Melina. And so many others." Tears roll down her face. "I trusted you. I ordered Angel to be killed when you were guilty."

"You did, yes, but I think you can safely lay the blame for that at my feet. No reason to fret that you're a bad person."

"It was your fault." She throws her dagger this time, but it's not nearly fast enough.

I catch it easily by the blade, and her total shock annoys me. "You thought I was kidding earlier, but I wasn't. I don't fight because no one else compares to me. That's not bravado or conceit. It's truth."

"Why?"

"I'm a rare, bizarre anomaly, genetically speaking."

"I don't understand."

"I think you will quite soon, unfortunately. And I'm very sorry for this too, but I don't see any other way. You see, I've been offered a reprieve, figuratively speaking. I've discovered that the love of my life actually survived."

For the first time, she's afraid, and I realize she really doesn't care much about her own life. I should have known that already—she did just race into a fight against two other empresses, knowing she'd likely be killed. "Who?"

"You think he's your father, actually. Eamon—and he was married to your mother when you were conceived, but he didn't father you and Judica, if Mother's journal can be trusted."

Her mouth drops open, making her look even more dopey than usual. "Wait."

She really had no idea. Mother hadn't told her a thing. "Yes, it turns out that our mother was a bit of a liar."

"You loved Mom's *husband?*"

"If you want to be outraged, maybe aim that indignation her direction. He was my boyfriend before she married him, and if she'd bothered to discover that before she ripped his clothes off—" Even thinking about that makes me quiver with rage. "It doesn't matter. That's all in the past now." My phone buzzes and I look down.

ALL FOUR ARE IN PLACE.

I text them back immediately. STAND BY. ALMOST TIME.

"I'm sorry," Chancery says loudly, "am I bothering you at an inconvenient time with my questions about my paternity and all the many murders you committed?"

She's such a ridiculous little girl, throwing a tantrum that I'm not showering all my attention on her. "Were you always this funny?"

She runs at me again, which I easily sidestep and in my irritation, I strike her elbow and back, sending her sprawling facedown in the sand. I shove the sole of my boot against her back. It's clearly time for me to break more than just her arm. "I have something you'll want to watch, I assume."

She snarls at me, for all the world like an adorable little cornered baby badger.

"I'll let you up, but I warn you. If you attack me again, I'm going to break your face. I'd rather this not get so ugly, but I'll do whatever it takes, as evidenced by my past behavior. Are we clear?"

"Clear," she snarls. Tedious.

I remove my foot and turn my phone to face her—so she can see the FaceTime call I've placed.

Edam, Judica, Alora, and Noah are bound, all of them staring at her, helplessly.

"How? Why?" Her eyes plead with me, as if I could reverse my course now. She'd execute me immediately. No, my only path now is through. I hang up the call.

"I'm going to need you to join the stones, but if I hand them to you now, you'll get all these ideas. Ideas about tossing me into the air, pelting me with fireballs, and then, I don't know, maybe exploding me into pink mist."

She's obviously already imagined all the ways she'd punish me for threatening her friends—that much is clear.

"Oh, I am a little bit proud of you in this moment, but hang on to that sense of anger. It's the best thing to get you through this next part."

"What part?" Her lip trembles, her eyes widen, as if she's finally processing what is about to happen—why I've gathered her largest supporters together in one place, away from the island. On a boat.

My heart contracts a bit, looking at that face. I think about the day I took her in my arms, the day I saved her from Melina. The day I intervened and helped Mother spare her life. And now I have to take it all back, undo my mistake.

I surprise even myself by mentally scrambling for

another way—any other way that I can salvage this and save Eamon, and carve out a future for us, a path through the misery. But all roads lead to Chancery, because she rules the world right now, and there's nowhere I could run or hide, not after what I've done.

I pick up the phone again and dial the number slowly. "Okay," I say.

Chancery whimpers and my heart nearly splits in two. Judica is on that boat. My own sister. Unwanted, the image of Melina, falling underneath my sword flashes through my mind. I've already killed my own mother, and my own sister. What are a few more?

But before, they were accidents. This is different.

A difference that doesn't matter, because I have no other choice. It's them, or Eamon. And that's no choice at all.

"Go ahead and do it." My voice is flat, emotionless. Or perhaps, guilt-ridden.

"But Wilhelmina and Quincy are still aboard the ship," Ephrata complains. "I'll give them the order, and then—"

"Absolutely not. Waiting for them to leave is too risky. Sacrifices must be made. Do it now." I end the call. Now that I've decided what to do, I can't allow it to go sideways. Too much is resting on this.

Chancery frowns, clearly about to ask me what's going on.

I helpfully direct her toward the ship floating just off the coast, halfway between here and Kauai. A blue boat, the one from the FaceTime call. Recognition dawns on her face, and she scrambles across the sand toward it. "No. Wait. I'll do whatever you want. I'll join the stones and hand them right back to you. I'll abdicate the throne." Her eyes are wild, her desperation almost pathetic. How are we this different? How far have I strayed from what I once was?

And then the ship explodes, which, knowing how she killed Rothgar and Melamecha, well, it feels almost poetic. "I've had this method in mind for quite some time, you know, even though I had no idea how you'd kill those two morons yesterday. It makes this whole thing almost elegant, really." But it doesn't feel elegant, not to me. It feels cruel, and depraved, and I did it anyway—what does that say about me?

Chancery howls then, like she's had some kind of mental break. It's almost disappointing, since it does nothing to help her free herself from her current predicament. Mother taught us to compartmentalize much better than this, to focus on the issues at hand before giving into our feelings—but then, Chancery was always overly coddled. I grab her by the forearms and shake her. "That's enough."

She can't seem to stop, however, and when she opens her eyes, they're filled with more sorrow than fury. Not very helpful for her right now.

Now it's time for me to kill her, and carry her back to the palace in horror. It's the last piece of my plan.

But when I raise my sword, she bows in front of me. Bows. Content to die. No fight in her at all.

And that baby face rises in my mind, her cherubic, trusting, angel's face—the eyes that stared into mine trustingly. The eyes that believed I would protect her from any threat.

And I can't do it.

I swallow. I tighten my grip. It must be done. Keeping her alive is too risky.

Only, what if it turns out that I do need the stones joined? I can hide her in the same way I hid Melina until I've decided what exactly to do with her and the stones.

"Normally I don't like holding prisoners, but I may have to make an exception." I tap my lip. "There must be some way I can force you to join these without putting myself and my new position at risk, but it's a conundrum for sure."

She begins to struggle, thrashing in my hands, and the last reserves of my patience evaporate. I pick up a nearby rock and bash her on the back of the head. I tranq her for good measure—can't have her waking up in the middle of the terrible pageant where I convince everyone that she's died. I adopt my most somber and terrified face as I carry her limp body back to the palace. Since the back of her head is covered in blood and the tranq has slowed her heartbeat to almost nothing, it's an easy sell.

"She swam toward the boat and got caught in the explosion," I say. "Her spine was severed. With Job gone." I shake. "I'll call him immediately. I'm sure something—" My voice cracks, and I dash into her room, and with a few orders, clear the path to the bunker. Once I've sealed off the way out, leaving her in the earthen water-runoff enclosure, I begin to run through the rest of my plan, one step at a time.

I deliver the bad news with great sorrow and devastation: Chancery, Judica, Edam, Noah, and Alora were killed in an insurgent attack off the coast.

Then I secure the support of the troops, rallying around the clear cause: eliminate anyone who objects to the joining of the stones. "We must carry out her purpose." My eyes even fill with tears as I address my new subjects. "The way forward is scary, it's hard, it's terrible, but we can't let her down. Chancery wouldn't want us to be crippled by grief. We're still on the same timetable she followed, and we can't flag in our purpose. We have to prevent the utter destruction threatening the earth."

Frederick proves the most irritating, publicly in fact. I can hardly kill a grieving man, but I badly want to. I settle for locking him up below, restrained in the holding chambers until I can dispose of him with fewer people watching.

My coronation should be quite the event. I've dreamt of it often enough. But without any empresses or heirs to invite, the excitement drains away. Besides, knowing that Eamon is waiting, possibly being tortured, takes a lot of the joy out of it. I wear one of Mother's gold and pink gowns, and the Sons stand in the positions of honor, Eirik crowning me.

"Our enemies will know the pains of defeat and the fear of our wrath," I say. It might not be the best motto of any empress in the last few thousand years, but it's fitting enough for me. With Chancery's death fresh on their minds, the citizens of Alamecha eat it up.

Finally, after nearly two hundred years of waiting, I'm empress. Of the entire world.

And it's finally time for me to go and get my Consort.

Mother hated Melamecha. I never knew how or when it began, but she's always hated her. Whenever Mother won, she rubbed it in Melamecha's face. When Mother lost, she'd gnash her teeth, knowing that Melamecha was celebrating.

But a part of Mother respected her most consistent enemy.

Melamecha was a brilliant, feared, and revered strategist. I knew that she was a sadist, that she reveled in the pain of others, and if she inflicted the pain herself, even better.

But I didn't understand it, not until I reached Moscow.

Most evians eschew living among the largest cities, put off by the sheer numbers of humans and all their messy foibles. Melamecha loved the teeming mass of humanity that surrounded her—she relished in spotting and even highlighting their flaws. Mostly she delighted in punishing the ones who were the worst.

"You said the last one was it," I practically growl.

Mischa ducks her head. "I did believe it was correct."

"I'm not going to hit you," I say. "Stop cowering."

She cowers more. "Yes, Your Majesty, Your Excellency, Your Most High."

Oh for the love. "But you think this one?" I look around her body at the sequence of black doors. It looks just like the last fifteen containment camps we've visited. "Keeping this many prisoners, didn't she worry that they would escape?"

Mischa laughs.

"Okay, you can tell me. She was *so* terrifying that the only thing worse than being held captive by her was being caught escaping."

Melamecha's steward is the most obnoxious person I've met in my two hundred years. "It seems Your Excellent Majesty would not like to hear that. I will only say that many of her prisoners grew to love her."

Love her? Obnoxious and clearly insane. "Okay, well, let's go."

I hate opening these doors as much as I hated opening the others, but with Mischa's recent revelation, my skin crawls a little. At least half of people behind the doors I open are *disappointed* when it's me, and they look practically desperate when I tell them Melamecha is dead. How did I miss that before? The people she tortured. . . *loved* her? I shudder. The world is a messed up place.

"He's not here." My tone is flat.

Mischa runs a hand through her tumbling russet curls. "There is only one other place he might be," she insists. "And you said he would have been a priority. That's the reason I never suggested this final location before. This is the place Melamecha sends prisoners she is. . .apathetic? That is the word, no?"

"She doesn't care about these prisoners?"

"Correct. She is not interested and rarely visits." That's promising at least. Hopefully Eamon won't be in love with

Melamecha. That's not something I ever worried about until this very moment.

"It's the last place in Moscow," I say.

She shrugs. "I only know of the places in Moscow, yes."

Which means that the three days I've spent visiting the most pathetic wretches I could have imagined might have been for naught. Eamon could be anywhere. Every time I close my eyes on the ride across town to the last set of cells, I see his face, curled into an expression of desperate longing. . . for Melamecha. Will he mourn her death? Will he regret leaving to return home with me?

I shake my head. Surely not. He sent me that message—asking me to save him. Not my Eamon. He won't be wrecked. He won't be destroyed. He can't be. And if he is, well, we will deal with it. Together, finally. There's nothing we can't do together.

At last.

I imagine his shock at seeing me, how his gorgeous eyes will widen. He'll inhale quickly, sharply, and his pupils will dilate. His heart will accelerate. He'll be dirty, thin, and depressed, like all the prisoners I've freed, but he'll also be the most beautiful thing I've ever seen. He always has been, every single minute of every day of every year that I've known him.

I try not to get my hopes up when I stand at the end of the hallway this time, staring down the same stretch I've seen over and over, a dozen black painted doors all locked tight. Mischa dangles a heavy roll of keys, and I snatch it irritably out of her hands.

The first three doors contain humans—two of whom are dead. I cover my nose. "You said she didn't care about them, not that they were abandoned here to starve."

Mischa shrugs. "When the master is away. . ."

The servants ignore their tasks. Gruesome. I shake my

head and hand her the keys. "You check the rest. Wave me over if the occupant is alive."

She reaches for the keys, and I realize that I'll spend the next decade wondering if I do that.

Could he have starved to death? Could Eamon be lying in his own filth, emaciated to the point of death? "Never mind." I shove the keys into the next lock, ignoring Mischa's disrespectful snort. She should be more careful. Now that she's shown me every place she knows about in Moscow, she's expendable. The hinges creak, and I prepare myself for another grotesque corpse. Perhaps this one will be desiccated, or dangling from the rafters. We found one inventive prisoner who hadn't loved Melamecha enough to prevent his committing suicide in exactly that way three prisons back.

This one is at least alive, his face so dirty that it's hard to tell what he used to look like. "What's your name?" I try not to worry about things that aren't my problem, but it's hard not to feel sympathy for these prisoners. They may not have been abused, but neglect might be worse in some ways.

"Inara?" The filthy man shoves upright. His eyes flash toward mine, bright, light, almost unbelievably golden. He runs a hand through grimy, but undeniably ebony hair.

My breath catches in my throat. My heart races, no, it sprints. I force myself to swallow, to breathe, to process what I'm seeing.

His collarbones protrude sharply as he uses painfully bony arms to leverage himself onto his feet. "I knew you would come." His voice is raspy, as if he hasn't used it in a very long time. "I knew it."

I blink and blink. "Gideon?"

He nods.

"Is that really you?"

When he smiles, his teeth are unbelievably shiny and

white. It's startling, against his full beard, cracking lips, and dirt-stained skin. Grey rags are knotted around his waist, keeping him decent, barely. His hair falls in a tangled tumble down his back.

I ignore the smell when he wraps his arms around me, and I pull him tightly against me. "I'm so sorry."

His hand brushes against my jaw. "For what?" His brow furrows.

"I should have come so much sooner."

He shakes his head. "You didn't know."

"Is Eamon here too?" I ask. "Do you know? Or did Melamecha keep him somewhere else?"

"Eamon?" His shoulders slump. "You don't know?"

I shake my head this time. "Know what?"

"The bomb killed Eamon instantly—he was closer than me—too close. I lost half my arm, but slowly, so slowly, it regrew."

I blink, my brain rejecting his words. "No." I stumble back. "That can't be. He sent me a message."

Gideon tilts his head. "I sent you a message."

The words flash through my head. *The only thing that has kept me alive all this time is regret that we missed our chance— George Town still haunts me. But no matter what torture I've endured, I never shared your secret, and I never will.*

"But Eamon said that George Town haunts him. . ."

Gideon has been tortured for two decades, but his eyes aren't angry when he discovers I thought I was rescuing Eamon. When he finds out I didn't come for him, he's merely sad—not for himself. For me. "I'm sorry," he says. "I didn't mean to mislead you. I mentioned your secret so you'd know it was me."

My secret—I assumed it was what I told Eamon, that I'm a berserker, but I realize with total clarity that Gideon kept a secret of mine as well. He never told a soul that I loved Eamon, my mother's own Consort. But the soul-rending pain that strikes me when I realize Eamon isn't alive. . .

I killed Mother.

I killed Melina.

I killed Judica and Alora.

And I would do it all again to save Eamon—but I didn't save Eamon. He was dead all along. Every line I crossed, it was all for nothing. He's never coming back.

This time Gideon's the one comforting me, his bony, frail arms squeezing as tightly as they can. "Oh, I'm so sorry. I never meant to. . . I can only imagine how upset. . ."

My tears drench his filthy chest, mixing with the grime and making a paste that stains my shirt. "It's not your fault, Gideon. Of course it's not." I'm surprised that a tiny, minuscule part of me is relieved.

Because I knew that Eamon might not have forgiven me.

He might have condemned me for what I did to save him, for what I did for us.

But Gideon would never condemn me, no matter what I've done.

"We have a lot to discuss," I say, gesturing for Mischa to clear a path out to our car. "Free the others," I say. "Free them all."

She nods.

Gideon stares at me on the ride back to Melamecha's palace, not even speaking. He may look like no more than a shell of himself, but his eyes, they're identical. They're the eyes I've always known. He wastes no time when we reach the palace, eating everything the servants bring, and once he's entirely stuffed, he ducks into my shower.

Nearly an hour later, he emerges, still painfully thin. Still rough around the edges, with dark circles under his eyes, but the grime is gone, and he's clean-shaven, and his hair is shaved on the sides and pulled back into a neatly trimmed ponytail in the back.

His eyes burn when he looks at me. "You're devastated," he says. "To find me and not him."

I think about the pull I always felt to Eamon, the inexplicable connection. I think about the dreams I fashioned around him. I spent the past sixty years grieving our imagined future—a future we never had and we probably never could have had.

I've been grasping at smoke all this time. How many lives have I ruined longing for the impossible?

And yet, Gideon was always there, decapitating my horse, protecting me, fighting my fights, forgiving me, every single moment of my life. "I am upset," I say. "I hoped that Eamon and I might finally—" I swallow. "But you're my best friend, Gideon."

His eyebrows draw together. "Still?"

"Always. Forever. If you'll still have me."

"There has never been anyone for me but you," he whispers. "Never."

His words are a salve for my broken heart. "I'm not the same person I was."

He shakes his head. "Me either, but I don't care."

For the first time in a very long time, I wonder whether redemption is possible for me. Probably not, after what I've done, but it's long past time for me to try. "I've made a lot of mistakes," I admit. "Huge, epic mistakes."

"I'm sure it's not as bad as you think."

My laugh is bitter, even to my ears. "Oh, it's far worse than you could ever imagine. You saved my life, passing the information to me that allowed me to take over the Sons of Gilgamesh. But that much power. . ." I shake my head. "They say power corrupts, but I think the power allowed the existing corruption inside of me—"

"Wait," Gideon says. "Did you say you *took over* the Sons

of Gilgamesh?" His eyes are brimming with an emotion I don't expect.

I nod. "I did."

His frail shoulders shake. "I advanced very high within the organization, but I was never its leader."

I frown. "How can that be? Eirik said—"

"You've been issuing commands. . . with no one telling you what to do?" Gideon lifts one eyebrow.

"I have."

He closes his eyes. "The whole reason I almost died was that the real leader grew tired of my power and reach. The accident was created to eliminate me, not Eamon—Melamecha did me a favor by warning me, but her payment was imprisoning me to mine for information on Alamecha. If she hadn't made that decision, I'd be dead right now."

"I don't understand."

"Why did you think Eamon died?" His eyes are shadowed, haunted even.

"Mother killed him," I say softly. "She had another lover—the twins' real father."

Gideon flinches. "Are you one hundred percent positive?"

I nod. "Not that she set up the explosion that nearly killed you, I mean, but I know for sure that Enora was pregnant with someone else's children and she was relieved when Eamon didn't come back."

He sinks onto the edge of the bed, his shoulders slumped. "This is very bad."

"I've been running the entire organization for decades," I say. "With no one to contradict me. How bad can it be? Who was your boss? Maybe she died."

"How many members are there?" Gideon asks. "In the Sons?"

"Over three thousand," I say. "More than a thousand are within Alamecha of course, but we've grown to more than two thousand members that are spread across the other families." I'm almost proud of how it has expanded—with very little effort on my part.

He swallows slowly. "There were more than ten thousand members when I was sent with Eamon. You're not the real leader—he's toying with you."

Wait, he? I thought Gideon said he was recruited by a woman. "Who?" I ask. "Who is it?"

"He had me killed because I had expanded too far—too many of the men were loyal to me," Gideon says. "I often worried that you'd decide to use the information in the letters I left you. . . to take an active interest in the Sons yourself. That fear has tormented me."

My fingers curl into fists, my nails digging into the flesh of my palms until they hurt. "Who killed Eamon?"

Before he says the name, before he tells me what I should have seen all along, I already know. Deep down in my bones, in the dark place between awake and asleep, I always knew. It's the reason I never told him my secret—my foil, my mirror, my friend, my enemy. The one man Dad loved, but didn't trust *enough* to share the truth, no matter how badly I needed his help.

"Balthasar."

❦

I hope you enjoyed unRepentant! Destroyed is out now! If you have time to leave me a review on unRepentant or any other books in the series on your platform of choice, that would really help me out.

And if you like ya post apocalyptic, try my other ya series Marked.

And if you've already read that one, you can check out my Finding Home Series! (It will be hitting all other platforms in January!)

OR if you want a FREE BOOK, you can get Already Gone, a standalone ya romantic suspense, if you sign up for my newsletter. You can do that at www. BridgetEBakerWrites.com.

If you don't want another single email, I totally understand. You can follow me for updates on social media and simply buy Already Gone. It's a twisty ya romantic suspense.

APPENDIX

I. ALAMECHA: United States of America, England, Ireland, Scotland, Canada, Cuba, Puerto Rico
Eve
Mahalesh 3226 BC
Alamecha 2312 BC
Meridalina 1446 BC
Corlamecha 553 BC
Cainina 273 AD
Enora 1120 AD
Chancery 2002 AD
H. Judica 2002 AD

2. MALESSA: Germany, France, Netherlands, Switzerland, Norway, Sweden, Finland, Australia, New Zealand, Papau New Guinea, Iceland
Eve
Mahalesh 3226 BC
Malessa 2353 BC
Adorna 1451 BC
Selah 618 BC

Lenamecha 211 AD
Senah 1022 AD (Denah dead twin)
Analessa 1820 AD
H. DeLannia 1942

3. LENORA: All of South America (including Chile, Argentina, Brazil), Mexico, Spain, Portugal
Eve
Mahalesh 3226 BC
Lenora 2365 BC
Ablinina 1453 BC
Leddite 652 BC
Selamecha 379 BC
Priena 460 AD
Leamarta 1198 AD
Melisania 1897 AD
H. Marde 1987

4. ADORA: India, Japan, Korea, Indonesia, Thailand
Eve
Mahalesh 3226 BC
Adora 2368 BC
Manocha 1461 BC
Alela 590 BC
Radosha 192 BC
Esheth 638 AD
Lainina 1444 AD
H. Ranana 1967

5. SHAMECHA: Russia, Mongolia, Kazakhstan, Pakistan, Uzbekistan, Philippines
Eve

Mahalesh 3226 BC

Shamecha 2472 BC

Madalena 1639 BC

Shenoa 968 BC

Abalorna 299 BC

Venoah 333 AD

Reshaka 936 AD

Melamecha 1509 AD

H. Venagra 2000

6. SHENOAH: Continent of Africa, Saudi Arabia, Iran, Iraq, Turkey, Greece, Italy, Jordan, Afghanistan

Eve

Shenoah 3227 BC

Adelornamecha 2385 BC

Kankera 1544 BC

Avina 670 BC

Sela 467 BC

Jericha 135 AD

Sethora 399 AD

Malimba 708 AD

Adika 1507 AD

H. Vela 1990

ACKNOWLEDGMENTS

First I should thank all the people who help this book come together: my copy editor (Carla Stuckey), my developmental editor (Peter Sentfleben), my proofer (Carrie Harris), and my husband! He is tireless in his support and his dedication to helping me work on these stories.

Thank you to my advance readers and fans. Your enthusiasm and support is invaluable. I love you all!

And my children have become such supporters of my work—reading it, cheering me on, and being patient when it means Mom is busy in her room.

It is always a momentous day when another book baby comes into the world. Thank you to everyone who is cheering me on!

ABOUT THE AUTHOR

Bridget loves her husband (every day) and all five of her kids (most days). She's a lawyer, but does as little legal work as possible. She has three goofy horses, two scrappy cats, two adorable rabbits, one bouncy dog and backyard chickens. She hates Oxford commas, but she uses them to keep fans from complaining. She makes cookies waaaaay too often and believes they should be their own food group. In an attempt to keep from blowing up like a puffer fish, she kick boxes every day. So if you don't like her books, her kids, her pets, or her cookies, maybe don't tell her in person.

ALSO BY BRIDGET E. BAKER

The Finding Home Series:

Finding Faith (1)

Finding Cupid (2)

Finding Spring (3)

Finding Liberty (4)

Finding Holly (5)

Finding Home (6)

Finding Balance (7)

Finding Peace (8)

The Birthright Series:

Displaced (1)

unForgiven (2)

Disillusioned (3)

misUnderstood (4)

Disavowed (5)

unRepentant (6)

Destroyed (7)

The Sins of Our Ancestors Series:

Marked (1)

Suppressed (2)

Redeemed (3)

Renounced (4)

A stand alone YA romantic suspense:

Already Gone

My Children's Picture Book

Yuck! What's for Dinner?